Also by Leigh Greenwood

Someone
Like You

Leigh
Greenwood

sourcebooks
casablanca

Originally published in 2009 in the United States by Leisure
Books, an imprint of Dorchester Publishing, New York. This edi-
tion based on the ebook edition published in 2012 in the United
States by Ten Talents Press.

Published by Sourcebooks Casablanca, an imprint of Sourcebooks,
Inc.
P.O. Box 4410, Naperville, Illinois 60567-4410
(630) 961-3900
Fax: (630) 961-2168
sourcebooks.com

Printed and bound in the United States of America.
OPM 10 9 8 7 6 5 4 3 2 1

For Irma Vinson. Great teachers make all the difference.

One

Rancho los Alamitos, California

DOLORES JERRY TOSSED ASIDE THE EMBROIDERY FRAME and surged to her feet. "I can't believe Warren made Rafe his executor," she complained for the thousandth time in the seven months since her husband's death. She kicked at the small dog huddled against her skirts. "I thought he hated Rafe."

"I don't think Warren ever hated his son." Maria de la Guerra didn't look up from the piece of delicate lace she'd been working on for the last five weeks. "He never said so, but I think he regretted sending Rafe away."

"You only think that because you didn't hear what Rafe said to him before he left," Dolores told her sister.

Maria knew what had been said. The servants had recounted the argument to her many times over the last nine years. But Warren's actions of the last several years caused her to believe he'd regretted throwing Rafe out of the house. He'd never mentioned Rafe's name when Dolores was present, but Maria had often come upon him staring at a miniature of Rafe taken when he was a young boy astride his first horse. It had appeared on Warren's bedside table after years of being hidden in a cabinet with other reminders of Rafe.

"If the letter Rafe sent the lawyer is a reflection of his present feelings, I doubt he will come home," Maria observed.

"He's *got* to come home." Dolores threw herself down on a velvet-covered daybed. The little dog huddled against her feet. "Soon we won't have any money to buy food."

"It won't come to that. The lawyer is empowered to make necessary decisions until Rafe returns."

"That lawyer hates me. I swear it hurts him to give me my pitiful allowance. Do you know he had the nerve to suggest I use my personal money to buy food? I barely have enough to dress myself."

Dolores and Maria had been born into the wealthy and historically important de la Guerra family, but when their father lost his land to an upstart American who had successfully disputed the legality of their land grant, Dolores's fiancé backed out of the engagement. The humiliation was compounded when Mrs. Jerry invited Dolores to be her companion. For a woman who'd been brought up to believe she deserved to be waited on hand and foot, being forced to become a glorified servant was the ultimate humiliation. After Mrs. Jerry's death and Dolores's subsequent marriage to Warren Jerry, Dolores had invited her sister to live at the ranch.

"I can use *my* allowance for food if necessary," Maria volunteered.

"You don't need to. You have control of the household accounts."

Dolores had been happy to turn over the accounts and the household duties to her fifteen-year-old sister soon after Maria arrived, but she was furious when the lawyer wouldn't return control of them to her after her husband's death. *I'm only following the instructions in Mr. Jerry's will*, Henry Fielder had told her.

Dolores lay back on the daybed, her arm over her eyes. "Rafe was so in love with me, he went crazy when I told him I was going to marry his father. Do you think I should marry him now that I'm free?"

Maria was used to her sister's capriciousness, but this was a step beyond what she could accept. "After what happened, I think you should keep as far away from him as possible."

"He's much younger than his father, and a lot better-looking." Dolores smiled, petting the little dog who had jumped up on the daybed with her. "Besides, I like being Mrs. Jerry a lot more than the widow Jerry."

Rafe brought his horse to a stop on a ridge overlooking the big Cíbola Creek where it dropped into the valley below. He had never forgotten this view because it was one of his favorites. Unfortunately, it brought back a bitter memory as well. It was on this spot that he'd first told Dolores he loved her. The letter in his pocket burned like a hot coal. He wished he had never responded to the newspaper ad requesting that anyone with knowledge of the whereabouts of Rafe Jerry, son of Warren Jerry, contact the law offices of Henry

Fielder in Cíbola, California. He hadn't spoken to his father since he'd walked out of his house ten years ago, yet his father had made him sole executor of a ranch he'd inherited jointly with a half brother he'd never seen. Rafe was a thirty-year-old bachelor. What could he have in common with a nine-year-old child?

"Where is your ranch?" asked Rafe's closest friend, Broc Kincaid. During the Civil War, Broc had served with Rafe in a cavalry unit that conducted night raids on shipments of supplies, munitions, and gold. He'd come to California with Rafe in hopes of finding Laveau di Viere, the man who'd betrayed their unit to the Yankees.

"Down there." Rancho los Alamitos land stretched as far as Rafe could see. "Everywhere. All of it."

Broc's eyes grew wide. "I can see thousands of acres from here."

"My father owned more than two hundred thousand acres."

Broc stared dumbfounded at the fertile acres stretching into the distance until they merged with the horizon. "How could you leave all this? It's almost as beautiful as Tennessee."

How could he explain that he didn't want to be heir to a ranch worth millions, that he didn't want to be the guardian of a half brother he didn't know, that he wanted nothing to do with a woman who decided she'd rather be his stepmother than his wife? He'd been happy ranching in Texas with some of the other men from his cavalry unit. The work was hard, but the bunkhouse was comfortable, the food good, and the friendship the kind that couldn't be bought. Why would he give that up for the responsibility of a huge ranch, an undoubtedly spoiled child, and the conniving bitch who'd broken his heart?

Rafe hadn't told anyone that Dolores—the woman he'd once loved—had seduced his father while he was grieving over the death of his wife, or that Rafe had been thrown out of the house because he couldn't treat his stepmother with respect. As he gazed out over the lush acres, some of the anger inside him eased. He loved this place, and that was a large part of the reason he'd come back to California. To see the ranch again. "I didn't leave the land."

Broc shook his head. "Must have been something really bad to make you give up this."

"I thought so at the time." He hadn't changed his mind, so why had he come back? Why had he *needed* to come back?

"You going down there, or are we going to see if we can find any trace of Laveau?"

They had traveled up the coast of California, following the line of the old Spanish missions. They had found reports of Laveau in Monterey and San Francisco, but the traitor was always one step ahead of them.

"We're going into town to see the lawyer first," Rafe told Broc. "I hope he can explain why my father wrote that infernal will. When I walked out of here, I told him I never wanted to see this place again."

"You're his son," Broc reminded him. "Naturally he'd want you to have your inheritance."

Rafe had lost all desire for his inheritance ten years ago—his half brother could have it all. Rage burned hot within him. He could feel the life he'd spent ten years building for himself slipping away. He was being drawn back into a quagmire of blighted love and shattered idealism, of lust, avarice, lies…and hate.

"He has another son, one he wanted more than me." Rafe reminded himself he wasn't angry at the boy. Even though his creation was the source of the enmity between Rafe and his father, the child was innocent. He would not judge this child until he'd seen him. It was possible he didn't take after his mother. "The last words my father spoke to me were to order me out of the house."

Broc turned his horse away from the cliff overlooking the ravine. "Apparently he changed his mind. Let's head into town."

∞

Henry Fielder was middle-aged, gaunt, and inhabited a law office as small and cluttered as an old maid's closet. Clean shaven and nearly bald, he looked at Rafe out of clear, piercing blue eyes. "You can't turn everything over to me," he said. "The will specifically states that you, and you alone, must be executor of the estate."

Rafe had nothing against Henry Fielder, but he had never liked lawyers. They lived in a world of their own, creating rules no one else could understand. They said these laws benefitted the average citizen, but as often as not, a man discovered what he wanted to do was the one thing he *couldn't* do.

"That may be what my father wanted, but I can turn around and go back to Texas. I'm sure Dolores will pay you anything you want if you can figure out some way to get around the will."

"First, the will states that the present Mrs. Jerry is never to have control of any portion of the ranch or its management. She has her allowance and nothing else."

Rafe found it hard to believe that his father would make such a provision. He had loved his first wife, but Dolores had captivated him with her youth and beauty when he was grieving and vulnerable.

"If you reject the provisions of the will," the lawyer continued, "I'm directed to sell the ranch. A portion will be set aside to increase your stepmother's allowance tenfold. She will retain that allowance even if she should remarry. The remainder of the proceeds will be used to create a park in honor of your step-mother. You will, in essence, disinherit your brother and yourself."

Rafe's fury at the net his father had woven around him was so hot, he was sure his temperature had risen ten degrees. He had no doubt his father had added that provision to make sure he didn't ignore the will and just disappear. Rafe wouldn't care whether he lost his half of the ranch and he might not care whether he was disinheriting his brother, but his father knew Rafe would do whatever was necessary to prevent the creation of *anything* that honored the whore who'd become his stepmother.

A question gradually penetrated his rage, a question he'd asked before, but which now assumed added significance: What had happened to cause his father to make such a will? As much as he wanted nothing to do with Dolores or his half brother, he needed to know what had changed.

"Why?"

A veil dropped over the lawyer's eyes. "I beg your pardon?"

"Don't fence with me. This is the opposite of what I expected. You've got to have some idea what caused him to change his mind."

The lawyer lost all signs of affability. "I was your father's lawyer, not his confessor."

The man had to know, or at least suspect, what had happened, but he wasn't going to say anything. Rafe would much rather be chasing Laveau, but Laveau would have to wait until he solved the puzzle of what had happened at Rancho los Alamitos.

Damn. How did a small ad in a Chicago newspaper find its way to Texas? Five more months, and I could have been richer than I'd ever imagined. I can't give up now. I'm too close.

∽

"Rafe is coming to the ranch. That horrible lawyer said he'll be here sometime today."

Maria couldn't understand her sister's excitement. Dolores had been running around the house giving instructions to every servant she saw. She'd changed the dinner menu three times, discussed and discarded a half dozen ideas for which dress to wear, and had driven poor Luis into a nervous state with a string of instructions about how to behave so he wouldn't upset his brother.

"Did he say anything about the will?" If anyone had consulted her—and Dolores rarely did—Maria would have suggested meeting Rafe in the lawyer's office. The decision as to whether he would be the executor was more important than any impression they might make on a single visit.

"He said Rafe had agreed to be the executor." Dolores looked at the dress she was holding up with disfavor. "I've got to get him to increase my allowance. I can't keep going around in this rag."

The *rag* she was talking about had been worn only once. The black velvet glittered with hundreds of tiny glass beads in swirling designs that made the gown seem alive when Dolores moved.

"If you want to convince him you need an increase in your allowance, don't wear that dress," Maria advised. "Not only does it look expensive, but it makes you look especially young and beautiful."

Maria had never envied her sister's beauty or her need to be the focus of attention. Managing the household and overseeing Luis's education was a big job, but she enjoyed the responsibility. The servants were hardworking and loyal, and she loved Luis like her own son.

Dolores paused before her mirror, critically studying her reflection. "I can't welcome him home looking like a faded old woman."

"You look neither faded nor old."

"He last saw me when I was nineteen. That was ten years, one husband, and one child ago." She made a face. "His father kept telling him I was his stepmother. I'll die if he still thinks of me like that."

"I'm sure he doesn't. And if he did, one look at you would change his mind." Maria smiled at her sister's pleased reaction to her comment. "Now get dressed. I'm going to see about Luis."

"Rafe never liked children. Maybe Luis had better stay in his room."

"I'm sure Rafe will expect to see his brother." Maria hated to use that word to describe the relationship between Luis and Rafe. She'd promised herself she would be cordial because this meeting was important to Dolores and Luis, but she wasn't sure how she could be pleasant to a man she despised. She wasn't a good actress like her sister. It had always been easy for people to guess her feelings.

"Very well, but don't let him stay more than a few minutes."

"I'll take care of that. Now get dressed. You've got to be downstairs when he arrives. You're the only one he knows."

Maria left her sister's room and tried to put Dolores and Rafe out of her mind. His mother's strictures had upset Luis so much that he couldn't eat his lunch. He was well grown for his age, but he was so shy, his sunny temperament and natural inquisitiveness could disappear at a moment's notice. He wasn't so young that he didn't know his father had wanted little or nothing to do with him. Maria could understand that, but she couldn't forgive it. Unfortunately, it was impossible to explain the reason to Luis. She knocked on the door to his room before entering.

Luis was seated next to a window with a view of the road leading up to the house. He looked so darling in his formal clothes, Maria was tempted to hug him. He never stinted in his show of affection for his aunt, but recently he had become uncomfortable with the hugs and caresses he'd enjoyed so much when he was younger. At nine, he was already showing signs of the young man he would grow up to be.

Luis turned when Maria entered the room. "Do you think Rafe will like me?"

"Of course he'll like you. You're his brother." Maria tried to sound reassuring, but she didn't know Rafe, so she could only guess how he might respond.

"Maybe he doesn't want a brother he's never seen. Mama says he hates children."

"I don't know what he was like when he was growing up, but maybe he's fond of children by now. He'll surely be happy to know he has a brother as smart and handsome as you."

"Rosana says he's so handsome, every señorita from here to Sacramento will be sighing over him. Juan says he can outride and outshoot anybody in California. I can't do anything like that."

Maria hated it when people compared Luis to Rafe. "He's a grown man. You're still a boy. I'm sure he couldn't do any of those things when he was your age."

"Juan said he could ride a horse before he could walk."

Maria laughed. "I bet he rode sitting in his father's lap and holding on tight." She regretted the words the moment they left her mouth.

"Papa never took me in his lap. He didn't teach me how to ride."

Maria had been grateful to Warren Jerry for giving her a home, but she would never forgive him for the way he'd treated Luis.

"Your papa was older when you were growing up, and he was sick a long time before he died. I'm certain he would have taught you to ride if he had been younger and in good health." She knew that wasn't true and suspected Luis knew it as well. The picture Warren had kept by his bedside, and his will, confirmed Maria's belief that he'd spent his last years regretting his separation from Rafe.

"Will he send me away to school?"

The question caught Maria off guard. "What do you mean?"

"Juan says all boys are sent away to military school when they're ten or eleven. He says it turns them into men. He says it's a Spanish tradition."

"Your father was not Spanish."

"Both my grandmothers were."

Maria deplored the pattern of Spanish fathers marrying their daughters to Anglo men, even though it had proved to be the best way to hold on to Spanish land grants after California became part of the United States. She rested her hand on his shoulder. "I promise I won't let him do anything to make you unhappy."

"Maybe I should go to military school. All the boys on the ranch ride better than I do."

"Only because riding is part of their work."

"I wish I could ride well. I wish I could do *something* well."

Maria had done all she could to give Luis confidence in himself, to make him feel loved and valued, but that was next to impossible when neither his mother nor his father showed any interest in him.

"You do lots of things very well," Maria assured him. "You're a brilliant scholar, you—"

"No one cares about that." He sounded dismissive of his own achievements. "They only care about how many tricks you can perform on horseback or how well you can shoot."

Maria had always enjoyed the contests the local men indulged in during festivals, but she disliked that they used such stunts as a measure of manhood and character.

"Is that my brother?" Luis pointed at two men approaching the house along the lane from town. The darker one was leading a pony.

"I've never seen him. The lawyer didn't say anything about someone being with him."

"He looks like the man in the picture Papa had next to his bed."

Maria didn't know when Luis had been in his father's room, but she couldn't deny that even at a distance, the rider looked like Rafe. "You go on downstairs. You don't have to meet him by yourself," Maria said when the boy looked stricken. "I'll be down as soon as I tell your mother he's here."

Maria wasn't surprised to find Dolores sitting in front of her mirror, inspecting her makeup. "Rafe is here."

Dolores didn't take her gaze off her reflection. "Do you think I have too much color? I hear Southern women often use buttermilk to keep their perfectly white complexions."

"You look beautiful, as always. Now come on downstairs. He'll be at the door any minute."

"I need to put on more powder. I swear, this California sun can penetrate the walls."

"Stop imagining faults that aren't there and come downstairs."

"I'll be down soon."

Maria knew her sister wouldn't stir from her room until she was satisfied with her appearance. Since that might take five minutes or half an hour, there was nothing to do but go down and meet Rafe Jerry by herself. It annoyed her that Dolores would neglect her role as hostess, but her sister had always left the unpleasant and uncomfortable duties to Maria. Maria figured it was part of the price she had to pay for being rescued from poverty. "Come down as soon as you can. You're the only one he knows."

Dolores was too absorbed with her reflection to answer. Maria squared her shoulders and marched downstairs.

Luis was standing inside the parlor just a few steps from the wide hall that ran through the center of the house. Maria held out her hand and forced herself to smile. "Your mother will be down in a minute. You and I will meet your brother together."

Taking Luis's hand, she walked to the door. Luis opened it, and she stepped forward to greet the man who was coming up the steps. When he saw her, he frowned.

"Who the hell are you, and where's the bitch who ruined my life and sent my father to an early grave?"

Two

MARIA'S INITIAL IMPRESSION WAS THAT SHE'D JUST MET the most overwhelmingly handsome man she'd ever seen. He was tall, with broad shoulders that tapered to a narrow waist and powerful thighs. The look in his eye, the way he carried himself, bespoke a man who was sure of himself. Unfortunately, he was also the rudest man she'd ever met.

"My name is Maria de la Guerra," she said with as much calm as she could command. "I'm Dolores Jerry's sister. This is my nephew, Luis Jerry. I'm afraid I don't know your name or that of your companion."

Rafe's presence was so commanding, she'd almost forgotten his companion.

"I expect Dolores makes you do all the work. Too bad you aren't more forceful—but if you had been, Dolores wouldn't have brought you here."

If the first speech had shocked Maria, the second rendered her mute.

"Where is Dolores? Does she still sit in front of her mirror for hours before she'll let anybody see her?"

He glanced down at Luis, who was virtually cringing at Maria's side. "You must be Luis."

That remark galvanized Maria. "Sir, I still don't know your name, though I expect—"

"I'm Rafe Jerry. Unless Dolores has thrown them out or burned them, there are enough pictures of me in the house for anybody to recognize me. May I come inside?"

"Before he makes you so angry that you show him off the property, I want to introduce myself. I'm Rafe's friend Broc Kincaid. He's not always this rude."

Maria swung her gaze to the man standing next to Rafe, only to receive another shock. She could see that the perfection of the right side of the man's face was counterbalanced by terrible scars on the left. Guessing they were the result of a war wound, she found it remarkable that a man of such outstanding looks could be so cheerful in the face of such disfigurement.

"I'm Maria de la Guerra. This is my nephew, Luis Jerry."

Broc extended his hand to Luis. "Glad to meet you, young man. You look rather big to be just nine years old. I bet you end up being taller than Rafe. Then he'll be *your* little brother."

Broc couldn't have said anything that could have made Luis feel better about himself. He had lived in awe of Rafe most of his life.

Maria moved back inside the door and to one side. "Please join me in the parlor. My sister will be down in a moment. May I offer you something to drink?"

Broc flashed a smile that tugged at Maria's heart. "Bless you. I've been thinking of beer for the last hour."

"We also have wine," Maria said.

Rafe surveyed the chairs in the room before crossing to a leather-covered captain's chair with a high back. "Rancho los Alamitos was always known for its wine." They waited for Maria to be seated. "We'll have whatever you're having."

Maria picked up a small bell on the table next to her and rang it. "I'm not thirsty."

"What's Luis having?" Broc asked.

Luis swallowed. "I would like some lemonade."

Rafe winked at Luis. "When I was your age, my father would occasionally give me wine or beer with enough water in it to make it safe."

Uncertain how to respond, Luis made a feeble attempt to smile.

"I don't believe children should be given strong drink," Maria told Rafe. "It encourages them to indulge in spirits far too early."

"Or takes the mystery out of it so they learn to drink with moderation."

She supposed that was possible, but all the men she knew drank too much. "We need refreshments for our visitors," she said to Margarita when the young servant entered the room. "Luis and I will have lemonade."

"I will, too," Broc said.

Maria turned to Rafe. "What would you like?"

"Water will be fine."

"We have a wide selection of wines, and your father's liquor cabinet is just the way he left it."

Rafe put up his hands. "I seldom drink spirits."

"He's not much fun at a party," Broc said. "He remembers everything we do."

"Water for Mr. Jerry," Maria said, dismissing Margarita. An awkward silence would have ensued if Rafe hadn't asked Luis what he was learning. In a few minutes Rafe had coaxed more out of the boy than anybody but herself. Maria wondered if Rafe might be less of an ogre than Dolores had said. Maybe he'd changed over the years.

When she thought Luis had talked enough, she intervened. "Did you have a difficult journey? I've never been out of the valley, but I'm told the places south of here can be extremely hot."

"You get used to the heat in Texas."

"What were you doing in Texas?"

"We're cowhands for a friend who has a large cattle ranch."

"We're a little more than that," Broc started to explain, only to be interrupted by Dolores's entrance.

Dolores paused in the doorway before surging into the parlor, the rich fabric of her dress rustling softly. Maria thought her sister's lips were too scarlet, her cheeks too heavily rouged, her brows and lashes too dark, but she looked magnificent.

"Rafe," she exclaimed with a brilliant smile that lit up her face and caused her eyes to sparkle, "it's so good to see you." She advanced toward him, her hands outstretched. Broc got to his feet, but Rafe didn't move.

Maria was familiar with anger, but she'd never seen the white-hot rage on Rafe's face. It was so virulent, even Dolores felt it. She appeared to stumble as though hit by something solid. She recovered but came to a stop a few feet from Rafe, her outstretched hands falling to her sides. She made a valiant attempt to recapture the smiling enthusiasm of her entrance, but the result was forced.

"I see you've lost none of your looks." His tone was sharp enough to cut. "What poor fool do you have your talons into now?"

Maria had never approved of the way her sister ignored her husband and flirted with handsome men, but she was proud of the way Dolores regained her poise.

"It's flattering to know you think I'm still attractive." Her smile was back in place. "You always were a very critical judge."

"I was nineteen and a fool."

"I haven't been nineteen for a very long time," Broc said, "and I still think you're beautiful."

When Broc spoke, Dolores turned, screamed, and stumbled backward. That brought Rafe to his feet with a growl of fury so fierce, Luis clutched Maria's hand. Dolores put one hand to her throat in a dramatic gesture, leaned against a table for support, and managed a tremulous smile.

"My God, you scared me half to death. I didn't see you when I came into the room."

The welcoming smile remained plastered on Broc's face. "I didn't mean to scare you."

"Of course not. I'm sorry I didn't notice you, but I was so excited to see Rafe I didn't have eyes for anyone else."

"This is Broc Kincaid. He works with Rafe in Texas." Maria hoped her interruption would give Dolores time to recover her composure.

"Pleased to meet you." Dolores was careful not to look at Broc when she spoke. The way her fingers nervously picked at her heavy silver and turquoise necklace belied her words.

Maria was irritated when Dolores chose a chair so Broc was out of her line of vision. "I was sorry you couldn't be here for your father's funeral," she said to Rafe, "but we didn't know how to contact you. The lawyer said it was the merest good fortune that you saw the notice in the Chicago newspaper."

"I didn't. It was sent to me anonymously. I wouldn't have responded if Pilar hadn't threatened to do it herself."

"Who is Pilar? Are you married?"

Maria was embarrassed that Dolores should expose herself so obviously. She might as well have stated that she was terrified Rafe might be married and thus beyond the influence of her beauty.

"She's Cade's wife, the man I work for."

"You shouldn't be working for anybody. You're a wealthy man."

"You've always valued people in terms of dollars." Rafe's words were infused with disgust, but they appeared to leave Dolores unscathed.

"A woman has to look out for her children."

"If you love your son so deeply that you'd make his welfare the deciding factor in choosing a husband, why is he huddled against your sister rather than you?"

"He adores his aunt. Besides, she's closer to him in age than I am."

"You're not his playmate, Dolores. You're his mother."

Dolores pouted. "Why are you being so mean when we're all so glad to see you? You have no idea how difficult your father's will has made everything."

"Then take consolation in the fact that it's made my life even more miserable."

"How can that be?"

"Because it's forced me into contact again with a woman I despise."

Dolores picked at one of the crystals on her dress. "I know you were unhappy when I married your father instead of you, but I was an impressionable young girl, overawed by a handsome and powerful man."

"You were a scheming fortune hunter who took advantage of a man grieving over the death of his wife."

"I'm older now and have had time to see things more clearly."

Rafe's response was forestalled by Margarita's return with the beverages. By the time everyone had been served, some of the tension had dissipated. Broc said he'd never been to California before and asked if it was always so hot. He found the weather surprising considering they'd crossed mountains still covered with snow.

"We get virtually no rain in the valley during the summer," Rafe said to Broc. "After the spring rains are over, we depend on snowmelt to carry us through the summer and fall. We also get water from wells that tap into underground rivers flowing from the mountains."

Maria wasn't surprised at Rafe's knowledge of the valley's climate. Both Juan and Rosana had said Rafe had been doing as much work on the ranch as his father before he left.

"Mr. Fielder gives me an allowance so small it would hardly keep a child alive." Bored by the conversation, Dolores had almost finished her glass of wine. "He told me I have no power to make any decisions concerning the ranch, that I can't even order food for the household. I told him it was ridiculous, that a wife should have the right to make decisions about her own property. That's when he told me I didn't have any property, that Warren had left everything to you and Luis. When I told him that as Luis's mother I could make decisions for him, he told me the will had made you and Maria his joint guardians."

Rafe stared expressionlessly at Dolores. "What's so hard to understand about it?"

"The whole thing!" Dolores exclaimed. "I tried to make Mr. Fielder understand that your father was sick, that he would never have written any of those things if he'd been in his right mind."

"I interpreted the way he wrote the will to mean he was in his right mind for the first time in ten years."

Any woman less self-centered than her sister would have been daunted by Rafe's words.

"He wasn't," Dolores insisted. "He would hardly look at Luis. I don't remember the last time he spoke to me."

"Apparently his lapse in judgment was only temporary," Rafe said. "I wish I had known."

Maria couldn't decide whether he spoke with regret or anger. He appeared to be a very self-contained man. She wondered how someone as cheerful as Broc would want him for a friend. She found it nearly impossible to imagine Rafe laughing.

"Warren never did recover his right mind. It was all very sad and I was heartbroken, but one has to go on." She flashed the smile that had dazzled so many men before. "I have to think of my son."

Maria was certain this callous speech would wring a response from Rafe, but he continued to watch her sister with the unblinking gaze of a predator. Just when Dolores opened her mouth to continue, Rafe did speak.

"You've never had any consideration for anyone but yourself in your entire life."

"That's not true." Dolores's indignation was genuine. "I thought of your mother when she brought me here to comfort her during her illness. And of you and your father when she died."

"Only of which one had the most money."

Dolores plowed ahead, ignoring Rafe's remark. "I thought of Luis when I asked Maria to move here and help me take care of him. I thought of your father when he was sick—I would gladly have stayed by his bedside night and day—but I'm convinced he was afraid I'd catch his malady." She sniffed, and a tear appeared on her eyelid before it swelled and rolled down her cheek.

With a look of fury that was frightening in its intensity, Rafe surged to his feet. "I'm going to take a ride. It's been so long since I was here, I don't know how much of the ranch I remember."

Dolores asked, "When will you be back?"

"I'm not coming back tonight."

"Of course you are. It's your home. I'm sure your friend would prefer to stay in Cíbola." Dolores didn't look at Broc. "He'd be bored here with nothing to do but watch me embroider and Maria make lace." Her laugh was light and transparently insincere.

Rafe turned to Dolores. "It's kind of you to be so concerned about Broc's entertainment."

"I don't mind staying in Cíbola," Broc said. "We have other business to attend to, and we can't do it from here."

Rafe's gaze never left Dolores. "That business can wait. I need you here."

"Cade said—"

"I know what Cade said."

"What can your friend possibly do that someone who knows the ranch can't do better?" It was bad enough that Dolores couldn't look at Broc, but she should at least have used his name.

"He can provide me with the companionship of one person I know I can trust." He turned to Maria. "What time do you dine?"

"Why didn't you ask me that?" Dolores was affronted.

"Because I was certain you were still too broken-hearted to have the energy to make arrangements for a meal you were probably too dispirited to eat."

"I have to eat. I owe it to Luis to keep my strength up."

"We dine at seven thirty," Maria said before her sister could make more of a fool of herself. "Is that acceptable?"

"Seven thirty will be fine. Does Luis occupy my old bedroom?"

"No. He sleeps in the room next to mine."

"I'll sleep in my father's room. Broc can have my old room. Will it be difficult to get them ready?"

"Rosana has cleaned your room faithfully ever since you left. She has always believed you would return."

"So Rosana is still here." She thought she saw a softening in his eyes, but the velvet curtains at the windows kept out the light as well as the heat. "How about Juan?"

"He and Miguel are both here. Juan has filled Luis's head with stories about you." This time she was certain of the softening in his eyes. That surprised her as much as his change in attitude when he talked about the ranch.

"I'm sure he's exaggerated my accomplishments and ignored my failures."

"He says you can do anything," Luis said.

Luis had been so quiet, she'd almost forgotten he was present.

"My father used to say Juan and Rosana spoiled me rotten." Rafe's smile was so genuine, Luis managed a faint smile in response.

"Would you like me to show you to your room?" Maria was sure he didn't need her help, but it was polite to offer.

"Thank you, but I remember the way. I'll see you at dinner."

"Juan will press your evening clothes," Dolores said. "I'm sure they're wrinkled from being packed so long."

"I didn't bring evening clothes. I haven't worn any since I left here ten years ago."

❦

"Warren never came to the table unless he was dressed properly," Dolores complained after Rafe and Broc left.

"Warren hadn't just arrived from Texas," Maria responded. "What are you trying to do? First you act as if this is the return of a prodigal son. Next you act as though he's still in love with you. Then you end by trying to send his friend away and insist on evening clothes for dinner. Are you trying to make him dislike us even more than he already does?"

"How can you stand to look at his friend?" Dolores's body quivered with disgust. "He makes my skin crawl."

"I think he's nice," Luis said.

"So do I." Maria was surprised Luis would speak up for a man he'd just met. Normally the boy was reluctant to voice an opinion contrary to his mother's. "And he has a name. Common civility requires you use it."

"How can I be civil around him when looking at him makes me feel unwell?"

"Broc was probably wounded in the war. He must have been remarkably handsome at one time. I think he's quite extraordinary to have accepted his scars so well."

"Then *you* look at him and use his name." Dolores appeared to think for a moment, a slight furrow marring her perfect brow. "I think Rafe is still in love with me. I wouldn't mind being married to him. He has a bit of a temper, but he used to worship me."

"I doubt he feels that way now." Maria knew it was useless to argue with her sister when she got an idea in her head. She hoped that given time, Dolores would see reason, but for the moment she hoped Dolores wouldn't do anything to set Rafe against them.

She wondered how he would react to the servants. Over the years, they'd filled Luis's head with tales of Rafe's limitless abilities, trying to inspire Luis to grow into the man Rafe had been when he left. Maria hoped he wouldn't become anything like his brother. Rafe was physically very appealing—she hated to admit that her first response had been one of attraction—but she was at a loss to understand why Warren had decided to make his son heir to half the ranch, executor of the estate, and Luis's guardian. How could he trust a man who had raped Dolores, impregnating her with a child Warren had been forced to call his own in order to protect Dolores and Luis from a life of disgrace?

She could tell Luis had been powerfully impressed by Rafe, but she intended to do everything she could to shield the boy from his influence. His behavior was as shameful as his body was fine-looking.

She had to stop thinking like that. Not even Rafe's good looks could compensate for the blackness of his past deeds.

❧

Rafe wasn't prepared for the welter of emotions that swamped him when he entered his father's bedroom. The huge mahogany bed, the Turkish carpet that muffled his footsteps, the fireplace with the blue-veined marble surround, the curtained windows that looked out over the foothills of the neighboring mountains... For ten years his memories of his father had been dominated by their last confrontation, when angry words and fierce accusations had ended with his father ordering him out of the house. Not even the horrors of a brutal war had blunted the edge of pain in his heart or excised the memory of those words.

He'd been prepared to feel renewed anger at the man who'd broken a bond he had thought was unbreakable. He wasn't prepared for a flood of images from his childhood: waking up early and pouncing on his still-sleeping father; sitting next to the fire on miserable, cold, rainy winter days and talking of the things they would do when summer came; reading together while the wind howled outside. It was in this room that the bond of love had been forged and tempered into steel. Or at least he'd thought so.

"I never expected such a big house." Broc had followed Rafe.

"My father built it for my mother. She was from a wealthy family of Spanish ancestry. He wanted her to be proud of her home."

"I grew up in a house so small, I had to share a room and a bed with three brothers. You must have had a powerful reason to leave all this."

Rafe had never told anyone why he'd left California, but he felt it was time to tell Broc. "My mother invited Dolores to be her companion when she got sick. I was nineteen, idealistic, and Dolores was even more beautiful than she is now. I fell hopelessly in love with her." Unwilling to face Broc while he exposed this painful part of his past, Rafe walked over to a window that looked out over a small creek. The water sparkled in the sunlight as it tumbled over rocks on its way to the flat valley floor that would take it to the

Sacramento River. In summer its waters were used to irrigate the rows of poplars and elms that shaded the house from the fierce summer sun. "She said she returned my love but devoted herself to consoling my father. Fool that I was, I thought she was wonderful for giving so much time to an old man grieving over his wife. It never occurred to me that she had set her sights on marrying him instead of me. I probably wouldn't have believed Dolores and my father were having an affair if I hadn't caught them in bed."

Three

HE COULD STILL REMEMBER FEELING AS IF HIS HEART had stopped beating even as the blood pounded in his temples so hard he could barely think. He turned to Broc. "I was ready to forgive her, to put all the blame on my father, until I learned she was already pregnant. She had managed to divert my father's attention so artfully from my mother's death that he felt she was necessary to his happiness. When he announced he was going to marry her, I lost control." The pieces of a porcelain statuette he'd thrown at the fireplace had been cleared away long ago, but the scar where it had hit the mantel remained. "I don't remember half the things I said to him and Dolores. I didn't care what I said, whom I hurt. I'm not sure whether my father threw me out or whether I left. It probably doesn't matter."

Rafe had expected to feel uncomfortable after this revelation, to feel exposed, but he felt better now that someone else knew the truth.

"You must have had plenty of relatives you could have stayed with."

"I hated myself for being so stupid. I went to Mexico and worked as an ordinary vaquero until the war started."

Broc whistled. "After being the pampered son of a rich man, that must have been hard."

"I was too angry to care."

A knock at the door was followed by the entrance of a middle-aged man carrying Rafe's saddlebags. The moment Juan saw Rafe, his face lit up with a smile that made him look a decade younger.

"I was afraid I'd never see you again," Juan said. "Never in this room."

Rafe's spirits lifted as he crossed the room to greet one of the family retainers who'd known him since his birth. He would have embraced Juan if Rosana hadn't burst through the doorway. As tall and ample as Juan was short and thin, she enveloped Rafe in a bosomy embrace. Words tumbled out of her mouth so rapidly, Rafe couldn't understand half of what she said.

"I prayed to the Virgin every night for your return. This is your home. I knew you wouldn't stay away forever."

Rafe couldn't tell her he didn't intend to remain. She'd learn that soon enough.

"When Margarita told me who was in the parlor, I broke into tears." Rosana supported her assertion by breaking into tears once more. "I would have brought the drinks, but I knew I'd probably drop the tray." She released Rafe and held him at arm's length. "Let me look at you." She studied his face a moment before saying, "The years have been hard on you, but you've gained some peace."

He had before he'd received the letter from Mr. Fielder.

"We've needed you here," Juan said. "Miguel has complained of your absence every day."

"He had my father. He didn't need me."

"Your father lost interest in the ranch after you left," Rosana said. "The last years before he died, he hardly left this room." She pointed to a small picture on the table next to his father's bed. "I'd bring him his dinner and find him so lost in his thoughts, he didn't know I'd entered the room even though I'd knocked first."

"That's not like him." His father had always been active.

"It's all the fault of that strumpet." Rosana's voice was like a hiss. Her black eyes flashed and her mouth grew hard.

Rafe had wished many times he could have taken back the words he'd spoken to the man he'd loved so much. After a few months in Mexico, he probably would have gone back and begged his father's forgiveness, but he knew his father would still require Rafe to treat Dolores with respect. Rafe couldn't do that. The hurt had burned too deep.

"If it hadn't been for Maria, I'd have left long ago," Rosana admitted.

"Why? The same blood runs in their veins. You can't trust either of them." When she'd opened the door to him, he'd found himself staring into the darkest brown eyes he'd ever seen. She was pretty, but it wasn't her attractiveness that struck him so much as the look of hard-held anger in her eyes. He hadn't known who she was or why she should be angry. He had been the one wronged.

"I thought the same thing at first, but she's shouldered the responsibility of Luis's education, the running of the household, and seeing that your father was comfortable during his illness."

It was to her credit that she had handled herself well enough to win Rosana's confidence, but she was still Dolores's sister. "She has a well-feathered nest. I'm sure she doesn't want to lose it."

"Everybody likes her," Juan said. "She doesn't take advantage of her position the way her sister does."

"I don't know what she's like, but she can't be half bad," Broc said. "Did you see the way Luis pushed up against her when he was frightened?"

"She's the only one who gave him any attention," Juan said. "His mother can't be bothered and his father couldn't bear the sight of him."

"Why?" Rafe couldn't imagine his father turning against a child.

Rosana rested her hand on Rafe's forearm. "I think it's because the child stood for everything that had gone wrong after your mother died."

"None of it is the boy's fault. It was Dolores. And my father," Rafe added reluctantly.

"It'll be up to you to make Luis believe that," Rosana said. "His mother has brought him up to fear you."

"Why?"

"How would I know?" Rosana replied. "She only talks to me when she wants me to do something for her."

Rafe didn't plan to be here long enough to make his brother believe anything. Luis could have the ranch. Dolores and her sister could live in all the luxury they wanted. As much as he liked Rosana and Juan, he didn't intend to let them draw him back into living at the ranch.

"If you intend to return in time for dinner, we'd better get going."

Rosana and Juan looked from Broc to Rafe.

"We're going to ride over the ranch. It's been a long time since I was here."

"Take Miguel with you," Juan said. "He's been hoping you'd come back for years."

Rafe didn't want to see Miguel because the old man would try to get him interested in the ranch all over again, but he'd take Miguel with him because it would break his heart to be left behind. It had been Miguel who taught Rafe to love the land, to love planting crops and watching them grow, to look for ways to improve the quality of the livestock. His father had been more concerned with business. Their diverse interests had meshed into a smoothly working partnership.

Until it had been destroyed by Dolores's greed and ambition.

❦

"You can't seriously think Rafe is still in love with you, that he will marry you." Having dressed for dinner, made sure Luis was fed and in his room, and that preparations for dinner were complete, Maria had gone to her sister's room. Dolores had dragged out more than a dozen dresses, all discarded in her search for the perfect gown for the evening. Maria started returning the dresses to the closet. "He's still furious at you." After what he'd done, Maria couldn't understand why Dolores would even want Rafe back.

"I refuse to wear mourning." Dolores flung a dress from herself in disgust. "I hate black."

"You don't have to wear black, but choose something in good taste." Maria frowned over a lilac creation, which fit her sister's body far too snugly.

Dolores didn't avert her gaze from the dresses piled on the bed. "Rafe is still angry I married his father, but he'll get over it."

Maria picked up an emerald-green silk dress and put it away. "How can you forgive Rafe for raping you to keep you from marrying his father?"

"That was a long time ago." Dolores hunched her shoulders. "It doesn't matter anymore."

Maria was used to her sister's vagaries, but this was too much. "How can you say that? That man stole your honor."

Dolores avoided her gaze. "He was in love and desperate." She held up a ruby-red velvet dress and studied her reflection in the mirror. "What's the point of holding it against him now?"

"Because any man who would commit rape is untrustworthy. It's impossible to tell what he might do the next time he loses his temper."

"He's too old to do anything like that again. He's like his father. He will grow calm and indifferent and life will be as it has always been."

Dolores sometimes indulged in absurd fantasies, but Maria was a realist. Her sister was probably hoping Rafe was still in love with her because that would be the easiest way to ensure her future. As soon as she realized Rafe disliked her too much to ever consider such an alternative, she'd come to her senses. Maria fretted over what Dolores would decide to do then.

Maria had always wished Luis had a brother he could respect, admire, learn from, but that wasn't the case according to Dolores, and Maria had made up her mind to keep them apart as much as possible. She didn't doubt that Juan's stories were true. Rafe had impressed her as a man who could do anything he wanted, exactly the kind of man a boy like Luis would come to worship. With his father absent from his life and the men who were drawn to Dolores a dissolute set, he had no male role model he could admire. She was determined Rafe wouldn't be that person.

Why couldn't Rafe be like Broc? Broc had suffered a terrible loss, one that was physically as well as emotionally painful, yet had managed to remain cheerful and smiling. She could only imagine what a devastatingly handsome man he must have been. It didn't make her any happier with herself to realize she preferred Rafe's brand of looks.

"What do you think of this dress?" Dolores held up a cream satin dress that was more suitable for a girl than a mature woman. "It was once Rafe's favorite dress."

"You were nineteen then, not twenty-nine."

"I can still wear it."

"It makes you look like you're trying to be a girl again. You'll look silly in it."

"Rafe won't think so."

Maria was fearful that *silly* wouldn't be the word that sprang into Rafe's mind. "It's inappropriate."

Dolores grinned, pleased. "Your opposition makes me certain it's the very dress I ought to wear."

Maria threw up her hands. She was positive Rafe's affections couldn't be resurrected, not even by a cream satin dress that lent Dolores an air of youth and innocence, but her sister would have to discover that for herself. "Don't be late coming down. Men hate to have their dinner go cold because a woman couldn't make up her mind which dress to wear."

Dolores favored her sister with a self-satisfied smile. "I'll be down early. I don't intend to compete with Rafe's dinner for his attention."

Broc looked his friend up and down when they met in the hall outside their rooms. "I thought you weren't going to dress for dinner."

Rafe hadn't brought evening clothes because he didn't have any. It had been Juan's suggestion that he see if he could wear any of his father's suits. Rafe was surprised to find his scrawny teenage body had filled out and now his father's clothes fit as if they'd been made for him. He was reluctant to wear them at first, but what the lawyer had told him, what Rosana and Juan had said, encouraged him to believe his father had changed his mind before his death and held Dolores responsible for the breakup of his family rather than Rafe.

"I think I'd have wounded Juan beyond hope of recovery if I'd come down in Levi's and a clean shirt."

Broc laughed. "He insisted I wear some of your old clothes." Broc twisted his body to show that the pants were tight about the hips and the coat snug across the shoulders. "It's a good thing I'm a skinny son of a bitch, or I'd never have managed to wiggle into these. Don't they ever throw anything away in your house?"

"It's not my house and apparently not."

Broc patted his stomach. "I can't eat too much or I'll pop a button."

"Mama used to say I ate as if I had a hollow leg." The memory cut through him like a sharp pain. His mother had been a semi-invalid most of her life. He'd loved her for her kindness and her boundless pride in him. Many times in the past ten years, he'd wished he'd been mature enough to have spent more time with her.

"Let's go down and dazzle the ladies," Broc said.

"Nobody ever dazzled Dolores except herself."

"She seems willing to be dazzled by you now, but you'd better stay clear of her sister. I think she'd be happy to stick a knife into you."

"That's not surprising considering what Dolores has probably told her."

Rafe was surprised by how familiar the house felt. Little had changed since he'd left. The rugs on the floor, the pictures on the walls…even the squeak in the stairs was like an old friend welcoming him back. He cautioned himself against getting too comfortable, against letting himself become attached. He wasn't going to stay.

Broc held back to allow Rafe to go down the stairs ahead of him. "That's a pity. She's a very pretty young woman. I think she likes you."

Rafe turned when he reached the bottom of the stairs. "A minute ago you said she looked like she wanted to put a knife in me. That's not my notion of *liking* somebody."

"She's conflicted."

"You're crazy."

Broc turned Rafe around and gave him a push toward the parlor. "You're too involved to be objective."

Rafe didn't get a chance to respond. The moment he reached the parlor, Dolores rose gracefully to her feet and crossed the room toward him, her face wreathed in a smile so brilliant it almost deflected his attention from her dress. Remembering that dress, and how it had affected him nine years ago, caused him a pang of remorse at his lost innocence.

"You're a naughty boy for teasing me about not dressing for dinner. You look so handsome, I could believe only ten minutes rather than ten years have passed."

"These are my father's clothes. I wore them only to please Juan and Rosana." He glanced at Maria, who had remained seated, but her gaze was directed toward Broc. Why did that irritate him? Maybe because he didn't want Broc falling for Maria as he had Dolores. She wasn't beautiful like her sister, but she was very attractive, more appealing than Dolores in a way he couldn't yet define.

Dolores used straightening his tie as an excuse to put her hand on his chest. "You're better-looking than your father. You've got your mother's eyes and nose." She looked thoughtful. "Maybe her mouth, too."

Rafe removed her hand from his chest more roughly than necessary. "Don't speak my mother's name. You aren't worthy to have it pass your lips."

Dolores's hand was back in an instant. "She thought I was worthy to be her companion, to entrust me with her secrets."

Rafe had never been naive enough to believe his mother would entrust her secrets to the ambitious daughter of a first cousin. "You're lying. Now get your hands off me."

Dolores appeared unmoved by his accusation. She reached for a glass of red wine, took a large swallow, and turned to Rafe with her familiar smile. He was beginning to feel like the victim of a snake, wrapped in its coils and unable to escape. He picked up a glass of whiskey and took it to Broc, who was standing close to Maria. "I don't want anything now," he said to Maria, "and I'd prefer water at dinner rather than wine."

"I've arranged for that."

Rafe was surprised by her thoughtfulness.

"You used to like whiskey and wine." Dolores's disbelief was apparent. "A little too much, as I remember."

"One time when I had too much to drink, I said things to my father I've spent years regretting. I won't take a chance on doing that again."

"You don't have to worry about that. Your father is dead."

He had to control an impulse to close his fingers around her lovely white throat and slowly squeeze the self-satisfaction out of her huge, mesmerizing eyes.

"I'm sure Rafe is aware of that, Dolores. It wasn't kind of you to mention it," Maria chided.

Maria hadn't left her seat, but she sat forward in her chair.

"I don't see why." Dolores didn't take the reproof well. "It's not as if he caused Warren's death."

Maybe he hadn't caused it, but he'd contributed to it.

"I think it's human nature to look back after the death of a loved one and regret you didn't do some things differently." Broc's angry look appeared to have little effect on Dolores.

Margarita entered the parlor to announce it was time for dinner.

"You will sit at the head of the table," Dolores told Rafe when they entered the dining room. "I'm seated on your right and Maria on your left. Your friend can sit at the other end."

Rafe suspected Dolores had deliberately placed Broc as far out of her line of vision as possible, but the steam was taken out of his burgeoning anger when he saw that all the extra leaves had been taken out of the table to reduce it to a size suitable for four people. Dolores's irritation told him that had been Maria's doing. He glanced in her direction, but her attention was on Broc, who was holding her chair. Rafe refused to hold Dolores's chair. She could sit on the floor for all he cared.

Dolores plopped into her chair with ill grace.

"Where's Luis?" Rafe hadn't expected to see him in the parlor, but he had expected him to be at the dinner table.

"He's too young to eat dinner with us." A second glass of wine had helped Dolores get over her pique. "We can't be expected to put up with childish prattle."

"Seven thirty is too late for a nine-year-old child to wait to eat," Maria said. "Rosana supervised his dinner, and I put him to bed before I came down."

Maria had looked at Rafe when she spoke, then dropped her gaze. He wondered if she was afraid he would criticize her choices. It wasn't that he thought the boy ought to be at the table. He'd just wondered where Luis was.

"That means he'll be up at the crack of dawn." Broc grinned at Rafe. "I'm going to leave a note on his door telling him to go straight to your room." He turned to Maria. "Rafe is the morning person on our crew. I like to sleep late."

"Maria is just like him. I don't understand how we can be so different." Dolores's glorious smile was back in place. Rafe could understand how his younger self had been dazzled by it. He might be just as dazzled now if he didn't know her character.

The rest of the meal passed without Dolores doing anything more annoying than talking to him while ignoring everyone else at the table. Rafe turned to Maria several times during the meal, but she was usually talking to Broc. He tried to listen to their conversation, but they spoke in low tones. When Broc laughed, Rafe was annoyed he didn't know what she'd said that was so funny. When Broc smiled and replied to her with enthusiasm, he resented that he was forced to listen to Dolores reminisce about times he'd rather forget. By the time the meal was over, he was out of patience. When the dessert plates had been removed, he pushed his chair back without ceremony.

"I'm going for a walk."

Dolores jumped up. "I'll go with you."

"You will not. Maria, would you accompany me?"

Four

IF MARIA HADN'T BEEN POSITIVE SHE HAD NO HEARING problem, she wouldn't have trusted her ears. "Me?" It sounded more like a squeak than a word.

"Yes, you."

His response was clear enough. It was his purpose that was obscure. "What could we have to speak about?"

"That's what I want to find out."

She wasn't afraid of him, but nor did she feel comfortable being alone with him. His behavior toward her was cool but correct. "I doubt we have anything to talk about that we can't discuss in the parlor."

"Maybe not, but I'd rather do it while I walk. As I remember, the nights here can be extremely fine on occasion."

The nights could be spectacularly beautiful, but she didn't see why that should be a consideration. "I'm sure you would enjoy the evening more in Broc's company."

"He's already spent too many nights in the saddle with only me and cows for company."

There didn't seem to be any polite way to continue to resist, so Maria slid her chair back and stood. She hadn't expected Rafe to hold it for her, but apparently he had been brought up to be a gentleman.

"What am I supposed to do?" Dolores asked.

"You could talk to Broc about living on a ranch in California. It must be quite different from Tennessee."

Broc hadn't let Dolores's temper spoil his mood. "California doesn't look much different from my home. It has mountains, valleys, and rivers. It just takes a lot longer to get here than to Tennessee."

Maria hated to leave Broc with Dolores, but she had the feeling he could handle himself around women even more difficult than her sister.

She left the dining room ahead of Rafe and turned down the hall toward the front door. Rafe went ahead to hold the door open. She was disinclined to take his hand when he offered to help her down the steps, but it was dark and she couldn't see the steps because her dress had a wide skirt. She probably shouldn't have been surprised by the strength of his hand or its roughness, but she hadn't really believed he worked as a cowhand. She wished she didn't find him so attractive and was angry with herself for feeling that way.

"I can't walk far without ruining my dress. We can use the gazebo." Maria had enjoyed sitting in the gazebo when Luis was a baby. It had been her refuge when the challenges she faced became too overwhelming. It had fallen into disrepair after the garden dried up, but she still loved to sit there in the early evening when it was cool. Now she seated herself on a bench that creaked under her weight. Rafe followed her into the dim interior. His shadow was imposing, his outline so close to what her ideal of a man should be that she had to remind herself he'd committed an unpardonable sin.

"What happened to my mother's garden?"

"Dolores didn't care for it."

"Probably because it reminded her of my mother. I'd say it gave her a guilty conscience, but Dolores doesn't have a conscience."

Maria decided it was best to ignore that comment. "It burned up during a particularly hot, dry summer."

"Until she got too ill to leave her room, my mother used to spend hours sitting in the garden, planning which flowers to plant, what trees or shrubs she wanted. One time the hands had to move a tree three times before they got it exactly where she wanted. She diverted the creek to flow through a rock garden. Sometimes she would sit next to it for hours. She said the sound of the water tumbling over the rocks was so soothing, it helped her forget the pain and the weakness."

It was impossible to be untouched by the sadness in Rafe's voice. She wished the shadows didn't obscure his face. She had a feeling he'd outgrown the lack of control that had caused him to attack Dolores. That didn't absolve him of the responsibility for his act, but it promised to make working with him less distasteful. If she could think of him as having reformed, she wouldn't be ashamed of herself for not hating him.

"You didn't bring me out here to talk about your mother's garden."

"Why do you want to hurry back? Luis is in bed, and dinner is over. Rosana can take care of the kitchen, and Margarita can take care of Broc and Dolores."

"There's always a lot to do in a house this size."

"Let Dolores take care of the house for a half hour, or don't you trust her?"

Dolores had never taken care of anything as long as Maria could remember. She had probably forgotten how to find the kitchen. On several occasions, Maria had been so upset by Dolores's selfishness that she'd been tempted to leave, but she owed her sister too much to desert her, no matter how difficult she might sometimes be.

Their father had been a member of an important Spanish family whose fortune was based on an old land grant. He'd never had to work or worry about where the money came from to support his extravagant lifestyle until an upstart Anglo named Solomon Grunge had decided to challenge the land grant in court. Knowing that many such grants had been overturned in the newly established American courts, her father had offered Solomon Grunge a portion of his land and Maria's hand in marriage if he would withdraw his challenge.

A shy and unworldly thirteen-year-old, Maria had been as much afraid of Solomon as she was repelled by him. He was more than three times her age, ill dressed, ill spoken, and given to staring at her while licking his lips. Maria had begged and pleaded, but her father said she had to marry Solomon to save the family. Dolores had told her father she wouldn't allow him to force Maria into such a marriage and had driven Solomon from the house. Dolores had placated their father by saying she would have more than enough money for everybody after she married Vicente Bandini.

It hadn't worked out that way.

Solomon pursued his case in court and won. The culminating blow came when Bandini broke his engagement to Dolores. Maria's father had never let her forget that her refusal to marry Solomon had beggared her family and destroyed Dolores's future. The invitation to live with Dolores had spared her poverty and daily recriminations. It had also given her a chance to compensate for what she'd done to Dolores.

She'd also stayed because of Luis.

"The only reason I'm here is to take care of Luis and manage the house." She wasn't just taking care of Luis until something better came along. She loved him. It would break her heart to lose him.

"As executor and heir to half the ranch, I think it's within my rights to request a small amount of your time."

She couldn't argue with that. He had the power to relieve her of her duties and order her to leave the house. She wondered if that was why he'd brought her outside. She had never considered living at the ranch to be a permanent situation, but over the last nine years it had become her home. Luis and Dolores were her family. As long as Warren had been alive, as long as she thought Dolores would inherit the ranch, there had been a clear expectation that she would remain. Warren must have intended for her to stay after his death, or he wouldn't have made her joint guardian of Luis. She shouldn't let her distrust of Rafe cause her to jump to conclusions. "You're quite right. I'm used to being the one to make decisions. It'll probably take me a while to change."

Rafe regarded her in silence for a moment. "I haven't said I want to make a change. I know nothing about taking care of a young boy, but I intend to learn."

Terror that she might lose Luis raced through her. "Are you saying you want me to stay on until you can find someone to replace me?" When she'd first learned about the will, everything Dolores had said about Rafe had led her to expect they'd both have to leave. But when months went by without the lawyer being able to locate Rafe, she'd started to believe he'd never be found and she would be allowed to stay.

"I don't know. I don't think you're like Dolores, but she's your sister so I don't know if I can trust you. You appear to have done a good job with Luis's education, but it seems he never leaves the house. How is that going to help him know what to do with a ranch?"

Rafe's criticism stung. She was aware Luis needed a much broader education than she could give him, but she'd done the best she knew how with the boy.

"I was only fifteen when Dolores invited me to live with her, so you might say Luis and I have grown up together. I knew nothing of horses, ranch management, or any of the sports and activities men find so necessary. I repeatedly urged your father to take an interest in the boy, but he refused."

"I can't understand that. My father put me up in the saddle with him before I could walk."

How could she tell him that Warren wouldn't see the child because looking at him reminded him of the son he'd lost, the son he apparently loved even after ordering him to leave the house? Despite what he'd done, Rosana insisted Rafe's leaving had broken his father's heart. She wondered if she'd feel the same about Luis. He was practically like her own son.

"I asked your father for his reason, but he never gave it. He became very reclusive after you left. During the last two years of his life, he rarely left his room."

"No doubt that was Dolores's doing."

It was hard for her to accept his deep dislike of her sister without throwing his own errors in his face. She'd never been in love, so she could only imagine how devastating it must have been to learn that the woman he loved planned to marry his father. But that had happened ten years ago. It was time to move beyond those past injuries.

"It hasn't been easy for Dolores. She's too young and too pretty to settle willingly into widowhood, and her allowance is too small to allow her the freedom she wants."

"Don't waste your time asking me to increase her allowance. If it were in my power, I'd eliminate it altogether."

"She was your father's wife, the mother of your... brother." She still stumbled when she said that.

"That woman destroyed my life and ruined my father's. She's cold, conniving, calculating, and utterly without conscience. I'm glad you were here to take care of Luis. There might be a chance for him despite the blood in his veins."

"The same blood runs in *my* veins."

"I haven't forgotten that." His tone was cold, unyielding.

"If you wish any changes in the household arrangements, just let me know. If you would prefer that I hand them over to Rosana, I'll do so."

"I don't want that."

She hoped her relief didn't show. She stood. "Is there anything more you wish to say?"

"We have to talk about Luis."

"It would be better if you spent some time getting to know him first."

Rafe had been leaning against one of the supports of the gazebo. Without warning, it cracked, splintered, and collapsed. Maria hardly knew how it occurred—it was such a surprise and happened so quickly—but she found herself in Rafe's arms, safely outside the gazebo as the structure collapsed on itself. It would have been hard to say which caused the greater shock. "You can put me down now." She didn't know how she managed to sound so normal. She felt anything but.

"Are you sure you can stand?"

"Thanks to you, I wasn't hurt."

"It must be a shock."

"I've had worse." But nothing more startling than finding herself in the arms of a man like Rafe. When he set her on her feet, her legs were wobbly.

Rafe knelt down to inspect the fallen timbers. Maria didn't know what he could see in the dark, but Rafe's inspection was thorough.

Rafe turned to look at her. "Have you seen anyone hanging around the gazebo?"

"No, but I can't see it from the house. Why?"

"Someone has worn down the wood in an unobtrusive way. Someone wanted the gazebo to collapse."

"Why? Nobody uses it but me."

Rafe's gaze narrowed. "Who could want you killed or badly injured?"

The thought that anyone could want to harm her

was too absurd to entertain. "No one. No one would have anything to gain by my death."

Rafe regarded the jumble of wood. "Someone must think he does.

"I'll look again tomorrow," he continued. "In the meantime, try to think of why someone would want you dead."

"Surely I wouldn't have been killed if it had fallen on me."

"The beams across the top are four inches thick, twelve inches wide, and about twenty feet long. Any one of them would have crushed your skull."

Maria couldn't make herself believe anyone would want her dead, but she didn't want to think about it anymore. "It would be nice if you would spend some time tomorrow with Luis. He needs to get to know you."

"Why?"

"You're the heir, the executor, his guardian. You'll be living here."

"I don't want to inherit this ranch or have anything to do with it. I'm heading back to Texas as soon as I can."

❧

Maria closed the door to her room and breathed a relieved sigh. Over the years she had come to feel that her room was a sanctuary, a place of quiet in the midst of constant drama. She was still reeling from Rafe's disclosure that he would be returning to Texas as soon as possible. It didn't make sense. Why should a man walk away from such an inheritance? In Texas he was an ordinary cowhand. Here he would own half of a ranch that would make him one of the richest men in California. No man in his right mind walked away from something like that!

How would his leaving affect her? Since she was joint guardian of Luis, she doubted she would be turned out. She'd hoped to see Luis grow up and assume his rightful position in society. She would be devastated if she had to leave. Luis had become an integral part of her life, the child she didn't have, the child she might *never* have. But running such a huge ranch on her own would be impossible.

Who would help her? Miguel was planning to leave at the end of the harvest to go live with his cousin near San Diego. There was no one to take his place, to teach Luis how to manage his inheritance, to keep the ranch prosperous until he was old enough to take over its management. Hundreds of people depended on Rancho los Alamitos for their livelihood. The town of Cíbola might wither and disappear if the ranch failed.

But the thing that worried her most was her opinion of Rafe.

Nine years ago he'd been the handsome, spoiled only son of an indulgent father, unable to accept that the woman he loved wanted to marry his father. Being driven out of his mind by grief, anger, and jealousy, he probably was trying to convince Dolores to choose him, got carried away by the passion of the moment, and ended up forcing himself on her. Unable to face his own guilt, he'd accused his father of having seduced her, had a terrible fight, then ran away. A classic case of a young man losing control while under the sway of volatile emotions.

The Rafe Jerry who'd appeared at the ranch earlier

today didn't fit that image. He was handsome, but there was nothing spoiled, overindulged, or self-pitying about him. He was still angry at Dolores, didn't trust Maria, and admitted he knew nothing about boys, but she had never seen anyone less likely to lose control, to rape a woman. He might have been a volatile youth—though Rosana said he never was until Dolores came into the house—but he wasn't any longer. And that impressed her.

What scared her was knowing that being impressed with him was even more dangerous than being attracted to him. Any woman breathing would be attracted to a man like Rafe. His black hair, black eyes, and slightly olive complexion were gifts of his Spanish heritage, yet he had the height and broad-shouldered strength of his father's Scottish ancestors. He moved with the grace of a man who kept himself in good physical shape and wore his clothes like a second skin. He had the presence of a man who was supremely confident in himself, one who had no doubt he could handle any situation that might arise.

What woman wouldn't be impressed by a man like that? She supposed she'd always had reservations about Dolores's version of what Rafe was like. Everyone knew Rafe and his father had quarreled over Dolores. Terrible things had been said by both men, but the sympathy of the household was entirely with Rafe. What no one knew was that Luis was Rafe's son. Dolores said Warren had married her so the child would have a father he could be proud of. She said Warren was adamant that no one was ever to know. That made it difficult for Maria to understand why

Warren would give Rafe control of the ranch and everyone on it.

"What did he say to you? You were gone a long time." Dolores had entered without knocking, had eased the door shut behind her.

"Why are you sneaking into my room?"

"I don't want Rafe to know I'm here."

"We're sisters. What could be more natural than a chat before going to bed?"

Dolores drew up a chair next to her sister. "Rafe is a very suspicious person. He'll want to know what I've said to you."

Maria hadn't noticed Rafe wanting to know anything about Dolores, but she said nothing.

"He hates me," Dolores went on. "He'll do anything he can to get back at me for marrying his father."

Maria was sure he'd never forgive Dolores for what she had done, but Rafe didn't appear to be a man who would waste energy on things that couldn't be changed. "He didn't talk about you except to say that he doesn't trust you. I'm not sure he trusts me, either."

"Maybe so, but he's attracted to you."

Maria laughed at the absurdity of that notion. "He's not sure you and I are alike, but he doesn't intend to take responsibility for the household from me just yet. Apparently I'm to have a trial period before he makes up his mind."

"He'd be a fool to ask you to leave. No one loves this place as much as you do."

"I doubt that will be an important consideration with him. I don't know what he was like at nineteen, but the grown-up Rafe Jerry is a pragmatic man who won't allow sentiment to color his judgment or affect his decisions."

"He's a different person," said Dolores.

"We're all different from what we were ten years ago."

"Did he say he would increase my allowance?"

"He said he'd eliminate it if he could."

"He wouldn't do that," Dolores stated confidently. "He has too much pride to endure people criticizing him for being so brutal to his father's widow."

Maria doubted Rafe cared what anybody thought. "We agreed to talk about Luis tomorrow. He doesn't think I've done a good job raising him."

"Why should he care? He's never seen the boy."

"Luis is his son"—Maria didn't hesitate to speak the truth to Dolores—"joint heir to his father's estate."

There it was again, Dolores avoiding her gaze. Why did she do that every time Maria reminded her that Rafe, not Warren, was Luis's father? "Rafe won't share control of the ranch with anyone," Dolores asserted.

"He'll have to share it with someone. He said he's going back to Texas as soon as he can."

"He'll never leave. Inheriting the ranch will make him one of the richest men in California."

"I don't think that matters to him."

Dolores looked at Maria as if she'd lost her mind. "Of course it matters. He only left because his father disinherited him. He's back now because he got the ranch instead of me."

Maria wondered why, if Warren had disinherited Rafe, he'd changed his mind without seeing his son again. She hadn't known Warren as well as she would have liked, but he'd always struck her as a man who wouldn't change his mind without a good reason.

"I can tell you only what Rafe said."

"He's got some trick in mind. He was always crazy about this place. There were times when he would get so caught up in his work, he would forget he'd promised to meet me."

That didn't sound like a young man who was crazy in love. Usually adult responsibilities were the first things to be forgotten. "I wouldn't know anything about that. I can only take him at his word."

"Never do that!" Dolores sounded insistent. "Rafe won't stop until he gets what he wants."

If he'd wanted the ranch, why had he left? Why hadn't he come back, tried to regain his father's trust, tried to push Dolores out of favor? With her single-minded concentration on her own pleasures, he could have found a hundred ways to put a wedge between husband and wife. "I'm too tired to discuss Rafe any more. If I don't get some sleep, I won't be fit to talk about Luis tomorrow."

"Don't let him get Luis off by himself. You don't know what might happen."

"Are you implying that he might harm his own son?"

"Stop saying that!" She looked around nervously. "One of these days you're going to slip and say it in front of Rosana or Juan."

Maria wished she hadn't been told—it was hard to know the truth and have to face Rafe and act as if she didn't—but she'd never do anything that would cause Luis to learn about his parentage.

"I don't know that Rafe would do anything to hurt Luis, but I don't trust him." Dolores fidgeted in her chair. "How many men in his position do you know who would be tempted to do something to get the whole fortune for themselves?"

Maria could name a dozen, but rather than show a dislike for Luis, Rafe had seemed to want to draw the boy out, make him feel important. He was brusque and reluctant to trust people, but his swift action had saved her from injury when the gazebo collapsed. He'd said he was going back to Texas, but his interest in Luis's studies, his having bought him a pony, his disapproval of the way she was bringing him up, might indicate he wanted to take the boy back to Texas with him.

Still, Dolores was right. A fortune could cause a man to do any number of things he wouldn't consider in ordinary circumstances.

❧

"How did it go with the fair Maria?" Rafe remained standing next to the fireplace, leaning against the mantel in the room that had once been his father's, while Broc made himself comfortable. He had brought up a bottle of brandy for himself and a bottle of the ranch's rich red wine for Rafe.

"I don't think she's as bad as her sister."

Rafe hadn't wanted to feel that way. He'd wanted to think the two women were alike so he could banish them both from the ranch, leaving the lawyer to look after Luis, but that plan had begun to fall apart the moment Maria opened the door to him. He'd known immediately Maria was nothing like her sister. The instant attraction had been a shock to him. He wasn't immediately attracted to people, least of all women he had reason to distrust. It would have been natural to compare the feeling to his attraction to Dolores, but he wasn't nineteen, Maria wasn't as beautiful as her sister, and he wasn't tempted to fall to his knees and worship her. The thought made him smile.

Broc regarded him over the rim of his brandy snifter. "What's got you smiling?"

"It was just a silly thought I had comparing Maria and Dolores."

"Don't keep me in suspense." He waved the brandy bottle at Rafe. "I might take to drink in frustration."

"Nine years ago, I practically fell at Dolores's feet and worshipped her. I found the idea of doing the same to Maria amusing."

"I don't agree with you. I considered making a push to attract her attention, but I decided it wouldn't be a good idea."

"Why?"

"Because you're interested in her."

Five

"YOU'D BETTER LAY OFF THE BRANDY. IT'S OBVIOUS you've had too much to drink."

Broc's lazy laugh annoyed Rafe. "I didn't say you were ready to offer marriage. I just said you were attracted to her."

"You said *interested*. That's not the same as attracted. You are aware that you're talking about the sister of the woman whose duplicity ruined my father's life."

"Just because they share the same blood doesn't mean they share the same morals," Broc pointed out.

"I'd be happy to learn Maria is as admirable as her sister is despicable, but I'm heading back to Texas as soon as I figure out how to shift responsibility for this inheritance to someone else's shoulders."

Broc took a sip of brandy and leveled a hard look at Rafe. "If I were you, I'd think about that a bit more before I made up my mind."

"You aren't me, but for the sake of argument, why would you want the responsibility of a place like this?"

Broc looked at his brandy with affection. "For one

thing, to be able to afford brandy like this. It's a shame you don't drink it. It's remarkable."

In the first years after he left the ranch, Rafe had drunk to forget. When he couldn't forget, he drank so he wouldn't mind that he remembered. "Setting aside the money, which I don't care about, why would I want to stay here?"

"How can you say you don't care about money when you're rich enough to buy and sell Cade several times over?"

"My father was rich, but it didn't make him happy. My mother died after a long illness, his only son ran away, and he married a harpy."

"You wouldn't make the same mistakes."

"I would if I was as interested in Maria as you think."

"Forget being attracted to Maria. Forget being married."

"I forgot that long ago."

Broc ignored Rafe. "You've inherited half of the ranch you used to love. You liked the work, and you liked the people. Your family is here. Your roots are here."

"My family is in Texas with Cade and Pilar and their kids, and my roots are wherever I decide to plant them."

Broc set aside his brandy. "Cade may be an old friend, but he's not really family. Think of your responsibilities. You've got a ranch that needs your attention, and a half brother who needs a big brother."

"He has Maria, who's horrified he even likes me."

"All the more reason to stay long enough to prove to him you're his best friend, his strongest advocate."

"How can I be his best friend when he's twenty-one years younger?"

He knew he was being obnoxious, but he didn't want to think about his attraction to Maria. It could have only one end. Nor did he want to think about his responsibility to Luis. It wasn't the boy's fault, but he thought of Dolores's betrayal whenever he saw him. Most of all, he didn't want to think of Dolores. He no longer wanted to be her husband, but he didn't want to be her keeper, either. He knew she would involve him in debts, an array of undesirable acquaintances, and ill-considered escapades. It would be better to let the lawyer deal with her.

Broc poured some of the rich red wine into a glass and handed it to Rafe. "Have some wine. It might mellow your mood."

Rafe didn't take the glass. "I don't want my mood mellowed."

"I do. You're my host, so it's your duty to see to my happiness."

Rafe had never been able to keep up a sour front when Broc exerted himself to be charming—or persuasive. "You should have gone into politics. You could persuade the devil to vote for you."

"Maybe the devil, but I'd scare off the good, common folk. At least cows don't care how I look."

Rafe accepted the glass. The wine had a rich, hearty flavor and just enough bite to keep it from being too fruity. He had been the one to encourage his father to plant these grapes, but the vines hadn't yet reached maturity when he left. He was glad to know he'd made a good choice.

He'd been too angry at Dolores and his father to miss the ranch immediately. For the three years he spent in Mexico, he was too drunk. Volunteering for the Confederate army had given him a reason to stay sober, as well as a group of friends who'd taken the place of the family he'd lost. Rebuilding Cade's ranch had given focus to his three years in Texas. Whenever he felt the need for more, there was the search for Laveau, the man who'd betrayed their cavalry unit. Though Laveau was Cade's brother-in-law, each of the Night Riders had sworn the traitor would not go unpunished.

"What do you plan to do about the ranch when you leave?"

Broc's question brought Rafe out of his abstraction. "If Maria proves as trustworthy as you think, I'll leave Luis in her care. The lawyer can handle everything else."

"I thought you had to sign for every expenditure."

"Maybe he can send the papers to me, or I can come out once a year." If it had been just Dolores, he'd have said to hell with her and the ranch. He had the right to throw away his inheritance, but he didn't have to right to throw away Luis's as well.

"I don't know anything about wills, but if your father intended to write that will in such a way that you had to be here, I don't think you're going to get away with once-a-year visits."

Rafe took a swallow of the wine. He really liked it. He would have to talk to Miguel about increasing the size of the vineyard. With the gold fields mostly played out, the market for beef was decreasing. However, with railroads able to carry produce to markets quickly, nuts, fruits, vegetables, wines, grains, and a dozen other crops would more than offset the loss of profit from the beef side of their business. He'd have to spend more time riding over the ranch and talking with Miguel before he decided what changes to make. The biggest need of all was a comprehensive irrigation system, but he refused to let himself get involved in ranch problems.

"What are you going to do tomorrow?"

"I'm not certain, but it will involve spending some time with Luis. I thought I would start by seeing if he knows how to ride."

Broc raised an eyebrow. "Maybe I'd better do it. Luis seems to like you, but you're a scary man even when you're in a good mood."

"Carlos isn't frightened of me," Rafe replied, citing Cade's two-year-old son.

"He's too little to have enough sense to be scared of you. Besides, you become human when you're around him."

"I'm always human."

"Haven't you wondered why Nate always works with Ivor even though he went through the war with you?" Broc asked, mentioning two of their fellow Night Riders.

"Are you telling me Cade pairs you with me because nobody else wants to work with me?"

"When was the last time you worked with any-body but me or Cade?" Broc swallowed the last of his brandy and set the snifter aside. "You're an angry man, but you've been angry so long, you don't see it any longer. Nobody says anything about it because criticism makes you worse. Pilar has given up doing anything except encouraging you to play with Carlos. It's the only chink any of us have found in the wall you've built around yourself."

How was he supposed to work with Nate? The man was only twenty-three. He'd never been out of Arkansas or off the family farm until the war. He wasn't interested in anything but cows and possum hunting. Ivor's family had lost their Polish estates through a war or some political shenanigans. All he could talk about was Poland. Thirty minutes in Ivor's company, and he was ready to buy his damned estates and send him back to Poland.

"The only reason Cade and I put up with you is because we don't care if you don't talk for hours."

Okay, so he wasn't congenial. Even when he was living at home, he'd preferred to work with Miguel than to run around with boys his age. "If you think all this honesty is going to cause me to change, I'm sorry to disappoint you."

"Whatever it takes to change you is right here." Broc's index finger pointed down at the floor. "This is where it all went wrong, so this is the only place that can change it."

"My father is dead, and I've lost my innocence— paltry possession that it was—so how can anything be changed?"

"You've got the home you love, a ranch and work that excites you, a brother to get to know, and a woman who attracts you. I'd say that's enough to start with."

"When did you turn into a romantic?"

Broc laughed. "We all have the potential to be happy. We just have to have the courage to try."

Rafe drank the rest of his wine and set down the glass. "It's a good thing you don't talk like that all the time. People would swear you were coming down with a fever."

Broc got to his feet. "Act like you don't care, if it makes you feel better, but somewhere inside is the boy who got hurt so badly that he went into hiding because he couldn't stand to be hurt again. I know he's there because I see him every time you play with Carlos. You just have to find a way to let him out. Now I'm going to bed. If I'm not up in time for breakfast, don't wake me."

Rafe didn't move from his position by the fireplace. He didn't believe the part about his younger self being inside him, still trying to get out. He'd spent ten years trying to forget everything about his life in California. Over time his home had become so thoroughly identified with Dolores, he couldn't imagine living on Rancho los Alamitos again. After the war, he'd been happy to settle down on Cade's ranch.

Now he wondered if he'd been fooling himself. Could it be that his refusal to think about the ranch was a way to cover up his desire to return? That might be true, but it couldn't change the actions of the two people he'd once loved the most. He couldn't think of the ranch without thinking of his father. And if he could manage to get past that, Dolores was there as a constant reminder of everything that had gone wrong.

Growing up, he'd never been conscious of being rich. He'd considered going to school a waste of time when he could be working on the ranch. In the years since, he hadn't wanted anything beyond a place to sleep, enough food to stave off hunger, and a job to give him something to do. You had to want power or possessions to want to be rich. Or have someone you wanted to give things to. Without those, money was only a responsibility. All he had to worry about now was himself, and that was fine with him.

He moved away from the fireplace and started to undress. It would seem strange to sleep in his father's room. He wasn't sure why he'd insisted on this room. He just knew he couldn't have slept anywhere else. Was it a subconscious statement that he was stepping into his father's shoes? He didn't think so, but he'd spent years refusing to think about why he did things. He didn't really believe all of Broc's nonsense, but while he was here, he might as well exorcize some of the demons that had plagued him for so long.

He knew he wasn't happy, and he was getting tired of his own dissatisfaction. Not because it made other people uncomfortable. He was jealous of the happiness that Cade and Pilar had found with each other. It wasn't so much that they were happily married or that they had a healthy toddler and a newborn infant. It was everything in general. Cade was so happy with his life, nothing bothered him. Pilar couldn't do enough for all of them. And that was on top of taking care of the household and putting up with a grandmother who would tax the patience of a saint.

Broc was right about one thing: If he was to make his peace with the past, he had to do it here. And he suspected he couldn't do it without Maria's help.

The collapse of the gazebo puzzled him. He was

certain it wasn't an accident, but he couldn't see why anyone would want to harm Maria. If someone *had* meant to harm her, the gazebo was a poor choice. It was more likely to be blown down by a storm than collapse on a clear, sunny day. The damage could have been a simple act of vandalism, but his gut said otherwise. Something was wrong here, and he meant to find out what it was.

❧

"I told you to forget about Maria. Rafe is the one we have to worry about."

"I could have gotten them both."

"But you didn't get either." He uttered a string of curses. "We're running out of time. Get Rafe. I'll worry about Maria later."

❧

His early-morning inspection removed any doubt from Rafe's mind that the gazebo's collapse was an accident. He couldn't tell when the footprints he found had been made, but they were recent, possibly as recent as last night. Thinking that someone might have been watching him and Maria caused a frisson of alarm to run along his spine. Since the end of the war, he had stopped looking over his shoulder for unseen danger. He couldn't imagine why anyone would want to harm Maria or anyone else at the ranch, but he couldn't leave until she was safe. He would have felt that way even if he hadn't been attracted to her.

❧

It amused Rafe to see Maria's surprise when she entered the breakfast room to find he was down before her. She was dressed simply in a white blouse with a ruffled collar and a gathered skirt, with her hair pulled back in ringlets that fell to her shoulders, but she looked elegant. Luis followed in her wake, looking bright-eyed but unsure of his welcome.

"Cows get up with the sun," Rafe told her. "Cowhands have to go by their schedule, not the other way around." The coffee wasn't as good as in Texas, but Rosana had laid out a breakfast of gargantuan proportions.

Maria seated herself. Luis took the seat next to her. "Where is Broc?" she asked.

"Luxuriating in my featherbed. I have orders not to wake him."

"You didn't have to. The damned cockerels did it for you." Broc stumbled into the breakfast room and focused a sleepy eye on Maria. "Why do you need so many chickens?"

"Because people like to eat eggs."

"That's what Pilar always says. Her place is overrun with them. That's why I don't mind sleeping out with the cows. They aren't so proud of getting up at such a god-awful hour that they have to crow about it."

Maria's smiling response was exactly what Broc had no doubt expected. Luis forgot his nervousness long enough to giggle. Normally Rafe would have found Broc's banter entertaining, but this morning his friend's chatter didn't amuse him. His mood deteriorated even further when he realized he was irritated that Broc had made Maria smile, something he'd never done.

Maria served Luis, then herself, from platters of eggs, pork, and fried potatoes. "What do you have in mind for today?"

"I'm taking Luis riding. I'm going to pack into one morning everything he should have learned by now."

Maria looked hardly less dismayed than the boy. "Do you think that's wise?"

Rafe didn't like the way Luis looked to Maria as if he expected her to protect him. "I won't know until I see how much he can do. Do you ride a lot?" he asked the boy.

Luis didn't meet Rafe's gaze. "Not often," he mumbled into his plate.

"How often is *not often*?"

Maria answered for the boy. "Not at all since last summer. There was no one to take him."

"Don't you ride?" he asked Maria.

"I have no need. Whenever I feel the need for exercise, I take a short walk along the road to town."

"You've got some fine riding stock in the stable." Broc had helped himself from most of the dishes on the table. "But I didn't see Luis's pony."

"He doesn't have a horse," Maria explained.

Rafe could understand his father's withdrawal from the household to avoid Dolores, but he had bought a new pony for Rafe every year until he was big enough to ride a regular horse.

"Wouldn't it be better to wait for the riding lessons until you can purchase a suitable mount?" Maria asked.

"The pony I brought is for Luis. I'm sure one of my old saddles will suit him."

Luis's eyes grew wide. "Is it really mine?"

Rafe smiled. "Who did you think it was for?"

"I never had a pony. I won't know how to take care of it."

"Someone in the stable will do that," Maria said.

"A boy should know how to take care of his own horse. Take care of your horse, and it'll take care of you."

Luis didn't appear to know whether to be pleased he had his own pony or worried he would be expected to take care of it. Rafe decided that even if Maria were the most wonderful woman in the world, Luis needed a male role model. There were some things a woman didn't know about being a man.

Rafe could tell Maria wasn't happy with the idea because she ate almost no breakfast. He didn't know how much Luis normally ate, but it didn't seem like enough. He didn't take it as a good sign that the boy could be thrown off his feed so easily. A man ought to have the courage to face challenges, maybe even be excited by them. He blamed his father for ignoring the boy.

"Where would you like to ride?" Broc asked Luis.

"I don't know." The boy answered so softly, Rafe could barely hear him from across the table.

"There must be some place you like to visit."

Luis shook his head.

When he was Luis's age, Rafe had liked riding out to see the mares with their new foals, but most of his favorite places had been in the foothills east of their ranch. He'd found sunny meadows, one spooky cave, cracks in the rocks where he could hide, and several places that offered spectacular views of the valley below.

"I don't encourage Luis to wander far from the house." Maria's tone was mild, but Rafe sensed disapproval. "We've had several reports of cougars in the mountains east of the ranch."

He remembered the occasional loss of livestock to a bear or one of the big cats, but that had always resulted in a hunt for the offending animal. Those hunts had provided some of the most exciting moments of Rafe's teenage years. He decided not to mention them to Maria.

"I'm sure Rafe can show you a lot of interesting places," Broc said to the boy. "I had my own favorites growing up in Tennessee. I remember one particular swimming hole. It was just a deep place in the creek, but it was shaded by a bunch of trees. It was a treat to go swimming there on a hot August afternoon."

"Luis doesn't know how to swim," Maria told Broc.

"Why not?" Rafe asked.

"There's no one to take him."

When Rafe had once asked his mother why women didn't swim, she'd told him that no proper female would expose her body in such a manner. Since he had been seven at the time and girls still looked pretty much like boys, it had taken him a few years before he understood what she meant. "There are dozens of men and boys on the ranch who would have been glad to go with him and teach him all he needed to know."

"I'm sure there were, and still are, but I haven't had much opportunity to get to know the younger children on the ranch, certainly not enough to entrust them with Luis's safety."

No wonder the boy acted like he was afraid of his

own shadow. Rafe supposed he couldn't blame him. It was unfair that he'd been brought up in a way that would make him uncomfortable in the presence of other men. "I'll have Miguel ask around. I'm sure he can find several boys mature enough to be responsible for Luis."

Maria looked as if she wanted to say something but she bit into a pear instead.

"Don't you have contact with the families on the ranch?"

"My duties in the house don't leave me much time."

"How do you know when people are sick?"

"Rosana keeps me informed of anyone needing help."

"What does Dolores do?"

Maria took another bite of the pear. That proved to be a tactical error because it gave Luis an opportunity to answer for her.

"Mama says anybody who works on the ranch is beneath us, and that I'll end up being low class if I have anything to do with them. That's why I can't play with the other boys."

If Rafe had had any doubt that Luis might not have understood his mother correctly, Maria's blush would have banished it.

"No one is low class because he works for a living, just as no one is better who doesn't have to. Do you think I'm low class because I work for someone else?"

Luis blushed and dropped his gaze. "No."

Broc folded his napkin and pushed his chair back. "I think we've all had enough breakfast. It's time to teach Luis how to ride."

Maria turned to Rafe. "You'll have to teach me, too. I'm going with you."

Six

It took only a glance at the horse being led from the barn for Maria to decide she had let her irritation with Rafe cause her to make a foolish decision. How could she ride an animal so big she couldn't see over its back? She wasn't aware she'd turned to Rafe, her expression apparently asking a question, until he spoke.

"The stable boy assures me this is the gentlest horse in the barn."

Broc surveyed the horse with disfavor. "It looks asleep."

The horse in question threw its head to one side, knocking its groom off balance. Not the behavior, in Maria's mind, of a gentle, sleepy horse. Luis's pony watched her out of huge brown eyes, its body motionless except for twitching muscles and a swishing tail to ward off insects. "Where's your horse?"

Her question was answered when two horses were led from the barn, one a huge black stallion that pranced rather than walked, grabbing at the lead shank with its teeth.

"I wanted the black, but Rafe claimed him by right of ownership." Broc scowled at the dark bay that followed. "I get the runt."

The bay was only a couple of inches shorter than the black. He lifted his handler off the ground when he reared.

"At least he has spirit," Broc added.

Maria didn't see why men wanted to ride animals capable of lifting them off the ground. What was wrong with walking? Or driving a buggy? She looked to see if Luis was feeling the same way. A brightness in his eyes, a tautness in his body, indicated excitement rather than fear.

Of course, he would be excited. He was a boy, and every boy wanted to grow up to be a man like Rafe. She wanted to caution Luis not to place too much importance on his first ride, but any failure would assume enormous importance to a boy who wanted to be like his brother.

Rafe turned to Luis. "Ready to mount up?"

The boy nodded rather than spoke.

"Broc will hold the pony, and I'll help you mount. I won't let go until you tell me, all right?"

Luis's eyes went wide with apprehension. Maria wondered if Rafe had missed that, or if he noticed and ignored it to spare the boy embarrassment. Probably the latter. She was coming to the conclusion that he didn't miss much.

Luis put his left foot in the stirrup, and then Rafe lifted him so he could swing his right leg over the pony and slide his boot into the other stirrup.

"Is the saddle okay?" Rafe asked.

Luis nodded.

"Broc is going to hand you the reins, but he won't let go of the lead shank until you tell him to. Okay?"

Luis took the reins but kept his eyes on Broc.

"Broc will help you get used to your pony while I help Maria mount up."

Maria's throat constricted. She hadn't ridden since she was a girl. She'd never ridden much, and she'd never ridden well.

"I'll tell you the same thing I told Luis. I'll settle you in the saddle and not let go until you feel at ease."

The stable boy held her horse. "I'd rather use a mounting block." The thought of Rafe's hands on her body was more than she was ready to contemplate.

"I asked about the one my mother used, but no one could find it."

Now she remembered. After Luis was born, Dolores had bribed one of the stable hands to break it so she would have an excuse not to resume her rides with Warren.

"I won't drop you."

Maria wasn't worried about that, but rather that the feel of his hands on her body would further erode her resistance to the attraction she felt whenever she was around him. She couldn't understand how she could possibly be attracted to a man of his character, but there was no use denying it. She couldn't stop wishing and hoping something would happen to prove he wasn't as bad as Dolores said. She took a deep breath and prepared to feel nothing when he touched her.

She *did* feel nothing because he didn't touch her.

"You look ill. Are you sure you ought to ride?"

He'd offered her the perfect excuse to back out without embarrassment. She was afraid, but she wasn't a coward. "I'm fine. It's just that I haven't ridden in a long time. I'm more nervous than I thought I'd be."

"You don't have to go with us. Broc and I will make sure nothing happens to Luis."

"It's okay. I want to ride." She didn't *want* to, but she *had* to. She didn't trust anyone else to watch over Luis.

Rafe placed her in the saddle so quickly, she didn't have time to fortify herself against his touch. Despite the thickness of her riding habit, heat flowed from his hands into her body with a swiftness that left her flushed and breathless. It required an effort of will to focus her attention on settling into the saddle, arranging her skirt, and collecting the reins.

"Are you ready?" Rafe's expression implied no scorn, only a polite question.

"You can let go of the lead shank," she said to the stable boy. Her horse immediately threw its head from side to side, but it didn't move. She was able to recapture enough calm to watch Luis bring his pony to a walk under Broc's supervision.

"If there's nothing else, let's go."

Maria was afraid they would start out at a canter, but they left the stable yard at a walk. No doubt the slow pace was for her and Luis's benefit. Men who herded wild longhorns every day probably never walked their horses. Rafe rode on her left, Luis on her right, and Broc on the other side of Luis. The boy's pinched look had lessened until he appeared cautiously excited. He was on his own pony, riding with men guaranteed to fill a young boy's heart with admiration, even hero worship. He didn't even take fright when they broke from a walk into a trot. She was relieved when the horses moved into an easy canter. As long as she could ignore objects going by with increasing speed, she could imagine she was in a rocking chair.

After nine years on Rancho los Alamitos, she still knew almost nothing about it. She could see the mountains from the house and the fields that stretched into the distance, but she seldom had an opportunity to see the rich green of artichoke plants with their spiky leaves, smell the lime trees in bloom, or watch bearded heads of wheat wave in a gentle breeze. Workers moved through the fields, the near silence broken by an occasional voice lifted in song. They passed small houses where children played under the watchful eyes of mothers preparing spicy foods for the midday meal. This was the heart of the ranch, the reason it held Rafe's interest.

Over the next half hour, Rafe talked about what they saw and the changes he wanted to make. When she was finally able to get her mind off staying in the saddle, she was surprised to find how much he knew about the ranch, how strong his interest in it was despite his long absence.

"How will you incorporate all these changes if you go back to Texas?" she asked.

He favored her with a look of annoyance. "Miguel can handle any changes."

"But I don't want you to go away," Luis objected. "You're supposed to be my guardian."

Luis had always looked to Maria for everything. How could he have changed to Rafe so quickly? What was it about the man that made both of them look to him for answers?

"Maria will take care of you as she always has," Rafe assured Luis.

"I don't mean give me my lessons or make sure I eat my vegetables. I mean teach me to ride, how to run the ranch when I grow up."

Luis seemed to be changing right before her eyes. He'd never shown any interest in riding, much less in learning how to run the ranch. That was probably her fault. She'd been so concerned about protecting him, trying to make sure he grew up normally in a household that was far from normal, she hadn't given any thought to what would happen when he became a man. She'd thought Warren would still be alive. His death and Rafe's return had changed everything.

"I'll make sure Rafe stays here until he figures out something," Broc assured Luis. "It's a lot nicer to sleep on a featherbed than on the ground."

Luis had never slept on the ground, so he bombarded Broc with dozens of questions. The more Broc talked, the more questions he asked about Texas. When he asked if he could visit Rafe when he went back to Texas, Maria decided she had been bringing up a boy she didn't really know.

"Rafe seems to know exactly what to say to make Luis feel more comfortable," she remarked to Broc. She had never understood how some people grew up with confidence in themselves and others had to work at building it piece by painful piece. Dolores had her beauty to depend on. What did Rafe depend on? How had he survived being banished by his father and the years he'd spent away from the ranch?

"Rafe was the one who looked after the new recruits after their first battle had scared them out of their minds. Just being around him gave them confidence."

"Luis has beautiful manners and has made great progress with his studies. I think that's more important than knowing how to ride or manage crops." She hadn't meant for Rafe to overhear her.

"Luis will be owner of one of the largest ranches in California. He has to know how to manage it, or he'll lose it. He has to ride because he can't see two hundred thousand acres from the front porch. He may have perfect manners and book knowledge, but he's not comfortable around strangers. How will that help him as a businessman or a social leader?"

"Why don't you go ahead and say you think I've done a terrible job of raising him?"

"Because I'm damned glad it was you and not Dolores. He doesn't yet know everything he needs to learn, but he's not likely to destroy other people's lives just to get what he wants."

It was a small compliment, but more than she expected.

"His education was my father's responsibility, not yours," Rafe went on. "Luis should know how to ride any horse in the barn, have ridden over every foot of this ranch at least a dozen times, and know how to get along with boys his age, whether they're the sons of other ranchers or the sons of men who work for him.

He should be able to handle a gun, a rope, and a dozen other things expected of boys."

Maria opened her mouth to object, but he hadn't finished.

"He doesn't need these things to be a man. He needs them because others will expect it of him. It's hard to respect yourself when others don't."

"I wouldn't have expected you to care about other people's opinions."

His smile lacked humor. "I was never as confident as I appeared. If I had been, I wouldn't have been so devastated when Dolores chose my father over me."

She immediately regretted her harsh words. "That's not what I meant."

"It was close enough. I spent three years in Mexico wallowing in my misery. It took surviving four years of a brutal war to pull me out of my self-absorption. It has taken three years of working and living with friends I wouldn't hesitate to trust with my life to sort through my feelings and figure out what's important. I don't want Luis to have to go through any of that."

Why did she always end up sympathizing with Rafe? She might as well create a separate person to endow with all his misdeeds. As far as her emotions were concerned, they didn't count. "Then you have to stay here. It's obvious you don't think I'm the right teacher for Luis."

"If you don't stay here, would you take me to Texas with you?" Luis asked.

She hadn't realized Luis and Broc had stopped talking and were listening to her and Rafe.

"Would I like it in Texas?" Luis asked.

Broc laughed. "Not after living here. It's hot as hell in the summer, the bugs will carry off anybody as little as you, and Cade will make you sleep in a bunkhouse on a bed as hard as the ground. You'll spend all your waking hours in the saddle. Cade will say you're chasing the cows, but they'll really be chasing you. At night you'll be so tired you'll actually be able to sleep on your hard bed."

Luis turned to Rafe. "Is that right?"

"Some of it, but Broc used to be an actor. Everything an actor says is something somebody made up. Sometimes Broc forgets he's not onstage."

Broc laughed at Luis's confusion. "Don't listen to a word he says. He's just jealous because everybody likes me better than—"

The sound was so unexpected, Maria couldn't believe it was what her instincts told her it had to be. She knew it was a rifle shot when Broc crumpled in the saddle, and Luis's pony screamed and broke into a gallop.

Rafe appeared to understand the situation instantly. "Look after Broc. He was hit in the shoulder. I'm going after Luis. His pony is headed toward a place where a creek tumbles through a deep ravine. If he tries to jump it, they'll both be killed."

Maria had never been called upon to deal with a situation like this. Her precious child was galloping toward instant death, and she'd been left to deal with a man who'd been shot. She'd never even *seen* a person who'd been shot. She had no idea how to take care of one.

"It's not a fatal wound," Broc managed to say,

"but if we don't stanch the bleeding, I could bleed to death."

"Tell me what to do." Her brain could at least follow orders.

"Take off my shirt. Rip it, cut it, get it off any way you can. We can use it to pack the wound."

She didn't know how she managed to help Broc out of his shirt any more than she knew where she found the strength to tear it into pieces. When she forced a piece into the wound, Broc looked like he would pass out.

"Harder." He could barely whisper. "It hurts like hell, but that's better than being dead."

Maria gritted her teeth and forced the now-bloody piece of cloth into the hole torn in Broc's shoulder.

"You've got to pack it tighter to stop the bleeding." He must have understood her hesitation. "It's not as bad as having my face blown off."

Broc's groans nearly stopped her, but she took strength from his courage. For a moment she thought she would have to stop packing the wound to hold him in the saddle, but he gripped the pommel and held on. She was still trying to stuff more material in the wound when Rafe returned with Luis.

Rafe took in the situation immediately. "You and Luis get back to the house as quickly as you can. Tell Juan to send for the nearest surgeon. We need to get the bullet out as quickly as possible."

Maria had intended to go back at a canter, but Luis kicked his pony into a gallop. "Wait!" Her cry might as well have been flung into the wind. Her precious baby boy, who had rarely been on a horse, was galloping down a rough trail on a runaway pony. Less than an hour ago, he hadn't been sure he wanted to get on the animal. Now he was galloping. It was all Rafe's fault.

Taking her courage in her hands, Maria urged her own mount forward until she came alongside Luis. "Slow down before you kill yourself!"

The boy didn't pause to glance at her, but kept his eyes straight ahead. "We've got to get a doctor for Broc. We can't let him die."

Maria wanted to tell Luis that Broc wouldn't die. Rafe had appeared calm, but he'd seen men shot, gravely wounded...he'd seen them die. If he said it was imperative to get the bullet out as quickly as possible, that probably meant Broc was in real danger.

The trip back to the house seemed endless, but once they reached the stables, Luis threw his leg over without waiting for help. He fell to the ground virtually under his mount's hooves. Maria's heart was in her throat until he scrambled to his feet and set off for the house at a run.

Several men came hurrying from the stable. "What's wrong?" one asked.

"Mr. Kincaid has been shot."

By the time she reached the house, Luis had alerted everyone. Juan passed her on his way to the stables.

"I'm going for Dr. Andrés. Rosana is already tearing sheets into strips."

Dolores met her in the main hall. "Luis said someone shot Broc? Surely he's wrong."

Maria kept walking toward the stairs that would

take her to Rafe's old bedroom. "He's not wrong. Someone did shoot Broc."

Dolores hurried after her. "Where were you? What were you doing?"

"We weren't off our land. I have no idea why he was shot."

"It must have been an accident. Someone was hunting and hit him by mistake."

That was possible. They had been riding near the foothills where a hunter was most likely to find deer, but they'd been out in the open, easily seen by someone pointing a rifle in their direction. Not for a moment did Maria think anyone on the ranch could be responsible for such a terrible mistake.

"I have no idea why it happened. I have to make sure Broc's room is ready."

The next minutes passed with agonizing slowness. While Maria organized the household to gather linens, hot water, and any salves and medications the doctor might request, Dolores asked questions and gave orders in alternating bursts. Luis stood out of the way, the color drained from his face, wanting assurance that Broc wasn't dead.

Margarita burst into the room. "They're here. They're bringing him up now."

Maria's first thought was that Broc was dead. She was relieved when she heard him threatening the men carrying him that if they dropped him before they laid him on the bed, he would shoot every one of them as soon as he could hold a pistol.

"He never misses," Rafe informed them. "You might as well be dead already."

They settled him in the bed with great care, then nearly stumbled over themselves getting out of the room.

Maria thought she saw a smile flit across Broc's face. "See if you can refrain from scaring the doctor," he said to Rafe. "I don't want his hand shaking when he cuts into me."

Once Rafe was sure Broc was as comfortable as they could make him, he pulled Maria aside. "How long before we can expect the doctor?"

"I don't know."

As the minutes passed without Juan's return, Maria sensed Rafe's growing anxiety. She breathed a sigh of relief when Juan hurried into the room.

"The doctor is away taking care of a miner who was attacked by a grizzly. His apprentice is coming."

Broc raised his head from the pillow. "I'm not having some apprentice sawbones work on me."

"That bullet has to come out," Rafe told him.

"If some amateur has to cut into me, I'd rather it be you. At least I know you won't murder me with stupidity."

"I'm not a doctor."

"But you've seen enough army doctors work to know what to do. Bring me some of that brandy I had last night. A couple of swallows of that, and I won't care what you do."

"I'm not taking that bullet out."

"If you let me die, I swear I'll come back and haunt you."

"You can't let him die!"

Maria had forgotten Luis was still in the room. She should have sent him out before Rafe returned with

Broc. "Go stay with your mother. I'll let you know when the bullet is out."

"I want to stay." Luis inched away when she attempted to lead him from the room. "My fingers are small. Maybe I can reach in and get the bullet out."

Rafe knelt down in front of Luis. "The bullet might be buried in the bone, which would make it very hard to get out."

"I'm not afraid."

"I'm sure you aren't, but I think you'd be more comfortable with your mother."

"No, I wouldn't. She doesn't like Broc. She says she can't look at his face. I don't care about his face. I think he was very brave to fight in a war."

Luis had never talked so much or so forcefully, not even to people he'd known all his life. Maria didn't know whether to be pleased he was finally asserting himself or upset he was going through a nerve-racking situation at such a young age.

"Let the boy stay," Broc declared. "If he throws up his breakfast, he won't make a bigger mess than I have already."

Rafe fixed Luis with a steady gaze. "Broc wants you to stay, but you've got to keep out of the way. If you feel like you're getting sick, you have to leave. Can you do that?"

Luis nodded.

Rafe stood and turned to Maria. "This is against my better judgment, but I'm going to try to get the bullet out."

"Wouldn't it be better to wait?"

"I would if I knew the doctor would be here instead

of his apprentice. I know the damage an inexperienced doctor can do."

"What if you run into trouble?"

"I'm already in trouble." That protest from Broc.

Maria couldn't begin to guess what Rafe and Broc had been forced to do during the war. Most doctors learned their craft by working as apprentices. The war could have been Rafe's apprenticeship. He needed to know only how to extract a bullet. He probably had seen that done more times than the apprentice. "How can I help?"

Seven

WHILE BROC SWALLOWED ENOUGH WHISKEY TO blunt the pain, Maria and Rosana gathered everything Rafe would need for the operation. Luis stayed out of the way, but his gaze followed Rafe's every move. He looked confused when Rafe insisted all the implements be placed in boiling water.

"During the war, patients of doctors who washed their hands and boiled their instruments had fewer infections," Rafe explained to Luis. "More soldiers died from infections than from the wounds."

Maria knew the danger of infections, but she had never heard of boiling instruments and washing hands. She wondered if the local doctor did that.

"Luis, run get Juan. Tell him I need him to help me. Taking the bullet out is going to be very painful," Rafe explained. "If Broc jumps or moves about, it could cause me to hurt him worse. I need Juan to hold him still."

Luis nodded and darted from the room.

"I wish you wouldn't encourage Luis to stay," Maria said. "He's too young."

"I agree, but he wants to stay. And it might help Broc to have him here."

"Like the little fella. Got spunk."

Broc's words were slurred. Maria would have been happier if he'd been too drunk to talk at all.

When Luis returned with Juan, Miguel came as well, bringing the implements in a pan of boiling water. Using a doubled cloth, Rafe laid the implements out on a table next to the bed.

"Make sure that damned knife is cool before you stick it in me."

"I'm going to use my fingers first. I'll use the knife only if I can't get it out otherwise."

"Don't poke around in there forever thinking you're sparing me pain. I'd rather you cut the bullet out and get it over quickly."

Maria found it difficult to believe Broc could talk so casually about Rafe cutting a bullet out of him. What horrors had these men witnessed that could have hardened them against such suffering? How could she ever understand a man like that?

Rafe folded a square of cloth and handed it to Broc. "Bite down on this, but not too hard. I'm not a dentist. I have no idea how to fix a broken tooth."

Broc took the cloth. "Just do it quickly. I'm no good with pain."

Maria thought Broc was the bravest man she'd ever seen to be able to talk about his wound like it was an inconvenience rather than a life-threatening injury. Dolores had screamed her way through Luis's birth even though the doctor said it was one of the easiest deliveries he'd ever seen.

"Juan, hold his shoulder. Don't press too hard but keep him still."

She wanted to avert her eyes when Rafe unpacked the wound, but she forced herself to move closer, to be ready to hand him any instrument he might need. Rafe inserted a finger in the wound to probe for the bullet. Broc lost color and bit down on the cloth, but he didn't move.

"Did you find it?" Anxiety caused Luis's voice to rise half an octave.

"Not yet. Hand me the knife."

"What are you going to do?" Luis sounded small and frightened.

"I have to open the wound."

Maria willed her hand not to tremble as she handed the knife to Rafe, willed her gaze to remain on the wound as Rafe cut into the flesh. Broc groaned and flinched.

"Hold him tighter." Juan looked nearly as pale as Broc. Rafe handed the bloody knife to Maria. "Wash it. I might need it again."

Rafe probed the wound with two fingers. Broc groaned and clamped down with his teeth on the cloth, but he didn't move.

"The bullet is buried in the bone. I'll need pliers to pull it out." Rafe signaled Miguel to help Juan. "Rosana, hold his feet. Maria, you hold his arm."

"I want to help." Luis had left his position by the wall and approached the bed.

Rafe answered without looking up. "Take one leg. Rosana will take the other." Rafe reached for the pliers, then turned to Broc. "Take a good bite on that cloth. This is going to hurt like hell."

Broc turned white when Rafe inserted the pliers into the wound, but his body went limp when Rafe gripped the bullet and pulled.

"Good. He's fainted. With luck, I'll get the bullet out and have him bandaged up before he regains consciousness."

Maria thought she might faint, too. She was nauseated from watching Rafe struggle to pry the bullet loose, blood halfway up his arms and all over Broc's chest, shoulder, and arm. Rafe put his knee against Broc's chest, gripped the pliers with both hands, and pulled. Broc's body rose from the table, then fell back when Rafe pulled the bloody pliers out of the wound. He held them up for everyone to see.

"The bullet's out. Now let's clean him up so I can bandage the wound."

Maria was relieved to have something to do. Wetting one of a stack of cloths in the hot water, she started to clean the blood from Broc's body, patting rather than rubbing.

"Don't worry about being gentle. It's more important to get it done before he wakes up."

She was still attempting to clean the wound when Rafe finished washing and drying his hands. "It keeps bleeding," she said.

"It won't stop until I pack it."

Rafe packed the wound and the bleeding stopped. After she cleaned up the last of the blood, Rafe treated the wound with carbolic acid and bacillicum powder.

"I'll have to change the packing at least once a day for a week. Can you see about having plenty of clean packing available?"

Rosana paused in her task of gathering up all the bloody cloths. "I'll see to it."

"I'll need long strips for bandaging."

"I can take care of that," Maria said. There were sheets available in the house that were too worn for further use.

"I want to do something."

Maria didn't know what it was about Rafe that had reached out to Luis so forcefully that the boy had overcome his shy disposition. Was it possible he really wasn't shy, that all he needed was the presence of a man he could admire? It irritated her to think being a woman made her in any way deficient, but there were differences between men and women. Ignoring the dissimilarities for fear of hurt feelings would be stupid. She wasn't inferior. She was just different.

"Broc isn't going to be able to get out of bed for a while, and that's going to make him cranky," Rafe said to Luis. "Reading to him would be a real help."

"I have lots of books. I'll get some." He started for the door.

"You don't need to get them now. Broc can't—" Maria began.

Rafe put a hand on Maria's arm, stopping her as Luis darted through the doorway. She could hear the boy's footsteps fading away as he ran down the hall to his room. "It won't hurt him to get them now."

"But Broc is still unconscious."

"That won't make any difference to Luis. He's reading more for himself than for Broc."

"What do you mean?"

"He's probably starved for companionship."

"I have never neglected Luis."

"I'm sure you haven't, but it's only natural he wants to be around men."

She could understand that, but she didn't have to like it. "I'm still not sure you're the best model for him."

"I've never set myself up as a model for anyone. No one should ever do some of the things I've done."

At least that was one thing they agreed on.

❦

"Have you had any trouble on the ranch since my father's death?" Rafe asked Miguel.

"Everything has been quiet." Miguel stood despite Rafe's invitation to take one of the comfortable chairs in his father's office. "No one who works for the ranch would do such a thing. The ranch has given them a better life than they had before."

"Is there someone who has had a setback and holds the ranch responsible?"

"No one."

"Anyone who's been fired?"

"Only Roger Anderson, but his family wouldn't let him do anything to hurt you. The last years have been good for them, for everyone who works on the ranch. Your people are happy."

Rafe didn't think of them as *his people*. A lot had changed in ten years. With births, marriages, deaths, and people leaving for other opportunities, he doubted he'd recognize half the ranch workers.

"Well, somebody's not happy."

"It could have been an accident."

"How? Nobody hunts this time of year, and the game is in the foothills."

"Not all of it. Deer wander onto the ranch all the time. They like to eat what we grow."

"I didn't see a deer the whole morning." There was a knock at the door. "Come in."

Maria entered the room. "Rosana said you wanted me."

"Miguel and I are trying to figure out who could have shot Broc and why. I thought you might be able to help."

Maria remained in the doorway. "I don't know anything about the ranch."

"You may be able to think of something we haven't." When Maria hesitated, Rafe said, "Come in anyway. You and Miguel will be in charge after I leave."

"You're leaving?" Miguel looked stunned.

"I have a job in Texas, a kind of partnership," Rafe explained. "I can't just leave it."

"But you're coming back, aren't you? This is your home now," Miguel said.

"This hasn't been my home for ten years. I don't know why my father left me any part of the ranch."

Miguel cast a quick glance at Maria. "Your father was a proud man. He would never admit to making a mistake, but he felt it." Miguel pointed to a picture of Rafe on his father's desk. "Why do you think that picture is there?"

Rafe shrugged.

"Because he knew he'd done a terrible thing when he let you leave. He never said so, but he thought you would come back."

"He knew I wouldn't because he knew what he asked was impossible."

Miguel's gaze sank to the carpet. "He wouldn't have asked it again."

The temptation to dwell on what might have been was a waste of time and could only make Rafe more bitter. "We've wandered from the question of who shot Broc and why."

"Every man has enemies," Miguel suggested.

"Broc doesn't. He's never been here before."

"They could have followed him."

"Nobody followed us."

"Maybe Broc wasn't the intended target."

Rafe turned to Maria, who'd taken a seat by the window. "Why do you say that?"

"Broc was wearing some of your clothes. That bullet could have been meant for you instead."

"Dolores is the only person who wants me dead, but she was still in bed when we left." Rafe was convinced Broc was the intended victim. He just didn't have any idea why. The man had no enemies. Everybody who knew him liked him.

"Are you sure the shooter couldn't have been aiming for you and missed?" Maria asked Rafe.

"I was too far from Broc for that to happen. Besides, I haven't been in California for ten years. Anything I might have done to make an enemy would have been forgotten by now."

"Is there somebody in Texas?" Maria asked.

"Do you think I go around making enemies wherever I go?"

"I was talking about Broc."

"Everybody likes Broc. You and Luis do, and you've hardly known him twenty-four hours."

"Broc is a charming man. It would be impossible not to like him."

Why did it irritate Rafe that Maria thought Broc was charming but not him? He knew he wasn't charming. He didn't try to be. Hell, he didn't *want* to be.

"Could someone be trying to hurt you by hurting your friend?" Miguel asked.

"Who would do anything as twisted as that?"

Rafe had a perfect answer for Maria's question: Laveau di Viere. But Laveau didn't know he and Broc were in California. "I'll go into town tomorrow and have the lawyer ask about any new arrivals. Miguel, you can do the same. Unless there's somebody on the ranch who doesn't want me to return, it's got to be a stranger."

"If the attacker wanted to get rid of you, wouldn't he shoot you instead of Broc?" Maria asked.

"I don't know. This doesn't make any more sense than the gazebo collapsing." The illogic annoyed Rafe. He had always been one who gathered facts and studied them until he found an order that made sense. The only plausible explanation for the shooting was that it was an accident, that someone had been firing a rifle at random or firing at a target and missed. The miscreant would probably never come forward for fear of what would happen to him. It was possible he didn't know what he had done.

Yet Rafe still couldn't rid himself of the feeling that he was missing something. He had been gone for ten years. Did he really know anybody anymore? Dolores could have hired an assassin. The lawyer could want to run him back to Texas so he'd have a free hand with the ranch. Maria could want him out of the way so she could retain her influence over Luis.

Now he was being foolish. He needed to put all these ridiculous notions out of his head and just deal with the facts.

"I don't have any idea why this happened, and apparently the two of you don't, either. All we can do now is keep our eyes and ears open for anything that seems unusual."

"If we don't know what we're looking for, how will we know when we find it?" Maria asked.

"We might not right away. That's why we can't overlook anything. Ask Dolores. See if she has any idea who might have done this."

Maria stiffened. "Are you sure you don't suspect my sister?"

"I'm sure Dolores would be happy to see me dead, but she has no reason to kill Broc."

Uneasy with the tension between Rafe and Maria, Miguel edged toward the door. "Everyone on the ranch will know what happened by this evening. If anyone has heard anything, I will be informed of it by tomorrow."

"Thanks, Miguel. And thank you for all you did while my father was sick. I know it wasn't easy."

"It wasn't hard because whenever I asked, he would say, 'Do what Rafe would do.' After all the years we worked together, I always knew what that would be. You took your work on the ranch very seriously. We've all been hoping you would do that again."

Rafe couldn't give Miguel the assurances he wanted, so he let him leave without further comment. Maria got to her feet.

"I'd better be going, too. I want to check on Broc before I start Luis on his lessons. When do you want lunch?"

"I don't. I'm going into town to see what I can find out. Let me know what the doctor says when he finally gets here."

                             ❧

"Fool! Imbecile! I said shoot the handsome one, not the one with scars on his face."

"I could see only one side."

"You should have gotten closer."

"That ranch is as flat as your hand. There's nowhere to hide up close and still get away unnoticed."

"There has to be some place. You didn't look hard enough."

"I worked there. I know every inch of it."

"Then find a better place next time."

"I can't risk going back. Rafe is too restless to stay on the ranch. Sooner or later he'll leave."

"Then make sure you're right behind him. I want this over soon."

"Then I can go back to the woman."

"You bungled that."

"It's hard to make it look like an accident when she hardly ever leaves that house."

"I'll think of something. You just concentrate on getting rid of Rafe."

                             ❧

Maria knocked on Broc's door.

"Come in if you're a friend. If not, go bother Rafe."

She was pleased to see him sitting up and looking cheerful. "I hope Luis hasn't bored you with his stories."

"Broc says I read very well." Luis glowed with happiness. "He says I should read for Rafe, that he'd be proud of me."

"I'm sure he would be. I've always been proud of you."

"You're my aunt. You're supposed to be proud of me."

Maria didn't like having her approval valued so lightly, but she was rapidly learning that she ranked far behind the glorious man who was his brother. If only Rafe *were* his brother.

"It's time for your lunch. You can read to Broc again after you've done your lessons."

"Broc said he'd help me."

"Maybe tomorrow. He needs to rest before the doctor gets here."

"Why does he need a doctor? Rafe has already fixed him."

Maria was getting a little tired of Luis thinking Rafe could do everything better than anyone else. "It's best to let the doctor check Broc to make sure. Now, your lunch is getting cold."

Luis grimaced. "Yes, ma'am." He rose and left the room.

"You don't like him looking up to Rafe, do you?" Broc asked.

The question startled and embarrassed Maria. She hadn't realized her feelings were so obvious. "I don't know Rafe as well as you do, or even as well as Rosana and Juan. I had been led to believe—"

"I don't imagine your sister had much good to say about him. She must have been mad as hell when she read that will."

Dolores had thrown a fit that was so embarrassing, Maria blushed to remember it even now. When Maria had tried to reason with her, Dolores had told her about the rape. After that it was hard not to commiserate with her even when her behavior was unreasonable. "It came as a great shock. She had expected something quite different."

"I'm sure she did. After causing Rafe's father to throw him out, I'm sure she expected to be left the ranch, or at least control of it until Luis came of age," Broc said.

"It's only natural that a wife would expect her husband to leave her more than an allowance in his will. I'm sure Rafe has told you—"

"Rafe never talked about his life before he joined the Army. All any of us knew was that his father owned a ranch in California. I never heard Dolores's name until we got here."

"After the way he took out that bullet, I can understand why you're so loyal to him, but that doesn't excuse the rest of his behavior."

"What behavior?"

She had let her temper cause her to say more than she intended. "I can't tell you, but I know of something that would alter your feelings."

Broc's gaze intensified. "I've never put much faith in secrets that couldn't be brought into the light. They leave me with the feeling there's a foul underbelly I can't see. Let me tell you a few things that are beyond dispute because many people saw what I saw."

Eight

BROC SAT UP A LITTLE STRAIGHTER, THEN DRANK FROM a glass of water before he began.

"Rafe and I served in a cavalry troop of thirty-six hand-picked men. We made night raids on wagon trains, supply depots, gold shipments, anything we could to delay and disrupt the Union Army. We lost only five men before one of our number betrayed us. Twenty-four men died that night, most of them in their sleep." Broc turned his face so Maria could see the scars. "I was shot in the face as I woke up. I couldn't see the man standing over me because of the blood in my eyes." He returned his gaze to Maria. "I would have died with his second shot if Rafe hadn't stopped him. The campsite was overrun with Union soldiers and a few escaping Night Riders returning fire. Rafe risked his life to drag me into a ditch. He stood over the doctor while he tried to put my face back together. Rafe was ready to kill the man, but saving me was the best he could do."

Maria wouldn't have tried to change Broc's opinion of Rafe if she could. She was sure Rafe had changed, had improved, since he'd left the ranch, but nothing could alter the fact that he'd raped Dolores. She had no trouble believing Dolores had exaggerated Rafe's faults over the years, but as much as she'd like to see him as Broc did, she couldn't.

"You don't think he's a good model for Luis, but he will be. Rafe isn't always easy on people, but he's really soft when it comes to kids."

"Luis isn't a little kid anymore. He's becoming a young man."

"Rafe was always the one to look after the new fellows in the troop. He was rough on them, but what he taught them saved their lives."

She could believe that. Rafe showed every indication of being the kind of man who could handle any situation. It was his ability to take charge at a moment's notice that made it difficult for her to imagine him working for anyone, even a friend.

"You ought to see him with Carlos. That's Cade's two-year-old son. He actually gets down on the floor with him, lets the kid ride him like he's a big dog."

Maria couldn't picture that. Not the Rafe Jerry she knew.

"You don't believe me, do you?"

"It's not that. It's just..." How could she explain that the image was too far from what she'd been led to expect?

"Come sit down. I keep thinking you're going to back out the door and run away."

She didn't want to sit down. She didn't want to listen to any more stories of how wonderful Rafe could be. She had been comfortable with her picture of him as a spoiled, selfish, untamed youth. Then she could think he was handsome without any danger of being attracted to him. She could handle that. But how could she handle an attraction to a man everyone seemed to think practically walked on water?

"I can't stay. I just wanted to make sure you were comfortable and advise you to take a nap before the doctor gets here."

"I don't need a doctor. Rafe can take care of me."

"I'm sure he can, but he doesn't have access to the medicines and ointments the doctor has because we don't stock them in the house."

Broc held out his hand to Maria. Reluctantly, she stepped forward to take it. "I'll see the doctor if it will make you feel better, but I'm not going to do anything he advises unless Rafe thinks I should."

"How can you have so much confidence in his medical ability? He's not a doctor."

"Rafe worked with the doctor in our troop so often, he said Rafe could have set up his own practice if he limited it to amputating limbs and treating gunshot wounds." He squeezed Maria's hand. "Don't be too hard on him. He didn't want to come back. Doing so has opened up old wounds he's spent years trying to heal. You like him. No use pulling away," he said when she jerked her hand from his grasp. "He likes you, too, though he nearly bit my head off for mentioning it. You could look a long time without finding a better husband."

Maria was certain she flushed crimson. "I'm not looking for a husband."

"Every woman wants a husband just as every man wants a wife."

"I don't know why I'm letting you talk to me about such an absurd notion. You need to rest, and I need to make sure Luis eats his lunch and starts on his studies."

"Luis can do without your undivided attention for one day," Broc announced. "You know, Rafe loves this place despite the bad memories. It's clear the people here want him back. You care about the ranch and Luis. You wouldn't have worked so hard if you didn't. Rafe belongs here, not in Texas. He'll never be the man he was meant to be if he leaves."

"Why are you telling me this?"

"Because I think you're the one person who might be able to convince him to stay."

"You're wrong. There are reasons I can't tell you why I—"

"I know. The secret."

"—could never have any part in the decisions he makes."

She didn't like Broc's smile. It made her feel as if she'd done something wrong.

"I trust you to figure out the right thing to do." His grin was pure mischief now. "You might need a little help, but that's what I'm here for. Now you can run away and convince yourself everything I said is the result of being shot. I promise to take a nap as long as you promise to keep all sharp objects away from that doctor when he arrives."

There were a dozen things she needed to do, but she hurried to her bedroom and locked the door behind her.

Her room was sparsely furnished—a bed, a large wardrobe against the far wall, an oak chest with a pitcher and basin, a dresser with a small mirror, and a couple of chairs—but she had no need for more. Her duties kept her in the rest of the house except for the hours she spent sleeping. A closet less than half the size of Dolores's and a room with a claw-footed tub made up the rest of what was her personal domain. Today she felt very much in need of the limited privacy it offered.

She didn't want to admit she was attracted to Rafe on a physical level, but as long as it was only physical she could accept it. He was a handsome man. Any woman would find him attractive.

To say she was *interested* in him elevated her predicament to a new plateau. She didn't know what she had done to give Broc the impression she had ever thought of marrying Rafe. She had begun to question Dolores's version of a lot of things that had happened, but rape didn't allow for any interpretation.

Unfortunately for her peace of mind, she couldn't reconcile that act with the man she was coming to know.

Everybody liked Rafe. She could see why the servants would—they were loyal to the family. Yet Luis had never been completely comfortable around anyone but her. She had taken pride in that without realizing she was limiting his ability to learn to get along with all kinds of people.

Luis's shyness made the fact that he felt at ease around Rafe all the more surprising, especially since she found the man intimidating at times. She had expected Rafe to be resentful of Luis. Not only was he the son of a woman Rafe disliked, but he'd cut Rafe out of half of a very large fortune. Since he had never seen the child, it wouldn't have been surprising if he'd shown strong resentment. And yet he'd accepted Luis without protest. He'd said he intended to leave everything to Luis and go back to Texas. She'd discounted that statement at first, but now she was beginning to wonder.

Liking Broc as much as she did made it difficult to ignore the things he said about Rafe. If there was any one thing that convinced her he believed what he said, it was his complete faith in Rafe's ability to remove the bullet. You didn't let a man you couldn't trust cut into you with a knife.

Then there were the servants. They had known Rafe when he was a boy. If Luis was any example, children were incredibly open and honest when they felt safe and loved. Rather than waste his time in typical teenage pranks, Rafe had taken up learning how to manage the ranch for his father. He'd succeeded so well that by the time he left, his father had made him responsible for all of the day-to-day operations. According to Juan, he was well loved by everyone who worked for him. According to Miguel, they'd lynch anyone who hurt Rafe.

It was impossible to know just how Warren had felt about Rafe, but everyone said he'd adored his son, that the dispute would never have happened if Dolores hadn't jilted Rafe for his father. The picture Warren had kept by his bedside, his increasing unwillingness to be anywhere near Dolores, and the way he wrote his will indicated that any ill feelings for his son were a thing of the past. But had Warren simply forgiven his son, or had he come to the conclusion that Rafe was right?

That left just Dolores claiming Rafe's villainy, but

her actions had precipitated the crisis. Shaking her head, Maria realized she was more confused than ever.

She sat down at her desk and pulled out her house-keeping book. She needed to bring the accounts up to date. That would keep her mind off Rafe at least until dinner. After that she'd have to come up with something else. One way or another, she had to put an end to this attraction.

∴

Rafe wasn't impressed by Cíbola's sheriff. He looked big enough to handle the job, but seemed out of shape and uninterested, as if he spent too much time in the saloons and not enough walking the streets. He seemed annoyed he'd been called to Henry Fielder's cramped office to meet Rafe. "There's nobody around here who would shoot at you or anybody on your place."

"I wasn't thinking of people who've lived here for years." Rafe leaned back in his chair and willed himself to relax. He was trying to keep ahold of his temper, but it was hard when faced with the sheriff's lack of interest. Fortunately, the lawyer intervened.

"Mr. Jerry was wondering if you've noticed any-body new about town. It hardly seems likely that a stranger would show up and start shooting at random, but Mr. Jerry has been back only two days and his friend has never been to California."

"It was an accident. Someone was hunting and a bullet went astray."

"We considered that." Rafe was annoyed at having to repeat what he'd said earlier. "My manager says no one was out hunting or doing target practice. I know looking for a stranger with a reason to shoot Broc is a long shot, but we've run into dead ends with every other line of questioning."

"You've run into a dead end here, too," the sheriff said irritably. "Only three men have come into town during the last week. Two were hands hired to work on a ranch north of here. They were picked up as soon as they got off the stage. The other is a gentleman who has taken the finest room in the hotel. You might as well question me as him."

"What is he like?" Rafe didn't want to overlook any possible suspect, no matter how unlikely.

The sheriff fidgeted impatiently. "If you hang around, you're liable to see him for yourself."

"I have to go back to the ranch. The doctor was supposed to see my friend this afternoon."

The sheriff huffed. "He's young—about your age, I'd guess—nice-looking, dresses well, and likes the best of everything."

Rafe realized that description could apply to hundreds of men...and also to Laveau di Viere. "Does he appear to be of Spanish descent?"

"Nearly everybody in California does. I didn't pay attention to that."

"Would you mind keeping him under observation for a few days?" the lawyer asked.

"I've got too much to do to spend time watching some young man romancing the ladies." He directed an angry look at Rafe. "You've got hundreds of people working for you. Get one of them to do it."

The sheriff's suggestion was made out of laziness

and annoyance, but it was an excellent one. "Thanks. I'll do that."

The sheriff clambered to his feet. "If there's nothing else, I got duties to attend to."

"Thank you for coming." The lawyer was more polite than Rafe would have been. "We'll let you know if we find anything."

"Don't expect you will. The shooting was an accident. Some kid playing around with a rifle and afraid to tell anybody."

Rafe wished Cade were here. The man had an uncanny instinct for things like this. Rafe couldn't find any logical reason to completely discount the accident theory, but for some reason he couldn't accept it as the right explanation.

The lawyer returned to his seat after showing out the sheriff. "He's not as bad as he seems," he said.

"Let's not waste any more time on the sheriff. I'd like to talk about my father's will. I don't want this inheritance, and I don't want the responsibility for the ranch or for my brother. Tell me how I can get out of it or at least limit my visits to once a year."

"You can't." The lawyer leaned back in his chair. "Your father made me go over the will several times to make sure there was no way you could get out of having to stay here."

It infuriated Rafe that his father would tie him to the ranch with the threat of using the entire fortune to create a memorial to Dolores. "Then go through the will again, line by line. There has to be something you can find." He needed to get back to Texas before his attraction to Maria turned into a true interest.

Maria was caught between a desire to stay and enjoy Rafe's company and the need to hurry Luis off to bed and get herself safely ensconced in her room. The doctor had praised Rafe's work but ordered Broc not to leave his bed until the next day. Dolores had gone into Cíbola to visit a friend, leaving Rafe, Luis, and Maria to spend the evening together. Maria had expected Rafe to excuse himself as soon as dinner was over. She hadn't been prepared to spend an enjoyable evening with him.

He'd started by asking Luis about his studies. For a man who placed little value on formal education, Maria found him remarkably well-informed, with a quick mind that was willing to consider any side of an argument, even those presented by a nine-year-old boy who was so excited by Rafe's attention that he occasionally betrayed his ignorance. Maria had listened in amazement as Rafe guided him through a discussion so cleverly, Luis believed he'd reached the final answer on his own. Luis was blossoming under Rafe's encouragement. She had no trouble believing Broc's assertion that the young soldiers had turned to Rafe for support. He had a way of focusing that made you feel like the most important person in the room. She hoped he was serious about returning to Texas. It was the only way she'd ever get Luis back to normal.

It annoyed her even more to realize she didn't want him to go back to Texas.

"I win."

Luis's exclamation of delight refocused her attention on the mathematical game her two companions were playing. Rafe settled back in his chair, a smile slowly forming. Luis's grin of childish glee transformed itself into a question.

"Did you let me win?"

Rafe's expression didn't change. "Why would I do that?"

"To make me feel better. I heard you tell Maria I didn't have confidence."

"I don't know why not. You're a smart young man."

"I can't ride or shoot like other boys. I can't play their games. I can't—"

"You can't do everything. No one expects you to."

"You can."

That was what worried Maria. Luis really thought Rafe could do everything. Luis was leaning forward in his chair, his elbows resting on the table and his legs swinging because they didn't reach the floor.

"No one can do everything," Rafe told him. "You decide what's important to you and concentrate on that. Someone else will handle the other things. That way we all have something that makes us special."

"But I'm not special."

"Yes, you are. You're the only brother I have, so that makes you special. And you're your aunt Maria's favorite person. Plus you're your mother's only son."

"But I can't *do* anything."

"That's the nicest thing about being special. You don't have to *do* anything to deserve it."

Did Rafe really believe that? Maria wondered. In her experience, men wanted to do something concrete, be richer, stronger, meaner than the others.

They didn't put any stock in emotions. They didn't even like to talk about them.

"Are you special?"

"I hope my friends think so."

"Do you have lots of friends?"

"Luis, that's not a nice thing to ask."

When Rafe turned to Maria, the expression on his face made her feel guilty. "Are you afraid I'll have to admit I don't have any friends?"

She tried hard not to blush but doubted she succeeded.

Rafe turned back to Luis, his expression softening. "I *don't* have many friends because I want only friends I can trust."

"You can trust me."

Maria's heart started to melt. The child wanted very badly for Rafe to love him.

Rafe reached out, took Luis's hand briefly. "I know that. We're brothers. That's even better than friends."

"It is? Why?"

"Being brothers is like being part of each other. No matter what happens, brothers will—"

The sentence was cut off by a laugh coming from the front hall. Dolores was home. Judging from the murmur of a deep voice in response, she'd been escorted by one of *her* friends. Maria hoped the man was neither drunk nor an obvious miscreant.

"Come on in." It was Dolores's voice. "Rafe and Broc are from Texas, too. You might know them."

Maria hadn't heard much about Texas, but she did know it was so big, it was doubtful Dolores's friend would have run into Rafe or Broc. She hoped the man would refuse the invitation.

"I really need to get back to town."

"Then come in for just a minute. My sister likes to meet all my new friends."

Maria never liked any of her sister's friends. She had no reason to expect she would like this one.

"Okay, but just for a minute. I need to get back to my card game."

"Haven't you won enough money for one night?"

"One can never win enough money."

Maria was pleasantly surprised when Dolores entered the salon followed by a tall, attractive, almost elegant, well-dressed man who smiled pleasantly to everyone in the room.

"Hello, everybody." Dolores's words were a little slurred. "I want you to meet my new friend, Laveau di Viere."

Nine

Rafe had recognized Laveau di Viere's voice from his first murmured response. He'd heard it for three years during the war, dreamed of it for three more. He stifled an impulse to rise up and strangle the man, to beat his head against the wall until he was as dead as their comrades.

He did none of that because Laveau was protected by the United States Army. Anyone who attempted to harm him would most likely be hanged.

He didn't turn as he watched Maria rise from her seat to greet the visitor. He could tell from her expression she was relieved. Apparently Laveau was a cut above the usual man Dolores brought home.

He listened to the polite exchange of meaningless words, Maria's welcome, Laveau's polished response, and Dolores bubbling with drunken excitement over her new friend. Luis regarded his mother with a look of embarrassment; Laveau he regarded with dislike. Rafe wondered how many times he'd been forced to be polite to the men Dolores dragged home.

"You have to meet my son." Rafe wondered if

Dolores sounded happy because of the wine or the companionship of a person more evil and corrupt than she. "Come here, Luis. I want you to shake hands with Mr. di Viere."

Luis glanced at Rafe, hesitated before getting out of his chair. Laveau's compliments on Luis's looks, size, and presumed intelligence sounded oily and insincere. He was an idiot to think even a nine-year-old boy would believe him.

"Don't sit there scowling, Rafe. Come meet Laveau."

Rafe stood and turned to see Laveau's familiar face smiling at him, his black eyes revealing the nature of his soul. "There's no need to introduce us. I know more than enough about Laveau."

"I see you're as friendly as ever." Laveau's smile was overtly insincere.

"I used to think we had something in common. It was a mistake."

Dolores clapped her hands in delight. "I was sure you would know each other. Now you can stay, Laveau, instead of going back to your card game."

"Dolores, it's not fair to put pressure on Mr. di Viere if he feels he has commitments elsewhere," Maria said.

"It wouldn't matter whether he had commitments or not. Laveau isn't welcome in this house now or at any other time." Rafe turned to Laveau. "If you set foot on the property again, I'll have you arrested."

"Rafe!" Dolores exclaimed. "Are you out of your mind?"

"No. I've been so only once."

"You can't tell Laveau to leave. This is my house. I can invite anyone I want."

"If you paid proper attention to the will, you'd know this is not your house."

He ignored Dolores's sputtered objections. He was more curious about the expression on Laveau's face. It looked too much like triumph for his comfort.

"You should thank me rather than throw me out."

"Why should I do that?" Laveau looked so pleased, Rafe knew he was about to hear something he wouldn't like.

"I'm the one who sent Pilar that ad when I saw it in the Chicago paper."

Rafe had wondered why it was sent anonymously. Knowing Laveau had been the sender made him even more apprehensive.

"I was certain my clever and curious sister would make you reply." Laveau's words virtually dripped with sarcasm. "She could never confine her interests to things that concern her."

"Get out, Laveau. You're fouling the air I breathe."

Laveau's smile deepened. "As charming as ever. In this world of change, it's nice to know some things remain the same."

"You can pat yourself on the back for having settled me with a load of responsibility I don't want. Now, I'm sure your friends are growing impatient for you to return to the game."

Rather than move to leave, Laveau seemed to grow more rooted to the spot. "Dolores tells me a friend of yours was shot while out riding this morning. I believe she said his name is Broc. I couldn't be sure. It's an unusual name, and Dolores is very fond of wine."

"You know very well his name is Broc."

"I trust he will recover soon. Dolores tells me you removed the bullet so quickly, he is strong enough to endure being read to." He cast a condescending glance at Luis. "Broc must have remarkable powers of survival. But then his face is a testimony to that."

Rafe had had all of Laveau he could tolerate. "It's time for you to leave. I'll see you to the door. Maria, would you ask Juan to send someone from the stable to escort Mr. di Viere to town? I wouldn't want him to lose his way."

Dolores grabbed Laveau's arm. "I refuse to let you run him off."

"If you enjoy his company so much, you can leave with him." The sudden brightness in her eyes amused him. "Just know that if you do, you can't return to this house."

Dolores's magnificent eyes flashed with anger, the first genuine emotion Rafe had seen in her since his return. "You know I can't leave."

"Then I suggest you allow Mr. di Viere to go on his way."

She gripped Laveau's arm tighter. "What will you do if I don't let him go? Hit me?"

Laveau cast Rafe an amused look, then carefully removed Dolores's hand from his arm. "It's never wise to annoy the man who holds the purse strings. I think it's best I go. Rafe doesn't like it when he doesn't get his way."

It was a remark cast at random to catch anything that might be there to catch. Rafe's expression didn't change, but Dolores didn't exercise the same control.

"He never has. Why do you think he ran away?"

Laveau's eyebrows rose. "He ran away?" He turned to Rafe. "I'm sure it must be a fascinating tale."

Dolores grinned. "I'll be happy to tell you every detail."

Laveau's eyes glowed with anticipation. "When you're next in town. Shall we say tomorrow at six?"

Dolores threw a satisfied glance at Rafe. "I'll be there."

Laveau brought Dolores's hand to his lips. "Until then, my enchantress."

Dolores was about to say something when Maria reentered the room. "Juan is at the door."

Laveau nodded to Maria. "You're most gracious." He ignored Luis and turned to Rafe. "I'm sure we'll see each other again. Give Broc my best wishes for a speedy recovery."

Rafe said nothing because anything he wanted to say would have made the situation worse. Laveau seemed to understand and be amused by Rafe's self-imposed silence.

"No final words to speed me on my way?"

Rafe didn't move.

Laveau sighed dramatically. "He never was much of a talker."

"How can you be so rude?" Dolores demanded when Laveau was barely through the doorway. "He said you were friends during the war."

Rafe felt a sudden desire for a large whiskey, but getting drunk would solve nothing. "I've made two big mistakes in my judgment of people. You were one. Laveau was the other."

"Everyone in Cíbola thinks he's wonderful. You

can't believe the jealous looks I get because he has a preference for me."

Rafe was tired of Laveau and tired of Dolores. "Laveau betrayed our troop to the Union soldiers. He compounded his treachery by stealing money from one of his fellow soldiers."

His words had no effect on Dolores. "You'd say anything about him if you thought it would hurt me. Do you still love me that much?"

Rafe found it impossible to plumb the depths of Dolores's powers of self-deception. Hadn't she heard a word he'd said, seen the revulsion in his eyes when he looked at her?

"I don't love you, Dolores. I got over that when I found you in my—" He remembered Luis was still in the room. "—when you decided to marry my father. What I said about Laveau is the truth."

Dolores stomped her foot. "Everybody in Cíbola thinks Laveau is a perfect gentleman."

"Everybody in Cíbola wasn't sleeping in the apple orchard that night in the Shenandoah Valley. Everybody in Cíbola didn't have to bury their friends the next morning." He still felt the grief of those losses. "Laveau killed the man standing guard and rode out before the attack."

"I don't know why you'd lie about a man who was your friend, but I don't believe you. I'm going to my room," she announced to Maria. "I won't be home for dinner tomorrow. Tell Juan I'll need someone to drive me into town after lunch." She left without saying a word to Luis.

"Can she drive a buggy?" Rafe asked Maria.

"I think so."

"I'll see she gets one." If Dolores could drive herself to and from town, Luis and Maria would be spared having to deal with the kind of men who attached themselves to widows like Dolores.

"Why did he do it?" Luis asked.

Rafe turned to Luis. "He wanted to be on the winning side. His family had lost some land, and he believed the Union Army would get it back for him."

"Did they?"

"No. Nobody on either side liked traitors."

"Did you know all those people who died?"

Maria was visibly upset at the direction of the conversation. "Luis, I don't think these are suitable questions for you to ask."

"He already knows too much to stop now." Rafe understood Maria's concern, but Luis's birth was the result of lies and treachery. He would have to learn things that would hurt him far more than hearing about the duplicity of strangers. "Yes, I knew them. We rode, ate, and slept together. It was like losing my family." For a second time.

"It's time for you to go to bed."

Luis tried to protest, but Maria was firm.

"If you want to have enough energy to ride with me tomorrow, you have to get your rest," Rafe put in.

Now that Rafe had given Luis a good reason for going to bed, the boy said good night, allowed Maria to kiss him, then left the room. Maria turned to Rafe, a worried look in her eyes.

"Do you think it's wise to ride tomorrow?"

"Are you worried someone will shoot at us again?"

"Yes, it makes me nervous."

"I'm not going to let the shooting confine me to the house. I'm not a coward."

"No one thinks you are, but the rest of us haven't gone through a war. We're not used to having people shoot at us day and night."

Rafe knew he shouldn't smile, but her eyes flashed when she got irritated. It made her look even more attractive. "I never got used to being shot at, but sometimes it's necessary to take care of my responsibilities."

"But you don't intend to take care of them. You're going back to Texas and leaving us at the mercy of that lawyer."

The outburst was unexpected. Maria usually seemed so calm, so controlled. Did this agitation mean she was changing her mind about him?

"I won't leave you and Luis in such a risky situation."

"But you won't know if something dangerous happens, will you? Texas is a long way off."

He could tell she was upset, but he wasn't sure he understood why. He reached for her hand. "Tell me what's wrong."

Maria jerked her hand from his grasp. "I wish you'd never seen that notice. I thought we could go on for years by ourselves until Luis grew up. I don't know why Mr. di Viere sent it, but I wish he hadn't."

"I don't know why, either, but I'm sure it was for no good reason."

"You don't like Dolores, or me, either, for that matter, because you think I'm like my sister, and you don't think I've done a good job bringing up Luis. Now you've got Luis determined to be just like you.

Do you know he galloped his pony back to the ranch this morning? That brings me to Broc getting shot and my having to help you take the bullet out of his shoulder. You may be used to cutting into your friends, with blood everywhere, but I'm not. And all of this has happened in little more than one day."

Rafe tried not to laugh, but he couldn't help it. The more vulnerable Maria appeared, the more unlike her sister she seemed, and the more he was attracted to her. He took her hand again. She tried to tug it away, but not as vigorously as before. He didn't let go.

"I'm sorry I've upset your life so badly. I never meant to do so."

"I don't suppose you did, but you *did* upset it, and you've kept on upsetting it, so your apology doesn't do much good."

She really was charming. There wasn't any challenge she wouldn't tackle, no person she wouldn't confront, yet she also had an endearing quality of vulnerability that made him want to protect her.

"And now you've brought that terrible man down on us. And don't pretend it's not your fault that he's here making Dolores think he's some sort of paragon."

Rafe was certain he was the reason for Laveau's presence in Cíbola. He just didn't know yet what the man hoped to gain. "You believe what I said about him?"

She looked directly into his eyes. "I can see the memory still gives you pain."

He hadn't expected that remark. He didn't think she was insensitive, but he was certain she thought he was. "I'm sorry about Laveau. I don't know what he's doing here, but he's as evil as his sister is good."

"I can't blame you. Dolores was the one who brought him here." Maria eased her hand from Rafe's grasp. "If you'll excuse me, I need to go upstairs."

"It's not terribly late."

"I have to make sure Luis is in bed. I'm certain I'll get a visit from Dolores as soon as I go to my room. Before I can do that, I have to go over tomorrow's household chores with Rosana."

"You have too much to do."

"You're the first person to think so."

"Your sister doesn't know how fortunate she is to have you."

"She does take me for granted sometimes, but that's partly my fault. I was so grateful when she brought me to live here, I felt I couldn't do enough for her."

"Was your life so bad?"

"It was worse, but I don't intend to tell you because I don't want you to feel sorry for me. Now I really must go. Juan will close up after you."

He could close up on his own, but he wanted to talk to Juan. It was time he learned more about Maria de la Guerra. It was time to throw out all his preconceived notions and start over again. Broc was right. He was interested in her.

Maria sighed when Dolores entered her room without knocking. She was tired, frustrated, confused, and angry at Dolores for bringing Laveau di Viere to the house. She couldn't have expected Dolores to guess the man's connection with Rafe or to have known about his treachery, but it was just like Dolores to bring home a man most women wouldn't want their son or their younger sister to meet.

Not waiting to be invited in, Dolores settled herself on Maria's daybed. "What were you and Rafe talking about for so long?"

Maria sat before her mirror and began to take her hair down in preparation for bed. "Nothing important. We can't seem to agree on anything."

"It had to be something. Rafe was never much of a talker."

"You know him better than I do."

"That was ten years ago."

"I doubt he's changed much." Yet he must have. She couldn't imagine Dolores falling in love with a man of Rafe's serious disposition.

"He's completely changed." Dolores waved her hand as though pushing aside any remnant of the past. "He used to be so in love with me, he would do anything to get me to marry him."

"He doesn't want to marry you now." She hoped Dolores wasn't going to ask her to help rekindle Rafe's old feelings for her. It was impossible, but she wouldn't have participated in such a scheme in any case.

Dolores shrugged. "I could get him to change his mind, but I've decided I don't want to marry him. He's turned into his father. *You* ought to marry him."

Maria removed the last pin from her hair and turned to face her sister. "Setting aside my feelings as well as his, how could you suggest that I marry the man who raped you?"

Dolores studied her hands. "He was young and upset."

Maria picked up a brush and began to work the

tangles out of her hair. "Nothing can excuse an act of such brutality."

Dolores met her sister's gaze. "He wouldn't do anything like that again. He's much too dull."

Maria gave her hair a hundred strokes each night. She began counting. *One, two, three...* "It wouldn't matter if he got down on his knees and begged your forgiveness. I still wouldn't marry him even if I loved him. In fact, I find it hard not to dislike him." No, that wasn't the truth. She *tried* to dislike him. She thought she *ought* to dislike him, but she couldn't.

"I think you *do* like him. I know he likes you."

It upset her that Dolores could see she couldn't control her feelings when it came to Rafe. *Nineteen, twenty, twenty-one...* "You're imagining things. Neither one of us likes the other."

Dolores didn't look ruffled by her sister's denial. "You understand how to take care of a house, how to teach Luis, how to deal with servants. I understand men, women, and their feelings for each other. If Rafe didn't like you, he wouldn't spend so much time talking to you."

Twenty-eight, twenty-nine, thirty... "He had to talk to me about Luis."

"And you wouldn't have gone riding with him?"

"I went to look after Luis."

"You're afraid of horses."

"I'm not afraid of them. I just haven't had much occasion to ride. I think I could learn to like it. I never realized the ranch was so beautiful."

Dolores sat forward. "You think the ranch is beautiful? Rafe is crazy about it."

Forty-one, forty-two, forty-three... "I think the *setting* is beautiful. I don't get excited by acres and acres of crops." She knew nothing about the seasons, planting, irrigating, harvesting, or marketing, but she wondered whether it would interest her. She'd have to learn if she expected to help Luis manage the ranch. Would Rafe stay long enough to teach her?

Dolores settled back. "One plant looks like another."

Fifty-three, fifty-four, fifty-five... "I doubt Rafe or Miguel would agree. The difference in plants is what makes the ranch successful."

"See, you already know more than I do."

That wouldn't be hard. Maria doubted Dolores could tell an apple tree from a grapevine. "I have all I can do to take care of Luis and manage the household."

"I could do that."

Sixty-eight, sixty-nine, seventy—Ouch! She was pulling her hair too hard. "You know nothing about managing the house. You know even less about Luis's lessons."

Dolores sat up again. "You ought to get Rafe to help you with Luis."

Eighty-two, eighty-three, eighty-four... The last thing she needed was another reason to spend time with Rafe. "If he really is going back to Texas, he has other things to do with his time."

"You can't let him go back to Texas."

Ninety-one, ninety-two, ninety-three... "And how am I supposed to stop him?"

"Make him fall in love with you."

"Don't be absurd. No one can make another person fall in love. Besides, you'd hate living in the same house with him."

"Maybe he'd give me a bigger allowance to get rid of me."

Ninety-nine, one hundred. She should have known Dolores wouldn't propose any scheme that didn't benefit her. Maria laid her brush aside and got up to take off her dress. "I'm not going to talk about this anymore. It's too far-fetched to consider."

"But our situation is desperate."

Ten

"No, it's not," Maria told Dolores. "You can live on your allowance if you're careful. Once Luis comes into his inheritance, neither one of us will have to be concerned with Rafe Jerry ever again."

Why didn't that thought give Maria comfort? Rafe's arrival had destroyed the tenor of their lives. She ought to long for the days before his arrival. Instead, she found herself dreading the day he would return to Texas.

"You've got to be worried about him. Our lives depend on him."

Maria stepped out of her dress and laid it across the bed. "We managed before he arrived. We'll manage after he leaves."

"I don't want to *just manage*. I'm tired of having too little money. I want to have fun while I'm still young."

The whole time she was growing up, their parents had told Dolores her beauty would win her a rich husband who would do anything he could to please her. That promise had not been fulfilled and Dolores was determined to have what she felt was *owed* her.

"I don't mind your enjoying yourself, but must you ask people like Laveau di Viere to bring you home?"

"I don't *ask* men to bring me home. They offer. What's wrong with Laveau? You don't believe what Rafe said about him, do you?"

Maria took the time to put her dress in the closet before she answered. "I could see the anger in Rafe's eyes, see the pain the memories caused him."

Dolores clapped her hands with delight. "That's exactly why he'll marry you. You believe everything he says."

"I don't—" she began, but she couldn't remember that he'd lied to her. "This conversation is absurd." She removed her petticoats and draped them across a chair. "Now, I'm tired, and I have to get up early. Rafe is taking Luis for a ride, and then we're going into Cíbola to buy clothes. Apparently according to Texas standards, the boy doesn't have anything decent to wear." She knew nothing about Texas, but if Rafe and Broc were any example, Texans knew how to wear clothes that made a woman acutely aware of their physical presence.

"Don't let Luis get on his nerves. I don't want him to drive Rafe away before he does something about that horrible will."

"Rafe seems to enjoy the boy."

"No man enjoys being around children."

"I'm not going to argue with you. I'm too tired."

Dolores pushed herself up and stood. "Think about what I said. If you married Rafe, you'd be a rich woman."

"I don't want to be rich badly enough to marry

Rafe. Now go to bed. You don't want wrinkles or bags under your eyes."

Only concern for her looks could sidetrack Dolores from a goal. In the meantime, Maria would get a reprieve from thinking about Rafe.

⤳

"How soon will I get my new boots?"

Luis should have been tired after spending an hour in the saddle, but buying new clothes had him dancing with excitement. Maria wondered how Rafe thought he was going to leave the boy behind when he went to Texas. The relationship between them seemed so natural, she ached to tell them they were father and son.

"They'll probably be ready in a couple of weeks. You can wear the others until then."

Luis looked with disapproval at his pair of ready-made boots. "They aren't real boots."

Maria nearly laughed aloud. Luis didn't know anything about boots, but if they weren't like Rafe's, they were not real.

"They're fine boots," Rafe assured Luis.

"Did you ever wear ready-made boots?" Luis asked.

"When the war was over, I had to wear my army boots for nearly a year. I thought my feet would never recover."

Why was it so hard for her to remember he hadn't always been the pampered son of a rich man?

"Did you have a horse?" Luis persisted.

"My friend's father had lots of horses. All we had to do was catch them."

"Weren't they in a stable?"

"No. They'd been allowed to run loose during the war. It was more than a month before most of them stopped bucking every time we saddled up."

"Did your horse buck?"

"Sure did."

"Did you fall off?"

"I came close a couple of times, but I'd been riding almost since I was able to walk."

"Papa said I was too little to ride."

Maria wished she had known riding was so important to Luis. He had always been such a biddable child. He never questioned what people told him. She hadn't wanted to admit it, but it hadn't seemed normal for a healthy boy to be so content to stay inside and read. What was she going to do with him after Rafe left? There was no one else on the ranch who could take him under his wing, and she didn't want Luis to be drawn to the men Dolores brought to the house. She needed to convince Rafe to stay. At least for a while.

"Where would you like to eat?"

Rafe had promised Luis he could choose the restaurant, but there wasn't much choice in Cíbola. After looking inside two restaurants that placed platters of food on long tables to be fought over by the patrons, he settled on the hotel. It was fun watching Luis order his first meal. It was even more intriguing to watch Rafe guide him through the process. When he asked about the difference between dressing made with oysters and dressing made with clams, Rafe drew the waiter over to explain how the dish was prepared. Luis decided on pork chops with clam stuffing, something he'd never had before. Maria hoped he didn't hate it.

"I'll have chicken," Rafe said.

"Maria likes beef," Luis informed Rafe. "We have it a lot."

"We also have pork, poultry, and fish."

"I know, but we have beef a lot."

Apparently she needed to vary their menu.

"I imagine you have beef a lot because you raise cows," Rafe said. "It's easier to eat what you raise."

"We also have pigs and chickens," Luis responded. "Broc said he saw a flock of geese. Do we have geese?"

"We raise geese, ducks, and turkeys—whatever people will buy," Maria answered. "We—"

"What a quaint family gathering."

Maria looked up to see Laveau di Viere approaching their table. Rafe stiffened and all the animation went out of Luis.

Laveau's smile was falsely amiable. "I'd invite you to join Dolores and me for lunch, but our table isn't big enough for five." He indicated a table for two tucked away in a discreet corner. "Should I ask for another table?"

"We've already ordered." Rafe's voice didn't reveal the anger Maria could see in his eyes. "Our food would be cold before yours arrived."

"You always were so sensible." Laveau subjected Luis to a momentary scrutiny. "Is this your son?" he asked Rafe.

"This is my half brother. Dolores married my father after my mother's death."

"I suppose your being brothers explains the extraordinary resemblance."

Maria wanted to say something, to do something

to ease the tension, but she suspected the animosity between these two men went too deep for her to change it. Rafe had his temper well in hand, but she could see the effort it took. Laveau, on the other hand, appeared to be frustrated that Rafe wasn't responding as he had hoped.

"I look like my father," Luis told Laveau.

Laveau scowled. "I would have said you looked like your mother."

"You would have been wrong," Rafe said. "But then you should be used to that by now."

It pleased Maria to see a momentary tightening around Laveau's mouth. Just then Dolores entered the hotel.

"I was hoping you would still be in town," she said with a satisfied smile. "Now we can all have lunch together."

Dolores was wearing a stylish new outfit topped off by a hat with a feather that curved provocatively against her chin. Maria didn't need to ask the price to know it had cost more than Dolores could afford.

"We've already discussed that," Rafe told her. "Your table is too small, and our food is already on the way."

"We can get a bigger table."

"It would be impolite to eat before you were served, but our food would be cold before yours arrived."

Dolores continued to argue with Rafe while he calmly explained why each of her proposed solutions wouldn't work. Considering how much he disliked her, Maria was amazed at his forbearance.

"I'm reluctant to say so, my sweet, but I think Rafe prefers your sister's company."

"You do occasionally get something right." The words were spoken calmly, but Rafe's eyes were hard as agate. "You should claim your table before someone else is seated there."

"The hotel has reserved that table for me for the duration of my stay." Laveau's smile was sickly sweet. "They value my patronage."

"Then don't give them reason to change their minds."

Though she didn't like him, it was hard for Maria to envision Laveau betraying his entire troop. She could easily believe he had poor character, but it was hard to imagine him causing the deaths of men who'd been his constant companions for three years.

"I don't like that man." Luis's eyes had followed Laveau across the room. "I wish Mama didn't, either."

"I'm sure she doesn't really," Rafe said, "but he thinks your mother is very beautiful, and she likes to be admired."

Maria smiled at Rafe. He had made some mistakes in the past, but bless the man for doing his best to shield Luis from the imperfections of his mother's character.

Luis appeared to be considering something. He pursed his mouth, looked at Laveau, who had said something to make Dolores laugh, then looked back at Rafe. "Mama is very pretty, but I don't think he cares about that."

Rafe glanced at Laveau's table; he paused before responding. "Mr. di Viere lost something he valued very much. He likes to make other people as miserable as he is."

"What did he lose?"

"His home, his inheritance, and the vision he had of himself."

"I don't understand."

Maria wondered how Rafe would have responded, but the arrival of their food spared him. Ignoring his vegetables, Luis cut off a piece of pork, put it in his mouth, and chewed slowly.

"This is really good. Can we have this at home?" he asked Maria.

"I don't know how to make it."

"Can we ask the chef?"

"Some cooks don't like to give away their recipes."

"Could you figure out how to make it if you tasted it?"

"Maybe."

Luis cut off a slice and put it on Maria's plate. "Taste it."

It was good, but Maria couldn't identify all the spices. "I don't know which seasonings are in the dressing."

"I'll give some to Rafe. He can tell you."

Maria was certain Rafe had never been near a kitchen except to steal a cookie or beg a bone for a favorite dog. She kept a straight face while Rafe carefully chewed the portion Luis had given him.

"It *is* good. I second Luis's request that you have Rosana fix it for us soon."

"If I can get the chef to share his recipe." She frowned, pretending to ponder the spices. "I know he used nutmeg and parsley, but there's something else."

"I think he used a heavy sherry and a dash of tarragon. I would have used thyme."

Luis looked from Rafe to Maria. "Is that right?"

She couldn't believe Rafe even knew of such herbs. "Don't tell me you spent your teenage years in the kitchen watching Rosana cook."

Rafe grinned. "I talked to Rosana and nearly every woman on the ranch about cooking." His smile faded. "I learned more during the war."

"You cooked during the war?" Luis asked.

"All of us did. We were a mobile unit, so we cooked for ourselves in small groups. Most of the younger boys didn't know how to boil water when they showed up. For a while, I did a lot of cooking. Now eat up. I'm going to show you one of my favorite spots when we get home."

Luis's eyes lit up. "Can we ride there?"

"We have to if we want to get back in time for dinner."

Maria was so intrigued by the conversation between Luis and Rafe, she paid little attention to the food she ate. Maybe it was because Rafe's being his older brother caused Luis to accept him so quickly. Maybe it was because he longed for the attention of a man he could look up to and admire. Or maybe it was that Rafe had immediately attributed to him a quality of masculinity no one else had seen. It could have simply been because Rafe treated him as an equal rather than a little boy. Whatever the reason, Luis had a case of hero worship.

It was hard for Maria not to feel the same way.

Except for that momentary loss of control years ago, he was the kind of man to cause any woman's heart to beat faster. He was handsome, kind, and thoughtful. There didn't appear to be much he hadn't done or couldn't do if needed. He gave her the feeling his life would be a carefully laid out mosaic instead of a series of accidental happenings. He acted like a man whose principles were so firmly fixed, he wouldn't compromise even if he faced hardship as a result. A man who would fight equally hard to get what he wanted and to protect it afterward. She suspected his loyalty, once given, would never be taken back. In short, he was exactly the kind of man she could fall in love with.

Unfortunately he was the one man she couldn't allow herself to love. It was good he was taking Luis off for the afternoon. She needed some time alone to get her feelings under control. She'd let Dolores's foolish suggestion that she marry Rafe get lodged in her head, and now she couldn't get it out.

"Do you think we ought to invite Maria to go with us?" Rafe asked Luis.

Feeling rattled by his question, she said quickly, "I've got too much to do."

"Surely you can delegate your work or leave it until tomorrow."

"You've never had to run a household," she pointed out. "You don't know—"

"When my mother was sick, I learned the list of things that really had to be done was short. The rest was just to make life more comfortable. I don't put much stock in comfort anymore."

The way he smiled at her caused her resistance to waver.

"Please come with us," Luis put in. "Rafe said he'll take us to his favorite place."

How could she resist when Luis looked at her as if

she alone had the power to grant the wish closest to his heart? Or when Rafe looked as if this was no polite invitation, as if he really *did* want her to go with them?

"I'll do all my lessons before I go to bed," Luis promised.

Rafe's eyes were alive with amusement. "I don't have any lessons, so I'll groom all three horses when we get back."

Her resistance, never strong, collapsed. "I'll go, but we can't stay long."

∽

Rafe worried that he might be on the verge of making a big mistake, but he wasn't sure he could stop himself. The more he was around Maria, the more he was convinced she was different from her sister. He didn't like to admit that Broc had been right, but he'd been attracted to Maria from the start. He knew he wasn't beyond being made a fool of by a woman, but he'd studied Maria's words, actions, even her expressions and the inflections of her voice, in search of discrepancies, of any careful concealment of her true nature, without finding any. He'd come to the conclusion that Maria was exactly what she appeared to be. And what she appeared to be was very attractive to Rafe.

So much so that his mind leaped all the way to thoughts of marriage.

That was something of a shock. He wasn't sure he wanted to get married. Unless he changed jobs, he wouldn't be able to support a wife and family. He liked his life in Texas. Not even his inheritance had made him want to change it. So what was it about

Maria that was causing him to question his plans for the future?

For one thing, he'd just spent one of the most pleasant afternoons of his life with Maria and Luis. Dolores had stayed in Cíbola, Broc was taking a nap, and nothing on the ranch needed his attention. The day had been unusually cool for summer, the sun behind scattered clouds. A breeze coming down from the mountainside stirred the leaves and set the tall, dry grass that covered the steep hillsides to waving.

Luis had ridden between them, his curiosity about everything seemingly boundless. He would question Rafe in detail, then turn to Maria and tell her everything he'd just learned. She didn't betray by as much as a smile or a raised eyebrow that she'd heard his questions and Rafe's answers. Seeing her patience, her pride in Luis, her love for him, had performed a special kind of magic in Rafe's heart. This was a good woman, the kind a man was fortunate to find even once in his life.

Maria kept smiling at him. Every time she did, he felt a little short of breath. He told himself not to do anything foolish, not to act too quickly, but it didn't do any good. There was something about this woman that spoke to him in a way no other had, not even Dolores. *Especially not Dolores!* And it didn't hurt that Maria had loved his favorite place.

It was a small outcropping where two ridges came together, looking out on a panoramic view of the valley for miles in all directions. Luis liked it because everything down below looked so small. *It's like a toy ranch*, he'd said. Maria seemed to understand Rafe's feeling for the place, where the ranch could be seen as a whole rather than a collection of parts.

"I can see why you love this spot," Maria had said to him. "It makes the ranch feel like a lot more than dirt, plants, and animals."

He had wanted to ask her what the ranch meant to her, but Luis had asked him a question and he'd gotten side-tracked. On their way back to the house, it hadn't felt like the right time. There would be a right time eventually. In the meanwhile, he had to search his mind and his heart. The latter organ hadn't been used in such a long time, he couldn't be sure it was working right. It was important that he find the right answers to his questions. He didn't want history to repeat itself.

Rafe decided he was getting soft. He couldn't remember when he'd spent a more enjoyable evening and all he'd done was listen to Broc recite bits from the roles he used to play on riverboats, listen to his friend sing while Maria accompanied him on the piano, and watch Luis's delighted enjoyment of the entertainment. Dolores had gone into town again, as she had for the last three nights.

Thinking of Dolores reminded Rafe that Laveau's presence in Cíbola had raised questions that needed answers. Why had Laveau come to California and why had he ingratiated himself with Dolores? Laveau wasn't one to spend money on anyone but himself unless he thought he had something to gain. Rafe wanted to believe Laveau was behind the shooting of Broc, but he couldn't think of any reason for the man to shoot Broc, and Laveau never did anything without a reason. If Rafe had been the one who had been shot, he'd have been certain Laveau was behind it and Dolores was somehow involved. Yet his father's will made it impossible for either of them to benefit from his death.

None of it made sense, and trying to figure out the mystery was giving him a headache. He was relieved when Luis spoke.

"That's enough singing," the boy said to Broc. "Say something funny."

"You've had him reciting bits from his plays every night," Maria said. "He's bound to be out of material by now."

"He's never out of material," Rafe said, "because he makes it up."

Broc defended himself, with Luis and Maria taking his side.

"If it's so easy to make up stuff, would you make up something for me?" Luis asked Rafe.

"Luis, my child, don't let your admiration for Rafe's horsemanship make you think he has a brain," Broc chided. "Whenever he has a question or needs advice, who do you think he goes to?"

"Cade," Luis said, then crowed with delight when Broc looked deflated. Even Maria laughed at his exaggerated shock and consternation.

"I'm hurt." Broc's pretense of being deeply offended was comic rather than serious. "I thought you liked me."

"I do like you, but Maria says I must always tell the truth."

Broc directed an accusing glance at Maria. "Stop

giving this child good advice. How am I supposed to steal his money?"

"You can't steal my money because I don't have any. Rafe has it all." Luis grinned as if he'd just won a prize.

"Then I guess there's nothing left for me to do but marry Maria and run away with her."

Maria giggled and flushed, which caused Rafe to feel an all-too-familiar stab of jealousy. He felt even more irritated when Broc started talking about all the children they would have and how Luis could think of them as his little brothers and sisters. Broc's description of several romantic trysts had Luis making faces of disgust and Rafe biting his tongue to keep from telling his friend to stop talking nonsense.

It threw him off stride when Maria said to Broc, "I need to talk to Rafe. Alone."

Eleven

As soon as Broc and Luis left the room, Rafe asked, "What do you want to talk about?" He couldn't think of anything Maria would want to say that required privacy.

"About Luis, the ranch, and you."

"That covers a lot of territory. Does that include you, too?"

"In a way. I mean, yes, it does."

Rafe hadn't expected Maria to blush. What could that mean?

"Can we go to your father's room?"

Rafe didn't know how much privacy Maria wanted, but he was surprised she would suggest his father's room. That implied a degree of intimacy Rafe hadn't thought existed between them. As he followed her up the steps and down the upper hall, he wondered if it was a reflection of the change in their relationship over the last few days.

She had insisted upon going with him every time he took Luis riding. At first he'd thought she didn't trust him with the boy, but she seemed more concerned about the ranch than overseeing the boy's safety. She had encouraged him to tell Luis everything he could about the ranch, how things had been when Rafe was a boy, and what he thought should be done in the future. He'd assumed she was trying to get as much information as possible about Rancho los Alamitos before he went back to Texas.

Yesterday her questions had been directed to his plans for the future. She'd questioned him about his partnership with Cade and the kind of work he did. Today her questions had focused on how he intended to run the ranch from Texas. She hadn't seemed upset when he didn't have answers.

He held the door to his father's room for her. "Take any chair you like."

She settled in a deep chair next to the table where his father had kept Rafe's picture. He stood by the fireplace. They were separated by less than ten feet.

"What did you want to talk about that requires so much privacy?"

"I want to convince you to stay here, not go back to Texas."

In the beginning she hadn't wanted him there. He wondered why she'd changed her mind. "That will take a lot of convincing."

She looked genuinely bewildered. "I don't understand. This is your home. You grew up here. Everybody says you loved the ranch. From what I've seen riding with you these last few days, you still love it. You already have dozens of ideas about changes you want to make."

She'd hit him at a weak spot. He liked his work in

Texas, but at heart he was a farmer, not a cowman. He loved every acre of Rancho los Alamitos, but he could not remain. "Things happened here that make it impossible for me to feel the same way I used to."

"I can't imagine how much Dolores's marriage to your father must have hurt, but no teenage crush lasts forever. Surely you can see that you and Dolores would never have been happy together."

He was older and he did see that, but the realization didn't change anything. He couldn't forget finding his father in Dolores's bed, naked, in the throes of physical climax.

"I agree with everything you say, but it's not enough to change my mind."

"What about the money? Surely being a wealthy rancher and one of the most important men in the valley is better than being a cowhand on a Texas ranch. One day you will want to marry and start a family. I wouldn't think you could do that on a cowhand's salary. Here you could give your family all the advantages of wealth and privilege."

"I don't care about any of that."

"How do you think your family will feel when they find out you turned down such a life for one of drudgery and hard work? And you know they will. There's no way you can come back here several times a year without people finding out."

She was bringing up points he didn't want to consider because he had no answers. He'd move heaven and earth to keep the ranch from being sold and the money used to build a shrine to Dolores. There was little point in returning to Texas if he had to come back here every month or so, and even less point in working for Cade when his half of Rancho los Alamitos would make him several times richer than Cade.

"I'm not likely to get married, so that doesn't matter. My friends are in Texas. They're my family."

She had been sitting forward in her chair in her eagerness to convince him, but now she got up, walked over to him, and put her hand on his arm. "Then think of Luis. The ranch is his inheritance. Someone has to manage it for him until he's old enough to take over himself."

Her hand on his arm made it hard for Rafe to concentrate on what she was saying. How could he have known her touch would affect him so strongly? Or that looking into her upturned gaze would cause his pulse to thrum in his temples? He wasn't an impressionable young man. He couldn't tell whether her look of entreaty was entirely on Luis's behalf or if it represented her feelings toward him.

"The lawyer can manage the business end and Miguel can take care of the ranch."

Her grip on his arm tightened. "But someone has to teach Luis what to do, to love this place as you did. Nobody else could do the job as well as you."

"Maybe you could talk Broc into staying. He grew up on a farm, so he would know what to do."

She gave him a nudge of frustration before releasing his arm. He wished she hadn't let go. He'd enjoyed the warmth of her touch.

"Luis has fun with Broc, but you're the one he looks up to. He doesn't quote Broc, but he does quote you."

"I'll start him riding with Miguel."

"It wouldn't be the same as riding with you. You're his brother. He wants to feel like he's part of everything you're part of. If you care for him at all, you've got to consider what I'm asking."

She stepped closer, put her hand on his arm once more, and met his gaze with a look that practically took his breath away. It was as though she were saying she depended on him, that without him everything could crumble to dust and blow away. No one had needed him for a long time—he hadn't allowed himself to be needed—but now he wanted the responsibility. He didn't know what it was about this woman that appealed to him so strongly, but he had to find out just how much she was interested in him.

"Would you like me to stay?"

"I've just said that I would."

"You've said you want me to stay for Luis. You haven't said that *you* want me to stay."

Her gaze faltered. "I didn't ask you here to discuss what I want."

She tried to release him, to move back a step, but he covered her hand with his. "I know that. Nevertheless, I want to know what *you* want."

She appeared confused, embarrassed. He knew he could be too abrasive. Pilar had told him he'd never get a woman to spend more than five minutes in his company if he didn't learn to be more sensitive. "I'll make it easier on you by going first."

"What do you mean?" Now she looked nervous.

"It was unfair of me to think you are like your sister just because you're related. I was prepared to dislike you. I was wrong."

"What made you change your mind?"

Now she appeared more curious than nervous. "The first clue was the way Rosana and Juan talked about you in comparison to Dolores. They aren't easily fooled. The second clue was that Broc liked you right away. In fact, he accused me of being interested in you that first day."

"You hated me because of Dolores."

"I didn't trust you, but I was attracted to you from the beginning."

"I would never have guessed."

"I didn't mean for you to." He hadn't meant for Broc to guess, either, but maybe he wasn't as good at hiding his feelings as he thought. "The most important reason for me to change my mind was your obvious devotion to Luis. The fact that he turns to you whenever he has a question or is unsure of anything is the best proof that you're an honorable woman."

Maria looked slightly embarrassed by his praise. "Luis is sweet and gentle. He's easy to love."

"There's a lot of Jerry in him, and we can be hard and uncomfortable. You lived with my father long enough to know that."

"Your father was unhappy and sick, but he was never harsh to me."

"Which is further proof that I was wrong about you."

She tried once more to pull away, but he captured both her hands and held on firmly. She turned away from him, wouldn't meet his gaze. "You give me too much credit."

"I don't think I give you enough."

She turned back to look at him. "What do you want from me?"

He didn't know the answer to that question. "I'd like to know what you think of me. I hope your first impressions have softened."

She looked down at her hands in his grasp. "It was hard to know what I should think at first. You'd left home and hadn't communicated with your father for ten years, yet he kept your picture by his bedside. Juan, Rosana, and Miguel were anxious for your return, but Dolores told me a different story."

"And you believed her?"

"She's my sister. She had suffered, too. Why shouldn't I believe her?"

Because she was a liar interested only in herself. Because she thought nothing of seducing an old man while he grieved over his wife's death. "Do you still believe her?"

"I'm not sure it should be a question of whether I believe her, but more about what I think of the man you are now. Ten years ago you were young, very much in love, and grieving for your mother. It must have been incredibly painful to learn that the woman you loved wanted to marry your father. Anyone could be excused for going a little crazy."

Why did he get the feeling she was trying to convince herself more than him?

"The important part is what you've done since. According to Broc, you were little short of a saint during the war."

"To a civilian, anyone who saves someone's life is a saint. During the war we all did it more than once."

"That's something else I like about you. You never seem to think the things you do are out of the ordinary. You have no idea what an impression you've made on Luis."

"I'm more interested in the impression I've made on you." She looked down. Why did some women prefer to look at a man's shirt buttons rather than into his eyes?

"You impress me as a man who's sure of himself and takes his abilities for granted. Though I doubt you'll admit it, you're very much concerned for others. I think you regret some of the things that happened here, but have learned to accept the past and move beyond it. I think you take your responsibilities seriously, even the ones you don't want. I think this is your home, that you're looking for a reason to stay."

"Would you be willing to be that reason?"

Her gaze flew to his face, her eyes wide and questioning. "I don't understand."

He was going too fast, but his curiosity was riding him hard. "Few men will make a major change in their lives for another man, be it a father or a brother. Every man will do it for a woman."

Maria avoided his gaze. "I would never ask you to do anything like that for me. I don't have the right."

"What if I gave you that right?"

Maria looked up at him. "There's too much history between you and Dolores, between you and your father, to make that possible."

"What if the situation weren't complicated? What if we were two ordinary people who'd met for the first time?"

She didn't answer, just shook her head.

He had the feeling she knew the answer to his question and wanted to give it to him but was holding back. "Sometimes knowing what you want has a way of clearing up complications."

"How?"

"Understanding your needs puts everything into perspective. If you want something enough, even past pain can cease to matter."

"Is that how you feel?"

He would never be able to forgive Dolores for what she had done. She'd destroyed his life. She'd hurt his father, had a child she didn't want, and had turned her own sister into a personal servant. "I doubt some things in my past will ever cease to matter, but I hope I can reach the point where they won't affect the decisions I make."

"Do you think you can?"

"I can with a good reason, but I'm not asking you for one. Just asking what you might do if the past were different."

She started to speak, then stopped. She paused so long, he thought she wasn't going to answer. When she did, her response wasn't what he'd hoped for.

"You have to know you're an attractive man. Any young woman would be flattered to be the object of your attentions. I've already pointed out the qualities in you that I admire. If the past didn't exist, I can't imagine why any woman wouldn't welcome your attention."

Was she speaking of some hypothetical woman, or was she speaking of herself? Tightening his hold on her hands, he pulled her closer, until he could feel her brush against him, her hair smelling of lavender. "I'm not interested in what *any woman* would do, just what you might do."

Still she didn't look up. "I have a past of my own to forget. My father tried to force me to marry a stranger to save his land, but I refused. Dolores's fiancé broke their engagement when she no longer had a dowry." She paused, as though uncertain whether to continue. "If I'd married that man, my father wouldn't have lost his land and committed suicide, and Dolores wouldn't have lost her fiancé. I couldn't do anything to help my father, but when Dolores invited me to live here, I vowed to do everything I could to make up for what I'd done to her."

Rafe had had no idea Maria suffered under such a load of guilt. "You shouldn't blame yourself for what happened. It wasn't your fault that your father lost his land, and he had no right to try to sacrifice you to save himself. And Dolores's fiancé is responsible for breaking their engagement, not you."

"But if I had agreed to marry Solomon—"

"Did you love him?"

"No! Dolores was the only one who stood up for me."

Rafe couldn't imagine Dolores standing up for anyone, but he had to admit she might have been different before her dreams had been so brutally destroyed. "You can't judge all men by your father or her fiancé. A man of honor would never have done any of those things. I'm not without fault, but I hope you believe I'm honorable."

Her expression was unreadable except for one thing. Pain.

"Will you tell me what is hurting you so much?" She avoided his gaze, shook her head.

His patience snapped. "Would you stop mincing words and give me a straight answer?" Pilar would tell him that demand was a perfect example of why no woman would ever put up with him long enough to fall in love with him, but he never could understand why some people were satisfied to talk in circles without ever giving a straight answer.

"If the past didn't exist, I could very easily fall in love with a man like you." She tried to pull away from him, but he didn't loosen his hold on her. "However, the past does exist. Since we can't change it, your question is pointless."

Surely she didn't expect him to accept her conclusion as the end of their conversation. No red-blooded man who was this close to holding an attractive woman in his arms would give up. He released one of her hands and slipped his arm around her waist. "I don't think the attraction between a man and a woman, regardless of the circumstances, is ever pointless."

"I didn't say I was attracted to you." She tried to pull away from him, but not very hard. "I just said I could fall in love with a man *like* you."

"I know what you said, but I don't think you would have said even that much if you felt no attraction to me. I've admitted I was attracted to you from the beginning. Can't you admit to being attracted just a little?" What was wrong with him? He was practically begging. What had happened to his pride? When did he start needing a woman so badly?

"I've already said I think you're handsome. That pretty much means I find you attractive."

That answer didn't satisfy him. It was like catching a glimpse of something without being able to see the whole. "You could be speaking about a piece of furniture or a vase of flowers."

"I prefer furniture that is functional as opposed to beautiful, and I think flowers shouldn't be cut and brought inside to die."

He tightened his hold on her and was pleased when she didn't resist. That answered one of the questions she hadn't. "Does it bother you that I find you attractive?"

"No." It sounded like she wasn't entirely sure.

"Do you mind my arm around you?"

She hesitated before answering, "Not really."

He freed her other hand, then cupped her chin and lifted it until he could look into her eyes. They were huge, a warm brown, and looking straight into his own eyes. Why hadn't he noticed how attractive they were? Her beauty radiated from the inside, which made her appeal that much stronger. It would be the same regardless of the setting. "I would never hurt you."

"I know that now."

But she hadn't known it in the beginning. He couldn't blame anyone but himself for her initial wariness. He pulled her up against him, was surprised but pleased when she didn't resist. He wanted to ask why she would allow him such familiarity without protest, but he was finding it impossible to think with his customary precision.

It had been more than ten years since he'd held a woman in his arms. He'd forgotten how desire could disrupt his thinking, could catapult his body into a state of such excitement that it was impossible for his brain to remain in control. With the little remaining brainpower he possessed, he searched for a way to convince her that his change of heart was sincere. His body had no doubt about the best way to do that. A tiny shred of sanity warned that he was about to make a mistake, but the rest of him was beyond the point of listening to counsel. His last thought before going completely under was that avoiding women for so long probably hadn't been a good idea.

The next thing he knew, he was kissing Maria. He couldn't remember if he'd asked her or just pulled her into an embrace. He could remember every moment he'd spent in Dolores's company, but none of them had felt like this. Being with Dolores was like suffering from a fever. Everything was hot, delusional.

This was different because Maria was kissing him back.

Dolores had *allowed* Rafe to kiss her. He'd been too besotted to realize what a difference it could make if the woman in your arms kissed you back. The feeling of Maria in his arms, of her lips on his, had the blood singing in his head and his groin swelling.

It was hard to believe how wonderful it felt to hold Maria, hard to believe he'd gone without this for ten years and had expected to continue to for the rest of his life. Why hadn't he dried up and blown away? How could a man be really alive without a woman to touch that part of him no man could reach? How could he have gone so long without realizing he was dying a little bit each year?

His life had assumed a fixed shape, all hard lines

and sharp angles. Even his friendships had been carefully contained. Cade and Pilar's son had been the only exception he had allowed himself. Now that had changed.

Maria was soft and pliable yet strong and resourceful. She was the kind of woman a man could depend on rather than the kind who needed constant reassurance. She would build him up rather than wear him down.

Her lips were soft yet eager. There was nothing coy, no pretense. He didn't want to think about the future or the past, just the present, and the wonderful feeling of holding Maria in his arms. To luxuriate in the taste of her lips, the feel of her mouth, the warmth of her body. He knew he'd have to stop soon, but all he asked for was a few moments longer, enough time to—

"Rafe Jerry. Get your hands off my sister!"

Twelve

RAFE COULDN'T BELIEVE HE HADN'T HEARD THE door open. What a cruel trick of fate that the worst possible person should have been the one to walk through it. He didn't need to step back from Maria. She'd jumped away from him as though propelled by a hidden force. He turned to see Dolores standing just inside the doorway.

"How dare you dishonor my sister!"

"I've done nothing of the sort."

Dolores ignored his protest. "I can't believe you could hate me so much that you would ruin my innocent sister." Turning to Maria, Dolores crossed the room in a few strides and folded her in a protective embrace. "What did he do to you?"

Rafe expected Maria to tell her sister to stop acting like a fool. He was stunned when she buried her face in Dolores's shoulder.

Dolores held Maria close. "You don't have to hide your shame from me. I know what he's like, but I'll see he does right by you."

Maria's head snapped up at that, but Rafe didn't

wait to hear her hoped-for protest. "I've done nothing to dishonor your sister. She was trying to convince me to stay here to teach Luis how to manage the ranch."

"You expect me to believe my sister would stoop to trying to seduce you so you would teach Luis how to plant beans and peas?" Dolores's indignation was magnificent, seemingly heartfelt.

"She wasn't trying to seduce me."

"So you *admit* you were trying to seduce her?"

"Dolores, this is ridiculous," Maria protested. "You can't believe—"

"I won't listen to a word in his defense. He lured you to his room to take advantage of your innocence."

"He did not."

"He's so handsome and sure of himself, any woman would be dazzled by him. I know I was."

Rafe had had enough of this silly melodrama. "I was the fool who was dazzled."

Dolores ignored him. "Rafe will marry you. If he won't do the honorable thing, I'll spread his dishonorable behavior all over the county."

"To what end, other than ruining your sister's reputation?"

Dolores turned to him. "To force you to make an honest woman out of her."

Rafe was about to make a heated response when a jarring suspicion flashed through his mind. Maria had suggested that they talk in his room, had shown only token resistance when he put his arm around her, had shown none at all when he kissed her. Dolores was supposed to be in town and wasn't expected home until late. Why was she home early and how had she known where to find them? Only one explanation answered all those questions. The meeting had been a trap, and they had planned and executed it together.

He didn't know whether he was more angry at them for their duplicity or at himself for his stupidity. Was there some curse on Jerry men that made them helpless victims when confronted with de la Guerra women? He wasn't a lovesick boy and Maria wasn't a great beauty. What had been his undoing this time?

"I have to offer my congratulations," he said to Maria. "I came here already disliking you. Yet in one week you had me so convinced of the goodness of your heart, of the purity of your intentions, that you were able to maneuver me into kissing you so your sister could burst in and insist that I marry you to save your reputation. Your conception and execution of the campaign was brilliant."

Maria looked shocked, horrified, and embarrassed. Rafe hadn't realized she was an even better actress than Dolores.

"I didn't do any such thing. I'd *never* do anything like that."

He had to give her credit for staying in character. How did a woman project such hurt, such honest incredulity, when she had a heart as black as coal? Wasn't there supposed to be some sign, some small but significant detail to indicate a person's true nature? If so, he'd missed it with both sisters. "It doesn't matter what you would or wouldn't do. I'm not going to marry you."

"I wouldn't marry you if you asked me."

"He won't have to ask you," Dolores declared. "I'll

make sure the sheriff has him at the church if they have to put him in chains."

It was time to end this charade. "You miscalculated when you attempted to catch me in your trap," he said to Maria. "I don't intend to take as much as a penny from my inheritance. If you'd managed to force me to marry you, you'd have been married to a pauper."

"As your wife, Maria will be entitled to anything you inherit, whether you want it or not," Dolores told him.

Maria turned impatiently to her sister. "Be quiet, Dolores. Rafe did not dishonor me, and he didn't force me to kiss him. To my eternal shame, I kissed him back."

Rafe was too disgusted with himself, with the whole situation, and too mistrusting of both sisters to believe Maria's words were any more than an attempt to save face.

"You can stop the playacting. It won't do either of you any good." His gaze narrowed on Maria. "Here I was telling myself that Luis was lucky to have you, that I could leave him in your care with a clear conscience, and all the time you were plotting to get control of the ranch."

He had to give Maria credit for carrying on the pretense. Her show of anger and wounded innocence was worthy of a professional actress.

"Luis *is* lucky to have me, and you *can* leave him in my care with a clear conscience. In fact, the sooner you leave the better. I don't know what came over me to allow you to kiss me. Your past behavior is not something I can admire or accept."

"The prospect of a large fortune can make a woman overlook a lot of sins."

"Nothing can make me overlook rape."

It took a moment for Rafe to realize Maria wasn't acting, that she meant what she said. "What are you talking about?"

"I'm talking about your raping Dolores to try to force her to marry you. I'm talking about your being Luis's father but having run off and left your father to marry Dolores to give the boy a name."

Rafe didn't allow himself to move for several seconds. His understanding of the situation was changing so rapidly, it was like trying to walk on quicksand, but one thing was abundantly clear. Dolores had lied—again.

"I told you never to say anything about that." Dolores was clearly agitated.

Maria threw Rafe a contemptuous look. "I'm sure Rafe would be the last person to want this secret to become public knowledge. I'm sure rapists aren't welcomed even in Texas."

Rafe got his rage under control by intentionally closing Dolores out of his range of vision and focusing on Maria. "I didn't rape Dolores. Except for a few kisses, she never let me touch her." He held up his hand when Maria started to object. "I found my father in her bed in the act of…" He couldn't complete the sentence. The image still had the power to nauseate him. "You don't have to take my word for it. I created such an uproar, half the servants in the house had reached the room before they could separate." He took a deep breath to slow his racing heart. "I left when my father told me he was going to marry Dolores and that I couldn't remain on the ranch unless I could treat her with respect." He glanced at Dolores and was pleased to see her looking scared and unsure of herself. "I think I could have forgiven them if it had been the only time, but apparently Dolores's notion of helping my father through his grief had been to take him to her bed as often as possible."

During his recital, Maria's gaze had swung back and forth between him and Dolores. He didn't know if she was finally realizing her sister had lied to her, but he was so disgusted with himself that he didn't care what she thought. He did, however, wonder about Dolores's motivation. "Why did you tell your sister I raped you and I'm Luis's father?"

"I didn't lie." It was a feeble denial, but everything about it convicted her.

"Rosana and Juan will back me up. Miguel didn't see the actual evidence, but my father told him what he'd done."

"Is this true?" Maria demanded of her sister.

Dolores didn't answer.

"Why did you lie to me? I hated Rafe for what I thought he did to you."

"But you changed your mind when you thought you saw a way to get control of the ranch," Rafe accused.

Maria rounded on him. "I changed my mind when I got to know you. You were completely different from what I expected. Broc admires you, Luis thinks you're perfect, and everybody on the ranch thinks you can do no wrong. I convinced myself you'd run

away because of what you'd done to Dolores. I didn't
know your father had…" She didn't finish the statement. "Everything I saw in you led me to believe you
regretted what you'd done, would have changed it if
you could, would never allow yourself to lose control
like that again. It wasn't easy, but I was willing to
try to forget what I believed was a momentary and
uncharacteristic aberration in your behavior."

Rafe wasn't sure how he felt about what Maria had
said, but he was certain how he felt about Dolores.
"You've always been a liar and a manipulator," he
said, turning to her, "but this time you've gone too
far. I'm giving you one month to leave the ranch. I
don't care where you go, but if you're not gone by
then, I'll have you thrown out."

"I'm your father's widow," Dolores protested. "I
have a right to live in this house."

"That's not in the will."

"I can barely dress myself on the allowance your
father left me. I'll starve if I have to move out."

"You've got enough clothes for five women, and
the allowance is sufficient to house and feed you in
reasonable comfort."

"You live in Texas and herd cows. You have no
idea what reasonable comfort is."

That amused Rafe.

"Rafe, you don't have to—"

Rafe turned to Maria. "I should have done this as
soon as I saw she was bringing men like Laveau di
Viere to the house."

"Laveau is more of a gentleman than you'll ever
be," Dolores exclaimed.

"Laveau is a traitor. One day he'll be brought to justice. Now get out of my sight before I do something I'll regret."

"I'll see a lawyer," Dolores threw at him.

"See anybody you want."

"Come on," Dolores said to her sister. "You have to help me figure out how to stop him."

"I have something I need to say to Rafe."

"What can you possibly have to say to him when he's trying to kick us out of the house?"

"I'm not kicking Maria out. Just you."

"She won't stay here without me. You'll see. We'll take Luis, too. He's my son, not yours."

Rafe didn't bother to argue with her. He wouldn't allow Dolores to take Luis with her even if Maria went with her to take care of him.

"Don't believe anything he tells you," Dolores said to her sister. "He could talk the devil out of his horns."

That was an odd thing to say when he hadn't been able to talk her into marrying him or his father out of marrying her. He and Maria waited in silence until Dolores left the room.

"I don't know why Dolores lied about you," Maria said to Rafe when the door closed behind her sister. "I'm sorry I believed her, but her story fit too well with everything I'd been told."

"It wouldn't have if you'd listened to Rosana and Juan."

Maria looked stricken. "Dolores wasn't always like this. You should have seen her before my father lost his land, before her fiancé jilted her. She really loved him."

"Lots of women suffer tragic losses without losing their sense of right and wrong."

"Women don't have the same opportunities men have to rebuild their lives. We have to wait for some man to offer to do it for us."

Rafe didn't want to talk about Dolores. "Is that all you wanted to say?"

"Just that I'm sorry. In the future, I'll base my beliefs on what I see rather than what I'm told."

"Don't worry about it. Go rescue Broc from Luis. He's still not completely recovered from his wound."

Rafe could tell she wanted to say more, but his anger at Dolores was too strong for him to be able to deal with his conflicted feelings for Maria. He needed time to calm down, to work through his anger so he could regain his equilibrium. He had a lot to think about.

❧

It had been hard for Maria to pretend nothing was wrong when she went down to send Luis off to bed, but it took every bit of her strength not to lose her temper when Dolores started raving about the unfairness of Rafe's edict.

"How can you say it's unfair when you made an accusation that sheds doubt on the very heart of his character, his fitness to be accepted by others, to be a part of any community?" She shuddered at the thought of what could have happened had Dolores been unwise enough to spread her lies when she'd been drinking in town.

"It didn't matter because I didn't think he was coming back."

Maria had difficulty catching her breath. "Of course it mattered. What if I'd said something to someone who knew the truth?"

"I knew you wouldn't say anything."

Maria found it difficult to accept that while she was horrified she'd harbored such unfair thoughts about Rafe, Dolores could face her without a shred of remorse, not even mild chagrin, at having been caught in such an enormous lie. "I'm so embarrassed, I don't know if I can face Rafe again. If it weren't for Luis, I'd leave this house first thing tomorrow."

Dolores came out of her sulk in a flash. "You can't leave. You've got to help me convince Rafe to change his mind."

Maria gaped at her sister. "You must be crazy! If it hadn't been for Luis, I'm sure he'd have told me to leave along with you."

Dolores jumped up, grabbed Maria's hand to force her to listen. "He won't throw you out because he likes you."

"He may have before, but I imagine he can't think of me now without cringing."

"Rafe was kissing you. You can't deny it because I saw it."

Maria flushed hot to think of herself in Rafe's arms, returning his kiss, wanting even more. "You can be sure he won't kiss me again."

"You haven't done anything. He'll let me stay if you tell him you won't remain here without me."

"I can't do that."

Dolores stiffened with anger. "Why not? Are you hoping he'll marry you after I leave? What kind of sister are you?"

"A gullible one; one who felt so sorry for you, I refused to see what you had become."

"*You* sorry for me!" Dolores looked as if someone had slapped her. "I'm more beautiful than you will ever be."

"And what has it done but make you miserable?"

"I'm not miserable. I'm a rich widow, courted by lots of handsome men who can't do enough for me."

"You're angry and selfish. You don't seem to care who you hurt as long as you get what you want."

Dolores assumed her poor-little-me pose, the one that never failed to bring strong men to their knees. "I just want someone to love me."

"I believed that once, but I'm not sure anymore. I am sure you're still trying to get back at Vicente for jilting you."

"*Don't say that!*" Dolores looked wild-eyed. "I don't want to hear that man's name ever again."

"He turned his back on your lack of a dowry, not on you," Maria told her sister with a softened voice. "He couldn't have loved you as much as you loved him. You're better off without him."

Dolores's face twisted in anger. "Better off to end up with an old man who locked himself away in his room for years? Better off a virtual prisoner in this house with nothing to do but embroidery? It's like a living death. You've got to convince Rafe not to make me leave."

"I don't know Rafe as well as you, but I know he's not a man to change his mind once it's made up."

"You don't know Rafe at all if you think that," Dolores snapped. "If he likes you well enough to kiss you, he'll do anything you want."

"Even if what you say is true, my conscience wouldn't let me take advantage of him in such a way."

"Don't try to play the innocent with me. You like to give the impression of the sweet, kind sister, the one who stays in the background and does all the work."

"I *do* stay in the background and do all the work."

Dolores barreled ahead without pausing. "Do you remember what your life was like before I brought you here?"

"I remember it very well. I've always been grateful to you."

"Then show it by helping me with Rafe."

"Dolores, he's not going to change his mind. He gave up a fortune to stay away for ten years. He abandoned an easy life to work as a cowhand. He plans to go back to Texas. He won't be here to know or care if you're miserable or in debt."

Dolores pierced Maria with a flinty look. "Then you've got to help me kidnap Luis."

Thirteen

ANGER SUCH AS MARIA HAD NEVER KNOWN SWEPT over her with the speed of a wildfire. Before she knew what she was doing, she slapped Dolores. Shocked, she drew back her hand, stared at it in stunned disbelief.

Dolores was so furious she turned white. "How dare you strike me?"

Maria was too angry to feel remorse. "I was trying to bring you to your senses. I thought I knew you, but now I realize you've always been putting on an act. You're selfish, conniving, and manipulative."

"It's not me; it's Rafe. He has never liked me because I fell in love with his father."

"You don't know what love is." Maria had spent years defending Dolores because she believed her sister had loved Vicente so deeply she still hadn't gotten over the pain. Now it looked as if it had been a matter of wounded pride and greed. When had Dolores changed so completely? Had focusing on her loss, an injustice she couldn't forgive, robbed her of all ability to see the truth?

"You have to help me take Luis," Dolores insisted. "Rafe will let me stay if it means he can have Luis."

Maria had heard enough. Dolores wasn't going to listen to anything she didn't want to hear. "I'm not going to try to convince Rafe to let you stay, nor am I going to help you kidnap Luis. One plan is stupid and the other is cruel. Now go to bed. You're tired and upset. You'll be able to think more rationally tomorrow."

"I am rational. If I have to go to court to get custody of Luis, I will. I'm his mother. No judge is going to give him to a half brother who's a cowhand."

"I'm his other guardian."

"That won't matter. I'll get custody. You have to come with me, or you'll never see Luis again."

Maria didn't think she could endure losing Luis. She'd acted as his mother since he was born. She'd changed him, had sat up with him when he was sick, had answered his questions, and had done everything she could to protect him from his parents' lack of interest. "What makes you think a judge would give Luis to you?"

"I don't just flirt when I go to Cíbola. I have the assurance of a judge that a child is always given to his natural mother. A man is considered unsuited by nature to raise a child."

There was no way on earth Maria would let Dolores have Luis by herself. "I'll go with you."

Pleased with her victory, Dolores smiled and hugged her sister. "You'll have to convince Rafe I'll need a bigger allowance for the three of us."

"He won't increase yours, but I can ask him for an extra allowance for Luis. Now I'm exhausted so I'm going to bed."

After Dolores left the room, Maria washed her

face and dressed for bed, but her mind was too full of turbulent thoughts to allow her to sleep. She walked to the window, opened it, and looked out. The distant mountains showed like inky masses against the moonlit sky. An owl hooted and another answered. The *yip-yip-yip* of a coyote was barely audible. The night was alive with God's creatures, but she didn't feel like one of them. She stared at distant fields lush with fruits and vegetables that would soon be ready for market. Beyond them she could make out the darkened houses of farmworkers. The cool air, fresh with the scent of rain from somewhere in the foothills, refreshed her body, but the night provided no answers for her questions, nor did it calm the upheaval inside her.

She closed the window and turned away.

How could she face Rafe in the morning? She didn't know whether she was more embarrassed that she'd believed he had raped Dolores or that she'd yielded so willingly to his embrace. It would be impossible for him to believe she'd kissed him because she couldn't help herself, because she'd wanted to kiss him and have him kiss her. When had her feelings changed so drastically? She hadn't realized her heart had moved on until he'd put his arms around her. Her resistance had melted like winter snow in spring sunshine.

She was weighed down by what Dolores was forcing on her, but she would do anything she must to make sure Luis was never left to the sole guardianship of his mother. He would be better off with Rafe.

But Rafe was going back to Texas. She blushed at the memory of the kiss. Did he think that was part of her attempt to persuade him to change his mind? Did he think she might have been willing to go as far as her sister?

Rafe had made the first move, something he wouldn't have done if he hadn't felt some genuine emotion for her. He said he'd been prejudiced against her from the first, yet his feelings toward her had changed and grown into something quite unexpected. Much against her will, her feelings had undergone a similar transformation. But though the evening had given her ample reason to think better of him, it had provided him with plenty of reasons to believe his first opinion of her had been the right one. She didn't know what she'd hoped could develop between them, but now there was no possibility of anything at all.

⁓

Rafe was surprised to see Broc, dressed and combed, enter his bedroom before he'd finished shaving. "What got you out of bed so early? I haven't heard any explosions or felt an earthquake."

"Curiosity." Broc settled into a chair by the fireplace while Rafe washed the lather from his face. "I want to know why the fair Maria had to drag you away from the parlor last evening. I might have been able to keep my curiosity to myself—"

"When have you ever done that?"

"—but then the beauteous Dolores came home and rushed past the parlor so she wouldn't have to look at me. That in itself was intriguing, but the raised voices coming from Maria's room confirmed my suspicion that I was missing all the fun. Luis is a good kid, but I much prefer adult drama."

Satisfied that his face was dry and clear of lather, Rafe reached for a clean shirt. "You missed a scene that would fit perfectly in one of your melodramas."

"Don't leave me hanging. I'm waiting with bated breath."

"I'm reluctant only because I'm not proud of my own behavior. I took advantage of Maria's devotion to Luis and kissed her."

Broc crowed with laughter. "I'm never wrong when it comes to knowing when people are interested in each other."

"Dolores came charging into the room just as Maria kissed me back."

Broc slapped his knee with glee. "I'll stay for the wedding, but Pilar will never forgive you if you get married without telling her."

"Hold your enthusiasm until you hear the rest." Rafe finished buttoning his shirt and looked around for a collar. "Dolores accused me of violating her sister and declared that I had to marry her to save her reputation."

"I don't see anything wrong with that." There was a mischievous sparkle in Broc's eye.

"You will." Rafe struggled with affixing the collar to his shirt. "At first I thought the sisters had set this up between them. Why did Maria suggest using my bedroom and how did Dolores know when and where to find us?"

"You fascinate me. How?"

"Because it had been planned."

"I don't believe it."

"After a bit, I didn't either, but there was more to come. It seems that Dolores had told Maria that I raped her, that Luis is my son, and that my father married Dolores to give Luis a name."

"I hope you don't plan to make a practice of falling in love with such women."

Rafe grimaced and straightened his collar. "Once was enough. But just as I was starting to feel better, I realized Maria had kissed me when she still thought I'd raped her sister. What does that say about her character?"

"Did she tell you why?"

"I didn't ask, but something she said earlier might explain it." Rafe picked up several ties, unable to decide which one to choose.

"Put down the damned ties and tell me what she said."

"She said she thought I was an overwrought youth who'd been so upset by the betrayal of the two people I loved most that I had done something out of character. She believed I wished I could have changed what I did."

"That sounds like a good explanation to me. What's wrong with it?"

"I still haven't forgotten what happened to me. How can she overlook something even worse?"

"She's a smarter, more forgiving person than you?"

Rafe chose a tie and tossed the others aside. "Whose friend are you?"

"Yours, which is why I'm trying to keep you from cutting off your nose to spite your face."

"Just how do you figure you're doing that?"

"By keeping you from saying something stupid until you can get some perspective on last night."

"But she thought I'd done something truly reprehensible."

"I'm not so sure about that."

"Why not?"

"Maria loves Luis and is loyal to her sister despite her many flaws, but she must know what Dolores is like. After meeting you and finding you weren't anything like what her sister led her to believe, I imagine she started to have doubts about Dolores's version of events. I expect she believed you did *something* but couldn't make herself believe it was anything as awful as rape."

Rafe wasn't sure that was the truth, but he hoped it was. He'd spent a large part of the night trying to explain his continuing interest in Maria. "You like Maria a lot, don't you?"

Broc eyed him speculatively. "Is that a trick question?"

Leave it to Broc to be sure of his ground before he committed himself. "No. I was going to ask how you think I ought to act toward her."

A slow grin spread over Broc's face. "You're asking me for advice on how to handle a woman?"

Rafe returned Broc's grin. "It was touch and go there for a bit, but I managed to get the words out without choking. Now stop being obnoxious. You know I don't have much experience with women."

"If Dolores is an example of your past attempts, I'd say you're in desperate need of guidance."

"Dolores is my *only* attempt."

"So you're beginning again with her sister. An interesting approach."

"It wasn't planned." Nothing about this trip was planned. Maybe that was the problem with his life as a whole. He had drifted along in one direction, then drifted in another. He was thirty years old. It was about time he stopped letting circumstance decide what he did.

In order to change, make a plan, he had to have an objective. He had to *want* something. For years all he'd wanted was to avoid *wanting*. He'd used drinking, fighting a war, and working for Cade to keep his emotions at bay. His father's will had forced him to deal with all the conflicts he'd been avoiding. Dolores. His father. Luis. The ranch. Now Maria.

"I think you ought to act like nothing has happened."

"She's got to know things have changed."

"Then let her be the one to say what those changes will be."

"She wants me to stay here long enough to teach Luis how to take over when he's older."

"What are you going to do?"

"Go back to Texas."

"Will you take Luis with you?"

Luis couldn't live in the bunkhouse with him, and it wouldn't be fair to expect Pilar to take care of him. "It makes more sense to leave him here with Maria. This is his home. Besides, he can't learn how to run the ranch from Texas."

"Have you thought about staying here for a year or so?"

Rafe laughed. "You think if I stay that long, I won't ever go back to Texas?"

"I think you'd end up marrying Maria and running the ranch. It's your home and your inheritance."

"I don't want to get married, I don't want the inheritance, and it ceased to be my home a long time ago." He wasn't as sure of those statements as he had been a few days ago.

Broc got to his feet. "I think you're making a mistake, but it's your life. I'm hungry. Are you going down to breakfast, or would you rather stay and wrestle with that tie?"

Rafe had almost forgotten the tie in his hand. "I can handle the tie. It's everything else that I can't."

∽

Maria could have eaten in her room, but she was so tense that just the thought of food made her stomach heave. She had told herself she would have to face Rafe sometime, but she was relieved when she found only Luis in the breakfast room.

"Where are Rafe and Broc?" the boy asked.

"Maybe they slept late."

"Rafe never sleeps late," Luis stated emphatically, "but Broc does. Broc says in Texas he has to get up early because his cows get up early. Do our cows get up early?"

Maria had no knowledge of the nocturnal habits of livestock. "I don't know, but the chickens do."

Rosana entered from the kitchen bearing a pot of coffee. "What can I get you to eat?"

"Nothing. My stomach isn't feeling right."

Rafe entered in time to hear Maria's response. "Are you getting sick?"

The concern in Rafe's voice made her feel even worse.

Broc, who had followed Rafe into the room, subjected her to close scrutiny. "She doesn't *seem* sick. Why don't you take a look and tell me what you think?" he said to Rafe.

Rafe took Maria's chin in his hand, turned her head from one side to the other while he peered into her eyes. She felt so much like a criminal caught in the glare of a spotlight, she had to force herself to sit still. Why hadn't she stayed in her room?

Rafe released her chin. "I don't think she's suffering from anything more serious than a poor night's sleep brought on by her inability to find a satisfactory solution to a problem that's bothering her."

"Mama didn't sleep, either," Luis informed everyone. "She woke me up. Did she wake you when she went to your room?" he asked Maria.

Maria had lain awake most of the night listening for any unusual sounds from Luis's room. "I was already awake." She was relieved when Rosana deflected Rafe's attention from her to ask what he would like for breakfast.

"Bring me the same," Broc said when Rafe said he liked the looks of Luis's breakfast and would have some of that.

Luis beamed. "Mama says I should have only fruit for breakfast, but I like sausage and potatoes, too." He also had stewed tomatoes and corn muffins.

By the time the men had poured their coffee and taken places at the table, Maria had herself under control. Rafe didn't mention anything about last night or ask about Dolores. Instead he and Luis planned what they wanted to do for the day. Maria decided she would stay in the house to give Luis as much time as possible with his brother.

Watching Rosana bustle in and out of the room,

fussing over the men, making sure they had everything they wanted and that it was *what* they wanted, Maria realized she would miss Rosana, Juan, and all the others who worked in the house. They had become her family. They had formed a partnership, each respecting the others' strengths and areas of responsibility, all working for the benefit of the whole. And now Dolores's foolish lie was threatening to bring that happy alliance to an end.

Luis pushed back his chair. "I've finished my breakfast," he said to Maria. "May I go?"

"Go where?" Knowing Dolores had threatened to kidnap the boy, she couldn't be entirely at ease with his being alone.

"I have to change my clothes. Rafe is going to teach me how to saddle my pony."

Rafe, barely half through his breakfast, smiled at her unspoken question.

"He can spend the time getting acquainted with his pony. It's important for a man to build a relationship with his horse."

Luis swelled with happiness when Rafe referred to him as a man. Leaving the ranch was going to be very hard on him. "Okay." She wanted to say no, but she couldn't hover over Luis all the time. Besides, Dolores couldn't kidnap him by herself, and no sane person would help her. "Just make sure one of the stable hands is with you."

Luis nodded and hurried from the room. She turned back to Rafe. "It's good of you to spend so much time with him. I never realized how important it was to him to have a man around."

"I don't understand why my father ignored Luis. That was so different from how he was with me."

"I think he was ill for a lot longer than we knew. I doubt he had the energy to do for Luis what he did for you."

"Then he could have asked Miguel to teach him." Rafe looked almost angry. "I'm sure he never forgave Dolores for having deceived and entrapped him, but that was no reason to take his anger out on Luis."

She was relieved to know Rafe was so concerned about his brother. It would make it easier to say what she had to say. "We need to talk about a living allowance for Luis."

Rafe's brow knitted. "Why? If you need to buy anything extra, like clothes or another pony when he outgrows the one I bought, the lawyer will give you the money."

Maria had spent hours deciding what to say to Rafe only to have the words desert her when she needed them. "You've told Dolores she has to leave the house within a month. I don't agree with your decision, but I can understand why you made it." It took all of her courage not to break eye contact with Rafe. He looked baffled by her request.

"I don't see what that has to do with Luis needing a living allowance."

Maria swallowed. "I know you have little sympathy for Dolores, but she is my sister and she did invite me to live here in luxury compared to what I would have had to endure at home."

"You've more than paid for any *luxuries* you allowed yourself."

She had worked hard, but that wasn't what she had meant Rafe to understand. "Dolores wasn't brought up to take care of herself or anybody else, much less a household. What I'm trying to say is that Dolores is incapable of living alone. She needs someone to take care of all the things she simply knows nothing about."

"Her allowance isn't generous, but it is sufficient to hire someone to help her."

Maybe being away from her had allowed Rafe to forget what Dolores was like. Maybe his own competence, his ability to adapt to any circumstance, had made him believe others could do the same. "Dolores can't live on her allowance, but the two of us can if I'm there to manage for her."

Both men stopped eating and directed stern looks toward her. "Are you saying you'll leave the ranch when Dolores does?" Rafe asked.

"Yes. She can't manage on her own."

"Then let her suffer the consequences." Broc's mouth was twisted in disagreement. "That woman is entirely selfish."

Maria was surprised at Broc's harsh response. "I know you can't understand, but—"

Broc pushed back his chair and got up. "It has nothing to do with *understanding*," he snapped. "I'm going to see how Luis is getting along with his pony." He left more of his breakfast on the plate than he had eaten.

The silence after he left was overwhelming. Rafe continued to eat his breakfast, studying her while he chewed. "Say something," she said when she could keep quiet no longer.

"I don't think you should go with Dolores. She'll

never understand that anything she's done, or is doing, is the cause of her unhappiness."

He didn't have to tell her that. For years she'd refused to face the true nature of Dolores's character. Her sister had found it easier to lie to get what she wanted than to alter her expectations of what life had to offer her. But not for one minute would Maria consider letting Dolores take Luis while she stayed at the ranch. "I admit that Dolores has her faults, but I can't abandon her."

"What does all of this have to do with a living allowance for Luis?"

"You can't expect Dolores to support both Luis and herself."

"We all agree that Dolores doesn't know how to support herself on her allowance. Why would I expect her to be able to support Luis as well?"

"You don't, and neither do I. That's why Luis needs an allowance of his own."

"If the household allowance isn't sufficient to cover his normal expenses, I'll increase it."

"This has nothing to do with the household accounts."

"Look, I don't know how you manage the accounts, but if it would be easier for you to have all of Luis's expenses in a separate account, that's fine. Though I don't see how you can decide how much of this morning's breakfast could be considered his expense."

Maria felt guilty for not coming right out in the beginning and saying why she needed a separate allowance for Luis. "I need the extra money because Luis will be living with Dolores and me."

Fourteen

RAFE'S EYES PRACTICALLY DRILLED A HOLE THROUGH Maria. "You're free to do what you think best for yourself, but under no circumstances will Luis leave this house to live with Dolores."

"I'll make sure he's well cared for."

"I'm sure you'd try, but you can't possibly believe living with Dolores is in his best interest."

"Dolores says she'll take you to court. She says a judge has told her no court will take a child from its mother, that the law considers men unsuited by nature to raise children. She says if I don't convince you to give Luis an allowance and go with her, she'll take Luis and I'll never see him again." She hadn't meant to say any of that, but it all came pouring out.

Rafe regarded her for a moment, his expression softening. "If necessary, I'll take Luis where no judge would ever find either of us, but I doubt I'll have to go to that extreme. I'm sure I can find enough evidence to convince any judge Dolores is unfit to raise a child."

Maria wasn't sure. Men couldn't say no to Dolores.

"I'd much prefer that you stay here and continue to take care of Luis," Rafe said.

She had been so afraid of losing Luis, his words made her dizzy with relief. "I'm surprised you would want me to care for him considering how you feel about the way I've brought him up." Maybe her reply wasn't fair, but she was angry and felt powerless.

"I didn't express myself very well."

Was he about to apologize?

"You've done a good job. It's just that he's lacking the influence of a man, and he's going to need that to be respected as a man."

"So you're saying that being able to ride and shoot well—maybe I ought to add fistfighting and performing tricks on horseback—are more important than being thoughtful and understanding of others?"

Rafe didn't appear annoyed by her outburst. "I doubt you'll find many women who appreciate those virtues in a man. They look for a man who's strong enough to protect them and provide for their children."

Maria hated the fact that he could undermine her position so easily, but she knew he was right. The gentler virtues were saved for women and the church.

"I know sisters are taught to help each other," Rafe said, "but I don't understand your continued loyalty to Dolores."

It was impossible to explain how she could still feel responsible for a sister who'd lied to her, who'd taken advantage of her and everyone else in her life, who cared for no one but herself, but she still did. Dolores couldn't adapt to the change in their circumstances any more than their father could. She was too strong to commit suicide, but not strong enough to accept her altered position in life.

Rafe took a swallow of his coffee and pushed back his chair from the table. "I intend to convince you to stay here and take care of Luis. Dolores can take care of herself. Now I'm going to see what Broc is teaching Luis. I wouldn't put it past him to tell him so many stories about what we did during the war, the boy will sneak out when we're not watching to try to copy some of them."

"Wouldn't that make him the kind of *man* you think he needs to become?" She realized her response sounded a bit childish, but she resented his telling her what to do.

Rafe paused briefly before answering. "We did desperate things because we had no alternative. I hope Luis never has to make the same kind of choices. I lost a lot of friends. I wouldn't want to lose my only brother."

His answer made her feel small. "I'm sure Broc would never do anything to hurt Luis. He seems like a very nice man."

Rafe smiled and Maria felt something warm inside. "I was only trying to ease the tension between us. I don't like it when you're angry with me."

All of her resentment melted. "I'm not really angry. I'm frustrated. I feel caught between my duty to Dolores and my responsibility for Luis."

"Let Dolores ruin herself if she wants. You owe her nothing. Now, before I make you too angry to forgive me, I'd better go."

Maria was left with her mouth open. Rafe wanted her to forgive him; he cared about her opinion of him.

Although Rafe was still determined to go back to Texas, he was truly concerned about doing what was best for Luis. Now it was up to her to do the same. There was no question in her mind about what she wanted to do. She wanted to stay at the ranch with Luis, but that decision would conflict with Dolores's demands.

Before Maria could decide which of her household duties needed her attention first, Dolores entered the breakfast room.

"I saw Rafe leaving the house. How much allowance is he going to give Luis?"

There would be no hours of rest, no period of relative quiet. "Rafe won't allow us to take Luis from the ranch, and he refused to consider an allowance for him."

"He doesn't care that I'll have to live in some squalid hotel room slowly starving because I don't have enough money to feed myself?"

"You'll have to budget carefully, but you'll have more than enough money to keep from starving."

Dolores threw up her hands. "You don't understand because you don't care what you look like. When a woman is as beautiful as I am, people expect her to look stunning all the time. I can't do that if I wear the same old dresses every night. You've got to talk Rafe into giving Luis a really big allowance. If I have his allowance to combine with mine, I won't feel so desperate."

Maria decided it was impossible to make Dolores understand. Her only choice was to do something she'd never done before: stand up to Dolores. "Rafe won't let Luis go with you. He said he'd go to court to prevent it. Nor is he going to give Luis a big allowance. But if he *did* allow Luis to leave with you, and if he *did* give him a big allowance, I wouldn't allow one cent of it to be spent on your clothes."

Paralyzed by shock, Dolores gaped at Maria.

"Since Rafe won't allow Luis to leave the ranch, I can't leave, either," Maria went on. "You will have to live on your own." Maria's conscience wouldn't allow her to leave Luis. Neither would her heart. She loved him too much.

"I've never had to live by myself. I don't know how," Dolores cried in panic.

Maria was shocked Dolores would make such an admission. Though Maria had made all the decisions, Dolores had always insisted she was the one in control. She'd acted as though every success had been of her own making. "It's not that hard to do. Before the first month has passed, you'll probably be wondering what I've been doing all these years."

"I don't care what you've been doing. You've got to come with me. Rosana and Juan can take care of Luis. They've been trying to do that ever since he was born."

It had been Warren's decision that Maria would have final responsibility for Luis.

"It's not just that I need to be here for Luis," Maria told her sister. "Someone needs to run the household as well."

"Rosana can do that."

"Rafe has asked me to stay. He can't take care of everything from Texas."

Dolores's eyes narrowed suspiciously. "When did Rafe start to depend on you to take care of the ranch?"

"Not the ranch. Just Luis and the house."

"That's the same thing."

Leave it to Dolores to ignore the ranch and the work required to support her expensive tastes. "Miguel will continue to oversee everything other than Luis and the house."

"How can you abandon me for Luis?" Dolores's eyes filled with tears, and for once her show of emotion was more than mere manipulation. "I thought you loved me," she whispered.

"Of course I love you."

"You love Luis more, or you wouldn't leave me to starve alone."

When did Dolores become such a child? Maria had coddled her and taken care of her, and just like a child who had been coddled too much, she'd turned into a spoiled, selfish adult. "It's not that I love Luis more than you. He's a child. You're a grown woman. It's time you started to act like one."

Dolores's tears stopped and her eyes turned hard. "Are you hoping Rafe will marry you?" Her laugh was mocking. "Why would he marry you when he could have had me?"

Maybe because he hates you so much he can't stand to be in the same room with you. "Rafe has made it clear from the beginning that he intends to go back to Texas as soon as he can."

"He won't," Dolores declared. "Laveau says Rafe and Broc hate him and are trying to find a way to drag him back to Texas so they can kill him."

"I don't think Rafe would kill anyone, but I can understand why he hates the man whose betrayal caused his friends to die."

"Laveau didn't betray anyone. That was just a lie Cade Wheeler and his friends used to steal Laveau's ranch."

"Whatever Laveau may or may not have done, and whether Rafe stays here or goes back to Texas, I am going to raise Luis until he's grown, and you are going to have to learn to live on your own."

The tears started to flow again. "I can't believe you're abandoning me, not after I brought you to live here instead of letting you sink into oblivion with our mother and sister."

Their sister had married a merchant who'd invited their mother to live with them. They weren't rich, but they were happy. "I've always been grateful that you convinced Warren to let me live here."

"I had to beg before he would agree. Do you have any idea how humiliating that was? And this is how you repay me?"

She had repaid her by doing all of Dolores's work for the last nine years. "It's not a question of my repaying you. It's doing what I think is right."

Dolores paused in her perambulations around the room, her eyes flashing in anger. "Do you think it's right for one sister to abandon another? Do you think it's right for Rafe to separate a mother from her child, for me to be cast out of my only home without enough money to feed myself?" With a flourish, Dolores sank into a chair, laid her head on the table, and burst into tears.

Dolores had overdramatized the situation, but she had the crux of it correct. She was being forced from her home and separated from her son and sister. That would have been very difficult to endure for a person far less self-centered than Dolores.

Dolores stopped crying abruptly and looked up at Maria. There were few women who could cry without looking red-faced and blotchy. Incredibly, Dolores looked even more beautiful. "You're not going to help me, are you?" she demanded.

"I can't leave Luis."

Dolores's expression hardened. "You wouldn't have to leave Luis if you convinced Rafe that the best place for him is with his mother."

Maria couldn't do that because she knew it wasn't true.

Apparently interpreting Maria's silence as a refusal to help, Dolores rose from her chair. "I don't need your help. I'll find a way to get Luis. You can have Rafe. I don't want him."

With that, Dolores marched from the room, leaving Maria to wonder if her sister was making an empty threat or if she really would try to find a way to take Luis with her. Maria's first impulse was to warn Rafe. Her second was to put it out of her mind as just another of Dolores's ploys to get her way. Dolores enjoyed picturing herself as a loving mother, but she didn't love anyone but herself. Maria wondered if Dolores would even want Maria to go with her if Dolores hadn't needed someone to do all the work of setting up and managing a new household.

It had taken Warren's death and Rafe's arrival to force Maria to face the truth about her sister. Sadly, it would be better for both of them if their lives continued along separate paths. Though it was hard for Maria to turn her back on her sister, Dolores needed to grow up and learn to be an adult.

And Maria would finally be free. She felt a little guilty for feeling that way, but she'd lived her whole life to please someone else. Hadn't she finally earned the right to please herself?

Rosana entered the breakfast room. She looked around before returning her gaze to Maria. "Have you finished eating?"

Maria realized she hadn't eaten anything, but she wasn't hungry. "Dolores and I were talking."

Rosana picked up the plates Rafe and Broc had left. "I just passed her in the hall. If I hadn't moved out of her way, she would have knocked me against the wall."

"She's very upset."

"I know. Rafe has told her she has to leave the house." Rosana loaded Luis's plate on the tray with the others. "It was a cursed day when she came to Rancho los Alamitos."

Maria understood why Rosana felt that way. She couldn't think of anything suitable to say so she didn't say anything.

"Are you going riding with the men? The stable is in a bustle. The hands haven't had this much to do in years."

Maria hated to think of what a dispirited place this was going to be when Rafe and Broc went back to Texas. Luis would be devastated. She refused to think about how she would feel. She'd known from the first that her attraction to Rafe could only cause unhappiness. She would mourn his loss like everybody else.

But it would be all the harder for her because she was the one person who would have to mourn in secret.

~❧~

"Come with us today?"

Maria looked up from her breakfast to meet Rafe's gaze. It had been nearly a week since Dolores had left the house to take up temporary residence in Cíbola.

"Why would you want me to go with you? I don't ride as well as you and Broc. Even Luis has outstripped me."

Luis grinned with pride. "Broc says I ride like I was born to the saddle, but Rafe says not to believe him, that Broc is just trying to flatter me so I'll let him live here."

"Would I do something like that?" Broc acted hurt.

Luis laughed at Broc. "Rafe says Broc is such a fine actor, I have to question everything he says."

"Which is a nasty way for a friend to give a back-handed compliment," Broc said to Rafe.

It seemed Luis couldn't say two sentences in a row without prefacing one of them with *Rafe says*. In his eyes Rafe could do no wrong. Maria felt the same way much of the time. Despite the tension created by Dolores's departure, everybody was happier.

"You can't use the excuse that you have too much work," Rafe said to Maria. "Rosana has promised to keep an eye on everything."

"Please come," Luis begged. "We have the most fun."

Maria didn't see anything fun about galloping about the ranch, but Luis wasn't happy unless he was riding as fast as he could. Maria guessed she wasn't cut out to be a horsewoman. It was just as well that Rafe was going back to Texas, where even women knew how to ride from the time they could sit astride a horse.

"I'll come if you promise not to gallop everywhere you go."

Luis laughed. "You're just afraid your hair will get tangled. Broc says that wouldn't happen if you would wear a bonnet."

"Brat!" Broc exclaimed with an apologetic grin at Maria. "You weren't supposed to mention that."

Maria fixed Luis with an amused grin. "I can comb out tangles. Broken bones are harder to repair."

"Will you come if I promise never to exceed a moderate canter?" Rafe asked.

"If you promise I don't have to gallop, I'll ride with you."

Luis gave a cheer, Broc breathed a sigh of relief, but it was Rafe's slowly forming smile that meant the most to her. She cautioned herself not to put too much meaning into the continuing signs that his interest in her was more than social, but she'd given up on her heart paying any attention. Their shared kiss made an appearance in her dreams at least once a night. His smile never left. She was slowly becoming obsessed with him. Her only hope was that she could hold out until he left. Then she'd have no recourse but to get over her foolish fascination.

"Can you be ready in half an hour?" Rafe asked.

Maria thought she could manage it in less time than that but decided she could use the extra minutes to counsel her unruly heart. It beat so rapidly whenever he smiled at her, she felt dizzy. Dizziness combined with being on horseback didn't sound like a good way to spend the morning. "I'll meet you at the stables. Just make sure I get a lazy horse."

❧

Rafe inspected the cinch on Maria's horse to make sure it was tight. He didn't really doubt that the stable hands could saddle a horse without his checking their work, but he still checked Luis's pony unless Broc had already done it. He supposed that was a carryover from the war, when it was essential to check and recheck every detail before setting out on a raid. Even a tiny mistake could cost lives. He decided to examine his own mount's feet, which accounted for his being unaware of Broc's approach until he spoke.

"Why did you insist that Maria ride with us today?"

When Rafe straightened, Broc was frowning at him. "I didn't insist."

"You kept at her until she agreed. I call that insisting."

"She still could have refused."

"Did you expect her to after the way you smiled at her?"

Rafe wasn't aware that he had smiled at Maria in a way that was significantly different from the way he smiled at everybody.

The soft nicker of a mare in a nearby corral caused Rafe's mount to stamp his foot and give an answering whinny. The young groom tightened his hold on the reins. Rafe reminded himself that he had meant to ask Miguel about his breeding plans for the young stallion. But that would have to wait for a time when

Broc wasn't questioning his motives. "What are you trying to say?"

"That it looks like you're trying to make her fall in love with you. Since you intend to go back to Texas, that doesn't seem fair."

A frisson of anxiety snaked down Rafe's spine. "Are you in love with her?"

Broc's laugh restored some of his sunny mood. "I like Maria a lot, but I'm not in love with her. Not that it would do me a lot of good, with her mooning over you."

Rafe tried to tell himself knowing that didn't please him, but it was useless. He had asked her to ride with him, Broc, and Luis because he was certain she wouldn't have agreed to go with him alone. "You're mistaken. She doesn't moon over me."

Broc rolled his eyes. "Surely you haven't been ignoring women for so long that you can't remember how they act when they're interested in a man."

The smell of sweet hay and saddle leather drifted from the barn, but not even the memories evoked by those comforting aromas could distract him from the troubling present. "Maria keeps a safe distance between us even when we're not alone."

"She wouldn't do that if she didn't feel threatened."

"I'm not threatening her."

"You kissed her, didn't you?"

"Just once."

"For some women, that's all it takes."

Rafe was becoming annoyed. "You're working up to say something, so go ahead and spit it out."

Now it was Broc's turn to look annoyed. "If you

don't mean to stay here and marry her, stop acting like you do."

"Are you saying I ought to be rude to her?" He saw Maria emerge from the house.

"No, not that you'd have any trouble."

"I like Maria, I think she's good for Luis, and I hope she will stay here as long as he needs her. She's upset about Dolores leaving. I'm just trying to mend fences." Was that truly *all* he was doing? If he was only trying to mend fences, would he be thinking of kissing Maria again?

"I'm not a fool and neither are you," Broc retorted in a low voice. "You've got to stop playing with her emotions."

Maria was too close to continue the conversation, so Rafe just frowned at Broc. He hadn't intended to smile at Maria, but his lips seemed to curve into a welcoming greeting on their own. "Right on time."

"I couldn't expect you to keep your promise if I didn't keep mine. Are you sure this horse would rather be in bed than out riding?"

He couldn't repress a laugh. "I promise to take hold of his bridle if he gets the least bit rambunctious."

"That won't do much good with your horse doing its best to tear off at a gallop."

"If I'm not up to the job, you can depend on Broc. He has lots of practice rescuing maidens in distress."

"Only onstage," Broc said with a grin. "This would be the first time I haven't had to memorize the lines."

Maria's laugh was so genuine, so lighthearted, Rafe felt guilty for having put her through a difficult week.

Maria looked around. When she didn't see Luis, she asked, "Where is Luis?"

"He was too impatient to wait for us," Broc answered. "I told him he could ride ahead if he didn't go beyond the first field."

Rafe could see Luis a few hundred yards ahead, riding his pony at an easy canter. He was comfortable allowing his brother to ride alone as long as he stayed on ranch land. He turned back to Maria. "Are you ready to mount up?"

She gave him a tight smile. "As ready as I'll ever be."

Broc held the horse while Rafe helped Maria into the saddle. Once she was settled, Broc handed the reins over to a stable hand while they both mounted. Maria took the reins into her hands and they were ready to ride.

"Where did Luis go?" she asked when she saw the lane ahead was empty.

"He probably rode to the far edge of the field," Broc said.

Which field? The acres of crops stretching far into the horizon never failed to give Rafe a sense of pride, but today he wished the valley floor had been barren. He searched as far as he could see but saw no sign of the boy. "Or he rode into the field itself. You didn't tell him not to do that."

"I never realized how many ways a boy could get into trouble and still stay within the rules," Maria said.

"Didn't you have any brothers?" Rafe couldn't remember that he'd ever asked Dolores about her siblings.

"No. Just two sisters. And we were never allowed

to play with our male cousins. My mother said they were too wild."

"My mother said the same thing about my cousins," Broc confessed. "Do you think all young men are the same?"

"Probably." Maria glanced at Rafe, broke into a smile, and turned back to Broc. "According to Rosana and Juan, Rafe was an exception. They have led Luis to believe he was the personification of all virtues."

Broc smirked at Rafe. "His father paid their wages. Did you expect them to say anything else?"

Maria laughed at Rafe's frown. "Probably not. They were too afraid of his scowl."

"I do not scowl," Rafe stated.

Maria laughed harder. "It's worse than that. When I opened the front door and saw you standing on the steps looking like—"

Rafe put his hand up for silence.

"What is it?" Broc asked.

"Luis. Something is wrong." An instant later, Rafe was thundering down the lane, his horse in a hard gallop.

Fifteen

RAFE'S BRAIN WAS WORKING ITS WAY THROUGH ALL the possible reasons for Luis's cry while berating himself for paying more attention to Maria than to Luis's whereabouts. Just then he heard another cry. It sounded like Luis was just beyond the cornfield rather than in it. Spurring his horse forward, Rafe rounded the edge of the field to see Luis struggling with a man trying to pull him from the saddle.

The man looked up when he heard Rafe approach, but he made no move to run away, just kept trying to pry Luis's hands loose from the pommel. It was a simple matter for Rafe to throw himself from the saddle and land a punishing blow to the man's jaw.

The man fell to the ground and lay there in an unmoving lump.

Rafe turned back to Luis. "Are you all right?"

Luis nodded, wide-eyed.

"Did he hurt you?"

Luis shook his head. "He said he didn't want to hurt me, that he just wanted to take me to my mother."

Rafe looked down at the man, who hadn't moved. "Get up."

The man lay still.

"I'm not going to hit you again unless you try to escape."

The man continued to lie still.

Rafe would have pulled the man to his feet, but just then Broc rounded the corner of the cornfield, closely followed by Maria. "Who is that?" he asked.

"I don't know who he is, but he told Luis he didn't want to hurt him, that he just wanted to take him to his mother."

Maria looked puzzled. "That doesn't make sense."

"A son should be with his mother," the man mumbled.

The smell of strong spirits caused Broc to look at the man more closely. "Did you knock the sense out of his head, or is he just drunk?"

"I only hit him once."

"Got to help a beautiful lady," the man mumbled again.

Rafe directed his gaze to the man. "Who are you?"

The man made an attempt to sit up, then nearly fell back before managing to get upright. "My name's Billy Cassius." His words were slurred but understandable. "Beautiful lady was crying that she couldn't see her son. That's not right. Offered to get him for her."

Maria's eyes widened in disbelief. "Are you saying my sister asked you to kidnap Luis for her?"

"Don't know your sister," Billy said. "Does she need a boy kidnapped, too?"

Rafe would have liked to take his anger at Dolores

out on this guy by pounding him, but the man was drunk. It was frightening to think Dolores had this kind of power over men.

"My sister's name is Dolores Jerry," Maria told Billy.

Billy frowned, shook his head slightly. "Can't be. My Dolores Jerry lives in Cíbola. Has a room at the hotel. Can't be two Dolores Jerrys."

Maria blushed at what that confession could possibly mean.

"I'm going to take him to the sheriff. Maybe he'll be sobered up by the time we get there."

"I'm coming with you," Maria said.

"Me, too," Broc added.

"Can I come?" Luis asked.

The boy had regained his color, but Rafe could tell he was still upset. "You'd better stay with Rosana and Juan."

Luis looked both disappointed and relieved at the same time.

Rafe reached down and dragged Billy to his feet. "Are you sober enough to ride?"

"Rode all the way here," Billy told him.

"Then mount up. I'm taking you to the Cíbola jail."

"Can't go to jail. Have to take the boy to Dolores."

It was clearly useless to talk to the man until he sobered up. "Fine. Just get into the saddle."

Much to Rafe's surprise, Billy mounted up without difficulty. Apparently riding drunk was something he did often.

∽

Rafe had accomplished little by taking Billy to the sheriff. He said Billy was a likable young man who had appeared in Cíbola recently with enough money to pay for the whiskey he drank and the room where he slept. He would keep the fellow in jail until he sobered up, but he wouldn't charge him with kidnapping because Billy was too drunk to know what he was doing.

Billy's rambling conversation during the ride to town had convinced Rafe that Dolores had chosen the drunk because he was so idealistic, he was virtually brainless. She'd cried on his shoulder and like some quixotic character in a romance book, he'd charged out to avenge her. Rafe wished he could laugh at him and forget the entire episode, but he couldn't forget it because he had no assurance Billy wouldn't come after Luis again. If his garbled conversation could be trusted, he wouldn't rest until he'd accomplished his mission.

They had left their horses at the livery stable and were headed to the hotel. If Billy could be believed, Dolores had taken a room there.

The town had changed considerably in the ten years Rafe had been gone. The single street running east to west had been extended to five with nearly that many crossing north to south. Wood-frame buildings stood side by side with those of brick, and there was even one of rough stone. Signs above a bakery, billiard hall, dentist's office, loan agent, even ladies' intimate apparel indicated that the town was serving the needs of a larger community. An Episcopal church, a newspaper office, and a theater advertising a dance troupe from San Francisco attested to a wider scope of interests than before.

"What are you going to do to Dolores?" Maria asked Rafe as they walked along the boardwalk.

"I can't *do* anything to her. It's not a crime to cry on a suggestible young man's shoulder. The sheriff didn't say so, but I could tell that in the eyes of the law—at least in *his* eyes—I'm more at fault than Dolores or Billy."

Broc's snort of indignation wasn't elegant. "As often as Dolores is in Cíbola, he ought to know what she's like."

"My father and I lived in the same house with her for two years, and neither of us knew what she was like." Despite his dislike of Dolores, Rafe wished he had held his tongue. He turned to Maria. "Sorry. I know she's your sister."

Maria didn't meet Rafe's gaze. "I should be the one apologizing. I've spent so many years being thankful she invited me to live at Rancho los Alamitos, I refused to see what she was really like. I should have known she'd do something like try to kidnap Luis. She doesn't want him. She wants more money. But she knows you'd give Luis a big allowance. If he was living with her, she could use his allowance for herself."

"She told you all of this?" Broc couldn't conceal his amazement.

Maria nodded.

Broc shook his head. "And you still defend her?"

"Not anymore, but I am still grateful for the opportunity she gave me."

"Don't be," Rafe said. "You worked for everything you got. You were no better than a paid servant. You were so grateful you would do virtually anything she wanted."

Rafe regretted the words as soon as they were out

of his mouth. No one likes to know their love has been wasted, their loyalty abused, their trust violated. He didn't know if it was harder when it happened with a sister or a lover, but it was painful either way.

The hotel came into view. It was one of the new brick buildings that helped give Cíbola the appearance of prosperity. The cool, dark interior of the lobby was a welcome change from the heat and bright sunshine of the morning. Dark mahogany furniture, velvet curtains, and thick rugs gave the lobby an appearance of opulence unusual in Cíbola.

Rafe stepped up to the desk. "I'd like the room number for Mrs. Dolores Jerry."

The clerk, a nondescript man probably somewhere in his forties, favored Rafe with a speculative gaze. "What is your business with Mrs. Jerry?"

Rafe stifled a desire to return a sharp reply. "I don't see that's any of your concern."

The clerk cleared his throat deferentially. "It's a policy of the hotel to guard our guests' privacy. Unless you're a relative, I can't give out that information."

Rafe had never had occasion to announce to anyone that Dolores was his stepmother. He was sure the words would stick in his throat. He was relieved when Maria stepped forward.

"I'm Maria de la Guerra. Mrs. Jerry is my sister. We're here to give her some news about her son."

"Mrs. Jerry isn't in just now. I don't know where she has gone. I expect she will return soon. Lunch is already being served in the dining room."

Rafe met Maria's gaze and they came to an unspoken agreement. "We'll wait."

They settled in a corner of the lobby with a view of the entrance. Broc drummed his fingers impatiently. Maria perused a few pages of a romantic tale of the West. Rafe was nearing the end of an article in the weekly newspaper about the expansion of the Southern Pacific Railroad into northern California when a familiar laugh brought his head up.

Dolores, accompanied by Laveau, had just walked into the hotel. Her laugh was cut off by a gasp when she saw the group seated in the corner of the lobby. For a moment she lost color, but then she regained control.

"What are you doing here?" She addressed her question to Maria. "Nothing has happened to Luis, has it?"

She should have been an actress, Rafe thought. With her beauty and ability to believe anything she wanted, she would have been a sensation.

"Luis is fine, but he's upset that Billy Cassius tried to kidnap him this morning."

"Who's Billy Cassius?" Had he not known otherwise, Rafe could have believed Dolores had never heard of the man.

"If I remember correctly," Laveau intervened, "he's the young man who was so entranced by your tale of a devoted mother who had been forcefully separated from her cherished son."

Rafe was fully aware of Laveau's ability to play both sides of the fence, but he couldn't understand why he was undercutting Dolores's position.

Dolores uttered one of those tinkling laughs Rafe so disliked. "How am I supposed to remember one besotted young man out of so many?" she asked Laveau.

"You aren't, my sweet. That's left for those of us who are beset with jealousy because we have to share your attention."

Dolores playfully slapped Laveau on the arm. "You know you're the only man I really care about."

"You'd be safer bedding down with a nest of angry rattlesnakes," Broc told her.

Dolores ignored him. "What did this man do?" she asked Maria.

"He was trying to drag Luis off his pony when Rafe got to him."

She turned on Rafe. "You're not a fit guardian if you can't protect him from drunken young men."

Rafe couldn't repress a smile. "I thought you didn't remember Billy."

"All young men end up getting drunk when I won't go off with them," Dolores said dismissively.

"I warned you not to talk to him," Laveau said. "I knew he was the type to do something foolish."

"That's probably why she talked to him," Broc said.

"Did you ask him to kidnap Luis?" Maria asked.

"No, I didn't."

"That's not exactly true, my love," Laveau said. "Though you didn't use the word *kidnap*, you did say you'd be forever in his debt if he returned your child to your bosom."

Dolores's feigned dismay was masterful. "Surely I didn't say that."

Laveau looked sympathetic. "You'd had a few drinks by that time."

Dolores turned to Rafe. "Well, I wish this Billy whatever-his-name-is person *had* kidnapped Luis. You have no right to keep him from me. I'm considering taking you to court to get him back."

"I wouldn't advise it. There's too much evidence of your neglect, of your near total lack of interest in him."

"Maria will tell you that I'm devoted to the boy."

Maria locked gazes with her sister. "*The boy* is named Luis. Since I've had sole responsibility for him almost from the moment he was born, I'll be happy to tell a judge exactly how devoted you are to a child you never ask to see, not even when he's sick."

Dolores stared at her sister in disbelief. "After all I've done for you, how can you say that?"

"Because I can't continue to ignore the truth. You don't care about me or Luis. You care only about how you can use us to your advantage."

"That's not true. I love you both."

"When I found out you'd lied about the rape, I knew I had to stop defending you. When you talked Billy into attempting to kidnap Luis, I knew I couldn't keep quiet any longer."

"Luis should be with me. I'm his mother."

Rafe didn't wait for Maria to answer her sister. "As far as I'm concerned, you abrogated any such right when you talked Billy into trying to kidnap Luis. Since I can't trust you not to make another attempt that might result in harm to him, I'm forbidding you to return to the ranch today or any other day."

Dolores clutched at Laveau's arm.

"I'll see that the rest of your belongings are packed up and brought to you as soon as possible."

"Rancho los Alamitos is my home," Dolores declared. "Warren should have left it to me."

"Maybe he should have, but he didn't. I'll ask Rosana to pack your belongings and have Juan bring them to you."

"I forbid you to let that woman touch anything of mine," Dolores declared. "She hates me."

"Margarita and I will put together your things," Maria offered.

"You can't do this," Dolores wailed. "I don't have a permanent place to stay."

"We found out today that you have a room here in the hotel."

"I can't afford a room on the miserable allowance you give me. That's Laveau's room."

Rafe turned to Laveau. "I hope you have a lot of space. Her gowns alone will fill a large room."

"I'll be happy to reserve all the space she needs."

The change in Dolores was instantaneous. From an outraged virago, she became a smiling seductress. "I'll need a full suite, not just another room."

"Certainly, my sweet."

Rafe didn't know what Laveau's game might be, but he wanted to set him straight. "I don't know what you're doing in California, but be assured a second kidnapping plot will not succeed."

Laveau's cheerful demeanor was undented. "I tried to talk Dolores out of that scheme. I hope I don't appear to be unfeeling, but I have an unfortunate dislike of children."

Rafe extended his hand and helped Maria to her feet. "I'm going to the lawyer's office now. I'll set up the terms under which you'll receive your allowance. He'll send it to you for your approval."

"I won't approve anything you send me."

"Fine. That will make things easier."

Broc left quickly. Rafe was ready to follow him but Maria lingered.

"You had so much. Why did you throw it away?" she asked her sister.

"What did I have besides an old husband who wanted nothing to do with me, and a house full of servants who hated me?"

Rafe reached out to Maria. "It's too late. She doesn't understand what you're talking about."

"She's not to set foot on Rancho los Alamitos land," Rafe told the lawyer. "Her allowance is to be paid on the first of the month with no advances under any circumstances."

Maria was uncomfortable listening to Rafe's strictures. She kept telling herself that her silence didn't mean she'd stopped loving Dolores or worrying about her. It meant that she had reluctantly accepted it was best that Dolores not have another chance to hurt Luis.

"All of her clothes, jewelry, and some furniture will be packed up and sent to her as soon as she has a place to live."

"What about visits with the boy?" the lawyer asked.

"She won't be allowed to see Luis."

"She's got to see Luis," Maria said. "She's his mother. She needs to see her child."

"I don't care about Dolores's needs. Luis will be better off without her."

"Maybe better off but not happier. He loves me and

he idolizes you, but neither of us is his mother or father. Those are two roles that don't allow for substitution."

"I agree with Maria," Broc said. "Find some place that's safe, make sure she's not alone with him, and let her see him for an hour once a week."

"It'll be more like once a month once she realizes he's no use to her," Rafe growled.

"Whatever." Losing interest in the conversation, Broc turned his attention to two attractive women walking down the street outside the lawyer's office.

"The meetings will prevent her from claiming that you're keeping him from her to damage their relationship and denying her rights as a mother," the lawyer pointed out.

"I'll stay with Luis whenever they're together," Maria offered. "Require her to see Luis for only a few hours and only when I am present." She could see his resistance collapsing and waited. He would make an unpleasant decision if he had to.

Rafe turned to the lawyer. "Set up the visits as Maria suggested. If anybody is with Dolores, they have to wait outside. I'll send one of the men with Maria to be sure there are no more kidnapping attempts."

Maria thought his strictures were unnecessary, but she didn't object. "I think it would be a good idea for you to give me a specific amount of money for Luis so you can track exactly how much I've spent on him and where it has gone."

"Why?" Rafe asked. "I don't think you'll steal from him or deprive him of anything."

Rafe's obvious surprise pleased her. "It was different when Warren was alive and even afterward when

Dolores was still living at the ranch. Now it's just Luis. I'd feel more comfortable if I had a specific amount for running the house and a specific amount for Luis. That way it would be easier for you and Mr. Fielder to see where the money goes."

"Okay. What about a salary for you?"

She'd never thought of being paid. "I don't need a salary. Dolores gives me her clothes when she's tired of them. Everything else is taken care of out of the household money."

"Taking care of the house and Luis is a big job and a serious responsibility. Anybody I might hire to do that would expect a substantial salary. There's no reason you shouldn't get exactly what I would have to pay a stranger. More, in fact, because you're much more than a stranger to Luis."

Maria was so overcome with emotion, she couldn't speak. Not even Warren had thanked her. Most of the time she felt more like a servant with privileges than a poor relation. She'd always tried to do a good job for Dolores and Luis. After she got to know Warren, she'd grown fond of him as well. They had become her family. It hadn't occurred to her to ask for pay for taking care of her family. That Rafe thought she deserved it was one of the nicest things that had ever happened to her.

"How much do you want to be paid?" Rafe asked her.

"Not much. I have nothing to spend money on."

The figure they settled on was so large, Maria felt like an heiress. She also felt uneasy about her relationship with Rafe. Now she would be an employee like

Rosana and Juan. Would she be obliged to do what he said just because he paid her salary, or would he still listen to her when she disagreed with him?

She was tempted to tell Rafe she didn't want a salary, but for the first time in her life, she would have money of her own. She would have some measure of control over her life. Her future wouldn't be entirely dependent on the whim of someone else.

"Are you ready to go?"

Maria hadn't realized Rafe and Mr. Fielder had finished their business.

"What are you going to tell the boy?"

Maria and Rafe turned back at the lawyer's question.

"The truth," Rafe answered.

⤜⤛

The man paced back and forth in the confines of the small room, a thin smile on his face. Rafe had driven Dolores from the ranch, and she had retaliated by broadcasting her mistreatment to anyone who would listen. When she'd got that young fool drunk enough to try to kidnap her son, she'd made herself the obvious suspect should anything happen to Rafe.

The man rubbed his hands together in anticipation. Something was going to happen to Rafe. He just hadn't decided what it was going to be.

Sixteen

RAFE, MARIA, AND BROC WERE SITTING WITH LUIS IN his room. His lower lip quivered when he turned to Rafe. "Mama wanted that man to hurt me, didn't she?"

Maria yearned to say something that would take that hurt and fear from his eyes, but he'd asked Rafe, the person who had most reason to give him the bitter truth.

"Nobody wants to hurt you," Rafe told Luis. "Especially not your mother."

"But she asked that man to take me away from you."

Maria marveled that Luis hadn't said *take me away from here* or *take me away from Maria.* He'd said take me away from *you.* In his mind, Rafe was the one to turn to when there was trouble or danger.

She shouldn't be surprised. She felt the same.

"Billy was a little drunk. When he heard her say how much she missed you and wanted to see you, he decided to kidnap you and take you to her."

Luis looked like he was digesting that information.

"I know it was frightening, but it just shows how

much your mother loves you. She would never have been so upset if she didn't love you very much."

Maria knew Rafe wouldn't say anything to hurt Luis, but it did surprise her that he would make Dolores's actions sound like those of a grieving mother. She'd been racking her brain for a way to keep Luis from knowing Dolores wanted him only as a way to get more money.

"Will I get to see her?"

"Yes, she'll visit you once a week at the ranch," Maria said.

She had mixed feelings about these visits. She felt Dolores should be able to see her son just as she felt Luis ought to be able to see his mother. But she worried that Dolores would have no idea what to do with Luis when they were together. She had ignored Luis when he was a baby, when he cried, wanted to be fed, or needed a fresh diaper. She was no better able to understand him now that he was older.

"When can I see her?" Luis asked.

"As soon as she gets a place to live. She's staying at the hotel now."

"I can go there. That's where we ate lunch the day that man came over with Mama."

Laveau's presence in the hotel was the main reason Maria didn't want Luis to meet his mother there.

"Is there something else you'd like to do when you're in town?" Rafe asked Luis.

"Can we go to the festival?" Luis's eyes grew bright with excitement. "Mama says all the young men race, ride bucking horses, and perform tricks for the ladies. Did you do that when you were a boy?"

"I was too busy working on the ranch."

Luis's face fell. "It's okay. You don't have to know how to do tricks."

A smile slowly spread across Rafe's face. "I didn't say I didn't *know how to* do tricks. I just said I was too busy working."

Luis's interest perked up. "Can you grab a hat off the ground while riding a horse?"

"Maybe."

"Can you throw a lasso?"

"Definitely."

"Can you ride without a saddle?"

"We're cowboys," Broc said. "They'd chase us out of Texas if we couldn't do all that stuff."

Luis was practically bouncing in his seat. "Mama says ladies go crazy for the men who win. I heard Juan tell Rosana that some of the young girls even gave up their honor."

Maria was sure she turned scarlet. She wanted to hit Broc for laughing. She had a feeling Rafe wanted to laugh as well, but his expression didn't reveal it.

"I expect Juan means they smile and throw their handkerchiefs at the young men."

"The young men dress up in fancy clothes," Maria said, trying to support Rafe's explanation. "When I was a young girl, I thought some of them looked very handsome."

"Did you throw your handkerchief at any of them?"

"At one or two," she confessed. "Festival is very exciting for a young girl."

"Can we go?" Luis asked Rafe.

"I don't see why not."

"Will you win something?"

"I don't plan to enter."

For a moment, Luis looked disappointed, but then an idea must have occurred to him. "Would you enter if Maria promised to throw her handkerchief at you?"

Maria felt herself blush; heat flooded her cheeks. She didn't dare look at Rafe, but looking at Broc wasn't any better. His eyes danced with amusement.

Rafe turned to Maria. "Would you like me to enter the contests?"

"That's not for me to say," she stammered. "I don't know what you can do."

"That's not what I asked. Would you *like* for me to enter the contests?"

"It would make Luis happy."

Rafe favored her with a lazy smile. "I don't know when I've have so much trouble making my meaning clear. Would *you* like me to enter the contests?"

How could she answer that question without betraying her feelings for a man who would soon ride out of her life forever? Well, since he *was* going to ride out of her life, it didn't matter what he thought about what she said. She would like to see him win some event.

"Yes, I would like for you to enter a contest."

Rafe turned to Luis. "I think that might be sufficient reason to change my mind."

Rafe was looking just as amused as Broc. She wanted to smack both of them, but she stayed glued to her chair. When Luis turned to her, a question in his eyes, she wished she'd gotten up and gone to do something. Even the laundry.

"Will you throw your handkerchief at Rafe if he wins?"

"I would be happy to do that, but you must not be disappointed if Rafe doesn't win anything. He's not as young as he used to be."

She heard Broc whistle under his breath. She thought she could hear Rafe's sharp intake of breath.

"Are you old?" Luis asked Rafe.

Broc's crack of laughter earned him a dirty look. "I may be old in spirit, but I'm still young enough in body to take on your young men. What events do you think I ought to enter?"

Luis beamed. "Everything!"

"His body's not *that* young," Broc suggested. "Nobody's is," he added when Rafe shot him a nasty look.

"Suppose Broc and I enter everything between the two of us."

"Wait a minute," Broc protested. "I doubt I know half the things you people get up to out here."

"You said Texas cowboys could do anything," Luis reminded him.

"So he did," Rafe said, grinning in a way that made Maria's stomach flutter.

Broc groaned. "Wait until I tell Cade what you had me doing. It'll be the last time he sends you to take care of business."

Maria didn't know what Broc was talking about, but his comment brought a very different look to Rafe's face.

"I haven't forgotten. I just haven't seen an opportunity to do anything about it."

"You haven't given it much time."

"Not yet, but I will."

Luis appeared as confused by this conversation as Maria felt. She'd always wondered why Broc had come with Rafe. Maria didn't know what the reason might be, but seeing the look that passed between the two men convinced her it was very serious.

"How soon can we go?" Luis asked.

Rafe turned to Maria, a question in his expression.

"Festival starts in ten days."

Broc swallowed the last of his wine and got up. "I'd better start practicing. I can't let the state of Texas down."

"May I watch?" Luis asked.

"You'd better. You're the reason I'm risking my neck."

"I'll ask Maria to throw her handkerchief at you, too."

Broc gave a shout of laughter. "Maybe you'd better not ask Maria to throw her handkerchief at me. I want to get back to Texas alive."

"Why doesn't he want Maria to throw her hand-kerchief at him?" Luis asked Rafe.

"Broc is a flirt. He wants all the women to throw their handkerchiefs at him."

"What would he do with so many handkerchiefs?"

Now it was Rafe's turn to laugh. "I don't know. You'll have to ask him."

Maria had never been more impressed with Rafe than when he made Dolores's actions look like those of a mother who loved her son and wanted to be with him. Now he had agreed to take part in the festival

to please Luis. She knew the events weren't easy.
Some of them were dangerous. From the time he
had arrived, he'd been doing things for other people.
How could Dolores not have married him instead of
Warren? *She* would have.

That thought caused her to blush furiously. When
Rafe looked at her, a question in his eyes, she felt
unable to remain there with her guilty thoughts practically plastered over her face. She rose. "I need to see
about dinner."

She was going to have to watch herself more carefully. If she had gone so far as to admit in her mind
that she wanted to marry Rafe, there was no telling
what she might do in a moment of indiscretion.

⁓

"See," Luis said, drawing Rafe's attention to the gaily
dressed young men who rode past them on their way
to Cíbola. "Everybody dresses up for festival."

They had spent a whole evening two nights ago
discussing what Broc and Rafe would wear at festival.
They had ransacked every closet in the house for
appropriate clothing. Rafe wanted to wear his own
clothes, but Luis had insisted that they had to look
as handsome as the other young men. Rafe ended
up wearing a red shirt with a scarlet serape over his
shoulders. Blue pants with gold embroidery from the
knees to the cuffs made a striking contrast to his black
saddle with its heavy silver ornamentation. A black
felt hat with a red band and black feather completed
his ensemble.

Determined to be equally colorful, Broc had

unearthed a pair of green pants in Rafe's closet and a bright yellow shirt. Maria thought it made him look like some kind of tropical bird, but she had to admit he looked extremely handsome.

As they approached town, the traffic increased. Men of all ages rode past in vividly colored clothes on horses covered with bright saddlecloths and saddles and bridles studded with silver. Women rode in carriages, some open and some closed, but nearly all of the occupants stared at the passing cavalcade and waved to friends and family.

In town, they saw dozens of booths set up to sell everything from food to clothes to equipment of all kinds. Chickens in cages and sheep and cows tied to trees and posts added their voices to the cacophony. People leaned out of windows, lounged in doorways, backed up against walls to watch the parade of riders. It was festival time, and everybody wanted to see and do as much as they could.

"When do the competitions start?" Luis asked.

"Not until tomorrow," Broc told him. "I have one more day in which to enjoy my body without bruises and broken bones."

Luis laughed, giddy from the excitement that filled him. "Rafe said you can ride anything with hair."

"He's the one riding. I have to wrestle a cow to the ground."

"Do you wrestle cows in Texas?"

"All the time—bulls, too. They don't know enough to lie down so we can chop off—" Maria nearly broke up at Broc's effort to avoid saying they castrated the young bulls. "We have to slap a red-hot branding iron on their flanks. You'd think they'd be more reason-able, wouldn't you?"

"They're no less unreasonable than the horses that try to buck us off every morning even though we rode them the day before," Rafe added.

Rafe and Broc continued to regale Luis with tales of Texas, each trying to top the other with the absurdity of their work, until Luis was laughing so hard he had tears running down his cheeks. Maria had never seen him so happy. It made her heart ache to think how miserable he'd be when the men went back to Texas. Though it would break her heart, she was beginning to think it would be best if Rafe took Luis when he left.

"There's the hotel," Luis pointed out.

Rafe had promised him they would stay in the hotel where Dolores had a room. Luis was nervous about seeing his mother, but when he insisted Juan pack a suit that his mother had picked out for him, Maria knew he missed her.

"Can I have my own room?"

"Rafe has already told you there aren't enough rooms during festival," Broc said, showing a rare sign of impatience.

Rafe brought the buggy to a stop in front of the hotel and went inside to claim their rooms. Broc vaulted out of the vehicle, grabbed Luis, and set him down on the boardwalk. When he walked back to Maria, he flashed a wicked grin. "I'd offer to carry you, but I don't think you'd let me."

"You're right. Now stop acting like you're Luis's age and let's go into the hotel."

"I liked being Luis's age. I haven't had this much

fun since then." He held out his hand to Maria but was jostled aside by Rafe.

"You can't let Maria get muddy."

There wasn't any mud in the streets, but Rafe picked Maria up before anyone had a chance to point that out, carried her over to the boardwalk, and set her down on her feet. He had a way of disconcerting her when her defenses were down.

The awkward moment was overshadowed by a cry from somewhere nearby. Startled, Maria turned to see Dolores coming toward them at a trot, calling the name of her son in a dramatic fashion guaranteed to make people believe she was nearly overcome with emotion at being able to see Luis again. She nearly smothered him in a motherly embrace.

"Let's go inside. I don't like being a spectacle for the public's entertainment." Rafe's voice was calm and controlled, but Maria could see the anger in his eyes. When Dolores ignored him, he pushed the two of them through the hotel doors and over to a relatively private corner of the lobby. Once there, he told Dolores, "Now that we're out of public view, you can stop acting."

"How can you accuse me of acting when I haven't seen my son for over a week?" Dolores demanded. "You can't begin to know how many hours I've spent wondering if he was warm and fed, if he was safe and happy." She subjected the wiggling child to another smothering embrace.

"You might as well save your breath, my sweet. Rafe is incapable of believing any person can care that much about another."

Maria turned to see Laveau standing at the edge

of their small group, impeccably dressed, and looking slightly sinister even though he was smiling.

"A mother is not just *any* person. You can't know the agony I suffered because I couldn't see my child."

Luis had been trying to wiggle out of Dolores's embrace, but he stopped at those words. "You could have come to see me at the ranch."

Maria hadn't expected Luis to be so blunt. From the blank look on her face, Dolores hadn't expected it, either. "I wanted to, my darling, but I couldn't bear to go back to a place that used to be my home, knowing I could never live there again."

"You don't have to come inside. We can go riding. Rafe says I'm good enough to go out on my own."

Fixing Rafe with a horrified glance, Dolores clutched Luis to her. "I never thought you would encourage this child to ride out alone." The sob that caught in her throat was a masterpiece of insincerity. "I can't believe you could be so cruel, so greedy, that you'd put his life in danger so you could have the entire ranch for yourself. You must come live with me," she said to Luis. "I'll keep you safe."

"Why don't you and Broc go up to our rooms," Rafe said to Maria, his expression unchanged. "I'll bring Luis up when he's through visiting with his mother."

Dolores was losing her grip on the struggling child. "I've hardly seen him."

"If you want to spend more time with Luis, you can join us for a picnic," Maria said.

"I'll go to your picnic," Dolores said with an air of one making a great sacrifice, "but I want him for the rest of the day. I'll bring him back after dinner."

"It causes me great pain to disagree with you, my sweet." Maria wondered why her sister couldn't hear the insincerity in Laveau's voice. "I can endure a child in some bucolic setting where he's able to run about and work off some of that annoying surplus of energy, but I can't endure a child at dinner. I regret to say that I must leave you on your own."

Luis finally succeeded in wiggling out of Dolores's embrace. He moved next to Rafe.

"It would be best if he eats dinner with us," Rafe said to Dolores. "He needs to get to bed early so he'll be rested for tomorrow."

"Rafe and Broc need rest, too." Luis turned to his mother. "They're going to race horses and fight bulls."

Laveau's smile was so haughty, Maria wanted to scratch it off his face. "Can't resist showing off, can you?" He looked from Luis to Maria, then back again. "I wonder whom you're trying to impress."

"You," Rafe said to Laveau. "I didn't want you to think I've forgotten any of my skills. Or *anything else*."

That must have been an unexpected answer. It took Laveau a few moments to regain his habitual appearance of disdain.

"Dear Rafe, I'm hurt that you would think I could have forgotten your many skills. I hope you don't think I've forgotten what I know, either."

"You have a remarkable mind," Rafe said. "Unfortunately it's cluttered with things that can hurt people."

"It's not my fault people are so vulnerable."

"No, but it is your fault that you take advantage of their vulnerability."

Laveau shrugged eloquently. "That's the nature of things."

"Just *your* nature."

Apparently Rafe had scored another hit because Laveau's eyes grew hard. He turned to Dolores. "As appealing as the invitation is, I believe I must forgo an afternoon spent with nasty insects and small woodland creatures. I'll reserve our usual table for ten o'clock." He kissed Dolores's hand. "My eyes will be famished until then."

Maria couldn't believe any man actually talked like that, or that such saccharine words uttered in a patently insincere manner could cause Dolores to glow with pleasure.

"We have to change our clothes before we go on our picnic," Rafe said to Dolores. "Will half an hour be enough time for you?"

"Not nearly enough, but I'll hurry for my darling boy's sake." She tried to pat Luis's cheek, but he moved out of reach. Dolores stepped forward, gripped him by the shoulders, and gave him a kiss. "I'm so happy to see you," she whispered. "I've missed you so much."

"I've missed you, too."

Maria knew Luis really did miss his mother. She didn't believe his mother had missed him at all.

❧

Broc leaned against the wall outside their hotel room. "After that big dinner I'm so full I think I could fall into bed and not get up for two days."

"You've got to fight bulls tomorrow," Luis reminded him.

"Not fight bulls," Broc corrected. "I'm just wrestling cows to the ground."

"Isn't it the same?" Luis asked.

"Not at all," Rafe said. "Cows just try to get away. Bulls try to kill you."

"Oh." Luis's eyes grew large. "Why would anyone want to fight a bull that was trying to kill him?"

"A good question," Broc said.

"Mama says bullfights are exciting."

"A lot of people agree with your mother," Rafe said.

Maria thought the afternoon had been one of the most nerve-racking of her life. She had been so angry at Dolores's postures and lies, she had been on the verge of returning to the hotel on the excuse that she needed to lie down and rest.

In addition to clutching Luis in a too-tight embrace so often he finally wouldn't go near her, Dolores had done her best to thwart Rafe's attempts to make the afternoon enjoyable. A long walk was too difficult in her shoes. Climbing low cliffs and walking across the shallow stream on protruding rocks was too dangerous. Exposure to the sun was undesirable because it would ruin her complexion. Any activity more strenuous than a slow walk was too tiring. Any person talking to Luis other than herself was limiting the little time she had with her son. Maria was tempted to tell Dolores to stop pretending and go back to the hotel. Broc *did* tell her. She acted as though she hadn't heard him.

Amazingly, Rafe never lost his temper. He achieved this miracle by ignoring Dolores. Luis soon followed his example. That had left Maria to bear the brunt of Dolores's complaints about Rafe's treatment of her, and her needling questions about whether Maria was in love with Rafe and if he had kissed her again.

"Luis needs to go to bed now," Maria told Rafe. "You can fill him in on all the details tomorrow."

"I don't want to go to bed," Luis protested. "Broc says I'm not a little boy anymore."

"I don't think Maria puts much faith in my opinions," Broc commented.

"Are you going to bed?" Luis asked Broc.

"I think so."

"Are you going to bed, too?" Luis asked Rafe.

"Not just yet." He looked at Maria. "Maria and I are going for a walk."

Seventeen

MARIA HOPED HER EXPRESSION DIDN'T REFLECT HER shock at Rafe's statement. She hadn't been alone with him since the evening Dolores had burst in on them in his father's room. She had tried to make sure there wouldn't be any reason for anyone to accuse them of impropriety again. She had thought Rafe felt the same.

She scolded herself for immediately thinking Rafe's intentions might be romantic. He was her employer. She was his housekeeper. They were joint guardians of Luis. There had to be at least a dozen things he could want to talk to her about that had nothing to do with their feelings for each other. Maybe she ought to change that to *her feelings for him*. He might consider a few innocent kisses merely an amusement for two people who were attracted to each other.

She felt very much at a disadvantage when he looked at her with that smile that always caused the muscles in her abdomen to tighten.

"I have to put Luis to bed." Taking care of Luis was part of the job for which she was now being paid. She was nervous about leaving him alone in a hotel room.

What if another of Dolores's drunken admirers tried to kidnap him?

Broc glanced at Rafe with a raised eyebrow before turning to Maria. "I'll see the little brat is tucked safely in bed."

"I'm not little, and I'm not a brat," Luis informed him.

"Maybe I'll even read him a story to put him to sleep."

Luis's eyes danced with excitement. "Will you tell me more stories about Texas?"

"I'm not sure I know many more stories."

Luis looked disappointed, then added, "What about the war?"

Broc's expressions sobered. "I think I can remember a few more stories about Texas."

"If you're really good," Rafe said to Luis, "maybe we can talk Maria into letting you enter the pony race."

Luis practically bounced with excitement. "Can I?" he begged Maria.

She'd have to talk to Rafe about pulling surprises on her, especially when saying no would make her seem like the meanest woman in California. "We haven't talked about that," she told Luis. "It could be dangerous."

"Rafe says I'm a good rider."

Clever of Luis to put her on the defensive because of her lack of knowledge about riding. That was something else she'd have to bring up with Rafe. "I've never ridden in a race," Maria said, "but I'm sure it's very different from riding around the ranch."

"It is," Rafe said, "but Luis will be fine as long as he remembers everything I've taught him."

"I can stare down the other riders," Broc offered

with a wink. "With this face, they'll be so scared they'll let Luis win."

Luis looked unsure whether to laugh. "I don't want to win unfairly," the boy said with surprising maturity. "I don't really care about winning. I just want to race. I've never done anything like that before."

"We'll talk about it tomorrow." That was all Maria was willing to concede at the moment. "But you have to get a good night's sleep for me to consider it."

"I'll make sure he's tucked in bed and snoring like a lumberjack in half an hour."

Luis looked indignant. "I don't snore." His expression changed. "What's a lumberjack?"

Broc put his hand on the boy's shoulder. "Your education has been sadly neglected." He cast Maria a mischievous grin. "I see I need to fill in some of the gaps."

"Remember he's just nine," Maria warned.

Broc only grinned more broadly. "A boy's education can't begin too soon."

Feeling a little uneasy, she turned to Rafe. "You don't think he'll—"

"Broc likes to tease people."

Now she felt guilty for questioning Broc's integrity. It looked like her education had been neglected as well. She had no idea what to do with men like Broc and Rafe. Did she have any idea what to do with *any* man?

In the traditional wealthy household of Spanish heritage, marriages were arranged by the parents. A young girl would be married by the time she was fifteen to a man of her parents' choosing.

The loss of her family's wealth and her father's suicide had meant that Maria's life had taken a different path, but she had been happy living at Rancho los Alamitos, bringing up Luis, taking care of the household for Dolores and Warren.

"You might want to get a shawl." Rafe's voice brought her out of her abstraction. "It can get cool and damp at night."

Entering the room she would share with Luis, she started to show Broc where to find everything the boy needed for bed. That incensed Luis, who announced he was perfectly capable of showing Broc himself. She watched with amusement as he systematically took out everything he needed and carefully explained its function to Broc. She wanted to laugh because it was funny, but she felt sad because her little boy was growing up. He would always love her, but he would never need her in the same way he once had.

"I think we can handle everything else ourselves," Broc said to her. "I don't want you to keep Rafe waiting."

She was sure she blushed, and that annoyed her. Deciding there was no response that wouldn't cause further speculation, she chose a shawl. "Don't keep Luis up too late telling stories. And don't make them too exciting, or he'll never fall asleep."

Broc promised to have Luis in bed and asleep before she and Rafe reached the end of the street. Rafe was waiting in the hall when she stepped out of her room.

"Giving Broc some final instructions?"

"He doesn't know anything about children, and Luis is still a little boy."

"Broc grew up the oldest in a family of nine. I expect he knows enough to put Luis to bed."

She would not blush for her ignorance. It was Broc's fault he'd never said anything about his family. "It isn't that he doesn't know how. It's that he enjoys telling stories too much, and Luis likes hearing them so much, he won't let Broc stop when it comes time."

Rafe put his hand on the small of her back and guided her down the hall that led to the lobby. "It won't hurt Luis to stay up late. Festival occurs only once a year."

She wondered if Rafe would come back next year at festival time. "It's a good thing, with you encouraging him to risk his neck in a pony race."

Rafe didn't respond until they'd crossed the lobby and emerged from the hotel. "So now it's my fault he's in danger."

She could tell from the tone of his voice he was teasing her. She wasn't sure she liked that.

"What events do you plan to enter tomorrow?" she asked.

Rafe's amused look served only to irritate her further. "Probably a race, performing some tricks, and bronco riding."

"All in one day?" The list seemed like a lot to her.

"They last only a few minutes each."

It only took seconds for something to go wrong. She didn't understand why men had to unnecessarily court danger just to show they were men.

As they walked along the street, she realized that Cíbola looked very different at night. The town throbbed with life. Even though it was dark, people filled the streets, some just walking as she and Rafe were. Others talking in doorways and courtyards. Still others eating on tables that had been set outside. The feeble light from the crescent moon was supplemented by multicolored lanterns lining the street, sitting on tables, and hanging from tree limbs or ropes strung from windows. Rich reds, brilliant yellows, and warm oranges gave the festival costumes a cheerfulness that was reflected in the laughter and excitement that filled the air.

Women strolled by, their hair coiled in tight knots and adorned with flowers, jeweled combs, or covered with lace. Many wore lockets at their throats and heavily embroidered shawls draped over their alabaster shoulders. Men were dressed with equal flamboyance in embroidered coats and vests sporting silver buttons, and flat-crowned, wide-brimmed hats decorated with colorful bands. They wore tight-fitting *calzoneras* of every color with red sashes tied around their waists. The sounds of violins, guitars, and voices raised in song competed with one another, first one then the other gaining prominence, only to fade out and be replaced.

The spicy smells of food of every description— tomatoes, garlic, beef, onions, chicken—filled the night air. Feeling a slight chill despite Rafe's nearness, Maria pulled her shawl more tightly around her.

"Are you cold?" Rafe asked. "Do you want my *serape*?"

Maria couldn't remember Rafe having ever worn a *serape*, a blanketlike garment that could be draped across the chest and thrown over the shoulders, with the ends falling down the back or wrapped around the body like a cloak. He always wore the shirt, vest, and pants that Broc said were cowboy gear in Texas. She wouldn't have admitted it to anyone, but his usual attire showcased his raw masculinity better than anything else.

"Thank you, but I'm warm enough."

She wondered where he was taking her, what he wanted to talk about, why he couldn't have done it in the hotel. They came to the bridge that crossed the creek dividing Cíbola in two.

"I remember the spring the creek flooded so badly it washed the bridge away," Rafe commented. "They found pieces scattered all the way to the Sacramento River."

The creeks always flooded when the snow melted in the spring. "What did you want to talk with me about?" she asked. "If it's about Luis or managing the house, we could have done it in the hotel."

"It's not about either."

"What, then?"

"Do I have to want to talk about anything in particular? Can't I just enjoy being with you?"

Maria's heart beat so rapidly, she felt breathless. "You've been with me all day."

"I wasn't with *you*. I was with everybody."

She understood. Hadn't she been trying to avoid being with him by surrounding herself with people? "Why would you want to be alone with me?"

"I enjoy your company."

"Really? Why?"

Rafe looked vaguely amused. "Do I have to have a reason?"

She opened her mouth to say of course, but closed it when she realized she couldn't say exactly what it was about Rafe that attracted her. "Most people do have a reason, that's all."

"What kind of reason?"

She started to mention the obvious but was certain Rafe wasn't talking about that. He wasn't attracted to Dolores despite her beauty. "I'm not sure," she confessed. "I haven't known many men."

"The only women I've known even reasonably well are Dolores and Cade's wife, Pilar. I completely misjudged Dolores, and I was never romantically interested in Pilar. That doesn't make me much of an expert."

Why had she always assumed he had wide experience with women? Was it his confidence, his decisiveness, his habit of command?

"You might say I'm trying to learn about women by being with you."

Maria felt bereft of speech. His words could have so many possible unspoken meanings...or absolutely none. She reminded herself that Rafe would be returning to Texas. If she had any sense, she'd go back to the hotel right now.

To give herself time to think, she walked onto the bridge. The water in the creek below tumbled over polished stones, eddied in twists of the creek bed, and pooled in places undisturbed by rocks. Against the backdrop of the celebration in Cíbola it seemed silent, going on its way without comment or notice of its surroundings. That was a lot like her life over the past ten years. She'd filled her days with her love for Luis and her housekeeping duties. She'd grown from a girl into a woman. She might never have noticed the changes in herself if it hadn't been for Rafe. But she *had* noticed the difference, and she now knew that she wanted things she'd never wanted before. "Maybe you ought to find a Texas woman. I doubt they're the same as Californians. There's a lot of Spanish blood in our veins."

Rafe had followed her onto the bridge. "One of Pilar's grandfathers was French and the other Spanish. Her grandmother is this fierce Spanish lady who tolerates me only because my mother was part of the Vallejo family."

"My father was Spanish; yours was an Anglo."

"Yours committed suicide, and mine closed himself up in his room until he died. I suggest we forget all our ancestors and think only of ourselves."

That was exactly what she was trying *not* to do. She needed to conclude this conversation and get back to the hotel. But if Rafe didn't have anything specific to say to her, only wanted to enjoy her company, there was no easy way to bring the evening to an end without just walking away.

"Why do you find it so hard to be around me?"

She'd never expected him to be so blunt. She didn't know how to answer his question honestly without revealing too much about her own feelings. "We're so different."

"I'm not talking about that. You've avoided me ever since Dolores accused me of trying to compromise you."

"Isn't that reason enough?"

"No. You were kissing me back."

It was foolish to think he wouldn't have realized that. "That's all the more reason to keep our distance from each other."

"Because of one little kiss?"

"In my culture, any action can be misinterpreted when it's between a man and woman who aren't married."

"Did you misinterpret that kiss?"

"I can't say. I don't know how you meant it."

"My meaning wasn't complicated. I like you and wanted to kiss you. What did you think I meant?"

Rafe didn't play fair. Men weren't supposed to be so direct. Honesty put a woman on the spot, gave her little or no room to be evasive, to keep from committing herself. She didn't have the same freedom as Dolores had as a widow, but she was old enough to make her own decisions.

"My experience of men is very limited," she confessed. "I've never had to sort through so many conflicting emotions." Rafe reached out, took her hand. She knew she should resist but didn't.

"Are you going to turn me away?" he murmured.

Maria couldn't breathe. Rafe hadn't asked anything of her, yet she felt he'd asked everything. Any answer could be the wrong one—for her and for him. "I can't give you an answer until I know what you're asking."

Rafe seemed to sense her confusion, her anxiety. He gently rubbed the back of her hand with his thumb. "I was only going to ask if I could put my arm around you, maybe kiss you again."

Only put his arm around her, maybe kiss her again! Didn't he realize granting him permission to do those things was the same as turning her world upside down?

"You say that as if it's no more important than asking whether I want to go for a ride." It was difficult to read Rafe's expression in the shadowy light, but she could feel the increase in tension through his grip on her hand.

"Then I didn't say it right. I like you very much. I'm not good with words, so I can't explain that because of things that have happened to me in the past, I'm not sure exactly what my feelings are."

Odd that she should be more attracted to a man who wasn't sure of his feelings for her than men who knew exactly what they wanted. She had questions of her own that needed answers, and she hadn't found any of them in the privacy of her thoughts. She didn't want to risk her heart, but she suspected it was already too late for that.

"I like you, too." Why was that so hard to say? It was only four words. She told Luis she loved him a dozen times a day. What was so difficult about admitting that she liked Rafe? Because loving Luis and liking Rafe weren't the same. They were miles apart. A universe apart. One emotion filled her with happiness, the other with terror and confusion. "One kiss," she agreed, "but that's all."

"You're going to limit me to one?"

She'd been kissed only once in her life—by Rafe. But that one experience had been enough for her to know how powerful a kiss could be. She felt herself flush. "I'm not trying to be coy."

His grip on her hand tightened and he pulled her closer. "I enjoy being with you. I have from that first night."

She started to protest, but he stopped her with a finger to her lips.

"I was angry at having to come back and face Dolores, and I was irritated I was attracted to you. I was certain you were like Dolores."

"What changed your mind?"

"Lots of things, even the way you looked out for Dolores although she took advantage of you."

She felt guilty she hadn't recognized sooner that her sister was a badly flawed woman. "I tried to make Dolores see reason, but I wasn't very successful."

"That wasn't your responsibility. Now, I don't want to talk about Dolores anymore. I'd much rather talk about you."

Maria didn't know what he could find to say about her. She wasn't beautiful, she wasn't young, she wasn't sophisticated, and she had never been anywhere or done anything. "That will be a short conversation."

"I disagree. You're a complicated woman, and I love your smile."

What could any man say about a smile that would take even half a minute? She didn't know how to tell him she wasn't amused, but he seemed to sense her change of mood.

"You don't believe me?"

"It's not that I don't *want* to believe you, but a smile is just the curve of two lips."

She had no trouble interpreting his expression this time. She heard his laugh, deep and slow. She felt his arm tighten around her. She could feel the heat of his body as he drew her closer.

"Your smiles reach beyond your lips and change

your whole appearance. They're never the same. Sometimes your eyes dance with merriment or become warm with emotion. At other times, they open wide in question or crinkle in agreement. I can't stop wanting to make you smile, to find out what it will look like, *feel* like, this time."

Once more Rafe had robbed her of the power of speech. Soon he would realize she was a very ordinary woman who was unlikely to hold the interest of such a complex man for more than a short time.

Rafe brushed her cheek with his fingertips. "You're very quiet."

His touch caused her to tremble so it took a moment before she could speak. "I can't think of anything to say."

A slow smile transformed Rafe's face. "We're making progress."

She opened her mouth to speak, then closed it again. She didn't want him to be wrong, but she couldn't bring herself to believe he was right.

He pulled her closer. "Maybe this will help to convince you."

She could feel the kiss before their lips met. It was in his eyes, in his touch, in the press of his body against her own. The joining of their lips was merely the culmination of the attraction that brought them together. She told herself she shouldn't yield to his embrace, that their attraction wouldn't last.

Throwing caution to the winds, Maria allowed herself to melt into Rafe's arms. She exalted in the feel of his arms tightening around her, pressing her firmly against the solid strength of his chest. She was surprised to find she felt small and helpless in a way that made her feel cherished, cared for, protected. She also felt desired. She could feel it in the heat streaming from his body into hers, the power of his embrace, in the hunger of his kiss, in the rapid swelling of his body where it pressed against her thigh. The intensity of his reaction frightened her as it thrilled her. How could she possibly live up to such an overwhelming emotion? How could she survive without it?

She focused on the feel of Rafe's arms around her, on the taste of his firm mouth, the sensation of his soft lips. His embrace comforted her at the same time it reached out to a need deep within her, a need she'd ignored for so long that she'd convinced herself it didn't exist. It rose inside her with the force of a powerful beast awakened from a long sleep. Her arms circled around Rafe's neck, pulling him deeper into their kiss, deeper into—

"Thank God I found you. You've got to come back to the hotel immediately. Luis is sick."

Eighteen

"WHAT'S WRONG WITH HIM?" MARIA ASKED BROC AS she and Rafe followed in his wake. She struggled to rein in her emotions enough to think of Luis. She could deal with the mortification of Broc finding her locked in Rafe's embrace later.

"I don't think it's anything serious," Broc said, "but he threw up his dinner. I put him back to bed, but he wants you and Rafe."

"Does he have a fever? Chills? Spots?" Luis had always been such a healthy boy she had virtually no experience with childhood illnesses.

"None of that," Broc assured her. "I think he just ate too much rich food too fast. He should be fine by morning."

She hoped Broc was right. Luis would be devastated if he had to stay in bed for the whole festival.

"Who's with him now?" Rafe asked.

"I asked one of the hotel maids to sit with him until I got back." Broc grinned. "She's young and cute enough that I don't think Luis minded being sick."

Maria was willing to let Luis grow up, but she wasn't ready for him to become interested in girls.

The walk back to the hotel seemed to take much longer than the walk to the park. Bigger crowds clogged the streets and were slower to move aside. Groups of merrymakers invited them to join in the festivities, offered them food and drink. One wandering musician tried to sing a song to her. At no time was she oblivious to the envious glances from women, young and old, who smiled invitingly at Rafe and Broc.

She chastised herself for such petty thoughts when Luis was lying sick in a strange room without any of his family nearby. By the time she reached the hotel, she could barely restrain herself from running up the stairs. She burst into her room only to find Luis's bed empty.

She turned toward Broc. "Where is he? You said one of the maids was sitting with him."

"She was when I left."

Despite her panic, she was able to see that Broc was as confused as she was.

"I expect there's a reasonable explanation for Luis not being here," Rafe said. "We just have to discover what it is."

Maria rounded on him, relieved to have somewhere to focus her anger. "How are we going to do that when there's no one here to ask?"

The appearance of a clearly distressed young woman spared Rafe the need to respond.

"What happened to the boy?" Broc asked the maid. "You promised not to leave him until I got back."

"His mother took him." The girl wrung her hands. "When she found he had been sick, she insisted nobody was going to care for him but her. The boy didn't want to go, but she called one of the men and had the child carried to her room. She said she wouldn't sleep a wink unless she was at his side."

Maria tried to reassure the young woman. "You did the best you could."

Rafe was already out of the room and headed toward the stairs.

"Rafe, wait."

He didn't slow down. She could only guess how he felt about Dolores taking Luis to her suite with Laveau present.

"Rafe's not going to wait for either of us," Broc said. "Let's hope we get there before he breaks her neck."

Holding her skirts high, Maria climbed the stairs as swiftly as she could. By the time she reached the upper hallway, she could hear Dolores's raised voice coming through an open doorway.

"You can't take him away, Rafe. He's sick."

Silence.

"He's *my* son, not yours. Stop him, Laveau. Don't let him take my son."

"Luis is his brother. It is his right to take care of him."

Maria reached the room in time to see Rafe, with a relieved-looking Luis in his arms, heading toward the doorway. Dolores pulled at his arm to stop him, but he shook her off effortlessly. Laveau stood to one side, watching with a detachment Maria found puzzling. Dolores turned to her sister when Maria appeared in the doorway.

"Tell Rafe it is a mother's right to care for her child when he's sick."

Maria didn't bother to remind Dolores that she had never cared for Luis when he was sick. Most of the time Dolores was unaware he wasn't feeling well, and wouldn't have known what to do in any case.

"He doesn't look dangerously ill. Broc thinks he just ate too much rich food too quickly." As far as Maria could tell, Luis's primary feeling seemed to be relief. He was a little flushed, but that was more likely the result of a stranger plucking him from his bed and carrying him to the suite of a man who clearly didn't want him there.

"What does Broc know about sick children?" Dolores demanded. "He's a man."

"He had eight younger brothers and sisters."

"I'm Luis's mother," Dolores reminded them. "I gave birth to him."

Maria had spent the last nine years making excuses for Dolores's faults, but she could no longer refuse to face the truth. Dolores didn't care that what she did hurt others or made them suffer. "I know you're his mother, but I'm the one who's always taken care of him. That's why you invited me to live with you."

"I invited you to live with me because I love you and didn't want you to have to live with our sister and her husband. I didn't want you to become a peasant like Mother."

"Tomás isn't wealthy, but he isn't a peasant. Mother was very happy to make her home with them."

"I can't believe my own mother could fall so far." Dolores shuddered theatrically. "She has the blood of

Spanish nobles in her veins. She was the chatelaine of an enormous hacienda with dozens of servants to do her bidding. During festival she gave parties for hundreds of people."

Maria tried not to dwell on memories of the rambling house with its cool, dark rooms decorated in a heavy Spanish style, her soft-spoken mother, or her imperious father. Nor did she tease herself with any longing for the days when she had had nothing to occupy her mind but clothes and parties.

Dolores had gotten so carried away with complaints about her mother and sister's fall from grace that she didn't appear to notice Rafe and Broc had disappeared with Luis.

"Not everyone has your exquisite sensitivity," Laveau said to Dolores.

"Not everyone can afford it," Maria snapped, out of patience with her sister's theatrics and Laveau's insincerity. She was sorry if her words hurt Dolores, but her sister needed a good dose of truth. "Now I have to go see Luis. Though I'm certain he's perfectly safe in Rafe and Broc's care, he's used to depending on me when he's not feeling well."

"How can you let Rafe keep me from my own son when he needs me?" Dolores wailed, piteously.

"I'm sure it's hard on you, my sweet," Laveau said, "but I think the boy is better off with Maria. Though I hesitate to mention such a mundane consideration, we don't have a bed for him."

"He's only a child," Dolores said. "He could have been comfortable on the couch."

Maria wasn't as bothered by Laveau's disclosure as

much as she was upset that it didn't cause Dolores to blink, not even to pause, at a statement that made it clear she had entered into a sexual relationship with Laveau for the sake of the material comforts he could provide.

"I'm sure he'll be more comfortable in his own bed," Laveau said. "You can see him first thing in the morning."

Dolores never rose early. It would probably be noon before she left her room. "I'll send you a message when Luis wakes up," Maria promised.

Making her escape before Dolores could think of some other complaint, Maria found herself wondering how she'd managed to avoid facing the truth all these years. She hadn't wanted to admit that her sister was such a selfish person, but Rafe's arrival had forced her to stop pretending. That left her in an awkward position.

She realized she disliked her sister.

The realization made her feel guilty all over again. Whatever Dolores's faults, she had invited Maria to share her home. Now Maria was siding with Rafe against Dolores for Luis's sake.

Luis was sitting up in his bed, laughing at something Rafe had said, when she reached her room. The boy turned solemn when he saw her.

"I'm sorry I got sick."

She couldn't get over how much he'd changed in the last several days. Before Rafe's arrival, he'd never thought of how his being sick might affect her. He glanced at Rafe. "Rafe says he's going to make sure I don't have anything but bread and water before the race tomorrow."

Maria had assumed riding in the race the next day

was out of the question, but apparently Rafe didn't think so. Now neither did Luis, because anything Rafe said was like a pronouncement from on high. She could understand why a little boy would be in awe of an older brother like Rafe, but she was the one who had loved Luis his whole life, taken care of him every day, had sat by his bedside whenever he'd been sick, shielded him from his mother's shortcomings, and had tried to compensate for his father's indifference. She felt like an old toy that had been shoved aside for a shiny new one.

In her mind she knew she hadn't been shoved aside, that Luis had just made room in his life for an extra person, but it still felt like rejection and she didn't like it. However, she did recognize that Rafe was the best thing to happen to Luis in years. "I don't know about the bread and water, but I think we ought to wait until we see how you feel tomorrow before we decide whether you can ride in the race."

His mouth falling in dismay, Luis looked from Rafe to Maria. "Rafe said he was sure I'd feel fine in the morning."

"I'm not a doctor," Rafe told the boy. "I could be wrong."

"But Broc says the same thing," Luis pointed out.

"And I agree with both of them," Maria said, "but we still have to wait until tomorrow to see how you feel."

It was clear Luis thought her pronouncement was practically the same as being told he couldn't ride in the race.

"The best way to make sure you can ride tomorrow

is to get plenty of sleep," Rafe told Luis. "Broc and I will go away and let Maria tuck you in."

"I want you to do it."

Maria thought she could sense a slight tensing in Rafe's shoulders. "Why don't all three of us do it? Then you'll be so tightly tucked in you won't be able to move."

Luis broke into a smile, and Maria felt a pang for what these two brothers had lost by being separated. Rafe was the bigger-than-life brother who'd transformed Luis into a smiling, active boy Maria had never known was there. Luis was the admiring little brother who could banish the black moods that descended on Rafe from time to time.

"Hop into bed," Broc said to Luis. "You're about to be tied up in a sheet."

Maria did her part in the fun that followed.

"Do you think that's tight enough?" Broc asked her with a wink.

The sheet was so tight across Luis, she could have bounced a coin off it.

"I don't know," Rafe said. "It looks a little loose to me. Maybe we ought to tuck it in at the top of the bed, too."

"I won't be able to breathe," Luis protested between laughs.

"He needs to breathe," Broc pointed out.

They joked a bit more until Maria was afraid Luis would be so worked up he'd never get to sleep. "We're going to leave now," she told Luis. "Remember, you need a good night's sleep if you're going to ride tomorrow."

Luis grinned up at Rafe. "I can't move, so I guess I'll have to sleep." Maria, Rafe, and Broc said good night and trooped out.

"Are you sure he'll be okay to ride tomorrow?" she asked Rafe as soon as she closed the door to her room.

"Ask Broc. He's the one with all the brothers and sisters."

"It wasn't just the food," Broc said. "It was the excitement as well. I don't mean to sound critical, but you didn't ever take the boy anywhere, let him do anything except study or read books, right?"

Guilt. How could she explain a situation in which she had appeared to have authority but in actuality had almost none? "I didn't know much more than that myself. Girls are reared very differently from boys, and I only had sisters. I guess I thought Luis was too small, that I could wait until later, that Warren would become interested in him when his son got older."

"No one is blaming you," Rafe said. "I'm sure you did the best you could."

She'd thought so, but if she had it to do over again, she would do some things differently. She knew so much more now than she had just a few weeks ago. Unfortunately, Luis had been the one to suffer from her ignorance. "I never realized how important it was for him to be around a man who was young enough to teach him all the things other boys take for granted."

"It's not too late. He's only nine."

She nodded. Luis had changed so much it felt as if he'd grown three years in the last three weeks.

Broc gave vent to an exaggerated yawn. "I don't know about you two, but I'm ready for bed."

Broc might be a very fine actor, but Maria was certain that yawn was an excuse to leave them alone. He probably felt guilty about bringing to an end one of the few chances they'd had to be together. "I'm tired as well," she said. "Luis always falls asleep in a few minutes. You don't have to wait up for me."

"While we're waiting for Luis to fall asleep, we can take a walk around the square," Rafe said.

"I'll leave a candle burning for you," Broc said.

"You're going with us." Rafe gave Broc a sly smile. "It's not every woman who has the opportunity to parade around town with two men in attendance."

Maria couldn't be sure of Rafe's reason for insisting that Broc accompany them, but she'd had enough stress for one day, and she could depend upon Broc to make the rest of the evening pass with lighthearted laughter. She hooked arms with Broc and Rafe. "Come on. I want everyone to see that Dolores is not the only de la Guerra woman who can capture the attention of handsome men."

Maria used to think the day Luis had been born was the most exciting and stressful day of her life. After today, that day was a distant second.

The day had begun with Luis waking up bright-eyed, bouncing with energy, and bubbling over with excitement about the pony race. She'd been hoping to find an excuse to keep him out of the competition, but it was obvious he was recovered from his indisposi-tion. Rafe and Broc had agreed he was in the pink of health, so there was nothing for her to do but send a note to Dolores saying Luis was fully recovered and steel her nerves so she could watch the race without acting like an overprotective mother.

It didn't help that Dolores had shocked her by turning up at ten o'clock, a good half hour before the race. Dolores declared she would watch the race with Maria. "Laveau doesn't get up this early."

Rafe had saddled Luis's pony, then rejoined Maria. "Are you nervous?"

"Of course she's nervous," Dolores answered for her. "My poor boy could be killed."

"I am a little nervous," Maria admitted. "Luis is barely nine and some of those boys look two or three years older." The fact that Luis seemed eager for the race to start didn't make her feel any better.

"They're off!"

The crowd of proud parents, family, and friends shouted their encouragement as the boys and their ponies jostled one another at the start. Maria gasped when a boy on a white pony bumped Luis's pony.

"That boy is a natural," Rafe said proudly when Luis held his pony together until he could regain his balance. "I'll have to get him a bigger pony before I go back to Texas."

It seemed half the boys didn't understand that they were supposed to race one another, not try to knock one another off the track.

"Those boys don't know how to ride," Dolores declared.

"They know how," Rafe said. "They're just trying to knock out the competition."

Maria thought that showed poor sportsmanship.

She was so worried about Luis's safety, she didn't know when she grasped hold of Rafe's hand. She became aware of it only when Luis emerged from the tangle and joined the leaders, who were more intent on winning the race than eliminating their competition.

"He's ridden himself out of trouble," Rafe said. "He's in a good position to win."

She would have withdrawn her hand, but Rafe didn't loosen his grip.

"He shouldn't be riding in this race," Dolores complained. "He'll be sick with exhaustion."

"You should be extremely proud of Luis," Rafe said to Maria. "The other boys used whips, but Luis hand rode his pony out of trouble. That takes real skill. Anybody can use a whip."

Maria didn't know what *hand riding* meant and didn't care. She cared only that Luis was in the middle of a group of boys trying to reach the finish line first. The shouts from the people around her rose to a crescendo as several boys crossed the finish line in a group.

"Did he win?" Dolores asked.

"I think he came in third," Rafe said, "but he's the best rider out there."

"He didn't win," Dolores said. "How can he be the best?"

She headed to where Broc was waiting for Luis. Maria started to follow, then realized she was still holding on to Rafe's hand. Embarrassed, she quickly pulled away, but he just smiled and said, "Let's go find Luis."

When they reached Luis, Dolores was fussing over

him, looking for possible injuries, and questioning how he was feeling. His gaze went straight to Rafe.

"I didn't win," he said.

"No, but you rode the best race of anybody," Rafe told him. "Nobody did a better job of steadying his mount during the rough start or of getting the most out of him at the finish line. I'm extremely proud of you for finishing third against boys with far more experience."

"See, didn't I tell you?" Broc said to Luis.

Rafe's pride in his accomplishment had the boy beaming. He had come out of the race with added confidence in his abilities. Maria realized it was worth a few moments of breathlessness to see the smile on his face, the way he walked with a bit of a swagger.

"Rafe said it would be easy," he told his mother. "And it was."

Maria had hoped Dolores would go back to the hotel, but she stayed to watch Rafe's race. She appeared to take great pleasure in seeing him lose. Maria, on the other hand, was never more proud of him. He lost because he'd helped a young caballero whose saddle cinch broke. The youth would have fallen into the path of the horses behind him if Rafe hadn't steadied him and stayed at his side until he'd been able to settle himself on the horse bareback.

Maria could tell Luis was disappointed. Rafe was his hero. He couldn't understand how his big brother could lose. Dolores attempted to use the opportunity to disparage Rafe to Luis, but that backfired when the young man and his parents came to thank Rafe for what he'd done.

"Would he really have been killed if you hadn't helped him?" Luis asked after the young man's father had thanked Rafe for saving his son's life and his mother had wet Rafe's shirt with her tears of thankfulness.

"He's a very good rider," Rafe said. "He probably could have pulled up on his own."

"Nobody can stay on a horse when the saddle slips out from under him," Broc told Luis.

Luis looked at Rafe with wonder in his eyes. "You saved his life."

That was too much for Dolores so she left to go back to the hotel. Besides, Broc's event was coming up. Dolores was still trying to pretend he didn't exist.

Maria couldn't understand what Luis found so enjoyable about watching Broc wrestle a steer to the ground, but the boy got so excited that he climbed up on his chair to cheer. For a time Maria thought the steer was going to win. How was any man supposed to wrestle an animal of that size? The steer dragged him around a bit, but once Broc got a good hold on the steer's horns, he used his weight to throw the animal off balance. Rafe explained that once a steer loses control of its head, it can be brought to the ground. Maria had been doubtful, but it happened just as Rafe said it would.

Which raised both Rafe and Broc in Luis's estimation.

Later in the afternoon, while they waited for Rafe's bronco ride to begin, Broc explained that all cowboys rode bucking horses practically every time they got into the saddle.

"My pony doesn't buck," Luis pointed out.

"Your pony grew up in a stable," Broc said. "Our horses ran wild during the war and haven't forgotten how much they liked it."

"My pony likes for me to ride him," Luis said.

"He likes to be taken out of his stall, but he'd be a lot happier if you weren't on his back."

"Oh." Luis looked thoughtful. "Does he hate me?"

"No. You feed him and give him a nice warm bed out of the rain and cold."

"One of the stable hands feeds him. I don't unsaddle him or put him in his stall."

Maria was certain Broc had backed himself into a corner.

"He knows he can depend on people, and you're a person. As long as you're gentle with him when you ride, he'll do whatever you want. Now watch carefully. When they open the gate, Rafe's horse will come out bucking as hard as he can."

"Will Rafe fall off? Will it hurt?"

Maria did her best not to hear any of Broc's explanation of what would happen when the gate opened. She could understand why a man would mount a horse that bucked if it was the only way he could get his work done, but how could being thrown about like a rag doll and probably sent flying through the air before crashing to the ground possibly be fun? There were times when she thought men had to be alien creatures. How else could you explain why they were so different from women? Then again maybe *she* was the alien creature. All around her women cheered the riders who stayed on longest and shook their heads at those who were thrown. Why didn't she thrill at the sight of a man testing his strength and skill against a powerful animal instead of cringing and praying it would be over soon?

The cheer that went up from the assembled throng signaled that the gate had been opened.

Maria didn't want to watch, but she couldn't take her eyes off the battle. The horse, a bony animal with brown and black spots against a dirty white coat, moved with rapidity that made her dizzy as it twisted its body into positions Maria would have thought impossible.

"That's what a horse would do to get a cougar off its back," Broc explained.

Broc told Luis the names of the various movements of the bronc. When he said that some horses had been known to attack the rider after they'd bucked him off, Maria was tempted to close her eyes until it was over. Much to her relief, someone blew a whistle, which apparently signaled that Rafe had stayed on long enough. He slid out of the saddle as if it were the most natural thing in the world and strode to the middle of the ring, where he acknowledged the applause of the appreciative audience. Luis was on his feet, clapping, shouting, and grinning from ear to ear.

Maria struggled to slow her rapidly beating heart. The ride had lasted just ten seconds, but she felt exhausted.

"Rafe is the best rider, isn't he?" Luis asked Broc. "He didn't fall off."

"Several of the others didn't fall off, either," Broc reminded him.

"But Rafe was better, wasn't he?"

"I think so," Broc said with an indulgent smile, "but we'll have to wait and see if the judges agree."

The horses bucked so fast and the rides lasted such a short time, it was hard for Maria to see any difference between one rider and another. She was just relieved that Rafe's ride was over. She wanted him to stop bowing to all those silly women. None of them had sat through the ordeal, heart in hand, unable to take a single breath. None of them had—

"Oh, my God!"

Broc's exclamation riveted her attention. "What's wrong?"

Broc was already disappearing in the crowd when Maria turned to him. Her attention drawn by a sudden hush, she turned back to the ring. What she saw caused her to gasp in horror.

Nineteen

RAFE'S EYES WERE CERTAIN OF WHAT THEY SAW, BUT his brain said it was impossible. A very large, very angry bull pawed the ground and glared at him from less than fifty feet away.

The fighting bulls were kept in pens at the edge of the arena so they could be released directly into the ring. All the bulls had already been brought to the holding pens because the bullfights were the next and final event of the afternoon. Through some incredible accident, one of the gates must have become loose or weak enough for the bull to get out. This was not the average bull with a natural antipathy for man. This bull had been bred for his willingness to fight anything he encountered, most particularly a man on foot. Instinctively, Rafe looked over his shoulder for a way to escape. He could hardly believe his eyes when a second bull emerged from its pen and trotted into the sunlit arena.

Nothing like this could happen—at least not by accident.

He didn't have time to worry about how it had happened, why it had happened, or who might have done it—accidentally or intentionally. He was in the middle of a large ring between two bulls, and he had nothing with which to defend himself. There were no picadors in the arena because the bullfights weren't scheduled to begin until later in the afternoon.

He was alone. It was up to him to save his own life.

It was natural for bulls to fight each other, but it was the practice of the people who staged the bullfights to irritate, agitate, and generally anger the bulls so they would be more eager to fight the humans who'd tormented them. Someone had driven lances into the shoulders of these bulls for the purpose of causing pain to escalate their anger to near-blind rage. And there he stood, a perfect target.

Rafe had seen bullfights, but he'd never participated in one. He'd always thought the fights were too cruel to the bull. The odds were stacked so it was almost impossible for the bull to win. Tradition dictated that the victorious matador conclude the fight by plunging his sword into the heart of his vanquished foe. But how could Rafe vanquish his foes? He needed something to attract the bulls' attention, to give them a target, and he didn't have anything.

If he could move out of the center of the ring, perhaps the bulls would see each other and forget about him. When he saw a third bull emerge from its pen, pinning him at the vortex of a lethal triangle, he was certain someone was trying to kill him.

A hush had fallen over the spectators. A child raised his voice, only to be cut off in midsentence. It was as if the whole world had stopped long enough to turn its attention on him, to watch with gaping mouths, waiting to see what would happen, certain of the inevitable outcome.

Rafe didn't move. He knew as long as he remained motionless, the bulls couldn't be sure he was a real person. But that strategy wouldn't work for long. Any moment an errant breeze could carry his scent to one of the bulls, and it would charge. Any movement would draw one or both of the other bulls into the fray. How was he going to get out of this alive?

He'd once heard someone say you could stare down a bull, but what did you do when you faced three? He racked his brain, trying to think of something he could use to distract the bulls, but he'd removed his vest when he mounted the bronc, leaving just the red shirt Luis had insisted he wear.

The red shirt!

He could use that as a cape if he could get it off before one of the bulls charged. It had at least six buttons and was securely tucked into his pants. Did he have enough time?

Being careful not to move too quickly, he brought his right hand up to the first button and undid it. At the same time he slowly turned his head enough so that, using his peripheral vision, he was able to see all three bulls. The third bull was more interested in the other two bulls than in Rafe. The second bull was distracted by the crowds. The first bull had stopped pawing the ground, but its eyes were focused intently on Rafe.

Rafe undid a second button.

The first bull grunted, exhaled through its nostrils, and lowered its head. Saliva dripped from its lips and the spear imbedded in its shoulder quivered. His action caught the attention of the second bull, which also focused on Rafe. It snorted and stomped the ground with a single hoof, causing the lance buried deep in its shoulder to wave about, undoubtedly causing even greater pain. Rafe could see no spear in the third bull. He hoped that would make it less dangerous than the first two, but he didn't need anyone to tell him that wouldn't matter if he didn't manage to get past the others.

He undid a third button.

The first bull raised its head and sent forth a full-throated bellow that seemed to shake the ground. That brought the other bulls to attention, ready for a challenge from any direction. The first bull bellowed again, pawed at the ground, and lowered its head, shaking it from side to side and flinging saliva in all directions. Its actions spurred the second bull to deliver an answering bellow before lowering its head and pawing the ground.

Rafe didn't bother to check on the third bull before undoing the fourth button.

Noise from the crowd penetrated his consciousness. He could hear men shouting and had a vague impression of running feet. There was no sound of a horse entering the ring, no picador coming to his rescue. The first bull sent a blast of air through its nostrils, lowered its head still more, and charged.

Rafe ripped open the shirt, sending the last two buttons flying. He jerked it out of his pants and pulled it off only a split second before the charging bull reached him. With no time to unfurl the shirt and use it as a target, Rafe threw himself to the side just as the bull thundered by. Using the agility bred in it through generations, the bull threw his head to the side and hooked the tail of the shirt with his horn as he passed.

The shirt was Rafe's only weapon, his only means of defense. As puny as it was, he couldn't lose it. Even as he lost his balance and tumbled to the ground, Rafe tightened his grip on the shirt. He heard it rip, prayed the tear wouldn't leave him with a scrap while the majority decorated the bull's horns. Both hands still gripping the shirt tightly, he came to his knees as the bull's horn ripped free of the tail of the shirt.

The sound of pounding hooves made him look up in time to see the second bull charging. Rafe wasn't sure how he got to his feet in time to face the second bull, but he managed to wave the shirt at the charging animal. It passed so close by, Rafe could feel the heat of its breath, could smell the odor of manure that clung to it.

The bull's furious charge carried it well past Rafe, but Rafe barely had time to regain his balance and face the first bull as it attacked again. He was caught between the two bulls. Only great luck would enable him to continue to face one at a time. That luck would vanish entirely if the third bull decided to charge. His only alternative was to get the first two bulls to attack at the same time from opposite directions. If they crashed into each other—it would be even better if they started to fight—he would have a chance to get them between him and the third bull. That might give him enough time to reach the edge of the arena and vault over the wall to safety.

He was vaguely aware of the sounds of movement outside the ring. Some of the spectators were shouting advice. Why hadn't he been interested in bullfighting when he was a young boy? Then he might have had some notion of what to do as he struggled to evade one attack after another.

Remaining in the center of the ring wasn't an option. Somehow he had to attract the attention of the first two bulls without drawing the third into the conflict. Waving the shirt in front of him, Rafe moved from the center of the ring in hopes of confusing the bulls and causing them to wait before charging.

It didn't quite work that way. He barely had time to spin away from one bull before the other was upon him. The second bull's horn caught his pants, ripped through the material to the flesh underneath, and spun him around and off his feet. Dragging his body up on his knees, he looked up just in time to see the third bull lower its head and charge.

The pain in his hip wouldn't let him stand and deploy the cape. He had to hope the bull was charging so hard, it wouldn't have time to change course when Rafe threw himself to one side at the last second—if he was able to judge when that last fraction of a second arrived. He didn't have time to determine the location of the first two bulls. He'd have to hope they would be distracted by the unexpected arrival of the third bull.

Rafe owed his survival to the help of an unknown confederate. Some object sailed through the air and struck the bull on the shoulder. Thinking it was being attacked by an unseen assailant, the bull skidded to a halt and whirled to face its challenger. Despite the pain from his injured hip, Rafe got to his feet in time to see the first two bulls eyeing him from opposite sides.

Grabbing what might be his only chance to escape without further injury, he waved the shirt, hoping to incite them to attack before the third bull could refocus its attention on Rafe.

He got his wish. Both charged at the same time. Now the problem became how to move his injured body out of the way in time to keep from being crushed between the two animals. The few seconds it took the bulls to reach him felt like the oddest moments of his life. One instant the bulls were moving in slow motion, getting only a little bit closer, and the next they were charging toward him at an unnerving speed. Abandoning any attempt to control the collision, Rafe tossed his shirt into the air and staggered to one side.

He could feel the concussion of the air against his skin caused by the impact of more than a ton of flesh as the two bulls came together. The impact was so powerful, it snapped one horn off the first bull and sent it spiraling through the air. Both bulls slumped to the ground, dazed and unmoving.

Rafe didn't have time to congratulate himself on his success. Finding only thin air rather than an opponent, the third bull had refocused its attention. His shirt impaled on the second bull's horns, Rafe took up the only defensive position he had. He limped around to the far side of the fallen bulls and hoped the third wouldn't leap across their bodies.

The pounding of hooves behind him sent his hopes plummeting. He had no defense against a fourth bull. He might be able to pull his shirt off the second bull's horns, but that would only give him a short respite. When he turned, he was stunned to see Broc racing toward him astride one of the picador's horses. Limping toward his friend, Rafe caught Broc's outstretched hand when he brought his horse to a standstill and somehow managed to mount behind Broc.

"What took you so long?" Rafe asked. "I'm out of shirts."

Broc's chuckle was more a release of tension than amusement. "I'm sure it seemed like hours to you, but you weren't out there more than a few minutes."

Finally safe enough to stop worrying about the bulls, Rafe looked around to see a half dozen riders with spears enter the arena. Thick pads over their mounts' bodies protected them from possible attack.

"I don't think they'll be having any bullfights today," Broc said. "Two of those bulls aren't in any condition to fight. How did you get them to charge at the same time?"

"Pure luck." He put his arms around Broc and held on. He felt so weak, he was afraid he'd fall off.

One thought prevented him from feeling a complete sense of relief at having narrowly escaped death. Someone wanted him dead badly enough to risk releasing three bulls with hundreds of spectators watching. Having failed, would his enemy abandon subtlety and ambush him or attempt to kill him outright? The only person he could think of who would want him dead was Laveau.

The moment he emerged from the arena, people surrounded Rafe to congratulate him on his narrow escape, compliment him on his strategy, say what a strange accident it had been. Rafe wanted to get back to his hotel and take care of his wounded hip. He didn't think he'd suffered much more than broken skin, but it hurt like hell. Besides, he wasn't accustomed to appearing in public without a shirt. He felt naked.

"Rafe! Rafe!"

Turning in the direction of the voice, Rafe saw Luis and Maria making their way through the crowd. Dolores followed them closely with Laveau trailing at a distance.

"You didn't tell me you were going to fight the bulls," Luis exclaimed when he got within shouting distance.

"It wasn't planned," Rafe said.

"Who do you think arranged that?" Broc asked in a low voice. "Laveau?"

"I don't think so."

"He'd be happy to see us both dead. Maybe he's the one who shot me."

"Laveau is smart enough to have pulled off the release of the bulls, but he wouldn't have wanted it to look like an accident. He'd want the rest of the Night Riders to know he'd done it."

There wasn't time to say any more. Maria and Luis had reached them, bringing a doctor who ordered Rafe to accompany him to a tent where he would check his injury. Rafe would have refused, but he knew that would upset Maria.

"Is he badly injured?" Maria asked the doctor.

"I haven't had time to look yet," the doctor replied. "He still has his pants on."

Many of his fellow soldiers had been wounded during the war and suffered the indignity of having to undress or lie naked before strangers. Having to bare his butt with practically everyone he knew on the other side of a cloth partition was just about more than Rafe could handle.

"Can I come in with you?" Luis asked.

"No!" Rafe, Maria, and Dolores responded at the same time.

"Oh." It took Luis a moment to digest their refusal.

"Get those pants off," the doctor ordered. "I can't see through cloth."

"Maria said those bulls weren't supposed to be in the ring," Luis said to Rafe through the partition. "Did you ask for them?"

"No."

"Laveau said you were a very good bullfighter. I thought you must have done it a lot."

"The wound doesn't look too bad," the doctor said, "but it's going to hurt for a while."

"Laveau threw a rock at that bull. Mama said you owe him for saving your life. Mama said he's a hero."

Rafe locked glances with Broc, who had accompanied Rafe behind the partition.

"I refuse to be turned into anything so hackneyed as a hero," Laveau remarked in his languid style. "I won't pretend to be fond of you, but I would prefer to see you expire in a fair fight."

Laveau's comment sounded genuine. Rafe wondered who *had* arranged to have the bulls escape.

"I hope you'll change your mind about letting Luis stay with me," Dolores said.

"Don't bother him with that now," Laveau said. "The man has been injured."

Rafe would force himself to thank Laveau for distracting the bull...if he didn't choke on the words.

"I ought to put a dressing on the wound," the doctor said.

"I don't need one."

"If I don't, the wound will weep and soak through your clothes. After that it will dry and stick to your clothes. You won't be able to remove your pants without ripping off the scab."

"Dress it," Broc said. "I'll make him lie still. Remember what you said to me when the doc was trying to put my face back together?"

Rafe had forced Broc to let the doctors save what they could of his face. He'd changed the dressing himself, ignoring Broc's protests that all he wanted to do was die.

"Let the doctor dress the wound," said Maria. "You have to set a good example for Luis."

Resigned, Rafe nodded to the doctor. How had he ended up being the one to set a good example for Luis?

"As soon as the doctor is finished with you, we're going back to the hotel," Maria informed him. "I'll decide later whether you're up to going out for dinner. I don't want you to do too much and come down with a fever."

"Listen to the lady," the doctor said.

Broc chuckled. "I've been telling him that for days."

Rafe groaned inwardly. Everybody was trying to domesticate him, and he wasn't even married.

✧

The man stormed around the confines of the small room, raging at fate, which had decreed Rafe would escape still another trap set for him.

"Damn it to hell!" he shouted. "How can one person have that much luck! God must be watching over the bastard. He should have been dead several times over."

"Did you know he was a bullfighter?"

"Shut up, you fool! He's no bullfighter. He's just the luckiest son of a bitch I've ever seen." The man drove his balled-up fist into an open palm. "He can't escape me forever." He turned to the man still huddled in the corner. "You'd better make sure he doesn't get away the next time, or they'll find your body in a ditch."

⌇

"Laveau must have had something to do with it." Broc had repeated that comment so many times, Rafe had lost count.

"It doesn't make sense for him to have helped me if he was trying to kill me."

"There were two other bulls."

"Still."

"Then who else could it be?"

"I've been cudgeling my brain for the last several hours, and I can't come up with anyone who wants me dead except Dolores."

"How could those bulls have gotten out without anyone knowing?" Maria asked.

After being released by the doctor, Rafe had spent the remainder of the afternoon in his hotel room. He had insisted on going out to eat, but he'd been relieved to get back to the hotel. Maria had put Luis to bed, then come to join Rafe and Broc.

The hotel couldn't aspire to compete with establishments in San Francisco or even Sacramento, but the management offered several suites. Laveau had the largest, so Rafe was installed in a sitting room featuring red velvet drapes with gold tassels, a thick Turkish carpet, and chairs that showed more style than comfort. Marble-topped tables and paintings in gilded frames added to the feeling of opulence.

The sheriff had promised to look into how the bulls had got out, but everyone had been too busy watching Rafe's ride and applauding his success to pay attention to the bull pens.

"I don't have an answer to any of these questions," Rafe said, "and I'm tired of racking my brain looking for some. I'm going to put it out of my mind."

"It wasn't an accident." Broc sounded aghast.

"You haven't been here in ten years," Maria said. "How can anyone have such a grudge against you?"

"My point exactly," Broc said. "That makes it all the more obvious Laveau has to be behind the attack. I know," he said when Rafe started to interrupt, "but maybe he decided to help you because he saw you were going to get away and he wanted to be above suspicion. You have to admit he's just about the craftiest man we've ever known."

"I'll agree with anything negative you say about Laveau," Rafe told Broc, "but I'm certain he wasn't behind that attempt to kill me."

"I think you're wrong," Broc said, "and I'm going to prove it."

"How?"

Twenty

"I'M GOING TO MOVE INTO CÍBOLA, FOLLOW HIM wherever he goes, know everything he does, everyone he meets. Sooner or later, he'll make a mistake. When he does, I'll have him," Broc said.

"No one will believe you," Maria said. "Laveau is handsome, rich, and free-spending. Having my sister as a companion just makes his acceptance by the townspeople more complete."

"Do you think he's handsome?" Rafe had never given Laveau's looks any thought.

"He's a low-down, conniving skunk," Broc said.

Maria's eyes twinkled when she smiled. "You only have to watch women's expressions to know they think he's very handsome."

"What about you?" Broc asked.

Rafe seemed very interested in the answer.

"Let me put it this way: A snake is graceful and sinuous, but I can still dislike it because it's poisonous. A flower can be beautiful and still give off an unpleasant odor."

Rafe laughed. "Don't ever play chess with her."

Broc failed to see any humor in her response. "Laveau is an ugly snake who gives off a foul odor. I haven't forgotten the reason I came to California was to bring him to justice."

Rafe had been surprised to find Laveau had come to Cíbola rather than San Francisco, but not as surprised as when he learned Laveau had sent him the clipping from the Chicago newspaper. He was certain Laveau was hoping to find some way to benefit from Rafe's inheritance, but that was a far cry from planning his murder. How could Rafe's death benefit Laveau?

"Neither have I," Rafe replied, "but I don't see what we can do."

"We could kidnap him and take him back to Texas."

"Why do you want to take him back to Texas?" Maria asked.

"To hang him for what he did during the war."

Maria looked stunned. "Wouldn't that be murder?"

"Yes," Rafe admitted, "a stumbling block that has stymied us from the beginning. Being a traitor isn't a crime unless you betray the winning side. Laveau is careful never to end up on the losing side."

"He didn't even lose his share in the family ranch," Broc said in disgust. "His sister sends him his percentage of the profits each year."

"He ought to be thankful for his sister and her husband rather than hating them," Rafe said. "Cade has made the ranch very profitable. Laveau would have run it into the ground within five years."

"He couldn't have done that because he wouldn't have been able to drive out the squatters in the first place." Broc told Maria the story of their return to

Texas and the fight to regain control of both the di Viere and Wheeler ranches. "Laveau thanked Cade for getting back the family ranch by sneaking into his bedroom at night and trying to kill him."

"That's terrible!" Maria's look of horror appeared to appease some of Broc's anger.

"Now you understand why we are determined to find a way to bring him to justice."

"Unfortunately, as long as he stays in the United States and its territories, he's protected by the Army," Rafe explained.

"You've got to help me find a way to keep him away from Luis," Maria said. "No telling what he might do to the boy."

"I'd be just as worried about his mother's actions if I were you," Broc said.

"I know Dolores isn't a good mother, but she'd never do anything to hurt Luis."

Broc didn't look convinced, but Rafe agreed with Maria.

"I'd better check on Luis." Maria rose from her chair.

"He's not a baby," Broc reminded her. "Besides, he's just down the hall."

"I suppose I'll always feel protective. He's probably the closest I'll come to having a child of my own."

Rafe wondered how she meant that and whether he could change her mind.

~

"Are you sure you want to make these changes?" the lawyer asked Rafe.

"Why would I ask you to do this if I weren't sure?"

"Possibly because you want to get back to Texas so badly, you haven't thought of all the ramifications."

After the attack in the bullring, Rafe realized he had to make provisions for Luis in case something happened to him. If his wishes were not spelled out, Dolores might get control of Luis and the ranch. He could imagine the boy being dragged after her as she flitted from one man to another.

"My father had enough confidence in Maria to make her Luis's guardian."

"His *joint* guardian."

"I made it clear to my father that if he married Dolores, he'd never see me again. In essence, he left Maria in charge of Luis and you as overseer of the ranch. What I'm doing changes that very little."

Rafe had decided to make Maria sole guardian of Luis if anything should happen to him. He was also giving her control of the ranch until Luis reached his twenty-first birthday. If anything were to happen to Maria, the lawyer would assume her responsibilities until Luis came of age.

He had considered taking Luis to Texas with him, but the ranch was the boy's inheritance. He needed to grow up here, to become so familiar with the land and the people that they became an integral part of him. All Cade's ranch in Texas and Rancho los Alamitos had in common was lack of rainfall.

Rafe wasn't about to disclose to anyone that the biggest question in his mind centered around his feelings for Maria and her feelings for him.

"So you're sure you want Maria to have control of everything?" the lawyer asked.

"Do you see any problem with that?"

"Your father's widow might object."

"I have complete confidence that you and Maria can take care of everything."

"I'll draw up the papers. They should be ready for you to sign sometime next week."

Rafe rose. "Send a message to the ranch. I'll come into town as soon as I can."

He paused outside the lawyer's office to rest his hip. The pain was gone, but his muscles were still stiff and the scab would pull off if he wasn't careful. The last thing he wanted while walking through the center of Cíbola was to bleed through the seat of his pants.

He wondered what it was about Henry Fielder that made him wish his father had employed another lawyer. The man had been the family attorney for as long as he could remember—and one of his father's best friends. He'd never done anything to warrant this vague feeling of discomfort.

Rafe shook off the feeling. He didn't have to like the man any more than the man had to like him. All he asked was that Fielder do his job. That way Rafe could go back to Texas with a clear conscience.

Well, almost.

⤜⤜⤜

This was an unexpected shift, but maybe it was better. He would have been happier if Rafe were dead, but there was always a danger of being caught when you killed someone—or hired it to be done. If Rafe was determined never to return to California, he could focus on Maria. She would be easier to dispose of and fewer people would care. He would have no trouble handling Dolores Jerry. She was doing everything she could to ruin herself. With a little help, she would succeed quite nicely. Then there would be nothing to stand in his way but a helpless boy. Whether he lived or died would depend on the boy's cooperativeness.

His chuckle was mirthless. He would finally have the wealth and power he wanted. Never again would he have to be subservient, pretend Warren Jerry wasn't an old fool when he'd let himself be seduced by a tramp younger than his son. The folly of marrying her to give his bastard child a name was beyond his comprehension. Knowing that child would inherit vast wealth and a position of power and importance caused him almost physical pain.

He would soon have the wealth and position in society he deserved. And Warren would get the justice he deserved.

❧

Maria stared at herself in the mirror. She didn't think the strain had begun to show, but it probably wouldn't be long. She turned away from the mirror and cast aside her dressing gown. It was time to get on with the business of running the household. Rafe and Luis would be back from their ride soon, eager for breakfast. She wasn't hungry, but she always ate with them. She missed Broc. His presence had served to break the tension between her and Rafe. She wondered if he was still following Laveau. From the information he sent Rafe, he hadn't yet uncovered any suspicious behavior.

Maria stepped into her skirt and fastened it around her waist. Try as she might to avoid being alone with Rafe, they were alone more and more. That meant he kissed her more frequently, held her in his arms more often, touched her all the time. She tried not to admit it to herself, but her body longed for him to take their courtship one step further. In her dreams he often did. She kept telling herself she needed to put distance between them. His arrangements with the lawyer made it clear he expected her to remain in California while he went back to Texas, never to return. It behooved her to get her feelings under control. Actually, she ought to eliminate them entirely, but she'd given that up as impossible until Rafe left.

She wasn't sure she would be able to do it even then.

She had asked herself whether she'd go with Rafe if he asked, but she hadn't come up with a satisfactory answer. She'd want to go with him, but taking Luis to Texas wasn't a perfect solution. He couldn't learn how to manage his inheritance from Texas. Having the lawyer manage it for him wouldn't teach him what he needed to know.

She picked a shirtwaist and began to button it.

Her whole train of thought was pointless and a needless irritant. Rafe hadn't indicated that he wanted her to go to Texas with him.

A knock on the door interrupted her musings.

She did up the last button before calling, "Come in."

Rosana entered the bedroom. "You're late coming down. Are you feeling well?"

"I'm fine."

"You didn't ride this morning."

"I'm not really very fond of horses or riding. Luis is, and he's taken to wanting Rafe to gallop every time they go out."

Rosana's smile was bright enough to light the whole room. "That boy has blossomed since Rafe came home. You wouldn't know he's the same child."

One more thing to throw her world out of balance. What was she going to do about Luis when Rafe left? She loved the boy as much as any real mother could, but that wouldn't take the place of having a brother like Rafe.

"He certainly has changed," Maria agreed.

"He's just like Rafe when he was a boy." A tear appeared at the corner of Rosana's eye. "I wish Senor Warren had lived to see it."

Maria wasn't sure he would have cared. She believed he'd lost the will to live when he finally realized Rafe wasn't coming back.

Rosana sniffed and wiped away the tear. "I didn't come up to make you sad. Rafe and Luis are having breakfast. They were asking for you to join them. Rafe was particularly concerned that you might not be feeling well."

That wasn't unexpected since she'd pleaded a headache as an excuse not to be left alone in his company last night. "I'm feeling fine. I'm just a little tired."

"Festival always wears people out. And worrying about the attack on Rafe and his injury hasn't helped, I'm sure." She brightened. "I wouldn't be surprised if Rafe is responsible. With him and his friend stirring things up, we haven't had this much excitement around here in a long time."

"It was certainly quiet during Warren's illness. I'm afraid that caused Luis to be more reserved than he really is."

"It's not good for a boy to be that quiet. He ought to be full of high spirits at this age. He'll have enough responsibility to settle him down soon enough."

Maria didn't feel like discussing the future. It seemed too dreary. "I'd better get down to breakfast before they send someone else after me."

"More likely they'll eat everything up. I've never seen Luis with such an appetite."

"Rafe let me gallop from the stable to the mountains," Luis announced as soon as Maria entered the breakfast room. "He says I'll win the pony race next time. He says I'll need another pony. I'll be too big for this one."

And who was going to buy that pony? Neither she nor Dolores knew anything about horses or ponies. As far as she knew, the lawyer didn't, either.

"Broc says I'm going to be big like Rafe." Luis paused. "Why did Broc move to town? I wish he was here."

"I'm sure we all miss him." Maria busied herself pouring coffee. "He was always lively company."

"Rafe says it's because Broc tells such big whoppers. Whoppers are things Broc makes up that aren't true," Luis explained.

Now the boy was talking like his brother. Didn't the man have any notion of what his leaving would do to Luis? What Rafe was doing for his brother was wonderful, but every increase in confidence, every new skill, even the silly stories made Rafe that much more important to Luis. He was going to be devastated.

"I'm not sure I approve of telling whoppers." Maria looked directly at Rafe. "It can lead people to hope for things that will never happen."

"It's okay if I don't get to be as big as Rafe. I'll still be taller than Broc."

That wasn't what she'd meant, but she couldn't explain to Luis.

"Now that Luis has given me a chance to get a word in edgewise"—Rafe gave Luis a playful punch—"is your headache better? Did you sleep well?"

"Yes to both questions." Maria had a feeling she was getting the beginnings of a real headache. "I was just slow coming down because I was being very lazy."

"Rosana said you never stay in bed late," Luis said. "She was worried you might be sick."

"I'm not, so everyone can stop worrying."

Luis swallowed the last of his breakfast and jumped up from his chair. "Rafe said if I finished all my studies this morning, he'd take me with him and Miguel this afternoon. Rafe says the ranch is going to be mine when I grow up so I have to know every corner of it."

"Your father's will gave half of the ranch to each of you," Maria pointed out. "You will actually share it with Rafe."

Luis's smile was radiant. "That's even better. Then I can ride with you forever."

After Luis had left the room, Maria said, "I didn't mean to make him think you'd be here forever."

"Do you really think I don't mean to give my portion of the ranch to Luis?"

"Luis won't reach his majority for twelve years. A lot can change in that time."

"True. I'll see the lawyer about making the transfer official."

"Don't!"

Rafe seemed startled at the vehemence of her words. "Why do you care what I do with my part of the ranch?"

"It was your father's will that you and Luis share it."

"A will is just a piece of paper. It's not the same as spoken words."

Maria had wondered how Rafe felt about not getting a chance to speak to his father before he died. She supposed the hurt of their separation was so great in the beginning he didn't want to see his father again, but would Rafe have come home if he'd known his father was dying?

"Your father still loved you when he died. He kept everything in your room the way it was the day you left. He kept your picture by his bedside. He would never speak to me of the sadness that was in his heart, but I could see it in his eyes. I saw him every day during those last years. I didn't need words to know he still loved you, missed you, wished you would come home."

"Then why didn't he write me?"

Was there a suspicious catch in his voice?

"Part of the reason was the same pride that kept you from writing him, not even to let him know you were still alive. Part was not knowing where to write. I expect he wasn't sure how to undo the mistake he'd made or unsay the words that had passed between you. I'm sure he feared you wouldn't come back even if he did write."

"We'll never know what he wanted, will we?"

"At least now I've told you what I saw. It's up to you to decide whether you think I'm right." She rose from the table.

"Don't go." Rafe had got to his feet, moved between her and the door.

"I have work to do."

"There's nothing that can't wait a few more minutes."

He moved closer and reached out to take her hand. She wanted to pull away, but her muscles wouldn't obey her command. Instead her fingers tightened around his until they gripped him as firmly as he gripped her.

"You can't stop trying to take care of people, can you?" he said.

"I haven't done anything someone else wouldn't have done."

"What about Dolores?"

"That's an unfair comparison," she replied.

"Not really, because you've done the things she should have done: raised her son, taken care of her husband, managed the household. You did all of that and took care of her as well."

"She gave me a home."

"She issued the invitation—out of her own selfishness, I might point out—but my father gave you a home. I'm talking about the care you put into your work, the love you have for people. You seem to have no idea how rare that is."

Maria didn't feel that she'd done anything rare or special. Anyone would have loved Luis. Warren had been more difficult to get to know, but he'd ultimately given her his complete trust, had depended on her when he got sick. It was only natural that she would care for her own sister. "I just did what needed to be done." That didn't sound like an adequate answer, but the way he was looking at her had shaken her to the core.

It was the way she'd always expected a man to look at the woman he loved.

"You did what your heart told you to do," Rafe said, "not what your mind told you was necessary."

"My heart and mind were in total agreement. How could I take care of Luis and not love him? How could I—"

She had no warning, no intimation, that Rafe intended to take her in his arms and smother her with a kiss that took her breath away. This sort of thing didn't happen in the morning, and it didn't happen in a breakfast room. Not in the civilized house of one of the richest men in California.

She'd told herself she didn't want Rafe to hold her or kiss her, that it would only make things worse when he left, but she couldn't stop herself.

Rafe was not a man to display his emotions. Knowing that made every kiss, every embrace, make her feel loved in a way that the attentions of other men never could. He hadn't wanted to like her or trust her, but his feelings for her had overridden all obstacles.

Knowing that, she wrapped her arms around his neck and kissed him back, giving free rein to the desire she had held back for so long. She felt overwhelmed by her need for him, her desire to be as close to him as possible. The feel of his arms around her rendered all her objections unimportant. If there were consequences— and there would be—she would deal with them later.

She couldn't find the words to explain how wonderful it felt to be close to him. It wasn't just that he made her feel safe. Or that he made her feel wanted and attractive. It was that being in his arms, having her arms around him, satisfied some unnamed need that lived deep inside her. Holding him tight, being held tight, felt so good, she needed more. Yet despite the yearning that came from every part of her body, it was a quiet need, a peaceful need, a restorative need.

There was nothing quiet or peaceful about Rafe's kisses. They were hungry, rough, demanding—and life-giving. They bruised her lips while they nourished her soul. They sapped her strength at the same time they unleashed a barely contained flood of energy within her. They threatened to obliterate her yet held out the possibility of happiness beyond all reasonable expectation. They overwhelmed her while redefining her more clearly than ever before. They threatened to absorb her yet whispered she had the power of life or death over him.

She let herself be swept away by the joy of being in the arms of a man who inspired the kind of love she'd always dreamed of. She wanted to wrap herself in the feeling until it became the air she breathed. She wanted it to seep into her bones and sinews until she felt formed, shaped, and defined by it. She wanted to—

The opening of the breakfast room door and the sound of heels on the wood floor destroyed the cocoon that had enveloped her. She and Rafe broke apart, turned to find Rosana had entered the room.

"They just brought Miguel up to the house." Tears streaked her cheeks. Her voice shook so badly it was difficult to understand her words. "They think he has a broken neck."

Twenty-one

"HAVE YOU CALLED A DOCTOR?"

"Juan sent one of the stable boys." Rosana led them from the ranch house toward the bungalow Miguel occupied.

"What happened?"

Rosana shook her head. "Nobody knows. A worker found him on one of the plantations farthest from here. He was lying in the middle of the lane. He must have fallen from his horse."

"Did the horse go lame or stumble?"

"They don't know. The horse was gone."

Rafe didn't understand that. All the saddle horses on the ranch were trained to stand when ground hitched and to stay near a fallen rider. Left on foot, an injured man could die.

Rafe steadied Maria as they practically ran down the stairs, out the door, and across the courtyard. Miguel had been a second father to him, teaching him to love the land, to know the people who worked for him, to understand how to make plants and animals grow and thrive. His father had trained him to be a businessman. Miguel had taught him what it meant to be a farmer.

Rafe's first glance at Miguel when he entered the man's bedroom was reassuring. His neck wasn't at an angle that would indicate it was broken. A second glance showed him Miguel was breathing, but he appeared to be unconscious. "Does he have any broken limbs?"

"I don't think so," Rosana said, "but I was too upset to check. Besides, I couldn't…I don't think…I decided it was better to tell you right away."

Rafe interpreted that to mean Rosana was uncomfortable touching Miguel's body. Rafe felt the same. He was a man everyone looked up to, respected, who held a position of authority on the ranch.

It was easy to confirm that his legs were okay. His arms looked fine as well, but Rafe was worried about internal injuries. "I'm going to undress him."

"Do you think you should?" Rosana asked.

"He'll have to be undressed before the doctor can examine him. Then he will need to be dressed for bed."

"I can help," Maria volunteered.

"I appreciate your offering, but Juan and I can do what needs to be done. You can be responsible for nursing him."

"I'll sit with him tonight," Rosana offered. "Somebody has to see that we're all fed and Miguel's medicines are prepared properly," she said when Maria started to protest. "With Miguel in bed, you'll have to take over running the ranch," she said to Rafe.

Rafe didn't feel like arguing with Rosana. "As soon

as the doctor has seen Miguel, I want him taken up to the main house so I can keep a close eye on him."

"I'll see that a room is prepared for him," Maria said. "Are you sure there's nothing I can do here?"

"Not until the doctor arrives. Rosana, tell the stable hands I want to know the minute they find Miguel's horse. In the meantime, send Juan to me."

Left alone with his overseer, Rafe began to undress him, taking care to handle his body as little as possible in case there were any internal injuries. He had undressed Miguel and covered him by the time the doctor arrived.

Juan still hadn't appeared.

"What happened?" the doctor asked as soon as he looked at Miguel.

"We're not sure. He was found lying in one of the farm lanes."

"He's getting up in years." The doctor ran his hands over Miguel's limbs. "There are a dozen reasons why he could have been unseated."

"There are none I can think of," Rafe said. "Miguel is an excellent horseman, and his horse is mature and well trained. They've been together for over fifteen years."

"Accidents happen to the most experienced riders regardless of what horse they're riding." The doctor checked Miguel's ribs, applied gentle pressure to several places in his abdomen. Apparently finding nothing to worry him, he gently rotated Miguel's head, then checked his eyes. "It's not a broken neck. From the bruising, I'm guessing he landed on his head. I'll know more about his spine when he wakes up. In the meantime, keep him warm and comfortable. Who's going to take care of him?"

"Go up to the house and ask for Maria."

The doctor smiled. "Miguel couldn't be in better hands. Maria took care of your father during his long illness. I've never seen anyone do a better job."

Rafe didn't like being reminded that Maria had been responsible for his father while he knew nothing of his illness.

Juan appeared as the doctor was leaving.

"Where have you been?" Rafe asked.

"I was helping some of the stable hands catch Miguel's horse. It knows all the forgotten paths and hiding places on the ranch better than we do. It took us almost an hour to corner it."

"What could have made it so skittish? Miguel hasn't said anything about cougar attacks."

"It wasn't a cougar or any other animal. We found a three-inch dart buried in his hindquarters."

"Why would anyone attack Miguel? He doesn't have an enemy in the world."

"It doesn't make any more sense than the other attacks."

Rafe had tended to think of the attacks as being unconnected, but now he wasn't sure, especially since he'd decided he had to include the collapse of the gazebo in the list. Who could have been the intended target? Maria, Dolores, Luis? Anyone could have been hurt by the damaged structure. He'd assumed the attack on Broc had been meant for him. He was obviously the intended victim in the bullring, but how could he explain the attack on Miguel?

Were all four incidents connected? If so, what was the purpose of attacking so many people in ways that might not kill them?

"What are you going to do?" Juan asked.

"Take Miguel up to the house and make him as comfortable as possible."

"I mean about the attacks," Juan said.

"I don't know how I can do anything until I figure out who's behind them and what the person is trying to achieve. It would have been easier to understand if all the incidents had happened since I arrived, but the gazebo must have been weakened earlier."

"Do you think that was planned?"

"Yes. Someone is out to cause trouble, but the sabotage seems to be aimed at the ranch rather than any one person."

"Do you think they're trying to drive you out?"

"Why? I've told everyone I'm going back to Texas."

"With you in Texas and Miguel out of commission, Maria would be left in complete control."

Rafe controlled the surge of anger. "Are you implying that Maria could have anything to do with these attacks?"

"No," Juan hastened to say. "I was just thinking that Dolores might think she'd have a better chance of moving back with you and Miguel gone."

Rafe could well believe Dolores would use her beauty to persuade some idealistic drunk she was a helpless female in need of his assistance, but he didn't think she was capable of planning the attack on Miguel or of finding someone to execute it.

"Let's get Miguel moved to the house. I need to talk to Broc."

"He doesn't strike me as a man who's likely to miss much."

Rafe would have said that about himself until these attacks started. Now it was obvious he had missed something important. At the very least, he had failed to see something in its proper context. There had to be a thread that connected the attacks, that explained the reason for all of them, but he couldn't see it. Nothing could explain the attack on Broc unless the killer had mistaken Broc for him. Still, what could the killer be trying to achieve? Even if Rafe were dead, the ranch would be managed by the lawyer and held in trust for Luis. No matter how he viewed what had happened, he couldn't put all four of the attacks in the same frame. He had failed to see a clue, had missed some piece of information that would tie everything together. Maybe Maria would know.

❧

"How is Miguel doing?" Rafe asked Maria.

"He was able to sit up to eat dinner." Maria shook her head at the memory. "He would have eaten a better dinner if he hadn't been worried about forcing you to do his work."

Maria had tried to convince Miguel that Rafe enjoyed the work, was good at it, that he should have been doing it. After a lifetime of selfless service, no one, least of all Rafe, would begrudge Miguel the time to rest and recover.

"Did he try to convince you he was well enough to get out of bed?"

"Three times."

They were in a room Maria had rarely entered—Rafe's mother's sitting room. Rafe preferred its sunny location and floral patterns to the heavy darkness of his father's office. He had encouraged Maria to make it her office rather than use a cramped corner in her bedroom. Luis had gone to bed. With Dolores and Broc in Cíbola, she and Rafe were alone each evening. It was a situation Maria knew she should avoid, but she'd given up trying.

"Do your best to convince him to stay in bed for two or three more days."

"I've done my best, but he insists he feels fine. He wants to be in the saddle tomorrow."

"Tell him that's impossible. I've given orders to everyone in that stable not to allow him near a horse. If he insists, they're to call me immediately."

Maria indulged in an inward sigh. Rafe had taken over management of the ranch as though he hadn't been away for ten years. The job fit him so naturally, she couldn't understand why he would ever want to return to Texas. Even if his sense of responsibility hadn't made him want to stay, his obvious enjoyment of the work should have. Yet he was going back to Texas because there was nothing in California he wanted, nobody he liked enough to stay.

And that included her.

The knowledge hurt, yet she had no one but herself to blame. He'd never made a secret of his plans. Though he was affectionate to her, he'd never promised anything more than some shared kisses. In fact, he'd admitted his lack of experience made it difficult to know the exact nature of his feelings, to know if he could learn to trust again. She wouldn't have minded the experimentation if she could have benefitted from it, but she didn't like being used to benefit some unknown Texas female in the future.

"What did you want to talk to me about?" she asked. "I ought to be sitting with Miguel."

"Rosana and Margarita can do that."

"Do you think they can take better care of him than I can?"

Rafe moved to the chair next to her, sat down, and took her hand in his. She wanted to pull back, to tell him to save his attentions for that woman in his future, but she couldn't.

"There's nobody on this ranch who can do anything better than you. That's what I wanted to talk to you about."

Maria's heart suddenly beat faster. What was Rafe going to say? Surely it would be about his staying in California. A man didn't say that kind of thing about a woman unless he was serious about her, did he? He wouldn't be holding her hand if he didn't want her to be part of his future. Nor would he be looking at her in a way that caused her heart to skip beats unless he felt about her the way she felt about him. She hadn't expected him to change his mind about going back to Texas, but perhaps Miguel's injury had caused him to rethink his decision. The ranch needed him. She didn't like coming in second to the ranch, possibly even third behind Luis, but only a fool would allow pride to get in the way of happiness. She'd waited too long to make that mistake. She gave Rafe's hand a squeeze. "What did you want to say?"

"Miguel would have been forced to retire soon even if he hadn't been injured. There's no one who knows this ranch better than you. No one I'd rather entrust it to. I want you to take over its management."

Maria was unable to speak. She was pleased Rafe thought so much of her abilities that he'd entrust the future of the ranch to her, but that in no way compensated for the almost unbearable sense of disappointment she felt. Her hopes had been crushed. Her future looked too bleak to be endured.

"You're probably trying to think of a way to tell me you can't handle such a job, but I know you can. You're the most capable woman I've ever met."

Then why didn't he love her? Was his love reserved for women like Dolores, women who were beautiful but incapable of taking care of themselves, much less anyone else? She couldn't pretend to be helpless. She didn't know how. Would that condemn her to spinsterhood for the rest of her life? It wasn't fair, but she already knew life wasn't fair. Not even to Dolores.

"Naturally you'll want to hire help," Rafe continued, "someone to do the kind of supervision you won't have time for. You can hire as many people as you want."

She had to stop sitting like a statue. She was sure her expression was so dazed, Rafe must be wondering if she was listening to anything he said. Maybe he was already regretting his decision. Maybe he would change his mind and let the lawyer make all the decisions.

"You don't have to worry about taking on all of

Miguel's responsibilities at once," Rafe assured her. "I'll ease you into the job."

"I can't do that," Maria said, finally managing to find her voice.

"It'll take you a while to become familiar with everything, but in a month or two, you should have everything under control."

If she couldn't control her heart, how could she tackle anything as vast and complex as this ranch? "That's not what I meant," she said. "I *can* do it. It would take more than a month or two, but I could learn."

Rafe gave her hand a reassuring squeeze. "Of course you could."

Maria snatched her hand from his grasp. "Stop talking to me like I'm a child. I've never considered taking on responsibility for the ranch, but I have no doubt I could handle it."

"Then what's the—?"

"Will you stop interrupting and let me finish!" He'd interrupted only once, but she was in no condition to be fair. She was fighting to keep from bursting into tears. She longed to lock herself in her room and not come out until she'd cried out the heartache and disappointment that was choking her.

"I won't speak again until you tell me what's wrong."

She wasn't sure whether he was hurt, angry, or simply tolerating her mood, but she didn't have the emotional energy to care right now. "I didn't mean to raise my voice, but my nerves are on edge."

He nodded but didn't speak.

"If something like this can upset me so badly, perhaps I'm not the best person to take on Miguel's responsibilities. Maybe you ought to put everything in the lawyer's hands."

He shook his head but didn't speak.

"There are several reasons why I'm not the right person for this job. My lack of experience is an obvious one."

He made no comment.

"Even if I could learn what to grow and when, how to balance produce against demand, and where to find the best markets, there's a real question about how the men would react to being told what to do by a woman. That runs counter to Spanish culture. As far as I've been able to tell, it's the same for Anglos."

She waited for him to speak, but he didn't.

"I don't feel I can give proper attention to Luis's education, manage the house, and oversee the running of the ranch at the same time. That's a job for at least two people. Say something," she said when he still didn't speak.

"I understand your concerns, but I think you can do it all."

"What if I don't *want* to do it?" She had to calm down. She was beginning to sound hysterical. Though hysteria might convince him she wasn't the right person to manage the ranch, it would also convince him she wasn't the right person to fall in love with. "I'm flattered you think I can take on so much responsibility, but I don't want it."

"Why not? You would be in a position to make all of your own decisions."

Why couldn't Rafe understand that being in a position of absolute power wasn't something she wanted?

She didn't want control over other people's lives, especially not when she didn't feel she had control over her own.

"What?"

"Rancho los Alamitos is your home and your inheritance. The obvious solution, the *right* solution, is for you to stay in California and step into your father's shoes."

Twenty-two

RAFE DIDN'T WANT TO HEAR HER SOLUTION. HE didn't even want to think about it. "You know I'm going back to Texas. I told you that from the beginning."

"I know what you said, and I understand why you said it, but the situation has changed. If you hadn't come back, all of us could have gone on as we were. Now that's impossible."

He hadn't wanted to return. He'd resisted when Pilar had insisted it was his responsibility. He'd agreed only when it appeared Laveau was headed to California, and Cade and the others had asked him to follow the traitor. He owed it to the members of his troop, especially those who had died, to do everything he could to bring Laveau to justice.

"I didn't come back to change anything here."

"Maybe not, but you have. Now it's your responsibility to make sure the changes are good ones."

How could he possibly do anything good? He hadn't forgiven his father or himself for being absent when his father died. Would he have come back if he had known? He'd been so filled with anger and bitterness it was hard to say.

"What are these changes?"

"The most important is Luis."

"He has you. He doesn't need me."

"He needs a brother, someone to look up to, a man he can learn from, model himself after."

"There are plenty of other men, better men to model himself after."

"None of them is a brother he adores and thinks can do no wrong."

"I'm only his half brother." He knew he was quibbling, but he didn't want to be drawn into a family relationship. That would lead to too many opportunities for hurt. Between the war and his family, he'd had enough hurt for a lifetime.

"That isn't the only reason I think you should stay," Maria said. "This is your home. You love this place, and the people love you."

"They have Miguel."

"He's really no different from them; he is someone hired to do a job. You're the owner, the one who has given them a home and a good life."

"My father did that."

"You're an extension of your father."

He rebelled at that thought yet was comforted by it. How was it possible to have two such opposite reactions to one man?

If Dolores had never entered his life, Rafe would have said his father was a man of integrity and concern for others, a faithful husband and a loving father, a successful businessman and a genuine humanitarian. He would have remembered only how much fun it was to work alongside his father, how happy and proud he was when his father praised him for doing a good job.

Yet one woman had changed all that and destroyed two lives in the process.

"You may not want to hear it," Maria continued, "but you are your father's son. That's how people here think of you."

He wasn't sure how he felt about that revelation. Nothing could break the physical link between Rafe and his father, but had the emotional bond been severed? No. Weakened, yes. Nearly cut, but at least one thread remained.

"Even if you do go back to Texas, you can't leave any time soon," Maria said. "Miguel can't get back in the saddle for weeks, maybe even longer. Someone has to oversee the day-to-day operation of the ranch. Even if I had agreed to accept your offer, someone would have had to teach me everything I needed to know about its management. That will take months."

"I'll stay until you feel you can handle everything by yourself," Rafe said.

"I still think you ought to put the ranch in the hands of your lawyer."

"He'd probably jump at the chance, but he would see it only as a job. I want someone who will see Rancho los Alamitos as a community of people, and running it as a commitment to Luis's future. You would do that. You couldn't do anything else."

"Yes, but you would do it so much better."

He wasn't sure, but it looked as if he was going to have a chance to find out.

"I haven't found a single piece of evidence to tie Laveau to the attempt to kill you," Broc said to Rafe, disgust evident in his expression and his voice. "He doesn't seem to care about anything but being seen with Dolores on his arm. He's forgotten we're here to bring him to justice."

"He hasn't forgotten," Rafe said. "He just knows there's not much we can do without getting into trouble ourselves."

"How are we supposed to catch him? It looks like we're wasting our time." Broc suddenly grinned. "The only fun I've had is seeing Dolores's expression when she catches sight of my face."

Rafe had come into Cíbola on business. He and Broc were having lunch in a little restaurant away from the center of town. It was quiet and offered some privacy. It was Rafe's intention to talk Broc into returning to the ranch. The attack on Miguel had convinced him Broc was wasting his time following Laveau.

"Have you heard anything else that might have some bearing on the attacks?" Rafe asked.

"Not really. There's one man named Anderson who hates your father, but nobody pays him any attention. He's drunk half the time."

That could explain the ineffectiveness of the attacks, but not their randomness. Besides, his father was dead, and Rafe didn't know anybody named Anderson. "This isn't the work of some dissatisfied worker. It's got to be somebody who thinks he has something to gain."

"Something really big to risk murder. Something like your whole ranch."

"Which is impossible. Even if they get rid of me, everything goes to Luis."

"What if they get rid of Luis?"

"Without a will, everything would go to the state."

"So they're not trying to get rid of Luis, only you."

"Don't forget Miguel, Maria, and you."

"No one is likely to be killed by falling from a horse or having a gazebo collapse on them. Being in the ring with three bulls is different. Besides, the shooter probably mistook me for you. Why would anybody have a reason to shoot me? I've never been in California before."

Rafe didn't know, but an idea was beginning to form in the back of his mind. It was like watching a group of seemingly random facts orbiting around a central core he couldn't see.

"I don't know who's doing this or why, but there has to be a reason. In the meantime, I want you to come back to the ranch. I'm tired of Luis asking when you'll return. He misses your stories."

Broc laughed. "You mean my tall tales, don't you?"

"He misses *you*. I'm such a dull, sober stick, I need your foolishness as a counterweight."

"I never expected to hear you say you needed anybody, especially not someone like me."

"Well, it is something of an embarrassment, but I can't deny you're more entertaining than I am."

They finished their lunch and left the restaurant. "Are you enjoying running things again?" Broc asked.

"Yes," Rafe admitted.

"Will you stay?"

"I'm trying to talk Maria into taking over, but she thinks I ought to stay."

"Do you agree with her?"

"I don't know."

"You used to love this place," Broc reminded him. "Maybe you can love it again."

Maybe, but there were too many painful memories attached to Rancho los Alamitos. It was easier to go back to Texas than to tackle so many ghosts.

❦

Rafe didn't want to admit it, but he was happier than he'd thought he ever could be again. During the last two weeks he'd spent most of his days in the saddle reacquainting himself with every part of the ranch, with all the crops and projects that were under way, with all the people who made the whole operation run smoothly. He loved being in the saddle at dawn. He loved watching the gradual maturing of a field of corn or the birth of a new crop of calves. He enjoyed his relationship with the people who lived and worked on the ranch. It was a feeling that they were joined together to create something really special and make all their lives better.

He had enjoyed working for Cade, but here he was the leader. Everyone looked to him to make the decisions that would determine their futures. He'd said he didn't want that responsibility, that he wanted to forget his job the minute he got out of the saddle, but he was discovering that wasn't true. He enjoyed discussing ideas with the workers. He got real pleasure from seeing their happiness when he accepted one of their ideas. He enjoyed long evenings talking with Miguel about the current problems, about plans for the future. The more he learned, the more he wanted to know. The more he knew, the more ideas he had. He looked forward to each day.

Luis was responsible for part of that. He wouldn't allow Luis to neglect his school work, but the boy rode with him every day. His curiosity was boundless and his enthusiasm infectious. He was as interested in the people as he was in the crops. He was beginning to develop friendships with boys his own age and be a spoiled visitor at their homes. The only worrisome element was his unceasing begging for a bigger pony, for a real horse.

But the most important part of Rafe's happiness was his relationship with Maria. He didn't want to admit it, but he might be falling in love. He couldn't understand how he had ever felt he was so hopelessly in love with Dolores. What he felt for Maria was stronger and different. There was nothing desperate about it, yet his feelings were so powerful that they were changing him in ways nothing in the last ten years had done.

Dolores didn't irritate him so much any longer. The stories that reached him from Cíbola caused him to shrug rather than fall into a rage. He could ignore her attempts to disparage his character or to convince people he was an unfit custodian for Luis. Most important, thinking of her betrayal no longer had the power to invade his dreams and keep him awake. Maria was slowly turning Dolores into a fading memory.

His attitude toward his father was also changing. Listening to Miguel and Maria had painted a picture of a man who had paid dearly for his mistake. Rafe would never know whether pride had kept his father from trying to find him or whether it was fear Rafe would refuse to return. It had taken Rafe a long time to realize it, but the love they had shared was strong enough to have overcome the bitterness of their separation. For the first time, he was able to remember the good times, to balance them against the betrayal. Much to his surprise the good times came out on top.

But Maria herself had brought about the greatest change because she had enabled him to feel love again. And to accept it. He had stripped Dolores's room of its furniture and turned it into an office where he consulted with Miguel during the day and with Maria after Luis had gone to bed. He preferred it to the rooms downstairs because it offered privacy, which allowed him to hug and kiss Maria without fear of anyone walking in on them. This had become his favorite room and this his favorite part of the day.

It was impossible not to compare his reaction to the two sisters. Dolores's beauty had so overwhelmed him, he couldn't see anything else. He worshipped the sight of her. His youth and innocence had endowed her with virtues that lived only in his mind. In retrospect he realized he had fallen in love with a creature of his imagination.

Not so with Maria. Her innate goodness had attracted him from the beginning. Even her blind allegiance to Dolores took on positive attributes in his mind. She didn't always agree with him, but she always believed in him.

Then there was the fact that she liked being hugged and kissed as much as he liked hugging and kissing her. There were times when Rafe felt their backlog of emotion might overwhelm them, obliterate all vestiges of common sense. There had been times when he hoped it would.

He was released from the tyranny of his thoughts when Maria entered the office. He kissed her before she could utter a word.

Maria's eyes gleamed with amusement. "I don't think Miguel would consider that a proper prelude to a business discussion."

"He would if he were thirty years younger and had found someone like you."

Rafe slipped his arms around her waist and pulled her close. He enjoyed few things as much as the way she seemed to melt into his embrace. He loved the way she came willingly, with no reluctance or pretense, no need to be persuaded. She never asked for more than he was willing to give, never tried to keep him at arm's length. She allowed him to set the parameters of their relationship. He'd never imagined a woman could be like this. Maria slipped her arms around his neck and looked up at him.

"I don't think Miguel would agree to meet a woman behind closed doors. He's much too proper for that."

"Thank goodness my father was an Anglo who didn't saddle me with the Spanish tradition of extreme formality. Think of how much we'd miss."

Rafe worried about how much *he'd* missed because of his bitterness over Dolores. If he had lived like a normal man, he wouldn't have come to Maria as a man who'd never been with a woman. He wasn't sure he knew how to take their relationship beyond the kissing and holding stage without doing something that would hurt or upset her. Having no carnal experience with women, he didn't know how important that would be to a relationship between a man and a woman. He grew up being told a woman tolerated a man's attentions for the sake of her husband's needs and for children.

Every male knew the basics of how to handle a relationship with a woman, but Rafe wasn't so stupid that he thought it was all about physical gratification. A woman needed to feel wanted, needed, appreciated, not that she was being used simply as the object of a man's desire. He had listened to enough youthful confessions from young soldiers missing their wives or the girls they were courting to know there were more ways to get it wrong than there were to get it right.

"I didn't feel I'd missed anything really important until I met you," Maria told him. "You're not like anyone I've ever known."

"For a long time I was so angry and bitter, I didn't want to risk caring about anyone. Every time I listened to a man talk about his troubles with his wife or his young woman, I congratulated myself on being smart enough to cut myself off from feeling. If my father hadn't died, I might never have known things could be different for me."

He kissed Maria. It wasn't the same as kissing Dolores. His feelings for Dolores were hot and desperate and impatient. He couldn't think of anything else, didn't *want* to think of anything else. His world gradually closed out everything around him until it focused so tightly on one person he felt there was no one else in the universe. He bounced between excessive highs and lows until he felt he was about to explode.

When he learned of Dolores's betrayal, he did.

His feelings for Maria were warm and comforting with no swings, just a steady glow that was gradually changing his pain and bitterness into a withering memory that no longer had the power to leach all the joy from his life. The nourishing warmth of Luis's happiness and Maria's goodness were slowly banishing the dark shadows that had hung over him for years. Whenever they threatened to reassert their hold, all he had to do was look at Maria, touch her hand, receive the gift of her smile. Whenever something caused him to remember his father's dishonorable conduct, he reminded himself that having Luis for a brother went a long way toward balancing out that betrayal.

Maria pulled back from his kiss, eyed him with a questioning smile. "You seem more intense today. If you hold me any tighter, I'll end up with bruised ribs."

"Sorry." Rafe loosened his hold. "There are times when I feel that by holding on to you I can see life more clearly."

Maria seemed surprised. "How? I've made mistakes of my own."

Rafe brushed her cheek with the backs of his fingers. "Trying to see the best in your sister wasn't a mistake because you didn't let it harm Luis or my father."

"I wasn't talking about just that."

Rafe kissed her on the end of her nose. "Rosana, Juan, and Miguel have nothing but praise for you. Luis loves you dearly, and you conquered Broc the first night."

Maria laid her head on his shoulder. "You weren't so ready to be conquered." She raised her head and looked into his eyes. "And I don't presume that I've conquered you yet."

"You conquered my fear of opening myself to the possibility of love."

"I think Luis is responsible for that more than I am."

"What I feel for Luis isn't the same as what I feel for you."

Maria lowered her gaze. "I don't know your feelings for me because we don't talk about them. I don't even know what your feelings for Luis are. Sometimes I think you see him as a toy to play with as long as you are here. You like to do things for him—buy him a pony and give him freedoms beyond what I've allowed him, but it's hard to believe you love him as a brother when you intend to go back to Texas and never see him again."

"Luis's future is here. I would be doing him a great disservice if I took him to Texas with me."

"Why don't you ask him what *he* wants? He might not care for this ranch any more than you do."

Rafe let his hold slip from around Maria to take her hands in his. "It's not that I don't care for this ranch, but it's not my home any longer. Why would I want the responsibility for anything as large as this ranch?"

"Because it was a home you used to love. Because there are many people who depend on this ranch, and no one can do a better job of making it successful than you."

Releasing her right hand, Rafe used his free hand to bring her gaze back to him. "I'm not doing this only because it's what I want. I'm doing it because I think it's right."

"Maybe for you, but what if it's not right for anyone else?"

"What do you mean?"

"Luis will be heartbroken when you leave. No matter what explanation you or I offer, he'll think you left because you like being with your friends in Texas more than being with him."

"Is that how you feel?"

Maria broke away and walked a few steps before turning to face Rafe. "I don't know what you think or feel about me. We spend hours together, but I don't know if you're interested in more than friendship or whether I'm just a woman to fill in for someone back in Texas."

"There's no one back in Texas."

"So what does that make me? I feel like the pony you bought for Luis, like you're using me to relearn how to be in a relationship before moving on to someone who will really matter."

Rafe wasn't any good at expressing his feelings—he didn't even know what they were half of the time— but he suddenly realized one thing: He was in love with Maria. He probably had been in love with her for days, maybe even weeks. Broc had seen it. Why hadn't he? How could he have planned on going back to Texas without knowing he wanted to take her with him, without knowing he couldn't leave her behind? How could he have made such a monumental mess of things? He crossed the distance between them, took Maria's hands in his grasp again.

"I've never thought of you as a substitute for anyone. You're the most remarkable woman I've ever known. There's no limit to your kindness, your willingness to give of your time. You never think of yourself, only of others, even when they're unworthy and ungrateful. You have boundless energy and never back down from a challenge. You have so much tolerance and patience, you make me feel like I have no right to any of your time or affection. You've bent over backward to put up with me and my bad moods. You never complain about the changes I've made even when they've made your work harder."

Maria's laugh was nervous and shaky. "Are you sure you haven't mistaken me for someone else? Not even Luis thinks that much of me."

"That would be impossible. There *is* no one else like you. I can't believe I was so fortunate to find you."

Maria swallowed twice. "I need to know what you're going to do about all these wonderful qualities."

Rafe decided he'd have to spend a lot of time studying how Cade related to his wife when he got back to Texas. It was hard to believe Maria had no idea he was in love with her. "Don't you understand? I thought you knew."

"Knew what?"

"That I want to marry you. I want you to go back to Texas with me."

Twenty-three

MARIA WAS JUST AS INEXPERIENCED IN MATTERS OF the heart as Rafe, but that didn't mean she was inexperienced enough to believe hugs and kisses were the same thing as a proposal of marriage.

"No, I didn't know you wanted to marry me," she managed to respond at last. "Nor did I know you wanted to take me back to Texas."

Rafe looked surprised. "What do you think I've been doing these last few weeks?"

Surely he must realize that if he wanted a woman to know he wished to marry her, it was necessary to say the actual words.

"I don't know what *you've* been doing, but *I've* been allowing myself to enjoy the attentions of a man I found attractive and admirable. You may say that's not appropriate for a respectable woman, but I'm not a young girl who needs protection or someone to think for her."

"That's not what I meant. I just meant, how could you think that I would act this way toward you, then simply walk away?"

She stamped her foot. "*Because you never said*

anything! Not even a child would believe a few hugs and kisses constitute a pledge of lifetime devotion."

Rafe's faced clouded over. "I guess I'm a child, because I thought they did."

She found it hard to believe a thirty-year-old man could believe such a thing. It was incredible unless…a surprising thought occurred to her. "Have you kissed anyone but me since Dolores?"

"I was never interested in any woman before Dolores. After her, I didn't want anything to do with women at all."

"I can't believe women weren't attracted to you."

"Some were, but I didn't return their interest."

"You're a hard man to understand. You don't talk about your feelings. Broc may understand you well enough to know what you're thinking, but you have to put things into words for me."

Rafe pulled her against him. "Then listen very carefully. I want to marry you and take you back to Texas." His smile revealed both humor and desire. "Is that clear enough?"

She nodded. "I think I can understand that."

She found it difficult to believe he actually wanted what she wanted. She felt stunned, unable to assimilate the change in their relationship. She had occasionally allowed herself to think of being married to Rafe, but she'd never once considered moving to Texas.

"Do I get an answer?"

Rafe was looking a little anxious. It was just like a man to drop something like that out of the blue and expect an immediate answer.

"I haven't had time to think about it."

Her answer apparently surprised him. "Does that mean you *don't* want to marry me?"

"It means I haven't had time to think about it."

He looked perplexed. "I thought a woman would know something like that."

She could hear the frustration in his voice, but she was so stunned by his proposal, she didn't know what to say. It would mean uprooting Luis and leaving Dolores. What about the ranch? Would they travel back and forth, would he hire someone to run it, or would he sell it? Her head was swirling so, she needed to sit down. "How can I give you an answer to that question without time to think it through? There are hundreds of things to be considered."

He didn't release her hands, but she could feel him beginning to withdraw from her. "It seems I'm not very good at this. Maybe I'm a fool, but I thought you loved me."

"I *do* love you. I have for weeks."

Now he looked really confused. "But if you love me, why won't you marry me?"

"I haven't said I won't marry you, just that I haven't had time to think about the hundreds of things we need to consider."

He looked relieved. "I don't need time. Knowing you love me is enough."

"Have you considered all the changes that will occur in your life? In my life? And what are we going to do with Luis?"

"Take him with us."

"What about the ranch?"

"I'll let the lawyer manage it."

"But what about—"

Rafe stopped her protest with a kiss that was so sweet, so filled with gentle passion, she forgot all her questions. Right now all she wanted to do was luxuriate in the knowledge that he loved her and wanted to marry her. She could loosen the restraints she'd put on her heart. She could set her imagination free, let hope soar, give wing to her happiness. Rafe loved her. He wanted to marry her. He wanted to take her to Texas so they would never be separated.

Buoyed by the feeling of happiness that enveloped her, by the sense of well-being that permeated every part of her body, by the physical need to be as close to him as possible, Maria allowed herself to kiss him back the way she'd been wanting to kiss him since the first time he'd kissed her. She wrapped her arms around his neck, pressed her body against his, and covered his mouth with needy eagerness.

In her inexperience, she'd underestimated the strength of the feelings, desires, dreams, hopes—all the things she'd buried inside because she thought she'd never need them. Everything came exploding to the surface. It seemed the force behind them was in direct proportion to the years she'd waited. The impact was making her a different person.

This new Maria wasn't afraid to acknowledge what she wanted, wasn't reluctant to demand that she get it. She didn't wait for Rafe to deepen their kiss, ratchet up its intensity, or decide its length. Nor did she wait for him to pull her firmly against him so she could feel the hardness of his muscles, the breadth of his chest, the strength in his arms.

She tried to reason with this new Maria, to tell her that Rafe loved her, wanted to marry her, that they would have years to explore what it meant to be together as man and wife, but the new Maria wouldn't listen. She wanted everything, and she wanted it now.

For a moment, she could feel Rafe hesitate, but she didn't mean to let him pull away. With slow deliberation, she dropped her arms from around his waist, reached up and placed one hand on each side of his head. She brought his face toward her and let her tongue invade his mouth.

All hesitation on Rafe's part stopped right there.

His arms closed around her so tightly, she wondered if her ribs would crack. She loved the idea that he held her so securely because he never wanted to let her leave his embrace, would allow no one to take her from his arms. She wanted to mold her body to his, every curve and angle fitted and matched, until she felt they had become one.

Until she felt she would never be alone again.

When Rafe first held her, first kissed her, she'd thought nothing could equal it. Now she realized that being held and kissed by a man *she* loved and being held and kissed by a man who loved *her* weren't the same thing. Nothing she'd felt before could compare with the feeling of being in the arms of a man who wanted to make her his wife, who wanted to share his life with her, who thought she was the most wonderful woman in the world. It didn't matter that she wasn't. It mattered only that he thought she was. That was more than enough to make her *feel* like the most fortunate woman in the world.

Her mind was nearly overcome with the abrupt change in their relationship, trying to cope with the changes at the same time it was cataloging all the differences.

The physical part of her had no use for thinking. It cared only how close they were, how passionately they kissed, how warm the feelings. It caused an ember of heat to ignite in her belly and begin its slow spread. Her nipples became engorged and sensitive to the pressure of Rafe's hard chest. Her muscles knotted and spasmed, her nerve endings shot sparks to random parts of her body, her heart beat faster, her breaths became short and uneven. It was the physical part of her that whispered there was more to be experienced, something so powerful and so exquisitely wonderful it couldn't be described.

Her mind overruled her body, declaring that she had to pull back and give some consideration to what was happening before things went any further.

Rafe relaxed his hold on her, leaned back until he could look into her eyes. "Have I scared or upset you?"

He'd done both but not in a bad way. "No. It's just that I had no idea you wanted to marry me. I thought I had everything worked out, what I would allow myself to feel when you left, what I would say, what I would do. You just tossed all that out the window, leaving me with no idea what to do or say."

His gaze narrowed. "Are you saying you don't want to marry me, or that you're not *sure* you want to marry me?"

"I'm not saying either," she hastened to assure him. "I *want* to marry you. I have for several weeks, but I'd accepted that it was impossible. I worked hard to keep my feelings under control, to keep my imagination from creating fantasies that could never be, to keep myself from hoping somehow you'd change your mind. Now everything is different. It's going to take a little while to get used to that."

He loosened his hold on her, let his arms start to fall away. "I don't want to pressure you. I'll—"

She gripped his arms, pulled them back around her. "How do I know this is real if you back away now?"

"I'm not backing away. I'm just offering to give you time to get used to knowing I love you and want to marry you."

Maria wasn't sure she'd ever get used to hearing those words. Or that she could ever hear them too often. They had transformed her world, changed her conception of reality. What had moments ago been a predictable future had now become a bewildering spectrum of possibilities she'd never allowed herself to hope for.

"It's easier to believe you love me when you have your arms around me." She clasped her hands behind his back and pulled him against her.

"I'm not sure whether I was reluctant to let myself fall in love because I was afraid what happened with Dolores would happen all over again," Rafe said, "or whether I was just too bitter and angry. Once I realized I'd fallen in love with you, I was afraid you wouldn't love me in return. I've held our *business* meetings in this room because it gave me a chance to be alone with you, to hold you, to kiss you, to convince myself that you loved me as much as I loved you."

"Why didn't you say something? I entered this room every evening trying to quell the hope that you did love me, that the only reason you didn't tell me was because you found it nearly impossible to discuss your feelings. I left each evening telling myself I was indulging in a foolish infatuation."

"I'm sorry. I fought it for a long time. Then when I didn't want to fight it anymore, I was afraid you wouldn't believe me."

"Why wouldn't I believe you?"

"There were times I was afraid you were only putting up with me until I left."

Maria didn't know whether she wanted to kiss him or give him a thump on the head. "Let me tell you something you obviously don't know about women. When a woman does the things I've done, she's not *putting up with you*. She's not going to commit herself until you do, but she's hoping for a commitment."

"Dolores didn't."

Dolores had let Rafe do everything except make love to her and had still rejected him. That was enough to make a naturally reticent man virtually inarticulate. "Most women wouldn't do what Dolores did."

"Intellectually I know that. I've just had a hard time accepting it where it counts."

The man couldn't even say the words *my heart*. She had a lot of work to do. She gave him a coquettish smile. "You don't have to worry about women any longer. Concentrate on me, and you won't be confused."

He returned her smile. "Is that an invitation or an order?"

She sobered. "I'd never order you to do anything."

His smile grew broader. "It might be easier than you think."

Where had this man been for the last ten years of her life? She brushed his lips with her right index finger, gave him what she hoped was a sassy grin. "I'll leave things up to you. I'll issue invitations only if you run out of ideas."

His smile grew broader still. "Is that a challenge?"

"No." She couldn't stifle a small laugh. How could a man so knowledgable of the world be so inexperienced when it came to women? "It's an invitation."

The grin that spread across his face said he might be inexperienced, but he wasn't stupid. His arms closed around her firmly. His kiss was gentle at first, then quickly transformed into a relentless exploration of her mouth. She felt captured and plundered...and hoped he would never stop. She tried to turn the tables on him, but now that she'd granted Rafe the freedom to do what he wanted, he didn't appear ready to yield the initiative to her.

She decided she didn't mind, especially when he began to scatter kisses over her cheeks and eyelids, to nibble her earlobe. The cumulative effect sent electrical charges arcing throughout her body in great bursts until she felt she would bounce out of her skin. It made no sense that a gentle nip on her ear would cause her legs to feel like they would go out from under her or that a series of kisses along her jaw would make her stomach feel like it had risen into her throat.

Maria had discussed marriage with her mother and both sisters. Her mother was of the generation in which marriages were arranged by the parents and the daughter given to a man she might never have seen before the wedding day. Maria had known there had to be more to a relationship between a man and a woman. She had often wondered what happened between lovers that could cause them to lose sight of all practical considerations, to turn their backs on old loyalties, to destroy the bonds of friendship and family, even to risk death.

Now she knew. She didn't find it hard to think of running off with Rafe in the face of parental opposition. Nor would she hesitate to follow him to Texas. There wasn't anything she wouldn't risk for him. She knew it like she knew being in his arms felt right. It was comfortable. They fit. She belonged here.

Rafe's kisses on the side of her throat disrupted her thoughts. For a man with little experience, he was quick to figure out how to reduce her to nearly mindless acceptance of anything he did. She couldn't decide whether her mind or her body was more helpless, but it didn't matter. Both had willingly yielded to Rafe. It came as a stunning surprise how wonderful it felt to give up all mental and physical control. She'd been responsible for so many people for so long, she'd forgotten what it felt like to have someone assume responsibility for her. It was a very seductive feeling, which drew her even deeper into Rafe's web of love.

She wanted to be closer to Rafe, to be part of him, to be absorbed by him without being lost in him. Her mind said that didn't make any sense, but her emotions said that was exactly right, that her mind should take a rest until it was needed again, which wouldn't be for some time.

Now Rafe was kissing her shoulder. Who would have thought that caress could make her weak in the knees? It could be because it was unconventional. Maybe her shoulders were extra sensitive, or maybe kisses placed there felt especially intimate. Whatever the reason, his kiss turned up the temperature of her body's response. She had a compulsion to touch and be touched.

She splayed her hands across Rafe's back. The play of muscles under her fingertips caused her belly to tighten in a not-unpleasant way. Pressure from his body heightened the feeling of coming together, of being molded into one. She knew that was physically impossible, but she wasn't interested in physical reality when her imagination enabled her to accomplish that and more. Despite the mind-sapping drug of Rafe's kisses, she retained enough presence of mind to know this had to be an emotional journey. Any attempt to bring it down to earth would destroy the magic.

She had never imagined she would fall in love with a man like Rafe, or that a man like Rafe would fall in love with her, but it had happened and she intended to explore every possible aspect of that love. An insidious voice in the back of her head whispered that something this wonderful couldn't last, that she had to grab everything while she could. She didn't doubt Rafe's sincerity, but the niggling fear wouldn't be banished.

When Rafe undid two buttons on the back of her dress to give him access to more of her shoulder, she didn't object. Instead, she undid three more to allow him to slip the dress completely off her shoulder. Her reward was a series of kisses that laid a blazing trail from her neck across her shoulder and down her upper arm. She marveled that her dull, ordinary body could be transformed into a symphony of sensations that had the power to suspend thought, to reduce her to a helplessness that she wouldn't have tolerated in any other circumstance. Now she welcomed it, willingly sinking into its velvety embrace.

She experienced a moment of hesitation when Rafe's hands moved down her back to cup her bottom and press her against him. The double sensation of his hands on her bottom and the swell of his groin against her inner thigh threatened to sweep her away on a tide of hunger so intense, she couldn't imagine how it could come from her body. Desire was like a sorceress with the power to make her believe that, at this time, she wanted him above all else. It scared her at the same time it inexorably propelled her forward at a pace that left her breathless.

Rafe tilted her head to give him access to her throat. But it was his hand on her breast rather than his kisses on her throat that took her to the next threshold. Like the rest of her body, her breasts were innocent of a man's touch. Their transformation from an ordinary part of her body to a source of sexual pleasure was a surprising yet pleasing discovery. Rafe kneaded her breasts until her nipples pushed against the restraints of the tight bodice of her dress. She offered no objection when Rafe slipped her dress over her shoulders.

The soft fabric of her chemise separated her from his touch, but it was no bar to the myriad of sensations that bombarded her when he covered both her breasts with his hands. For a moment it seemed as if all her sensory receptors were located under his palms. When his lips moved from her throat to suckle one nipple through the fabric of her chemise, she was certain of it. She moaned softly, arched her back, and leaned forward against him. Her hands moved from her sides to his shoulders and then to his head, pressing him against her. Every part of her being was so focused on what Rafe was doing to her breasts, she didn't realize he had undone the rest of her buttons until her dress fell to the floor around her feet.

His hands moved down her sides, across her back, over her buttocks, and down her thighs to the backs of her legs. Slowly he turned her whole body into an erogenous zone that needed no more than the brush of his fingertips to set off a storm of sensations.

When he pulled back and stood, she felt bereft, abandoned. Without a word, he led her through the door from the office to his bedroom. Coming to a stop before the bed he'd occupied since he arrived, he asked the question with his eyes rather than words.

She responded by stepping out of her shoes.

Rafe countered by untying her chemise and letting it pool around her feet. For a moment he stood looking at her, no words spoken, his gaze wandering over every part of her body. Just as she was becoming uncomfortable with his scrutiny, fearful he had found something to dislike, he released a long sigh. "Do you have any idea how beautiful you are?"

How could he think she was beautiful compared to Dolores? Even her mother had bemoaned the fact that Maria was cast into a shadow by her older sister. "You will never marry until your sister is married," her mother used to say. "No man will know you're in the room as long as Dolores is there." Faced with the irrefutable corroboration of her mirror, Maria had long ago accepted her lack of beauty—and her role in life as secondary in importance to her sister. Now Rafe was asking her to believe the impossible—that in his eyes she was beautiful, maybe even as beautiful as Dolores.

Rafe was in love with her, not Dolores. Just as she thought Rafe was more handsome than Broc, he believed she was more beautiful than Dolores. It was love that made the difference. This was one time when reality didn't matter. When Rafe looked at her the way he was looking at her now, she *felt* beautiful.

His eyes, wide and luminous, didn't waver. He stood, arms at his sides, unmoving. He appeared to be holding his breath, locked in a moment of immobility. The silence was so deep that she could hear the sound of her own breath, hear the sound of her heart beating against her ribs.

Rafe was the first to move. Reaching out with his hand, he drew her to him, wrapped her in his embrace. The feel of the rough cotton of his shirt, his belt buckle digging into her abdomen, made her acutely aware she was naked while he was still fully clothed. She reached between them to unbutton his shirt. Nerves, or excitement, caused her fingers to fumble.

"Let me do it."

Maria had seen the naked torsos of many men as they labored in the hot California sun, but none came close to matching Rafe's body. His skin was smooth with a slight olive cast to it. His arms, shoulders, and chest were developed in a way that implied being a cowhand was strenuous work. Maria couldn't stop herself from reaching out to touch him. She didn't know why she was surprised that his skin was soft and warm, incredibly wonderful to touch, to caress. He stood still while she ran her hands over him from collarbone to waistline.

"Let me take off my boots."

After removing his boots and socks, he stood to remove his pants...and underwear. When he stood, she was made acutely aware that his body was as stimulated as her own.

Rafe reached for her hand with his right hand. With his left under her chin, he lifted her head until she gazed into his eyes. "If anything makes you uncomfortable, just tell me and we'll stop."

She wanted to say something, but the words wouldn't come out because she wasn't certain what they should be. She didn't pull away when he led her to the bed. When he tugged back the covers, she allowed him to lift her onto the bed. Almost immediately the bed sagged under his weight as he joined her.

So you like you

Twenty-four

"ARE YOU NERVOUS?" RAFE ASKED.

Nervous didn't begin to cover what she was feeling. Nervous. Dazed. Excited. Scared. Curious. Eager. Hesitant. She didn't know what to say, but she knew she had to follow her heart. "No," she said.

"If anything bothers you, let me know."

"I will."

His touch was gentle as with his rough fingertips he brushed her arm from shoulder to wrist. He cupped her cheek with his hand, moved his thumb over her lips, before leaning forward to place a kiss on her forehead, then on her mouth. A moment later he lay back, gazing at her. "I could lie here for hours just looking at you."

She loved looking at him, being with him, but she knew it would be impossible just to lie next to him. She let her hand roam over his chest, along his arms, over his shoulders, and back down to his chest, where a small nest of black hair covered his breastbone. Yielding to an irresistible impulse, she rubbed his nipples gently with her fingertips. His body quivered.

"Does it hurt?" she asked.

He smiled. "No. I just didn't realize I was so sensitive there."

She didn't know where the urge to pinch his nipples came from.

"Ouch."

She giggled. She didn't understand how it was possible to be so aroused she could barely take a deep breath and still be able to giggle.

"What made you do that?" he demanded.

"I don't know."

He reached out, took one of her nipples between his fingers.

"Don't you dare."

"I want to try something more interesting."

He moved down until he could take her nipple in his mouth. Once more chills lanced through every part of her body, from her scalp to her toes. When he took the tip between his teeth and gently nipped at it, the chills turned to arrows of desire so powerful, her body went rigid, her muscles tight with a delicious ache. The feel of his hardened sex lying heavily against her thigh only served to heighten the sense of urgency building inside her. She wanted him, more of him, *all* of him.

Without releasing her nipple, Rafe let his hand move over Maria's back, along her side, across her hip, and down her thigh. His feathery touch caused her whole body to quiver with an ache so sizzlingly sweet, she feared she would melt. Being in control had been essential all her life; it was part of who she was. No one had ever caused her body to overpower her mind. No one had promised to take her on a journey so incredible, so much beyond anything she knew, that it would change her life forever. With a sigh, Maria gave herself up to Rafe.

It was a shock when Rafe released her nipple. She felt abandoned, rejected. She pressed against him looking for, and needing, a replacement for the excitement his attention to her nipple had created. She found it when his hand moved between her legs.

Her muscles tightened and her knees clamped together in an involuntary reaction. Rafe pulled back.

"Don't," she gasped.

"I won't."

"I mean don't stop." Her brain felt heavy, foggy, unable to focus. Her muscles gradually relaxed and her body sank deeper into the mattress. Rafe's hand moved gingerly along her inner thigh. Drawing on the minimal resources of her brain, she fought the urge to pull away, to defend she knew not what. Rafe loved her. He wouldn't hurt her. He would stop if she asked.

When his fingers parted her flesh and entered her, it was all she could do to keep from flinging herself from the bed. Instinct urged her to resist the invasion, to fight to protect her body. That was countered by an even stronger need to open up, to yield, to give herself to him.

It became harder and harder to complete even simple thoughts, thoughts that made her wonder why his touch seemed alien and natural at the same time, why she should feel so conflicted about what he was doing, what it would be like to touch him. Just as she felt she was about to get a grip on a thought, he would move his hand in a way that shattered the thought into unrecognizable fragments.

Then he found a spot that not only rendered her brain

useless but caused her body to go rigid and arch up from the bed.

"Did I hurt you?"

How could she describe something that made her feel like she was coming apart yet was so wonderful she would beg him to do it again? She managed to shake her head from side to side. "No," she said with a mere thread of her voice.

It didn't hurt when he did it again. And again. She was sure she would come apart, but it didn't matter. As his hand moved inside her with rapid or slow strokes, with deep or shallow penetration, all conscious thought narrowed until she was aware of nothing but the spiraling sensations inspired by Rafe's touch. Her body was moving inexorably beyond her control and into a realm where nothing mattered but sensation.

She felt like a spring being wound tighter and tighter. She writhed under the ministrations of Rafe's hand, her body moving first away and then toward the sweet torture. She wondered if the moans she heard were her own but didn't have enough energy to care. She cared only about the feeling that something inside her was growing, swelling, on the verge of consuming her in one enormous gulp. The spring wound tighter, her muscles so rigid she was sure she couldn't stand any more, yet she didn't have the power to move away. Didn't have the desire, either.

Then something inside her burst, overwhelming her with exquisite sensation, and she felt the tension drain away from her like water rushing through a gap in a blasted dam. A shuddering breath escaped her, and the tenseness began to seep out of her muscles, leaving her feeling limp and unable to lift so much as a finger. She didn't know how to explain what had happened to her body, but nothing had ever left her feeling incapable of thought or movement. She was only vaguely aware that Rafe had moved, that his shifted weight had caused the bed to move beneath her. Her thoughts weren't able to focus until she realized his body was suspended over hers, that something large and hot was pushing between her thighs.

"Let me know if this hurts."

It didn't hurt, but his entrance into her body stretched her until she was certain she couldn't contain him. When he started to move within her and the tension began to build once more, she forgot about everything else. She became a vortex, a single source of energy, slowly spinning into the outer rings of consciousness.

She didn't know when she started to move with him, to welcome him deeper and deeper into her body. The need to feel connected to him grew stronger, until having him inside her wasn't enough. She wrapped her arms around his neck and pulled him down so that their lips met in a series of kisses that stoked the fires deep inside her to a white heat.

Yet that wasn't enough. She wrapped her legs around his waist and pulled him still deeper inside her, but the more she got, the more she needed. Clinging to Rafe with all her strength, she drove him deeper in an attempt to satisfy the need raging inside her. She could hear his breath become labored, feel his muscles tense, his body stiffen. He seemed to swell inside her, filling her to bursting. At that moment, his body began to buck and she could feel the warmth of his seed as he exploded inside her.

That was all the stimulus she needed to carry her over the edge into sweet oblivion.

❦

Rafe slowly floated upward from the depths of sleep to the calm surface of consciousness. He marveled at the sense of peace that holding Maria in his embrace gave him. The hurt of Dolores's betrayal would never go away, but Maria's love for him had enabled him to put the past behind him, enabled him to look forward with eagerness to the future.

He'd rather thoughtlessly said he intended to take Maria and Luis back to Texas with him, but having made love to her, having felt the healing balm of her love, he knew it was not the life he wanted for Maria. He would have a family that would need a home of its own.

He would hate to leave his friends, but maybe he could buy a ranch within easy riding distance. He smiled at himself. Here he was making plans for their future and he hadn't asked Maria what she wanted.

He would need more money than he'd saved to buy his own ranch. Maybe he would consider selling his interest in Rancho los Alamitos to Luis. That ought to give him more than enough money to buy ranch land in Texas. Would it be better to leave Luis and Maria in California while he went back to Texas to buy a ranch and build a house? He didn't like to think of leaving Maria for such a long time, but if he didn't, she'd be forced to live in a cabin like the one Cade's grandfather still occupied, and that was unacceptable to Rafe.

Thinking about leaving her reminded him that he had no idea who was trying to kill him. Unless he was mistaken, that first attempt had been directed against Maria. He couldn't possibly leave as long as he thought she was in danger. Selling the ranch would be one solution, but Luis was too young to make such a decision for himself.

He had racked his brain, but couldn't figure out who could benefit from his and Maria's deaths as well as a serious injury to Miguel. If they were out of the picture, the ranch would still be under the lawyer's management until Luis came of age.

Suddenly the murky idea that had been lurking in the back of Rafe's mind came into sharp focus. He lay still for a moment longer, running the idea through several tests. Once he was satisfied that it had passed all of them, his expression turned grim. He reached out to shake Maria.

"Wake up," he said. "I know who's trying to kill me."

⌘

"Are you sure?" Broc asked.

"I've gone over every possibility numerous times," Rafe said, "and this is the only name that fits with everything we know. Laveau doesn't care about anything but money. Killing me won't make him a penny richer."

They were gathered in Rafe's father's office so no one in the house would be aware of their meeting.

"I can't believe it," Maria said. "Your father placed complete trust in Henry Fielder."

"So did I," Rafe admitted. "I knew of no reason to do otherwise."

"But why would he want to kill you as well as seriously injure Miguel and me?" Maria asked.

"Money. In case I couldn't be found or was dead, my father's will set him up to manage the ranch until Luis reaches his majority. He only has to incapacitate you and Miguel to have complete control. There's no assurance he wouldn't do something to Luis so he could keep stealing for the rest of his life."

"So how do you intend to prove it?" Broc asked.

"I plan to set a trap for him."

Broc's eyebrows rose. "What do you mean to use as bait?"

Rafe met his gaze. "Don't you mean *who*?"

"You can't seriously mean to set yourself up as a target," Maria protested.

"Can you think of a better way?" Rafe asked.

"No, but there must be one. Have you thought of what would happen to Luis and me if you got killed?"

Broc looked from Maria to Rafe. "Is there something I don't know?"

Rafe turned to Broc. "I've asked Maria to marry me. I'm taking her and Luis back to Texas with me."

Broc jumped up from his seat, strode over to Maria, and subjected her to a crushing hug. "I told him weeks ago he was in love with you." Broc released Maria, turned to Rafe, and wrung his hand while grinning so broadly that it nearly overcame the effect of his scars. "I hope you know she's too good for you, you old rascal. I have a good mind to cut you out to save her the ordeal of having to put up with you for the rest of her life." Broc mitigated the severity of his remarks by giving Rafe a hug even more bone-crushing than the one he'd given Maria.

"I know that better than you." Rafe gave as good as

he got. "She has too much sense to prefer an actor over a landowner."

"It won't make any difference to me how much land you own if you're dead," she said to Rafe.

"It would make you a rich widow." Broc's grin faded when he realized Maria was truly upset. "Sorry. Not funny."

"Isn't there some other way?" she asked, turning to Rafe.

"Not one I can think of."

"If you're planning to take everybody back to Texas, why do you care who's trying to murder you?" Broc asked.

Maria didn't want to go to Texas, but she would happily live in an even more disagreeable place if it would keep Rafe out of danger. "Forget all about traps and bait. We can leave for Texas anytime you want."

Apparently she had caught both Rafe and Broc by surprise. "You don't know anything about Texas," Broc pointed out.

Rafe's gaze was more penetrating. "I was certain you were going to do your best to convince me to stay here."

"Why would I want to stay here when someone is trying to kill you? The notion of using yourself as bait makes me crazy."

"We mounted this kind of operation several times during the war," Rafe told her. "It's not without danger, but Broc and I know how to take care of ourselves."

"How? You've never seen the person who's trying to kill you. Have you considered it might not be the lawyer?"

"I'm certain it's not," Rafe said. "He'd use someone else so he wouldn't be under suspicion."

"So you're going to set yourself up to be shot at when you don't even know who's doing the shooting?" There had to be something wrong when neither man would meet her gaze. "What are you going to do? I have a right to know."

"I haven't worked out all the details yet," Rafe admitted, "but I'll start by telling Fielder I'm going to be married and make you my heir. If anything happens to me, Broc will become manager of the property until Luis becomes of age. If anything happens to Broc, it goes to Cade."

"How is that going to draw him out?"

"I'll have to wait for the will to be drawn up before I can sign it. That will give him about a week to kill me."

"So you're just going to walk around as a target?"

"Not quite. I intend to invite him to go hunting with me."

Maria decided she'd fallen in love with a madman. "Wouldn't that be the perfect opportunity for him to kill you?"

"He doesn't dare do it himself while we're together. It would practically be an admission of guilt. He'll depend on the man he's hired to kill me."

"Do you know who that man is?"

"No."

Now she was certain Rafe was crazy. "How do you plan to discover this man's identity?"

"Broc and I haven't discussed a plan yet," Rafe said, "but I was thinking that Broc could wait out of sight to see who follows us up the trail. If no one does, he'll send me a signal that means I have to watch out for Henry Fielder."

"Suppose the killer is already on the mountain?"

"I plan to tell Henry we're going to hunt in one place, then change my mind and take him somewhere else."

"I think you should tell the sheriff and let him handle everything."

"I have no evidence," Rafe reminded her. "Unless and until we find the man actually responsible for the attacks—and we won't know we have found him until he makes another attempt—we have nothing to take to the sheriff but my suspicions."

She couldn't argue with that, but she had to convince Rafe to find another way. "At least let the sheriff help you."

"I wouldn't put it past the sheriff to warn Fielder. He's an important part of this community. I'm not."

"You would be if you stayed here." But she didn't want Rafe to stay if it would put him in danger. Why was everything so difficult?

"I still don't see why you want to bother if you're going back to Texas," Broc said. "Just appoint someone else to look after things and the lawyer is out of the loop."

"The will is written so I can't take Fielder out of the loop unless I get married and have a wife and children to inherit the ranch. Even then, if something were to happen to Maria and me, the lawyer would have control until the children came of age."

"You think he was planning this all along?"

"Yes. I think he thought I'd never be found or wouldn't come back. The only attempt to find me was a single ad in a Chicago newspaper. If Laveau hadn't sent it to me, I'd never have known my father had died and Henry Fielder would have had uncontested control for the next twelve years."

Maria felt guilty for having complete confidence in Fielder. Warren Jerry hadn't seen the ranch accounts for the last two years of his life. Neither she nor Dolores had seen any after his death. As far as she knew, every penny that wasn't necessary for the running of the household could have found its way into Fielder's pockets. She couldn't bear to think that Fielder had robbed the family blind and she hadn't known anything about it. "Maybe you could ask the sheriff to look into the lawyer's accounts. If large amounts of money suddenly started appearing, wouldn't that be enough to arrest him?"

"Embezzling is a lot less serious than attempted murder. I don't intend to let him off easily."

She didn't know what she was going to do, but she had no intention of standing aside while some greedy lawyer attempted to kill Rafe. She didn't know whether her future lay in California or in Texas, but she certainly wouldn't let some thieving lawyer ruin it.

❧

Henry Fielder cursed Roger Anderson. "Rafe wouldn't be changing his will if you'd killed him the first time."

"The man has more lives than a cat."

"Well, his are about to run out. He's invited me to hunt a cougar with him. You'll follow us. If I don't manage to push him off a cliff, you're to shoot him."

"How will you prove that you didn't do it?"

"We'll use different rifles. I'll carry a tan-colored coat to put on him so the sheriff will believe me when I say he was shot by another hunter."

"Maybe we should give up," Roger said. "You've already taken a lot of money."

"I mean to have it all."

❧

"Where is Broc?" From where Maria and Rafe were waiting near the stables, she could see Henry Fielder riding toward the house.

"He's hidden out of sight along the trail," Rafe explained. "I wish you'd stop worrying. We've got everything under control."

Nothing would be under control until Fielder and his cut-throat companion were in jail. "How do you expect me to stop worrying when you're going into the mountains with a man who wants you dead?"

"I know what Henry's up to, but he doesn't have any idea that I know."

She didn't see how that was going to help, but she didn't bother to say so. "I still don't see why you don't take someone else along with you."

"Because then the man might decide against trying to kill me."

Maria bit her tongue to keep from screaming that she thought that was a good thing. "Just be careful. Don't let Fielder get behind you."

"I'm the one who's leading. I have to be in front. Remember, Henry won't try to kill me himself."

Maria didn't know how Rafe could be so sure of that. She didn't know anything about killers, but she doubted they could be depended upon to behave according to expectations. After all, murder wasn't exactly normal behavior. She could think of a hundred perfectly logical reasons why Rafe should change his mind, but she wasn't able to put forth any of them because Henry had reached them.

"It's a perfect day for a cougar hunt," he said as he dismounted.

Maria eyed the rifle in a scabbard attached to his saddle. She saw no reason it couldn't be used on a man as well as a cougar.

"Most of the time cougars keep their distance from the ranch," Rafe said to Henry, "but this one has been giving us a lot of trouble recently. It might be injured or too old to hunt deer any longer."

"Let's go," Henry said. "I'm familiar with the lower canyon. I used to hunt there as a boy."

"We're going to the upper canyon," Rafe said. "One of my men sighted him there yesterday."

"I know that one, too."

As far as Maria could tell, Henry showed no sign of being upset or even vaguely concerned about the change in plans. That meant whatever he'd planned, he thought he could pull it off no matter what Rafe did. She racked her brain for something to say that would make Rafe cancel the hunt, but she knew it was useless. In many ways he was very modern in his treatment of women, but in instances like this, he expected her to sit patiently at home and wait for him to return.

"I'll let you lead the way," Rafe said as both men mounted up. "I've been in that canyon only once. I was a young boy and don't remember it well."

"I'll be happy to lead the way," Henry offered. "It'll give me first shot at the cougar."

Maria just prayed the first shot would not be fired at Rafe. She was still standing in front of the stables, watching the men disappear in the distance, when Luis came from the house. "Rafe told you to stay inside until he returned," she reminded him.

"I was using the telescope Rafe gave me. I wanted to see how far up the mountain I could see him," Luis said.

"Why did you stop watching?" she asked.

"I saw Roger follow them."

"Who's Roger?"

"He's the man Papa fired," Luis replied.

Maria had a vague memory of a man who had been fired making a bit of trouble, but Miguel had taken care of it.

"Roger's nephew told me Roger swore he wouldn't rest until every male Jerry was dead. I'm a male Jerry. Does that mean he wants to kill me?"

Maria tried to throttle the feeling of panic that threatened to choke her. "Go back to the house and don't leave for any reason until Rafe and I return."

"What are you going to do?"

"I'm going to follow Roger. And I plan to take a gun."

Twenty-five

MARIA WAS THANKFUL THE TRAIL INTO THE MOUN-
tains was so well traveled that even she could follow
it. Tree branches and vines constantly caught on her
skirt. She'd never realized so many bushes and trees
came supplied with thorns. She didn't care about her
dress, but untangling her clothes slowed her down.
She caught only an occasional glimpse of Roger, who
was far ahead of her. She wasn't good at hiding. If he
did spot her, she hoped he would ignore her the way
most men in California ignored women.

The holster she had belted around her waist felt
awkward. She'd never worn a gun. She hadn't even
handled one. She knew this one was loaded only
because one of the stable boys had said it was. She
had no idea what she would do when and if she confronted Roger, but it would have been pointless to go
after him without some sort of weapon.

She had to find Broc. She had to tell him Roger
was the man trying to kill Rafe.

A particularly evil thorn caught the sleeve of her
dress. Her forward movement caused it to dig deep

into the soft flesh of her arm. Resisting the urge to cry out in pain, she clenched her teeth and let the forward motion of the horse tear the thorn from her sleeve. She didn't look to see if she was bleeding. She couldn't do anything about it, so why bother?

She appreciated the shade of the occasional oak that cast a shadow over the trail, but she wished every tree and bush that blocked her view of Roger had been cut down. The trail was so full of sharp curves and switchbacks, she found it impossible to keep him in constant sight. It was no comfort to her that Roger would have an equally difficult time keeping Rafe in view. But it didn't take long to raise a rifle and shoot.

"What are you doing here?"

Broc's sudden appearance nearly caused her heart to stop beating. She jerked so hard on the horse's reins, he grunted and tossed his head in anger.

"You've got to go back to the house," Broc said. "You might scare off the man I'm following."

"Roger," she supplied.

"Is that his name? I've seen him hanging about town looking for handouts."

"Warren fired him some time back. Luis said Roger told his nephew he wouldn't rest until every male Jerry was dead."

Broc had a very surprised look on his face, but it gradually changed as a series of thoughts chased themselves through his mind. "Roger is always begging. I saw him come out of Henry Fielder's office one day, so I figured he was trying to get money out of Henry." Broc stared at Roger's figure growing smaller in the distance. "I don't see the man as a killer, but I can't take a chance on being wrong. If you won't go back to the ranch, stay well behind me. If you get hurt, Rafe won't understand why I didn't take you back to the ranch and make sure you stayed there."

"I wouldn't stay."

"That's why I'm not going to waste time trying."

Maria didn't like having to lag behind, but she didn't want to do anything that would interfere with Broc's preventing Roger from shooting at Rafe. She worried even more about Henry. What would stop the lawyer from shooting Rafe himself? She doubted anyone in town would believe a respected lawyer would kill his richest client. He could push Rafe over a cliff, start a landslide, or say a tree limb fell on him and cracked his skull. She was so busy torturing herself with all the things Henry could do to Rafe, it took her several minutes to realize Roger had disappeared.

Ahead, Broc rode with his rifle across his saddle, his eyes scanning the brush-covered hillside as he passed. Had Roger guessed Broc was following him, or had he assumed Broc was just another hunter who would ride past and disappear up the mountainside? Would he try to kill Broc so there couldn't be any witness to his attempt to murder Rafe? Did he know Maria was following both of them? If so, what would he do?

How had she ever thought she could help Rafe? The only thing she could have done was to let him know Roger was the one who was trying to kill him, but she didn't know where Rafe had gone. If she did find him, how could she tell him without Henry guessing? She was out of her depth, but she couldn't have remained safe at the ranch while Rafe was out here risking his life.

The morning seemed eerily quiet. Usually birds and small animals would be heard hunting among the dry leaves for seeds and other bits of food. There was no breeze to rustle the leaves of the trees. No distant sound of voices shouting to and fro or raised in song. The *plop, plop, plop* of her horse's hooves sounded unnaturally loud in the silence. She swayed gently in the saddle as the horse's shoulder blades rose and fell with strides so hypnotic it made it difficult to stay alert.

It took Roger's sudden appearance on the trail between her and Broc to bring her brain to full awareness.

Roger had left his horse and was on foot, but he carried his rifle. They had reached a point in the trail where a series of switchbacks made it difficult to keep anyone in sight for more than a short time. Roger was walking slowly, his gaze locked on the trail above him. Maria had to get closer. Afraid Roger would hear her horse as she approached, she slid out of the saddle and ran forward as rapidly as she could.

She'd never hiked or ridden in the mountains and had no idea how difficult it was to run up a steep incline. Twice she stumbled on loose gravel. Her dress protected her knees, but her hands were bruised, and blood was beginning to ooze from small cuts. She reached a spot where she could see Roger in time to glimpse him raising his rifle. She couldn't see what he was aiming at, but she was certain it was Broc. She couldn't hit Roger, but she could distract him. She reached for her pistol only to realize a strap held it in place. The stable boy had said the strap would make sure she didn't lose it. She lost precious seconds fumbling with the strap before she got it loose and yanked the pistol out of its holster.

She raised it in Roger's direction, closed her eyes, and fired.

The sound of something crashing through the brush above caused Maria to open her eyes. Roger's body tumbled down the mountainside, crashed through the low-hanging limbs of a stunted oak, and landed on the trail less than ten feet from her. When he didn't move, the shock of what had happened hit her.

I have killed a man!

Her brain refused to accept that. She could barely process the fact that she'd fired a pistol. She was still standing there, body stiff, gun held in unsteady hands, when Broc appeared around the bend in the trail. He went straight to Roger's body and knelt down to examine it.

"I killed him." Maria's voice sounded hollow. "I killed him."

Broc turned the body over and checked it carefully before standing to turn and face Maria.

"There's no bullet wound on his body." He pointed up at the boulder-strewn mountainside. "He must have thrown himself down to avoid the bullet and hit his head on one of those rocks. He has a crushed skull."

Maria's body sagged with relief. The fact that she hadn't killed him directly might not make any difference to some people, but it made a huge difference to her.

"You should go back to the ranch."

Broc's words brought Maria out of her dazed state. "Rafe is still up there with Henry. We've got to let him know Roger is dead."

"It's already been done. You did it."

"How?"

"A pistol shot was the signal Rafe and I arranged between us. Rifle fire could be an exchange between me and Roger or it might be another hunter on the mountain, but no hunter would carry a pistol. A pistol shot would tell him I'd caught the man who'd been sent to kill him."

"What was Rafe planning to do when he heard the shot?"

"Confront Henry with the knowledge that Rafe knew what he'd been trying to do and that I had captured the man, who would be forced to testify against him."

"But Roger is dead. He can't testify."

"I know that but Rafe doesn't. And neither does Henry."

Maria's attempt to help Rafe had deprived him of his only witness. The lawyer might deny the charges, and Rafe wouldn't be able to do anything about it.

Rafe would continue to be in danger.

❧

Henry had dismounted and was about to make his way to the top of a group of boulders that had been washed down from the mountain in some ancient rainstorm when Rafe heard the pistol shot. He was relieved. Now he didn't have to worry about getting shot in the back, but the knowledge didn't rid him of the heavy feeling in his chest. Henry had been his father's best friend for years. He couldn't understand what had caused the lawyer to turn on the one man who'd done so much to help him establish himself in Cíbola. He could understand greed, but he didn't understand the willingness to kill for money.

He watched Henry scramble around the boulders. He was in remarkable physical condition for his age. Why hadn't he been out enjoying life rather than sitting inside brooding over ways to steal money? Rafe felt sorry for him. A lifelong bachelor, Fielder probably had little to look forward to but his work.

"Henry, stop," Rafe called out. "I have something to tell you."

Henry paused, stood, and turned to look down at Rafe. "We can talk later. I've found some footprints."

"Forget about the cougar for right now. Come down. We need to talk."

It was hard to tell at this distance, but it looked as if Henry's body had gone rigid. Could he have guessed what Rafe was going to say?

Rafe wished he could have been close enough to Henry to see his reaction when he told him Broc had captured the man who would testify against him. He'd like to see at least a trace of remorse. He'd always thought of Henry Fielder as a kind man who was looking out for his father's best interests. Several times his kindness had extended to Rafe. It was hard to believe this man had tried to have him killed.

But there was no point in dwelling on the past. He had to put an end to this threat.

"Come down, Henry. I know you've twice tried to have me killed. I also know that you had the gazebo sabotaged so it would fall on Maria and that you are responsible for Miguel's accident."

Henry's expression didn't change. "That's absurd. Your father was my best friend. What could I hope to gain?"

"Control of Rancho los Alamitos so you could embezzle from it. I suspect you've been embezzling since my father became too sick to manage things himself."

"Nobody will believe you."

"They will because I have the man you hired to kill me."

"You don't have anybody. There's just the two of us out here."

"I figured you'd try to kill me before I could sign the new will, so I invited you on this hunt. I knew you wouldn't do it yourself, that you'd hire someone so you'd be above suspicion. I had my friend Broc wait along the trail to see who followed us. That gunshot you heard was our prearranged signal to let me know he'd caught the man."

"This is all a figment of your imagination," Henry said.

"My father helped you establish your business. Luis and I have done nothing to harm you. Why did you do it?"

Rather than come down to face Rafe, Henry started to climb the boulders again.

"You can't get away," Rafe called out. "You'll have to come down sooner or later."

Henry didn't answer, just kept climbing.

Rafe wondered if Henry knew another way down the mountain. His father used to say Henry knew the eastern slopes of the mountains better than anyone in Cíbola.

Rafe decided to follow him. He didn't think Henry would attempt to get down the mountain without his horse, but he wouldn't have thought the man wanted him dead, either. Deciding to depend on his pistol rather than his rifle—he could climb a lot faster with two hands—he started after Henry.

One hint that Henry didn't mean to let himself be caught came when Henry dislodged a rock that sent a small rockslide in Rafe's direction. None of the rocks was over a foot in diameter, but any one of a dozen could have easily killed Rafe if he hadn't taken refuge behind a large boulder.

"Broc and Maria both know what you've been doing," Rafe called to Henry. "It's impossible for you to get away."

That wasn't exactly true. If Henry could kill or wound Rafe, he might have time to get down the mountain and out of town before Broc could do anything to stop him. Rafe was certain Fielder had the stolen money stashed away in Sacramento or San Francisco.

"You can't escape. Broc will be waiting at the foot of the mountain. Maria may have already alerted the sheriff."

Henry's only reply was to send another rockslide toward Rafe.

After that Rafe climbed in silence. It wasn't long

before he became aware that working as a cowhand didn't prepare a man for climbing over boulders. Without gloves, the rough surface of the boulders scraped the skin off his fingers and inflicted dozens of tiny cuts that stung like the devil. Cowboy boots were about the worst possible choice for rock climbing. The tight pants and shirt that worked so well in the saddle didn't allow him the freedom of movement he needed.

Pausing to catch his breath, he looked up to see that Henry had changed direction and was headed toward a ledge that ran along both sides of the ridge. He'd forgotten all about any interest Henry had in the cougar in his desire to get away. If he was moving toward that ledge, it was because he believed it offered him a means of escape. Since Henry had stopped trying to kill Rafe with rockslides, he must believe he was nearing his goal. Rafe took another deep breath and started to climb again.

He didn't know how long he'd been climbing—it couldn't have been more than five minutes—when he heard a deep-throated snarl. Barely a second later, he heard Henry scream.

The next few minutes were destined to remain a horrible memory that would haunt Rafe for years to come. He climbed as quickly as possible toward Henry's screams, but silence had descended before Rafe reached the ledge. He approached with his gun out, but the cougar must have fled when he heard Rafe coming. The bloody and badly mauled body of Henry Fielder lay on the flat ledge.

Rafe wasn't sure whether he was relieved to find

the man still alive. From the extent of his wounds, it was apparent he wouldn't live long. It was also apparent that those last moments would be lived in great agony. "Why did you try to kill me? What have I ever done to you?"

"Your father." Henry's words were barely audible. Rafe had to kneel down to hear him. "He stole the woman I wanted to marry. She was mine, but he stole her."

Rafe knew the story of how his parents had met. Henry had introduced them during a festival, but his mother had never said anything about being attracted to Henry. His father had given his business to Henry in appreciation for the introduction, which had resulted in the young couple falling in love and marrying.

"But you weren't trying to kill my father. You were trying to kill me."

"You...weren't supposed to come back. I would have been rich."

Henry probably had never thought of killing anyone until Rafe's father had made the will giving the lawyer control of the ranch if Rafe didn't return. Henry had thought Rafe was dead and that he was entitled to Warren's wealth. Maybe he had been embezzling and didn't want Rafe to find out. Maybe he just wanted the money and didn't care what he had to do to get it.

"Were you going to kill Luis, too?" Rafe thought Henry shook his head, but the movement was so slight, it was impossible to be sure.

Rafe wanted to ask Henry if there was anyone he should notify, but he doubted the man had the strength to respond. Rafe couldn't save him and he couldn't do anything to ease his suffering. He could only watch as Fielder died.

It didn't take long.

❧

"He wanted me dead," Rafe said to the sheriff. "Why should he leave his estate to me?"

"The will stated everything was to go to your mother or her descendants," the sheriff said. "He made it before you were born. I can't understand why he didn't change it."

"I don't want anything of his," Rafe said.

"I can understand that, but this inheritance will give you a chance to find out how much money he stole from you and your father. I've only had a brief look at his accounts, but there are some substantial amounts in banks in Sacramento and San Francisco. Henry didn't have a practice that would have given him that kind of income. It's possible he was embezzling from other clients as well."

Rafe didn't want the responsibility of sorting out Henry's financial dealings. He hadn't wanted anything to do with the funeral, either, but when it turned out Henry had no known relatives, he didn't have a choice. Broc had laughed at the irony.

The sheriff was the only one who knew the real story of what had happened on the mountainside. Everyone else was allowed to believe Roger had died in an unrelated accident. Roger's family had taken responsibility for his burial.

"You'll have to look around for another lawyer,"

Maria said as she and Rafe left the sheriff's office. "There aren't many in Cíbola to choose from."

He didn't want to think about that now. He just wanted to go back to the ranch. If Henry had been embezzling from other clients, his several bank accounts would probably take weeks to unravel. "Do you know a lawyer to recommend?"

Maria looked at him in surprise. "You're asking me?"

"I've been gone so long that I don't remember anybody."

"My father would never have asked my mother's opinion in any business matter. I doubt your father would, either."

"I have three friends with very capable wives who've taught me a different way to look at women. You've been running a household since you were fourteen. In my mind, that qualifies you as a capable person. Now stop acting so surprised and tell me whom you think I should hire."

"You should ask the sheriff. Or better yet, Miguel. I haven't spent enough time in town to know people well."

Rafe thought Maria was probably being modest.

"Well, we're likely to be in town for another day or two, straightening things out. Is there anyone you want to see? Anything you want to do? Anything you want to buy?"

Maria hooked her arm in his and leaned into him as they walked. "What a generous offer. It could take days just to consider all the options."

There were many things Rafe liked about Maria, but one was her ability to take him by surprise. He had a feeling that once the serious issues in her life had been dealt with, she would have a lively sense of humor and would take great pleasure in keeping him guessing. He decided that wouldn't be so bad.

"I wouldn't want you to wear yourself out trying to do everything in one day. Make a list. What we can't do now we can do later."

Maria pinched his arm. "I don't want to do anything as much as be with you, but I expect Luis and Broc are getting hungry by now. Why don't we go by the hotel and take them out to lunch? I know Luis has a list of things he wants to do, and most of them have to do with a horse. I'm not sure I'm going to forgive you for turning my sweet, studious child into a horse-mad boy."

"Then I'll have to see about giving you a child more like you. How about a little girl with big brown eyes and a button nose?"

It amused Rafe to see Maria blush at the thought of having his children. He was equally surprised to find it gave him a funny feeling all over. A son or daughter would be his flesh and blood, his responsibility to support, to guide, to love no matter how difficult that might be at times.

"There's a lot to be worked out before we think about children," Maria said.

"What?"

They'd entered the hotel and Maria put her finger to her lips to indicate that she didn't want to talk about such personal matters where strangers could overhear them. But all thoughts of children went out of his head when he opened the door to Maria's room to find Broc lying on the floor, bound and gagged.

Twenty-six

"WHERE'S LUIS?" MARIA ASKED.

"Laveau kidnapped him," Broc said the moment the gag was out of his mouth.

Maria had never trusted Laveau, but his dislike of children had been displayed so openly and so often, she'd never thought he would kidnap Luis. From what Rafe and Broc had said about him, she should have realized Laveau would have abducted the devil himself for the sake of money. Yet that same thought afforded her slight comfort. Laveau would have no desire to harm the boy. He wanted only the money Rafe would pay to get Luis back.

"How did you end up gagged and lying on the floor?" Rafe asked, starting to untie the ropes that bound Broc's hands.

"Laveau. And don't tell me I should have kept an eye on him. That bitch Dolores was in on it. She smothered Luis in so much false affection, I was worried the boy was going to develop a fever. I was trying to get her to leave him alone when Laveau came at me from behind. When I came to, I was like you found me."

"Why did you let them in?" Rafe asked.

"Dolores." Broc rubbed his wrists to restore the circulation while Rafe worked to remove the rope tying his feet. "As much as I dislike her, Luis still loves her. Laveau was acting so cool and aloof, like he couldn't wait to be gone, I didn't pay him any attention. I know. I should never turn my back on that man, but Dolores got me off balance."

"Do you have any idea where they went?"

"None whatsoever." Broc kicked aside the loosened ropes and rose to unsteady feet. "They couldn't have left long ago. If we hurry, we should be able to find which road they took and maybe catch up with them before Laveau stashes the boy where we'll never find him."

"How did he know you were going to be alone with Luis?" Rafe asked. "Maria and I haven't been gone more than a couple of hours."

"I think he has spies everywhere."

"Do you mean he pays people to watch what we do?" It had never occurred to Maria to look over her shoulder.

"Not with money," Broc said as they hurried out of the hotel and toward the nearest livery stable. "He smiles and simpers and looks so damned superior that when he turns his fake charm on people, they can't stop themselves from telling him anything he wants to know."

When they reached the livery stable, Rafe ordered one of the stable boys to saddle his and Broc's horses.

"Mine, too," Maria said.

"Stay here," Rafe said. "Laveau is dangerous."

"Either I go with you or I follow after you've gone," Maria said. "Which do you want it to be?"

"Neither," Rafe snapped, "but I don't have time to argue. Wait here. Broc and I will see if we can find anyone who rented horses or a buggy to Laveau. I just hope we can find someone who saw him leave town."

"Everybody knows him," Broc said. "He's made sure of that."

Maria was worried about Luis. How was a child supposed to get over his mother's helping a man he distrusted kidnap him? How could she explain Dolores's actions in a way that wouldn't leave a permanent scar on the boy's heart?

Maria felt guilty about the many times she'd explained away something Dolores had said or done to hurt or disappoint Luis. She'd always finished by assuring him his mother loved him and would never do anything to hurt him. Now she wondered if it might not have been better if she'd let Luis see his mother as she really was. But how could she have done that when she herself had refused to see her sister for the selfish, manipulative woman she was?

Maria held herself almost as much to blame for Dolores's behavior as Dolores herself. Her loyalty, love, and continual forgiveness had enabled Dolores to indulge the worst attributes of her character. Maria's deep love for Luis had prompted her to keep the truth from him. A reluctance to tamper with a marriage that wasn't her own had kept her from asking Warren to take a stronger hand with his wife.

It was too late to be sorry now. All she could do was try to comfort Luis when Rafe found him. She never once allowed herself to think they might not find him. That possibility was too horrible to contemplate.

She was relieved when she saw Rafe coming toward her. "What did you find out?"

"Dolores picked up a buggy at the livery stable across town. Laveau was carrying Luis in his arms. The stable boy had no idea where they might have gone."

"Do you think Laveau would hurt Luis?"

"No. I'm sure his only interest in Luis is the ransom he's going to demand."

Maria didn't like the tightness around Rafe's mouth. He was trying to reassure her, but he didn't put much faith in Laveau having enough human decency not to hurt a child. She could only hope Dolores would see to it that nothing happened to her son. Despite her flaws, Maria couldn't bring herself to believe Dolores would knowingly let anyone hurt Luis.

Dolores must have believed Laveau was helping her gain possession of her son, that Laveau would marry her, and they would all live happily together. Maria knew her sister would do a lot to regain the lifestyle she had had when Warren was alive.

She was relieved when she saw Broc round the corner of the stable at a run.

"I know which road they took," he shouted. "They can't be very far ahead."

In a matter of moments they were mounted and on their way out of town. Maria had always wanted to ride slowly, but today she kept urging her mount forward despite Rafe's warning that it was necessary to conserve energy.

"If you drive him too hard now, he'll be exhausted after a few miles and we'll have to leave you behind."

It was difficult to throttle the fear that if they didn't ride as fast as they could, she would never see Luis again.

They rode by scenes that at any other time would have drawn her attention for their beauty, serenity, and sheer majesty. She took no notice of the forested flanks of the mountains or the snow-covered peaks in the distance. She saw no abundance of flowers in fields, along hillsides, or on creek banks. She heard no birdsongs, saw no butterflies, nor did she feel the warmth of the sun on her cheek, the breeze that ruffled her hair. She didn't smell the heady aroma of water lilies in a shaded pond or taste the crispness of fresh country air.

She heard only the rhythmic tattoo of the horses' hooves on the hard ground, the squeak of saddle leather, the clink of metal against metal. She saw only the empty road that stretched endlessly before her. She felt only the tears that ran down her cheeks. She smelled only fear, tasted only the bitterness of regret.

Her vision narrowed to a mental image of a frightened Luis being carried farther and farther from the people he loved and trusted. He was old enough to understand what was happening to him but not why. He was young enough to give unconditional love but not old enough to understand that love rarely came without conditions. He was too young to understand that for some people the love of money could be more powerful than love for a person.

He would never understand why his mother would

betray him; he might end up thinking it must be due to some fault in himself.

That single thought exploded in her head with a force that was almost blinding. Was that how Rafe had explained his father's choosing Dolores over him? Had he spent the last ten years feeling that the reason for the tragedy stemmed from some flaw in himself?

She had always seen Rafe as a strong, confident man who had no doubts about his worth or his ability. He seemed to have an answer for everything and make decisions without needless vacillation. He trusted friends implicitly and distrusted enemies with equal directness. He held no secrets and expected others to be equally open with him. Could all of that be a painstakingly pieced together defense to cover up a deeply buried fear that he might not measure up?

She glanced at the profile of the man who rode alongside her. He leaned forward in the saddle, the reins loose in his hands, the horse moving fluidly between his powerful thighs. He faced forward, his gaze focused on the trail ahead. She couldn't read his thoughts, but the hard set of his jaw, his compressed lips, the rigidity of his body all spoke of strong, focused determination to face the challenge ahead without hesitation. They spoke with equal clarity of a determination to succeed.

She didn't know whether he could see she was staring at him, but when he looked over at her, his expression changed instantly. Grim determination became a gentle smile. The hard gaze vanished and his eyes filled with the warmth of love.

"Don't worry." He rode close enough to give

her hand a comforting pat. "We'll get Luis back safe and sound."

She tried without success to smile. "I know, but he must be terrified."

Rafe's expression hardened. "It's my fault. I should have known Laveau sent me that newspaper ad for a reason. He knew my father was wealthy."

"Pilar still sends him his share of the profits from the ranch," Broc said. "And that doesn't count what he made rustling cattle or robbing that banker in Galveston. He ought to have plenty of money."

"No amount of money will be enough for Laveau as long as Cade has control of the di Viere property. He hates all of us for depriving him of his position as head of the family."

"Laveau hates cows. He ought to be glad Cade took over. At least he has an income."

"This has nothing to do with logic or fairness. Laveau betrayed us so he could be on the winning side. In his eyes, we cheated him by surviving. We cheated him again by making it impossible for him to go home. This is about vengeance as much as money."

"Do you think you have enough money to pay a ransom?" Maria asked.

"I'll pay whatever I must to get Luis back, but I doubt Laveau will be able to resist the chance to use Luis to hurt me even further."

Maria could have done without hearing that, but she took consolation in one thing: No matter what doubts Rafe might have had about himself ten years ago, he'd gotten over them. Maybe it was surviving the war. Maybe it was the love and loyalty of friends. Maybe it was becoming mature enough to know that even if he had been flawed, it didn't excuse what Dolores and his father had done to him. She hadn't fallen in love with a man racked by doubt or living with the fear he had a fatal flaw. He was strong and confident, a man a woman could depend on.

"How far ahead do you think they are?" Broc asked Rafe.

"I don't know. I can't read a trail like Cade. I grew up a rich man's son. I never had to trail cows over ground as hard and dry as clay."

Maria turned worried eyes to Broc. "You said they'd been gone only a short time."

"Don't worry," Broc assured her. "Rafe has a clock in his head. He can calculate how fast the buggy is probably going and how many miles it can cover in a given period of time. I'm not as good as Cade at tracking, but I grew up hunting in the Tennessee mountains. Between Rafe and me, we'll find them."

Dolores often said women weren't made to handle facts, that they dealt in emotions. But right now Maria would have appreciated a lot of facts. She had plenty of emotions, and none of them were contributing anything to Luis's rescue.

The minutes seemed to drag by. Maria questioned Rafe's decision to slow their horses to give them a breather.

"That will give Laveau time to get farther ahead," she protested.

"Laveau grew up on a ranch and spent three years with an army troop that fought on horseback. He knows how to spare his horses. He won't put them into a drive unless he sees us on his heels."

"He's got to know we'll follow him at some point," Broc added. "He'll save something for a chase."

Maria tried to be content with that answer. Nothing really mattered but Luis. He'd been the center of her life for so long, she couldn't imagine what she would do if anything happened to him. She breathed a sigh of relief when Rafe said it was time to put the horses into a fast canter once more.

She was as surprised as Rafe when the buggy tracks turned off the mail route onto a rough track leading up into the foothills. "Do you know what's up there?"

"No, but this was gold mining country before the war. I expect there are cabins or buildings still there."

"What would Laveau want them for?"

"To hold Luis while he negotiates with me."

"I can't imagine Dolores being willing to step inside an old mining cabin, much less stay in one," Broc said.

"Laveau won't give her a choice."

Maria wondered if Dolores realized by now she wasn't going to get whatever Laveau had promised in return for her support. Would she attempt to rescue Luis on her own? No matter how much trouble she caused, Dolores found a way to make sure she was never the one at risk.

The trail climbed farther up the hillside. It was rough and overgrown in places, but it remained passable. "Where's he going?" she asked Rafe.

"Most of the gold from this side of the mountains was extracted by panning in streams and gulches, but I remember there was a mine in this area. I don't know how Laveau learned of it, but I expect he's headed there."

"Why?"

"It was abandoned a long time ago, and I doubt anyone has a reason to come here. He's probably brought supplies to last for as long as he thinks it will take me to find the money to pay the ransom."

"Do you think he knows we're following him?"

"He will keep that possibility in mind."

Maria decided it would be easier to be ignorant of all the possible dangers and leave everything up to Rafe, but she'd been in a position of responsibility far too long to totally abdicate to anyone, even him. "What do you want me to do when we get there?"

"Stay back until Broc and I have time to assess the situation. If you were to fall into his hands, he'd really have me over a barrel."

"There they are!" Broc shouted.

"Where?" Rafe and Maria asked together.

"I got a brief glimpse of them through the trees."

Maria followed where Broc was pointing, but she couldn't see anything.

"The trail will get rougher as it goes higher," Rafe warned. "It could be blocked by a rockslide."

"Then he won't be able to reach the mine," Maria said.

"He'll reach it if he has to carry Luis and drag Dolores every step of the way."

Maria was torn between guiding her horse around rocks and ruts and straining for a glimpse of the buggy. "There it is," she said a moment later.

The trail had been built out over the side of the

mountain as it made a sharp U-turn. The trees had been cut down to serve as supports. A moment later the buggy disappeared behind a screen of willow and sycamore trees.

"They'll be easy to see soon," Rafe said. "The miners cut down everything on the upper slopes to use for supports inside the mine."

A moment later Maria got her first glimpse of the mine. Built into the side of a gulch, down which ran a small stream, the site had been constructed in a series of steps, starting from the scaffolding that supported ore-bearing cars as they emerged from the mine to the buildings lower down the slope that processed the rock. Other buildings might have been offices, shops, dormitories, and dining halls. "How can we find them with so many buildings?"

"It has probably been quite a few years since anyone has been up here. It ought to be easy to follow their footprints."

Maria tried to show as much confidence as Rafe, but it was hard when Laveau seemed so far ahead. What if he decided to hide Luis in the mine tunnel? A mine as old as this one could collapse at any moment.

"The buggy has stopped and Laveau has gotten out."

Maria tried to see what Broc was describing, but apparently he had better eyesight.

"What's happening?" she asked Rafe.

"Laveau appears to be trying to clear some rocks from the trail. I'm sure he's been here before, so that rockslide is recent."

Maria was thankful the rockslide had slowed

Laveau. Maybe they could reach him before he could hide Luis.

"He's having to look for something to give him leverage," Broc said. "I'm surprised he didn't bring something in the buggy. He's had to take off his coat." Broc chuckled. "I can just imagine how that must offend his sense of style."

"He probably doesn't want to get it wrinkled or dirty. You know how fastidious he is," Rafe said.

"He probably took more baths than everybody else in the troop combined."

"And had his mother provide him with uniforms. Regular army issue wasn't good enough for him."

This ridiculous conversation irritated Maria. Why weren't they figuring out how to rescue Luis? Why didn't they go faster? Laveau had managed to lever the rock off the trail. "We've got to hurry. He's getting back into the buggy."

"I'm saving the horses for the end," Rafe said. "The trail looks good for the last quarter of a mile."

Rafe must have meant the path was clear of debris. That was the only good thing about the dizzyingly steep trail.

They were now gaining rapidly on Laveau, but Maria wasn't sure it was fast enough. She was certain it wasn't when Laveau looked back. It was obvious he'd seen them because he took out his whip and laid it across the backs of his horses.

"He's a fool!" Broc exclaimed. "If he loses control of those horses, he could go off the mountainside."

"He'll drive them as hard as he can," Rafe said, "but he won't lose control."

Maria watched nervously as Laveau drove his horses at a canter. Moments later he had to stop.

"More boulders," Rafe said. "He'd have been smarter to come on horseback even if he had to tie Luis across the saddle behind him."

Maria was grateful Laveau hadn't made such a decision. She didn't want to think of the damage that Luis might have suffered in such a ride.

"That boulder didn't take as long to move," Broc pointed out unnecessarily.

Maria was hoping for a boulder so large Laveau couldn't dislodge it, but though his progress was slow, it was relatively unimpeded. She wondered whether Luis could see them, whether he knew they were following. What would Dolores do when she realized they were being followed? Was Luis tied up? She almost hoped he was. She wouldn't put it past the boy to attempt to jump from the buggy the moment he knew Rafe was coming after him.

"Time to go faster," Rafe said. "Laveau has reached the part of the trail that looks clear."

For the next short while, Maria had to struggle too hard to stay in the saddle to be able to concentrate on Laveau and the buggy. She understood the necessity for learning to ride a horse, but she couldn't understand how anyone could like it. She felt as if she was one lurching stride away from disaster at all times.

When they reached the relatively clear portion of the trail, Rafe and Broc put their horses into a hard drive. She tried to keep up, but they quickly outdistanced her. She cursed her own lack of riding skills. Even at the slower pace, her horse was laboring by the time she reached the first building. It appeared to be a small office, but its roof had collapsed and one side had disappeared.

So had Laveau and the buggy. All she could hear of Rafe and Broc was the rattle of their horses' hooves on the road that wound between two tall buildings that blocked her view.

She was alone.

Twenty-seven

RAFE NEEDED TO FIND LAVEAU BEFORE HE COULD disappear into one of the cluster of rotting buildings. There was danger in entering such a building, but Laveau had shown that not even the lure of money would cause him to expose himself to danger. Unfortunately that concern didn't extend to others.

Rafe knew he was in trouble when he came upon the empty buggy in front of a huge building that climbed halfway up the mountain toward the mouth of the mine. Most of the tin roof had been blown away by winter storms. The building would be riddled with decaying timbers and rotting floors. A slip could send any one of the three people dropping as much as a hundred feet. No one was likely to survive such a fall.

"He could be anywhere in there," Broc said.

"Or in another building."

"Do you think he left the buggy here to throw us off?"

"He had time. He knows I'm not going to leave until I find him and Luis. I'm sure he's trying to make certain he's in the best possible position to get what he wants." While they talked, they dismounted and made their way into the building through a door that had been left ajar. Two sets of footprints were clearly visible in the dust and dirt. It worried him that there weren't three. He had detected the faint odor of chloroform in Maria's room.

"How's Laveau going to do that?" Broc asked.

"I don't know, but I expect I'll be very unhappy when I find out. Let's split up. I don't want Laveau to be able to keep his eye on both of us. Besides, I don't know what Dolores's role in this might be." Dolores had a selfish streak so deeply ingrained, she couldn't be depended upon to go along with any plan if she decided another was more to her advantage.

Rafe followed the footprints in the dust. The bottom floor of the building was shallow and the prints soon led up a set of wooden steps to a second floor. Following the prints, Rafe was led to a third floor and then a fourth. Laveau was leading them to a part of the building where the flooring gave way to a narrow walkway over a grid of supports extending down to the first level. Many of the floorboards were half rotten.

Dolores stood about fifty feet ahead. Laveau had moved onto a narrow suspended walkway. He held an apparently unconscious Luis in his arms. There was nothing but air between him and the floor more than fifty feet below.

"Come closer," Laveau said. "I don't like to bargain with a man I can't see clearly."

Sunlight poured in where the tin roof had been

blown away. Laveau and Dolores stood in the sunlight, Rafe in the shadows. He approached slowly, his brain working feverishly.

"Let me make some things clear so there won't be any misunderstandings," Laveau said. "The boy is unconscious. I used chloroform. I couldn't take a chance on his waking up and upsetting my balance. You want to shoot me, but you won't because I would carry the boy with me to his death. You want to wrestle him from my arms, but you won't because that would cause us both to fall. Of course that wouldn't happen because I'd throw the boy at you. Not something a loving brother would want to consider."

"Cut the chatter and tell me what you want," Rafe demanded.

"You always were a man of few words and even less patience. I want a great deal of money to restore your brother to you unharmed."

"How can I be sure you'll return Luis?"

Laveau shook his head slowly. "I have nothing against the boy, nor am I a child murderer. It's you I dislike."

"Get to the point."

"I want fifty thousand dollars."

"There isn't that much money in Cíbola."

"I'm prepared to be patient."

"It would take days, possibly weeks, to raise that much money. I'd have to sell all my steers, possibly some land."

Laveau's expression hardened into one of dislike. "That's your problem. Don't bore me with the details."

Rafe wasn't going to leave Laveau alone with Luis for the time it would take him to raise the money.

He'd been watching the boy for signs that he might be regaining consciousness. He needed to find some way to outmaneuver Laveau before Luis woke up. Dolores gave him an idea of how to do it.

"The money is for me," Dolores said to Rafe. "I could barely survive on the miserable allowance Warren left me when I was living at the ranch. After you threw me out, I'd have been destitute if Laveau hadn't come to my aid."

"If you think Laveau is going to give you any money, you're not as smart as I thought."

"He's going to marry me," Dolores said with a mocking smile. "We're going to take Luis with us."

Rafe was relieved to see a look of disgust mingled with anger on Laveau's face. "Why should I pay you any money if you're going to take Luis with you?" Rafe asked.

"I'll let you see him," Dolores said, "more often than *you* let *me* see him."

Apparently Dolores liked the image of herself as a devoted and loving mother. Rafe didn't understand why this was important to her since she spent so little time with Luis, but he intended to exploit her fantasy.

"Laveau dislikes children," Rafe told Dolores.

"He only said that to fool you."

"The only person he's fooled is you. Laveau doesn't care about anything but money. He gets his share from the family ranch each year, yet he's wanted in Texas for theft and cattle rustling. He's in California only because he thinks there's some way to get money from me."

"I don't believe you."

"Look, I'll make a deal with you."

"No deal. I was distraught when you made me leave the ranch. I wouldn't have thought of asking for so much money by myself. You never should have thrown me out of the house."

"I admit that was a mistake."

"I'm a good mother. I love my son."

"That's why I'm going to give the money to you. You can move back to the ranch. I'm going back to Texas. Once I make arrangements to have the money transferred to you, you won't have to see me again. Take Luis back to Cíbola with you until you have the money."

"Don't believe a word he says," Laveau said to Dolores. "He's a liar."

"No, he's not."

Rafe had been concentrating so hard on finding a way to rescue Luis, he hadn't realized Maria had found them. It took a conscious effort not to turn toward her.

"Rafe told us the first night he arrived that he intended to go back to Texas as soon as he could," Maria said to Dolores.

"You're lying," Laveau said.

"Why should I lie? I don't stand to gain anything."

"You're in love with Rafe. Any fool can see that."

"If I were, it wouldn't make any difference. My place is with my sister and Luis at the ranch. I'd be a fool to accept an offer of marriage that would require me to move to Texas as the wife of a common ranch hand."

Dolores turned to Laveau. "Give me Luis. There's no need to hide now that Rafe is going to give me the money."

"You can't be fool enough to believe them," Laveau protested. "If you take Luis and go back to the hotel, what reason does he have to give you anything?"

"I heard you say Laveau wants to marry you," Maria said to her sister. "Has he actually proposed?"

Rafe didn't know how Maria had keyed into what he was trying to do so quickly, but his ploy was better coming from Maria. Dolores had little reason to trust him, but she'd been depending on Maria for ten years.

"Not yet, but he's going to."

"That's a lot of money, much more than most men would ever see in a lifetime. He'd have a lot more for himself if he didn't have to share it with a wife and stepson," Maria said.

Rafe thought he saw Luis's eyelids flutter. Just as he thought he might be mistaken, Luis moved in Laveau's arms. He was waking up.

"It would be easier if Rafe gives the money to you," Maria said to her sister. "Then you won't have to wait for Laveau to transfer it to you. I don't know about such things, but wouldn't you have to pay some taxes on it? You could end up with a lot less than fifty thousand."

"Don't listen to her," Laveau said to Dolores. "She's trying to play on your fears."

"My sister wouldn't lie to me," Dolores insisted.

"Anyone would lie for fifty thousand dollars."

Laveau's words fell like lead weights into the silence of the building. Rafe could practically see the thoughts forming in Dolores's mind.

"Would you lie to me for that much money?" Dolores asked Laveau.

"Never. I'm the one who took you in after Rafe threw you out. You know I want to marry you."

"I don't know how I would have gotten through the last weeks without you." Dolores favored Laveau with a brilliant smile. "But Maria is right. It would be easier if Rafe gave the money directly to me."

Rafe wasn't sure Dolores was strong enough to carry a sleeping Luis, but he was certain she couldn't handle Luis if he was struggling to get away. Laveau backed away from Dolores.

"The only way either of us will get any money out of Rafe is to keep the boy until he hands over the cash."

"What do you mean *either of us*?" Dolores's suspicions were fully aroused. "You said I would get all the money, that you didn't want any of it."

"I just meant that the only way either of us can force the money out of Rafe is to keep the brat."

"Is that any way for a stepfather to refer to a stepson?" Maria asked.

"Let me have Luis." Dolores held out her arms.

Laveau showed signs of losing control of his temper as the situation escalated. "I'm not letting go of him until Rafe gives me the money."

"He's giving it to me, not you," Dolores declared. "Now let me have Luis."

"Get your hands off the boy."

Rafe was surprised Laveau hadn't gained a better understanding of Dolores during the weeks she'd lived with him. Once she got something in her mind, she was as tenacious as she was selfish. Her sudden attack shocked Laveau so much he lost his grip on Luis and the boy's feet dropped to the planks. There wasn't much space on the narrow walk. Fearful of what might happen, Rafe started forward at a run. Out of the corner of his eye he saw Broc start forward from where he'd been hiding in the shadows.

As Laveau and Dolores fought, Luis broke free. Unable to go toward Rafe because Laveau and Dolores blocked his path, he started in the opposite direction. In their struggle, Laveau pushed Dolores into one of the timbers that attached the walkway to rafters overhead. Using the timber as leverage, Dolores launched herself at Laveau. The rotting timber broke under the force and a section of the walkway between them and Luis crashed to the floor more than fifty feet below.

A groggy and disoriented Luis was left suspended on a teetering section of walkway.

"You stupid bitch!" Laveau screamed. "You've ruined everything." He pulled a knife from inside his coat and stabbed Dolores. Then running the short distance to the main floor, he knocked Maria down when she tried to stop him, and raced for the stairs. Rafe could have intercepted him, but he had to reach Luis before the creaking walkway collapsed.

The inside of the building reminded Rafe of the inside of a tobacco barn he'd seen in North Carolina on his way to Texas after the war. The farmer had created a crisscrossing network of beams and trusses to support the poles of curing tobacco leaves. By using the stabilizing trusses, the farmer could climb to any part of the barn. If the beams and trusses in this building were strong enough to support his weight, that was how he planned to reach Luis.

If they weren't, he could fall to the floor below.

Rafe had helped Maria to her feet by the time Broc reached them.

"See if you can help Dolores," he said to Broc. "I'm going after Luis."

"What about Laveau?"

"We can worry about him later. Luis," Rafe called to the boy, "don't move. I'm coming after you."

The boy was still groggy, but he was alert enough to know the portion of walkway that remained was sagging under his weight.

As a child, Rafe could remember frequently scampering across a log that spanned a creek near the house, but he'd never crossed rotting beams fifty feet above a building floor. A tumble into the creek didn't compare to a fall here.

He tested the timber nearest the walkway but didn't like the way it felt under him. He tested the next one over with the same result. The first one that felt solid under his feet was thirty feet away from the walkway.

Keeping his footing on the twelve-inch beam wasn't a problem. Looking down without getting dizzy was. He held his arms out like a tightrope walker and, focusing on the massive support beam about twenty feet away, walked with slow and deliberate steps. He wasn't sure he breathed until he reached the beam. Wrapping his arms around the beam, he stepped from one timber to the next. He had to do this twice more before he could reach the portion of the walkway where Luis waited.

He'd never thought he suffered from vertigo, but every step of the way he had to fight dizziness and the feeling he was about to fall. At one point, he was

afraid he would have to get down on his knees and
crawl, but he couldn't bring Luis back if he were on
his hands and knees. He refused to look down, refused
to let himself think of the fall, refused to give in to the
fear that pounded on the outer limits of his mind. Luis
depended on him. He couldn't fail.

Once he reached the beam that supported the
crumbling piece of walkway on which Luis was
perched, he was faced with another problem. He
couldn't step onto the walkway to reach Luis. It
wouldn't support any additional weight. Luis would
have to crawl over to him. He could see the fear in
the boy's eyes. He gripped the walkway so hard that
his knuckles had turned white.

"It's okay," Rafe said, hoping to reassure Luis. "All
you have to do is crawl over to me and take my hand."
He wrapped one arm around the beam, leaned over,
and reached out for Luis.

The boy didn't move.

"I know you're scared," Rafe said, "but all you
have to do is take my hand."

"I can't let go." The swaying of the walkway under
him had terrified the child so badly, his body had frozen.

"I'm not going to leave until you're standing on
this beam with me. Now let go and start crawling very
slowly toward me."

Rafe could see Luis's fingers gradually loosen their
grip on the walkway. The shift in weight when the
boy started to crawl toward him caused the walkway
to sway still more. Luis froze.

"I know it's frightening," Rafe said, "but it's just
swaying back and forth because your weight shifts

when you crawl. The sooner you reach me, the sooner I can take you back to Maria."

"That man killed Mama."

"He didn't kill her."

"I saw him stick a knife in her."

"Maria and Broc are looking after your mother. As soon as you come to me, I'll take you to her."

"Mama didn't want me. She just wanted the money."

"Your mother does want you. Laveau is an evil man. He made her say things she didn't mean. Now don't think about that anymore. Just concentrate on coming to me. Maria and I love you as much as your mother does."

"Does Broc love me?"

"Of course I do, brat. Now come on down from there before you give me a heart attack."

Rafe looked over to see Broc turn his gaze from them back to Dolores. Maria was holding Dolores in her arms and pressing a piece of folded cloth against the stab wound. Broc had placed his hand over another spot. Rafe could see blood oozing from between Broc's fingers. Apparently Laveau had stabbed Dolores twice.

"Come on, Luis," Rafe coaxed. "We need to get your mother to a doctor as soon as possible."

Luis released his grip, but the walkway swayed worse the closer he got. Rafe leaned over as far as he dared. "Come on. Grip your fingers around my wrist and I'll do the same." He needed the strongest grip possible to swing Luis over to the timber.

The walkway lurched crazily as Luis covered the

last bit of distance. Rafe breathed a sigh of relief as he felt Luis's little fingers attempt to close around his wrist. He'd just secured his grip on Luis's wrist when the walk broke loose with a loud crack and crashed to the floor fifty feet below.

Its collapse left Luis dangling in midair.

"Don't panic," Rafe said as calmly as he could. "I'm going to pull you up. As soon as you can, reach out and hold onto my belt. I won't let go of you until you're standing on the timber."

Rafe had always had enough strength to do anything he needed, but he'd never tried to lift a one-hundred-pound boy with one arm. It took all his strength to keep his hold on the timber and pull Luis up. When the boy grabbed hold of his belt, he pulled so hard that Rafe had to dig his fingernails into the wood of the support to keep his hold from slipping. With one final effort, he swung Luis onto the timber. Once both his feet were on the beam, Luis wrapped his arms around Rafe's stomach, held on hard, and buried his face in Rafe's chest.

"I was scared."

Rafe didn't say it, but he was scared, too. The worst part was over, but they still had to cross three timbers before they would be safe.

"You don't have to be frightened any longer," Rafe said, hoping to ease some of Luis's terror. "Here's what we're going to do. You're going to get on my back. Once you're there, you're not going to move even one inch no matter what happens. Remember, you've got to be absolutely still so I don't lose my balance. Do you think you can do that?"

"Yes."

The boy sounded badly frightened, but Rafe gave him credit for being brave enough to act as if he weren't. He knelt down so Luis could climb on his back. Once the boy's arms were around his neck and his legs around his waist, Rafe slowly rose to his feet. "Remember, you're not to move until we reach the support."

Rafe took a steadying breath and started across the timber. He couldn't tell whether it was the extra weight, his imagination, or dizziness, but the beam didn't feel as steady under his feet this time. He forced himself to remain calm, to walk slowly and deliberately. He breathed a huge sigh of relief when he reached the support. Luis's arms had tightened around his neck until they threatened to choke him.

"Now, this is what we're going to do next," Rafe said to Luis as he knelt. "You're going to get off my back and squat down on the timber. I'm going to hold on to the support and step over to the next timber. After I do that, you're going to stand up, grip my arm like we did before, and I'm going to swing you onto the timber in front of me. Understand?"

He felt Luis nod his head.

Rafe knelt, and Luis hesitatingly slid off his back. When Rafe reached out to put his arm around the support, he felt sharp pains in his fingers. When he pulled them back, he saw several splinters. He'd gripped the aging support so hard he'd driven pieces of the decaying wood into his fingers. He pulled out the biggest splinters. He'd dig out the rest later.

They managed to make the transfer to the next timber without incident, repeating the process twice more before he and Luis reached safety. He supposed it was a reaction to all the stress and fear, but the moment he stepped onto the solid floor, he wrapped Luis in a bear hug and held on hard. In the moments that followed, while Luis held Rafe as hard as Rafe was holding him, the horror of all the possible consequences struck him with stupefying force. Luis could have fallen to his death, or Laveau could have used so much chloroform, Luis would never have regained consciousness. If Laveau had carried a gun, he could have shot Maria for turning Dolores against him. If Rafe's dizziness had been any worse, he could have fallen. The beams could have—

Broc must have been talking for a while before Rafe heard him.

"Dammit, Rafe, haven't you heard a word I've said? If we don't get Dolores to a doctor soon, she's going to bleed to death."

❧

Rafe hoped he'd never have to spend another such week in his life. It would be a relief to get back to Texas and the even tenor of his life there. If nothing else, people would no longer look to him for a solution to every problem.

Okay, that wasn't fair. He and Broc had been responsible for getting Dolores to Cíbola and to a doctor. The doctor had been responsible for keeping her alive and Maria had been responsible for nursing her sister. Dolores's injury had given Rafe a new reason to be angry at Dolores, because taking care of her kept Maria so busy that she didn't have nearly enough time to spend with him. Dolores was also back at the ranch, and Rafe wasn't sure how he could get rid of her.

Rafe didn't fully understand how a kidnapping could affect a child, but Luis wanted to be at Rafe's side from morning to night. Broc had been a great help, taking him riding, spending hours telling him stories, even helping him with his studies. Luis had suffered from mood swings over the last several days. Broc always seemed to know just what to do to coax him back to a more even temperament.

The accountant he'd hired to look into Henry Fielder's accounts had made his first report, one that promised to create even more responsibility for Rafe. It seemed Henry had kept meticulous records of all his financial dealings. They provided a detailed road map to the embezzlement he'd been involved in throughout much of his life. He had cheated most of his clients in one way or another, which promised a lengthy disposition of the estate. Rafe wasn't surprised to find Henry had embezzled large sums from his father. He was surprised to find he'd been doing it for years. The amount of money in the collective bank accounts in Sacramento and San Francisco was staggering. His father must have been incredibly rich and incredibly uninterested to have missed that. Most of the embezzling had occurred after Rafe had left, so maybe his father just hadn't cared anymore.

One adjustment Rafe didn't mind making was spending many hours each day riding over the ranch and talking with Miguel. He had expected that to be the most wearing of his responsibilities. Instead it had turned out to be the most rewarding. He couldn't pinpoint any one thing that had caused the change, but his anger at his father and Dolores was gone. It could be the transformation he'd noticed in Dolores. Coming close to death had wrought a change in her. She seemed to understand that she had been at least partially responsible for her own misfortunes. She would never be a person Rafe could like, but he no longer hated her. He finally understood that she must be a frightened and insecure woman to have behaved as she had most of her life. Her behavior had deprived her of any chance for love.

The kind of love he'd found with Maria.

Just thinking about Maria caused him to smile. He could be riding over the ranch, in the middle of a discussion about crops, or going over ranch records, and something would pop into his head that made him think of her. He'd spent too many years convinced he would never smile again, that he would never have any *reason* to smile. Now he welcomed every opportunity. Thinking of what Pilar would say if she knew he was sitting in the rebuilt gazebo waiting for Maria to join him made him chuckle. Watching Maria come down the path toward him, moonlight bathing her in its lustrous glow, caused contentment to spread through him. It was a feeling he'd never known, one he hoped he would experience for the rest of his life.

He didn't allow Maria to speak until he'd properly welcomed her. Since that involved numerous kisses, assorted hugs, and repeatedly telling her how much he'd missed her, quite a few minutes had passed before he finally got around to letting her speak.

"I want to convince you to stay in California…with me and Luis."

Twenty-eight

RAFE HAD LOOKED FORWARD TO A ROMANTIC INTER-
lude. He'd chosen to meet Maria in the gazebo because
the evening was cool and the sky littered with stars.
A lone rose that had survived the destruction to the
garden added its delicate fragrance to the gentle breeze.
A night bird's call brought to mind the melodious
timbre of Maria's voice. He hadn't gotten to the point
where he could wax poetic on the beauty of Maria's
eyelashes, but he never tired of looking at them. He
knew her hands were strong and capable, but in his
eyes they were dainty and fragile. Their touch was
the best medicine he knew. Moonlight glistening on
her hair made him want to run his hands through it.
Everything about her mouth made it eminently kiss-
able. Maybe he'd try to put his feelings into words
someday, but he doubted it. It was more fun to just
kiss her and forget about trying to explain why he liked
it so much. Anyway, he thought she probably knew.

He wasn't upset that she didn't want to go to Texas.
He'd had his doubts about that almost from the beginning. Then he'd had what he thought were excellent

reasons why he had to return to Cade's ranch. Now he wasn't sure.

Despite everything that had happened in the past, he'd enjoyed the past week. For years Rafe had told himself he didn't want anything to do with the ranch, but he had no sooner returned than he'd started having ideas about improvements he wanted to make. Money wouldn't be a problem. The money Henry Fielder had embezzled would cover the cost of everything. He could even set up the extensive irrigation system he believed could increase production as much as three to four times.

"Have you prepared a long list of reasons why I should stay here?" Rafe asked Maria.

"No."

That surprised him. "How do you expect to convince me if you aren't going to give me reasons to change my mind?"

"I think you've already changed it, but I'm not sure you know it."

"And what if I still want to return to Texas?"

"You know I'll go anywhere you go. It will never matter where that is as long as I'm with you."

Rafe wasn't sure he'd suffered enough to deserve a woman like Maria, but she was his now and he intended to keep her whether he deserved her or not. A sudden breeze bearing the scent of pine from higher up the mountain ruffled the strands of her hair, causing them to glisten like sable in the moonlight.

"There are many reasons for me to go back to Texas," he said to Maria. "For one thing, my life would be a lot simpler there."

"Now that your mind is clear of anger and bitterness, you'd soon be bored with simplicity."

He stroked the softness of her cheek with his thumb. "All of my friends are in Texas."

"There's no reason you can't visit them from time to time. Or have them come here."

"I have a stake in Cade's ranch."

"Which you have no intention of cashing in. Broc tells me you adore Cade's son, Carlos. Why don't you make it a gift to him?"

"There's another reason I have to go back to Texas." He cupped her face with his hands so she would have to look at him with her dark brown eyes glistening in the moonlight. He could sit here looking into them forever. "Pilar would never forgive me if she didn't get to meet my wife."

"I have no objection to going to Texas for a visit."

"I let Laveau get away, so it's up to me to find him. I don't know where he is now, but he'll return to Texas sooner or later."

"I don't intend to wait patiently here or anywhere else while you chase after a lying, cheating, thieving, murdering traitor." She pulled back, gazing at him with a hint of mischievousness. "If he's more important to you than Luis and me, then you'd better start for Texas first thing in the morning."

Maria had many moods, all of which Rafe liked, but he particularly liked it when she got feisty. It made him want to laugh, to hug her, to kiss her until she laughed as hard as he did. It made him feel alive in a way nothing else did. It connected her to him because the emotional response formed a direct link between the two of them. The stronger the emotion, the stronger the link. And he wanted to be linked to her.

Forever.

"There will be problems if I stay here," Rafe told Maria. "I'll have responsibility for this whole ranch on my shoulders. And for the hundreds of people who depend on it. I'll be gone long hours every day overseeing the regular work as well as the changes that need to be made. When I'm home I'll be tied up many evenings with account books and meetings with engineers and construction managers. Worse, I'll be cranky and tired."

Her eyes narrowed and she gave him an impish grin. "I'll send Luis to keep you company on your rounds. His excitement and enthusiasm will keep you in a good mood. And Miguel will help with those accounts and changes. As for being cranky, I think I can take care of that."

Time for the clincher, but he suspected she'd have an answer for that, too. "Dolores is still here. You know we'll never be able to live under the same roof."

She leaned against him, pulled his arm tighter around her. "Dolores understands she can never live with us. I would like you to build her a modest house on a part of the ranch nearest Cíbola. She would be close enough to see Luis, for me to keep an eye on her, and close enough to Cíbola to begin to build her own circle of friends. She'd be far enough away that you and she won't have to run into each other more than a few times a year."

Rafe didn't need more reasons to be in love with Maria, but she was fast providing him with new ones.

For the first time since the rupture with his father, he had someone who could share decision making with him. He hadn't thought he wanted that. Now he couldn't imagine doing without it. "Do you have any more reasons why I should stay here?"

"Only the most important one."

"What's that?"

She turned in his arms to face him. "You've started to think of the ranch as your home again. I can see the love you used to feel beginning to resurface."

"You've been listening to Miguel."

"I didn't need to. I can see it in your eyes when you look out over a field that's ready to harvest. I can hear it in your voice when you talk about what you've done each day. Even Luis can sense your excitement when you talk about the new irrigation system. I found him explaining it to Dolores this morning when he should have been doing his lessons."

"Did she have a relapse?"

Maria pinched him. "No, but she was beyond her depth. I'm afraid my sister has allowed herself to become a very shallow woman."

Rafe didn't want to talk about Dolores. He wasn't particularly interested in talking about Luis, either. This was his time with Maria, and he selfishly wanted to share it with no one. He wrapped her in his embrace and planted a kiss on her head.

"Is that like a pat on the head before you tell me I've got it all wrong?"

He squeezed her a little tighter and kissed her on the head again. "No. I just wanted to kiss you."

"Good answer."

He chuckled. He looked at the big house silhouetted against the night sky, at a vineyard growing up the side of the mountain, caught the scent of lime trees in the distance, and realized that no matter how much this place meant to him, it represented only a fraction of what Maria meant to him. He even had a little brother thrown into the bargain. He was one lucky devil, something he'd never thought he'd say about himself. He felt a catch in his throat and he buried his face in Maria's hair. "There's a lot about life in Texas that I'll miss, but I do belong here. When I came back, I never thought I could feel that way again, but falling in love with you changed everything for me. You gave me back myself. I'll never be able to thank you enough for that. Now you're all I need to be happy."

He scooped her up in his arms and kissed her so thoroughly, she came away breathless, but not so breathless that she couldn't get in the last word.

"Oh, I don't know. I remember your saying something about wanting a little girl with brown eyes and a button nose."

Read on for a sneak peek of
When Love Comes *by Leigh Greenwood!*

One

Texas, 1869

BROC KINCAID STOOD BEFORE THE SPARE, SOMBER figure seated behind a plain table in what passed for the sheriff's office. He didn't want to look the judge in the eye, but his own stupidity had gotten him into this mess. He wasn't going to compound his error by adding cowardice to his list of transgressions. Getting arrested for brawling in public was humiliating enough.

"Have you been arrested for something like this before?"

"No, your honor. I've always managed to keep my temper under control."

The judge looked at a sheet of paper in front of him. "If these witnesses' statements are correct, I'm surprised you didn't do more than break Felix Yant's jaw and fracture his arm."

Broc had tried to ignore the man's vicious taunts about his face even when Felix had followed him from his hotel to the restaurant to the saloon. Broc had tried to convince himself the man wasn't worth his attention, but it was the laughter that did it. "I didn't mean to lose my temper. I apologized to his wife."

"I understand you paid for the doctor's bill."

"Yes, your honor." The man had two children. They didn't deserve to suffer because of their father's cruelty.

The judge sighed. "It goes against the grain to punish you for doing what is essentially a public service."

"I understand, your honor."

The judge's features hinted at a smile. "I'm going to give you a job I expect you'll dislike even more than spending a couple of nights in the lockup. If you can accomplish it within two weeks, I'll wipe this case from the records. If not, I'll have no recourse but to send you to jail."

꠸

Broc pulled his hat brim lower to shade his eyes from the intense glare. It was only midmorning, but the Texas sun was so hot drops of perspiration had begun to trickle down his chest. It made him long for the cool days and evenings he'd spent in Rafe Jerry's home in California. Though Rafe had encouraged Broc to stay, he knew it was time to return to Texas. He wasn't sure he was cut out to be a cowboy—it was a long way from his days as an entertainer on Mississippi riverboats—but he was positive he didn't want to be a farmer like Rafe. Cabbages and artichokes held no fascination for him.

Laveau di Viere, a traitor to the crack regiment

they'd all served during the war, had escaped once again, this time after kidnapping Rafe's half brother and attempting to kill Rafe's stepmother. The only good thing to come from his latest crimes was that Broc and his friends finally had something any court in the country would accept if they managed to capture him. *When* they captured him. Every time Broc saw the reflection of his ruined face in the mirror, he renewed his vow that Laveau would not continue to escape justice.

Laveau's latest escape had left Broc in a rotten mood for most of the trip to Texas. Maybe that was why he'd gotten into the pointless fight with Felix Yant. He knew it was impossible to change the attitude of men like Yant, even by beating their faces in. The best course was to ignore them.

But he'd let his temper flare out of control, and now he was saddled with collecting a debt from a family he'd never seen before. That ought to make him about as popular as fire ants at a family picnic. It wasn't a small debt, either. Not many people in Texas had seven hundred dollars. If they did have something worth that much, it was usually difficult to turn into cash.

Virtually impossible in the thirteen days he had to complete his mission.

He couldn't go to jail. It wasn't the time he'd be forced to spend behind bars that bothered him. It was the damage it would do to his reputation. All he needed was to add *jailbird* to *scarface*, and his place in life would be fixed forever.

His unhappy ruminations were interrupted by the

sight of a bull emerging from a brush-filled creek bed that paralleled the trail at a distance of about fifty yards. The beast was clearly not a range bull but a valuable blooded animal brought to Texas to improve the quality of the owner's herd. Longhorns were hardy animals, but they didn't carry much meat. Broc wondered if the owner of the bull knew it had escaped. The animal looked strong, but if it got into a fight with one of the wild-eyed range bulls, it wasn't likely to survive without injury. He supposed the best thing to do would be to lasso the bull and lead it into town. He'd seen a sign a few miles back telling him a place called Cactus Bend was eleven miles ahead. Surely someone there would know where the bull belonged.

Cactus Bend was also where he was supposed to collect the debt.

Before he had time to uncoil his rope, a young woman and a boy emerged from the streambed. The way the young woman held the rope told Broc she didn't have much experience handling it. A rope dragged the ground from the boy's saddle. Maybe the rope that had been on the bull before it had escaped. Broc uncoiled his own rope and wheeled his horse to go after the bull. The bull made an attempt to evade Broc's rope, but it was too slow and Broc's horse was too fast. The bull tried to fight the rope, but the harder it fought, the more the rope tightened around its throat. Realizing its mistake, the bull decided to charge the creature that was threatening its freedom.

"Get a rope on him!" Broc shouted to the woman. "1 don't want him to gore my horse or me."

The next few minutes were some of the most challenging of Broc's short career as a cowhand. The bull was crafty and mean, but its weight slowed it enough that Broc's horse was able to avoid its horns. Deciding to fight fire with fire, Broc spurred his horse in a different direction from the bull's charge, pulling the rope taut and throwing the bull off balance. Before the bull could regain its balance, Broc changed direction. When he changed directions so quickly the bull went to its knees, he shouted to the woman, "Throw the rope before he gets to his feet." He was relieved when, after three previous failed attempts, the woman's lasso settled over the bull's head.

"Let's hold him between us." A needless directive, for the woman's lasso was already looped around her saddle horn. The bull was smart enough to realize fighting was a waste of energy. After bellowing its rage, it snorted twice and pawed the ground before giving up the struggle.

The boy was at Broc's side almost immediately. "That's our bull. You can't steal him." The boy looked torn between his desire to stop Broc and his fear that this strange man with the terrible face might do something to hurt him.

"My brother is right." Once she was certain the bull was under control, the young woman also turned her attention to Broc. "We've been trying to get a rope on him for the last two hours."

Broc's impulse was to turn away to spare the young woman the shock of seeing the disfigured left side of his face, but rather than recoil in horror or disgust, she seemed curious, even sympathetic. Broc wanted nothing to do with either reaction. He just wanted to forget he was different from everyone else.

"I wasn't trying to steal your bull," Broc said. "I got the feeling you weren't used to handling that rope much."

The young woman flushed. "Is it that obvious?"

"My sister could have roped that old bull any time she wanted," the boy said.

"Eddie, there's no use stretching the truth further than it will go. I just said I've been trying to rope him for two hours."

"You would have roped him fine if he'd stayed in the open," Eddie said.

"If he'd stood still with his head at just the right angle," his sister said. "Sorry," she said, turning to Broc. "Eddie thinks it's his job to defend me."

"Somebody's got to," the boy said, "'cause Gary won't."

"He would if I needed it," the woman said. "Please excuse my bad manners. My name is Amanda, and this is my brother Eddie. My family owns the Lazy T Ranch."

Broc had passed identifying signs of several ranches, but none of them were the Lazy T. If Amanda's bull made a habit of wandering onto other ranches, it could lead to trouble. Preventing trouble wasn't his responsibility, but he had nothing against helping a beautiful woman. "I'm Broc Kincaid. I'll be happy to help you get your bull back home and in his pen."

"I couldn't put you to so much trouble."

"It's no trouble if your ranch is on the way to Cactus Bend."

"It's just outside of town."

"We used to own a saloon there," Eddie informed Broc. "My sister sings there."

Amanda blushed again. "It would be more accurate to say I wait tables."

"You do sing," Eddie insisted.

Broc tightened the rope on the bull and clucked to his mount. "You can tell me all about it on the way into town," he said to Eddie. "I like singing. Do you know what her favorite songs are?"

Given an invitation to talk, Eddie proved himself up to the challenge. Broc didn't have a chance to get in more than a sentence or two before they reached the lane leading to the Lazy T.

"You really don't have to come with us," Amanda said.

"I don't think your brother is ready to take on a full-grown bull."

"I am, too," Eddied declared. "I've already done it."

"Only once," Amanda said.

Eddie stuck out his jaw. "But I done it."

"It's okay," Broc assured both of them. "I'm planning to spend the night in Cactus Bend."

"What are you doing here?" Eddie asked.

"Eddie, it's rude to ask a question like that."

"Ma's going to want to know before she lets him inside."

Broc laughed. "I'm not planning to go inside."

"You must meet my mother and allow her to thank you," Amanda said.

"If old man Carruthers had got hold of that bull, we'd never have got him back," Eddie said.

"You don't know that," Amanda said to her brother.

"That's what Ma said. I heard her."

"She was just upset. The bull is very valuable."

"She's going to be even more upset when *he* comes riding up to the house." Eddie pointed at Broc. "What happened to your face?"

Amanda gasped and flushed crimson.

"I got shot in the face," Broc explained.

"That was a mean thing to do. Who done it?"

"Eddie, you can't ask such questions."

"I already did."

"I apologize for my brother," Amanda said. "He's too young to understand that there are certain things it's not polite to mention."

"I do, too," Eddie said, indignant. "I know it's not polite to mention the black hairs on Mrs. Dunn's lip. And I know it's not polite to tell anyone that Niall Toby's thing is so small even the whores won't have anything to do with him."

Broc thought Amanda would faint from embarrassment. He knew he shouldn't laugh, but it was impossible not to be amused.

"I was shot in an ambush during the war," Broc explained.

Eddie's eyes widened with excitement. "Did you kill the man who done it?"

"No, but my friend did. He was about to shoot me again."

"That's enough, Eddie," Amanda said in a voice Eddie had obviously heard before.

"My other brother and I are out of the house a lot, which leaves Eddie to look after our mother,"

Amanda said to Broc. "She's something of an invalid. I'm afraid she indulges him too much."

"Ma says she can't get along without me." Clearly Eddie was proud to be so valuable to his mother.

Broc was impressed by the ranch house they were approaching, a rambling, wood-frame dwelling that appeared to have at least six rooms. The wide front porch reminded him of his childhood home in Tennessee. Three other buildings, all of rough-hewn timber, seemed to be a barn, a bunkhouse, and probably a henhouse.

"Nice place you have here," Broc said.

"It belongs to me, too," Eddie informed him.

"My father told us he bought it for the family," Amanda explained.

"Which part do you get?" Broc enjoyed Eddie's confusion.

"He gets the chickens," Amanda said. "That's his job."

"Chickens are for girls." Eddie's disgust with his job was plain to see.

"I gather you don't have a little sister," Broc said to Eddie.

"Just Gary and her," Eddie said, gesturing to Amanda. "Everybody bosses me around."

"Well, I won't," Broc said. "Now let's get this bull in his pen."

The pen turned out to be a large pasture. "We can't afford to let him run loose," Amanda explained, "so we bring the cows to him. We have a small herd. Without him, we'd have no hope of making the ranch pay."

"Gary doesn't want it to pay," Eddie told Broc. "He wants it to fail so he can spend all his time in the saloon."

"Mr. Kincaid doesn't want to hear about our problems," Amanda told her brother.

"I'm just passing through," Broc said. "I'll have no reason to tell anyone there's dissension in the family."

"You don't have to," Amanda said with a sigh. "Everybody knows it."

Broc decided it was time to be on his way. "I'd better go," he said to Amanda. "Be careful when you drive cows into his pasture."

"That's Gary's job," Eddie informed him.

It wasn't difficult to put the bull in its pasture. Eddie jumped down to open the gate. Keeping the bull between them, they led it into the pasture. Once Eddie had closed the gate, Broc released the bull, which ambled off as though its escape were a routine part of the day. Dismounted, the three of them leaned against the gate and watched the bull try to excite the interest of a young heifer.

"Is it a lot of work to round up cows for him?" Broc asked Amanda.

"Not really. Our ranch isn't very big, and we have a creek running through the middle. Since the best grass is near the creek, our cows never wander far."

"Old man Carruthers's cows eat our grass," Eddie informed Broc.

"You know cows are allowed to range free," Amanda said to her brother.

"Amanda, who is that strange man? What's he doing here?"

The sound of rustling skirts and footsteps on gravel caused Broc to turn and face an older woman he assumed was Amanda and Eddie's mother. Her features were those of a woman still shy of her forties, but her demeanor was that of someone much older. She walked with stooped shoulders and leaned on a cane. Her face was devoid of energy or expression. Even her voice sounded thin and frail. Unlike Texas women, who wore simple dresses with only a single undergarment, her gown of rich green was worn over many petticoats. Her adornments included a necklace made of a single strand of dark green beads and a cream-colored lace cap over immaculately groomed hair. She looked like the women Broc remembered seeing before the war. Her reaction to his face was to recoil so violently, she might have lost her balance had she not held a cane. Amanda looked horrified by her mother's reaction.

"This is Mr. Kincaid, Mother," she said quickly. "He caught the bull for us and brought it back home."

Taking a moment to recover her balance, Amanda's mother paused before lifting her gaze to meet Broc's. "I'm Mrs. Aaron Liscomb. Thank you for helping my daughter."

Broc hoped he covered his surprise better than Mrs. Liscomb. Aaron Liscomb was *the man* from whom he had to collect the debt. It was all he could do to keep from turning his head to see if Mr. Liscomb might be approaching.

Mrs. Liscomb turned to look at her daughter, but did it so naturally she didn't appear to be averting her face. "Where's Gary?"

"He sneaked into town," Eddie told her.

Amanda kicked her brother's ankle. Apparently she'd intended to keep that information from her mother.

"He wouldn't do that before he'd finished his chores," Mrs. Liscomb chided. "You've got to stop being jealous of Gary. You'll be a big boy like him one day."

Amanda laid her hand on her brother's shoulder to keep him from making the sharp rejoinder Broc was certain hovered on his lips. "I don't know where Gary is," Amanda told her mother.

"I'm sure he's with the herd. Earl Carruthers wouldn't miss a chance to run off some of our cows. He wants that bull almost as much as he wants our ranch."

Feeling he was being drawn too deeply into the private problems of people from whom he had to collect money, Broc thought it might be better to leave. "It was nice to meet you, but I need to be getting on my way. I need to find a room in town and hunt up some dinner."

"You must have dinner with us," Mrs. Liscomb said. "You won't find anything good in Cactus Bend."

"Thank you, but I don't want to put you to any trouble."

"It's the least I can do. We would be ruined without that bull."

Broc had the feeling Amanda would have preferred that he turn down her mother's offer, but he decided to accept for three reasons. For one, Eddie begged him to stay.

"I'll show you my horses," he offered. "I've got three."

Hoping to see Mr. Liscomb and finish his business quickly was his second reason for staying. The third was purely selfish. Amanda was a lovely young woman, and he hadn't had the pleasure of spending time with a woman that pretty since he'd left California. Putting up with Amanda's mother couldn't be worse than spending time in a saloon with a bunch of drunks he didn't know. "Thank you very much for the invitation. I'll accept if you're sure it won't be too much trouble."

"It's no more trouble to cook for seven instead of six."

Believing he wouldn't cause more than a mild inconvenience, Broc accepted.

"Let Eddie show you his horses," Mrs. Liscomb said. "Amanda will have dinner ready before you know it."

Too late, Broc realized it wouldn't be any trouble to the older woman because she wouldn't do any of the work. He turned to Amanda, intending to apologize, searching his mind for a reason to say he couldn't stay.

"It's not a problem," she said with a smile that made him feel better. "It'll be fun to have someone new to talk to. Cactus Bend is so small, we're all bored with each other."

"Cactus Bend isn't a suitable place for a young woman," Mrs. Liscomb told Broc. "There are too many rough men there."

"Cowhands," Amanda translated.

"You may insist that they're just as nice as Leo and Andy—they're the young men who work for us," Mrs. Liscomb explained, "—but I wouldn't want you to frequent their company if they didn't work for us."

"Don't let Eddie bore you about his horses," Amanda told Broc. "If you give him half a chance, he'll show you every horse on the place."

"You like horses, don't you?" Eddie asked Broc.

"I like them very much, and I'm looking forward to meeting yours."

Mrs. Liscomb offered a faint smile before turning back toward the house. "Come on, Amanda. We don't want to keep the young man waiting for his dinner."

Broc watched mother and daughter walk toward the house, confused by the mother but intrigued with Amanda. She didn't appear to mind his scarred face. That had never happened before.

"So," he said, turning to Eddie, "what makes these horses of yours so special?"

About the Author

Leigh Greenwood is the award-winning author of over fifty books, many of which have appeared on the *USA Today* bestseller list. Leigh lives in Charlotte, North Carolina. Please visit his website at leigh-greenwood.com.

RUNAWAY BRIDES: THE GUNSLINGER'S VOW

An exciting new historical Western series
about rugged cowboys and the runaway
brides who steal their hearts by
USA Today bestselling author Amy Sandas

Alexandra Brighton spent the last five years in Boston,
erasing all evidence of the wild frontier girl she used to
be. Before she marries the man her aunt is pressuring
her to wed, she's determined to visit her childhood
home one final time. But when she finds herself
stranded far from civilization, she has no choice but to
trust her safety to the tall, dark, and decidedly dangerous bounty hunter Malcolm Kincaid.

"Pure perfection."
—Romancing the Book for *The Untouchable Earl*

For more info about Sourcebooks's books and
authors, visit:
sourcebooks.com

COWBOY CHARM SCHOOL

Stop that wedding!

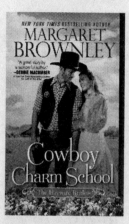

Texas Ranger Brett Tucker hates to break up a wedding, but the groom is a danger to any woman. So he busts into the church, guns blazing…only to find he has the wrong man.

Guilt-ridden, he's desperate to get the bride and groom back on track—but the more time he spends with Kate, the harder he falls…and the more he wants to convince her that he's her true match in every way.

Also by Leigh Greenwood

Night Riders

Texas Homecoming

Texas Bride

Born to Love

Someone Like You

Texas Pride

Heart of a Texan

Cactus Creek Cowboys

To Have and to Hold

To Love and to Cherish

Forever and Always

Christmas in a Cowboy's Arms

No One But You